David Caute is a novelist, histori[...] novels include *At Fever Pitch* (Au[...] Llewelyn Rhys Prize), *Comra[...] Brownlow as *Winstanley*), *The De[...] and *The K-Factor*. His most recer[...] *Sixty-Eight: The Year of the Barricades* and *Under the Skin: The Death of White Rhodesia*. A former Literary Editor of the *New Statesman*, he lives in London.

DAVID CAUTE

News From Nowhere

GRAFTON BOOKS

A Division of the Collins Publishing Group

LONDON GLASGOW
TORONTO SYDNEY AUCKLAND

Paladin
Grafton Books
A Division of the Collins Publishing Group
8 Grafton Street, London W1X 3LA

Published in Paladin Books 1988

First published in Great Britain by
Hamish Hamilton Ltd 1986

Copyright © David Caute 1986

ISBN 0-586-08675-7

Printed and bound in Great Britain by
Collins, Glasgow

Set in Plantin

To Edward, Daniel, Rebecca and Anna

PROLOGUE

Buhera and Beyond – a Report from the Future by Richard Stern

Liberty made herself my wife the night before the Rhodesians came on a narrow camp bed shrouded in coarse netting in a hot, stifling tent reeking of gun grease. Mosquitoes whined like angry dentists' drills from outside the net while the alien breath of a peasant girl whose diet was not mine assaulted me from within it. Liberty's bush-hardened muscles were uncompromising; she grasped my hips with calloused hands as practical and urgent as a midwife's and the transaction, though not soundless, was completed without verbal exchange. It didn't take long.

Yet Liberty was a most sensitive woman who loved, above all, to talk.

After the ceremony she dutifully re-coated my body in mosquito repellent, carefully fastened the net under the bed, coiled the bandoliers round her splendid body, took up her AK 47, and then settled down outside the tent on the hard, cooling earth of Buhera to guard me with her life. Again not a word had passed between us.

I lay tossing in the oppressive heat, increasingly awake, the luminous hands of my watch inexorably quartering what was left of the night – the Rhodesians would come soon after first light. But they were scarcely on my mind; I had spent ten years waiting for Esther. No inoculation – not anger, not even betrayal – could immunise me against that passion and that longing. Whether it was a real woman I loved or my own Hegelian 'idea' of her, I was hooked.

I may have fallen into a shallow sleep because I heard nothing until I became aware of a soft hand on my drenched brow, murmured words of affection, and the most extraordinary sense of

1

transport, as if my body had become weightless with happiness. It was almost three years since I had last folded my arms round Esther's naked body but what sounded bugles of triumph was the knowledge that I was now to possess her on the soil of Africa.

'Your jungle princess Liberty is fast asleep at her post,' Esther whispered. 'I stepped over her prostrate body – the sentinel who reminds us, hourly, that we must "ever be vigilant".'

'Poor girl, she's tired,' I murmured.

Perhaps Liberty's uncharacteristic dereliction of duty uncurled in Esther's mind a worm of suspicion; perhaps her gently roaming hands were worldly enough to discover evidence of the truth. Abruptly they recoiled in anger:

'Liberty was with you!'

My silence was my admission. One smells of the woman one has been with.

'It was her wish,' I said, 'I could hardly refuse.'

'You knew I was coming, Richard.'

'No, my darling. I received your cryptic note with its one-word message, but assumed that it represented another of your husband's dangerous jokes.'

'So you took Liberty in revenge?'

'Haven't I suffered enough for my love of you?'

Esther's head sank on to my shoulder, her rich chestnut hair brushing my face.

'I want a child, Richard.'

I understood at once.

'You mean I am the only man whose hair moves in the wind within a hundred kilometres. Why not wait for tomorrow – you'll have five hundred Rhodesian commandos to choose from.'

Her beautiful oval face touched mine.

'Whatever I say, you won't believe me.'

To which I might add: whatever I write about that night in Buhera will not be believed.

PART ONE

ONE

'Can you spell it?'

'Again?'

'Yes, spell it again.' Harry Marquis drove his ancient Ford Anglia with the impatient hands of a maestro pushing an orchestra to its destiny.

'P-e-n-r-y-n-d-e-u-d-r-a-e-t-h,' Stern said.

'Pronounce it.'

Stern tried but sank in the middle. His stomach had not felt good since they crossed the Welsh border and began to pursue the inescapable A5 along narrow, twisting passes between dry stone walls and small hills painted in shades of green and grey by gusting clouds. Harry's nature drove him to overtake everything, regardless of visibility, honking as if every turn in the road was a personal insult.

Their progress was halted by a mass of bobbing white fleeces. The shepherd boy grinned at them placidly.

'Bloody Galles,' Harry muttered as his engine boiled.

'Where are we now?'

'Cerrigydrudion.'

'What! I never cared for Dylan Thomas, all those baroque alliterations and quaint cadences aimed at sentimental English philistines.' Grumpily he reached for the magazines and books on the back seat, plucking from the pile the current issue of the *New Statesman*: June 1967. I told him there was a piece in the magazine, written by J. R. Tree, a gnome of villainous aspect, damning the planned Tribunal with faint praise. Harry snorted.

'More Cold War Natopology. The CIA got their claws into *Encounter* and this rag's going the same way . . .'

'He's waving you on,' Stern said.

Harry tossed the *New Statesman* over his shoulder and lurched forward into the bleeting, shitting sheep: the first soft bump was followed by others. Glancing through the rear window, Stern saw the shepherd boy gesturing angrily, confirmed in his view of the English.

'Two mutton chops, just what I need,' Harry said. 'Bertie won't give us a thing to eat, of course. He lives off seven whiskies a day and weighs barely a hundred pounds.' This trail of resentment evidently sparked another: 'You didn't bring Elizabeth, then?' – as if Stern had promised to bring her.

South of Betws-y-Coed they had a short argument whether to follow the A5 to the north or risk the unknown southern route along the A494 and the A4212. Approaching the west coast an hour later, Harry announced that he never wanted to see 'another bloody blue hydrangea or another bloody slate quarry' in his life; then, leaving the unpronounceable town of Penryndeudraeth, they got trapped in the long crawl of cars heading for the toll across the 'cob' to Porthmadog.

'Christ!'

'I suppose we could visit Portmeirion.'

'Why? Pseudo-Portofino. Pastel and pastry instead of pastel and pasta.' Harry chuckled at a comment clearly not invented on the spur of the moment. 'Bertie should be ashamed of himself trotting down to this barbarous shore in pursuit of post-Bloomsbury aesthetes with rouged cheeks.'

Harry, as always, suspicious of anything he wasn't part of.

'You didn't suggest it to Elizabeth, then?' Harry revived the subject.

'Suggest what?'

'That she come with us, of course.'

'It didn't occur to me.'

Harry's grunt was compounded of reproach and scepticism.

They had left the previous afternoon's faculty meeting in the best of moods. Seated side by side, as usual, Harry and Stern had shared jokes, raised points of order and enjoyed Dean Ramsay's rising distemper. 'The Fifth Column,' Ramsay called them. Harry had adopted the stigma: 'Speaking on behalf of the Fifth Column . . .' Half-way down the agenda paper lay a thin stick of dynamite: 'Student Council proposal to abolish grades, assessments and examinations.' Opening the debate, Harry said that the demand went too far, too fast:

—Which doesn't mean we can ignore it or reject it. We must listen.

—In other words, you want to eat your cake and have it, said John Ramsay, historian of Tudor England and Dean of the Faculty.

—The abolition of National Service was of course a disaster. After

6

two years of square-bashing and the Malayan jungle, no student ever protested about having to sit examinations.

—They still have national service in France, Stern smiled insolently. —They will also have a revolution. But no doubt your coming nuclear war will give us all a proper sense of proportion.

Ramsay accorded him a slow look of distilled hatred: Marquis's acolyte cellophane-wrapped in sycophancy. Only the mob outside the door could embolden a junior lecturer to address his Dean thus. Then spoke Dr Gough, Ramsay's ally, in his precise, funnelled anglo-scotese, once resonant with permanent authority but now marred by intermittent quavers – possibly the result of having his office ransacked by students of Stern's International Marxist Group, seeking hard evidence of collusion between the faculty and the military-industrial complex (C. Wright Mills, etc.) . . .

—The whole radical performance is of course a pantomime, said Gough, —a charade within a comfortable metropolitan landscape. Marquis knows it, but prefers to collaborate.

Harry was doodling Spitfires and Hurricanes on a blotting pad, insulated from the insult by the militant student delegation waiting outside in the corridor (but outside for how much longer?), demanding access, participation, democracy, and more besides. Presently Dr Gough would raise his favourite subject, 'our responsibility to the taxpayer', and Stern would leave the room to claim his seething constituency:—The Dean wants to bring back military service and send us all to Vietnam.

'Turn left here,' Stern said.

'Are you sure? There's no sign.'

'Perhaps Russell had it removed to baffle American journalists.'

Throughout the journey Harry had contested every one of Stern's navigational directives but only nominally, out of impish habit; invariably the professor would defer to his saturnine pupil's long, pointing nose. Roaring his Anglia up a lane wide enough to accommodate only one car, shoulders and hairy hands in constant motion, Harry came at last to the white, pebble-dash house commanding a hill high above the Glaslyn estuary. Here, on a glass-roofed verandah with metal pillars, they found the philosopher asleep in a rocking chair.

Harry shook him energetically, despite the twittering protests of Russell's male secretary.

'Bertie, are you asleep or dead?'

'Depends on the weather,' Russell said, instantly awake, his scrawny neck stretching like that of a fledgling alerted for the first time to the world beyond the nest.

'Wonderful view, Bertie.'

'The sands were reclaimed from the sea ten years before I was born.'

'Is that Snowdon?' Stern asked, pointing due north.

'Yes.' The former Cambridge Apostle and author of fifty-six books regarded Stern intently. 'Who's this young man of yours, Marquis? He looks ambitious. They always ask about Snowdon, the dangerous ones.'

'Richard Stern. You've met him before, Bertie.'

Russell was tugging at Stern's sleeve with fingers as brittle as twigs. 'Are you ambitious?'

'I confess I am.'

'We brought you a bottle of Red Hackle,' Harry said, clearly hoping for permission to open it. Russell smiled.

'Ten years ago they discovered a kink in one of my intestines. Since then I've lived off seven scotches a day. Why are clever boys like yourself ashamed of ambition these days? When I was an undergraduate there were many boys cleverer than I but I surpassed them all because I was consumed by a passion that I've recently been able to diagnose as ambition. Mm. I've lost it now. Harry never had it, not really. He's vain though, have you noticed? Harry's star pupil, weren't you? – I remember now. You'll stab him in the back soon enough and good luck to you. Where's the pretty girl?'

Harry looked embarrassed. 'I thought Richard might want to bring her.'

'He prefers to keep her for himself. A pity: I still enjoy a pretty face.'

'Are you quite sure you won't come to Paris, Bertie?'

Stern could almost feel Harry's hunger. The room was bare, not a cocktail biscuit in sight.

'I'm ninety-four. Ask Wittgenstein instead.'

'He's dead.'

'He may claim to be.'

'They expect de Gaulle to throw the Tribunal out of France, despite his anti-Americanism. If you came, he might think twice.'

Russell nodded. 'He might. But he'd still do it. You'll have my name and my cheque – can't do more. I had a silly creature from the *Los Angeles Times* up here yesterday. First she admired the view then she suggested I was being used as a tool, a "dupe", of the Communists. I told her that the first task of newspapers is to distort the truth and make common cause with mass murderers like Lyndon Johnson. Gleefully she wrote it down.'

As he spoke the old man's features refolded like wrapping paper, but his hands rested immobile in his lap, pensioned off. Stern thought of the torrent of prose that had flowed from those hands, but neither the man nor his work moved him to the concern he felt about rumours of Sartre's creeping blindness. If Russell declined to attend the War Crimes Tribunal in Paris, then Sartre's participation would be their only hope. Visiting Paris to sign a contract with Gallimard, Stern had called on de Beauvoir, who confided her fear that Sartre would be unable to compose once he could no longer monitor his own script across the page. 'We've tried dictation but he must move his hand in order to think.'

'Nothing to eat, I suppose?' Harry could no longer mask his need.

Russell half-turned his stiff neck towards his hovering secretary, who shrugged impatiently and left the room.

'Time you left the Communist Party,' Russell told Harry by way of retaliation.

'That was twelve years ago, Bertie. They threw me out, you may recall.'

'You should have resigned first.' He turned his beady eye on Stern. 'This one would never make the mistake of joining the Communists. You know why the Russians have kept quiet about the Tribunal? Because they're under the thumb of the Americans. Just count the nuclear weapons on either side. The Russians can count.'

Harry was clearly relieved that Russell would not be coming to Paris; his maverick utterances were always a liability. But another cheque would do no harm. When they left Penrhyndeudraeth an hour later, Harry's empty stomach swilling with weak tea and two biscuits, he had his cheque.

'Don't the Welsh ever eat?' he roared as they passed through one bleak, foodless, grey-stone village after another.

De Gaulle duly threw the Tribunal out of Paris. It moved to Stockholm.

In Stockholm Stern found himself caught in a punch-up on Wassgergatan between demonstrators carrying North Vietnamese flags and chanting 'Ho Ho Ho Chi Minh' and a dozen young men waving Stars and Stripes. Momentarily his arm encircled Elizabeth's slender shoulder as he pulled her away: 'This isn't for you.' The snow was fresh, even in May.

Within the Folkets Hus he sat in the press section observing Harry's grim scowl whenever the photographers closed to the foot of the platform to snap him in company with Sartre, Deutscher and Dedijer. Did Elizabeth, cool and detached at his side, understand that Harry's scowl masked a need of which he was ashamed?

At his side sat the impassive Sartre, listening through earphones when English was spoken, his hair parted at the side and brushed flat across his head, his oyster eyes askew, a cigarette permanently coiling smoke into Harry's irritated eye. Then Harry shoved his own earphones up into his long mane of prematurely white hair as the Vietnamese witnesses rose to deliver their devastating testimony with impassive dignity. Miss Ngo Thi Nga, from Quanghanh in Quanglinh province (the professional journalists scribbling intractable names on their pads, Stern leaning back easily in his chair), told the Tribunal how a pellet from an American fragmentation bomb had lodged in her brain while she was out in the rice field.

'How awful,' Elizabeth Halliday murmured.

Then nine-year-old Do Van Ngoc, the victim of third-degree burns while herding buffalo, calmy removed his clothes to display his ravaged skin.

'Bastards,' Stern said.

One of Sartre's eyes was focused on the boy. The other, possibly, on Gustave Flaubert, the master-work interrupted by man's mounting inhumanity to man. After the morning session Stern introduced Sartre, standing small and alone in the committee room, stranded among over-friendly American peace spokesmen, to Elizabeth, who shyly offered her hand.

'*Vous profitez de ces témoignages, maître?*' Stern asked Sartre, while Harry bit an empty pipe a few feet away, uncertain of his spoken French, and studiously ignoring Elizabeth.

Sartre nodded. '*Oui. Il y a deux espèces de pauvres, ceux qui sont pauvres ensemble et ceux qui le sont tout seuls. Les premiers sont les vrais.*'

Cameras clicking.

'How about something to eat?' Harry said. Stern lifted an inquiring eyebrow at Elizabeth; with a bird's appetite she was usually content to nibble a salad while Harry and Stern, the subject of her dissertation and its supervisor, swallowed steaks and moved giant pieces across the board of the world. Her pad and pencil lay dutifully beside her plate; when bored by the dialectic she would recross her legs and doodle cartoons, the swish of her thighs lengthening Stern's nose and penetrating Harry Marquis's unruly thatch of dissident hair.

Waiting for coffee, Harry heaved himself to the toilet. When he returned a man of his own generation had taken the empty chair at their table. He rose as Harry's corduroy jacket, its pockets loaded like a gypsy's, brushed through the closely packed tables, but cautiously withheld his hand, as Englishmen do to Englishmen.

'Professor Marquis, my name's Tanner.' He mentioned a newspaper. 'May I?'

Harry shrugged and sat down, as if importunate journalists were the burden of his life. Stern judged the man Tanner to be touching fifty, with the same indulgent stomach as Harry's, the same whisky pouches under the eyes, but he was dressed in a tie and grey business suit, with a 1950s hair cut and a hint of the common people in his accent quite different from Harry's plum baritone, rich with port wine and poetry.

'I covered the Nuremberg trials,' Tanner said.

'There, of course, the victors were judging the vanquished. With us it's the other way round.'

'Isn't that the common factor?' Tanner asked. 'The absence of an impartial judiciary. Isn't it a bit like Alice – the verdict first, the trial later? Call it theatre and I wouldn't argue.'

Harry dug into his sack pocket and rummaged for pipe, tool and pipe cleaner, scavenging for the filthy wet sediment at the bottom of the bowl. Stern glanced at Elizabeth's pad where Tanner was beginning to take the form of a sergeant major barking, 'Am I standing on your hair?!'

'Whatever I say you'll misquote me,' Harry said.

Tanner bridled. 'I think I know my trade.'

'Precisely.'

'The first task of the Tribunal,' Stern said, 'is to establish a formidable and incontrovertible dossier of evidence. For example, you heard Miss Ngo Thi Nga testify about the bullet in her head. We have X-rays, signed by three reputable Paris brain surgeons.'

'If you're telling me people get hurt in wars, I've seen enough wars not to argue,' Tanner said. 'I happen to have been in Vietnam myself.'

'Professor Marquis and I happen to have been in North Vietnam,' Stern said.

'Yes, yes, you're wasting your breath,' growled Harry, more irritated by Stern's usurpation of the interview than by the journalist's hostility. Elizabeth recrossed her legs and for a moment Tanner's attention was diverted to the line of thonged suede half way up her thighs.

'You don't believe the United States has a right to defend an ally against aggression?' he asked Harry.

'The South Vietnam regime is a puppet instrument of America's global imperialism. It doesn't require a tribunal or Bertie Russell or Jean-Paul Sartre to demonstrate that – merely an elementary grasp of the worldwide struggle between monopoly capitalism and the demand of the peasant masses for land and freedom.'

'You account collectivised agriculture a success? Where?'

'For starters, in North Vietnam.'

11

'You spoke of freedom. Does the Communist system of Ho Chi Minh accord with your own idea of freedom?'

'No. But it enjoys the overwhelming support of the Vietnamese masses.'

'I believe you left the Communist Party in 1956?'

'I thought we'd come to that.'

'Do I take it you regard Communism as more acceptable in Vietnam, or China, than in Europe?'

'It's not a question of what I regard as acceptable. It's a question of the right of peoples to self-determination without suffering napalm, CBY fragmentation bombs and, make no mistake, genocide.'

'What's your view of the British Labour Government's posture on Vietnam?'

'Shameful.'

Tanner made a cursory, token jotting in his notebook; clearly he was going to rely on memory, or invention. He glanced at Elizabeth who lifted her pad to shield the cartoons from his gaze.

'And the young lady, does she have an opinion? Miss Halliday, isn't it?'

Elizabeth's lightly mascaraed eyelids lifted in faint surprise.

'The man means,' said Harry, 'who are you sleeping with in Stockholm?'

Stern looked at his watch. 'We're late,' he said.

Standing with Harry in one of the large, cobbled courtyards of Hradčany Castle high above the Vltava River and the beautiful old city of Prague, he contemplated the soldierly lines of bulbous black Tatras belonging to members of the Czech Central Committee meeting in emergency session to depose Novotny. Dubček's socialism with a human face – and an invitation from the Philosophy Faculty of the University – had brought Harry Marquis to Prague. For twelve years (as Stern explained to Elizabeth during a brief tutorial before catching a taxi to Heathrow) Harry had been searching for socialism with a human face.

'Genuinely socialist, genuinely human. Sure you won't come?'

She appraised him. 'I've got classes. You may be able to take off in the middle of term but—'

'That's just bloody bourgeois bureaucracy. Join the university of life. I can square it with the Dean.'

Her eyelids dipped. 'I may join you later.'

In a large, cool room of the Charles University, Professor Marquis, distinguished author of *Reason and Revolution*, inter-

nationally renowned for his definitive study of the utopian socialists, addressed a packed audience confronting its historical – and
perhaps historic – moment in a mood of grave elation. The sealed
shelves of the Novotny era had suddenly yielded a thousand
flowers. Greeted like ambassadors from paradise, Marquis and
Stern had been eagerly questioned about C. Wright Mills, Sartre,
Marcuse, Aron, Althusser and the intoxicating ferment of the New
Left. It seemed to Stern that Harry's own mood darkened as his
lecture progressed. Starting with the rediscovery of the young
Marx, the recovery of alienation as 'the crucial concept', his tone
became increasingly distempered as he proceeded to the 'supermarket of ephemeral fads' displayed in 'the gaudy shop window'
of the New Left.

'Their slogans remind me of sartorial fashions. What sells is
good. Instant solutions. History is Now. Liberation is simply a
new form of conspicuous consumption – these sad children of the
capitalist market innocently condemn the market in the cultural
modes validated by the market. The ad men are delighted: if
"revolution" helps sell trendy gear in the boutiques of the King's
Road, then the entrepreneurs can regard Che Guevera as the patron
saint of the moment. The Stock Exchange loses no sleep when its
own children occupy the colleges in a conforming euphoria of drugs
and sex.'

The Czechs listened intently, faintly bemused, as if something
was being stolen from them. Reciting passages from Blake, Coler-
idge, Shelley and the young Wordsworth, Harry Marquis roamed
the terrain he loved and trusted, wise and sad like a St Bernard,
yet somehow at odds with the intensely urgent needs of an audience
which had only recently marched on Hradčany Castle and been
answered with tear gas and truncheons. Of the two English guests,
Stern proved the more popular; friendly and informal when
meeting small groups of intellectuals and writers in cafés and beer
cellars, he traded in gossip about famous contemporaries, Gunter
Grass, Rudi Dutschke – the intense Czechs wanted to know who
had really been responsible for the almost fatal attempt on
Dutschke's life – Daniel Cohn-Bendit, the leaders of the Free
Speech Movement at Berkeley. A vast love bonded these kindred
spirits and Richard Stern felt himself to be part of it.

Between Harry and Stern there were differences, even tensions.
A meeting with representatives of the Czech Writers' Union,
including Goldstucker, Havel, Vaculík and the editor of Literani
Listy, almost ended in disaster when Harry, galloping ahead of
a desperate and not entirely comprehending translator, abruptly
embarked on a diatribe against George Orwell. Accusing Orwell of
providing a whole generation with an alibi for swallowing capitalist

13

mythology 'hook, line and sinker' (the translator struggled), Harry denounced the author of *1984* for varnishing capitulation in the 'beguiling colours of English decency'.

The Czechs scratched their heads and gazed out of the large, Habsburg windows of the Writers' Union, perhaps listening for the Soviet tanks. Leaving the building, Stern remarked:

'I doubt whether Orwell means much to these people. I mean – their nightmares are not fictional.'

Harry's bushy eyebrows lifted. 'You should have stopped me,' he said sarcastically. 'Why not go back and tell them about the beauties of Orwell's clear, window-pane prose?' He paused to give careful examination to the foreign magazines on display at a newsstand. 'When your pupil, la Halliday, turns her little pen to my views on Orwell, I shall know what to expect.'

'She forms her own opinions.'

'With that in mind, you advised her not accompany us to Prague?'

Harry had orginally resisted Stern's suggestion that Elizabeth should devote her final-year dissertation to 'Harry Marquis: a Philosphy in Transition'.

—Smells of nepotism, he had warned. —No, of incest. The Faculty diehards will never buy it. Besides, she's not all that bright, is she?

—She's not flashy.

—She flashes her thighs enough. Having her, are you? Take a warning: Ramsay and Gough have been waiting to pin something on you ever since I brought you into the department.

But now, three months after Harry had gruffly warned Elizabeth, in Stern's presence, that he wasn't 'the soft option I look', he seemed distempered whenever Stern appeared without his beautiful pupil in tow. On one occasion Harry had taken Elizabeth on a short visit to Paris, where he had been invited to join a jury examining a *thèse de Doctorat d'Etat* on *Le Marxisme, les intellectuels, et le mouvement travailliste en Angleterre*. Stern regarded the trip with misgivings and rather fiercely cross-examined Elizabeth after her return.

—Professor Marquis didn't get much of a word in, the French examiners were all showing off madly. But he did rebuke everyone present for allowing the word 'Angleterre' into the thesis, and then proceeded to question the terrified candidate about Clydeside and South Wales.

—He loathes Scotland and despises Wales.

—That's something the French will never know.

—Did he make a pass at you?

—No. Should he have?

—If I'm not allowed to, he certainly isn't.
—Is that in the LSE regulations?
—Jealousy is part of the curriculum.

She tossed her blonde hair and recrossed her legs.

—You're certainly not short of female admirers. I see them queueing up in the corridor after your lectures, clamouring for your attention.

Partly severed from Harry in Prague by George Orwell, beset with suspicions about why Elizabeth had refused to accompany them, Stern found himself in the company of two avant-garde Czech painters visiting the Galeria Vaclava Spaly where the spirit of the Prague Spring burst into pyrotechnics of iconoclasm and heresy, a loud fart at socialist realism: futuristic Frankensteins, piles of foam rubber, American football helmets painted like lollipops, and a lifelike replica of Marilyn Monroe painted gold from head to toe with the invitation 'Touch me' in five languages. Stern was nervously patrolling a three-dimensional vagina worthy of Eskimo Nell when a small, delicate and faintly perfumed presence registered itself at his side.

'Hullo.'

'Elizabeth!' He couldn't conceal his delight. 'So you got around Ramsay after all?'

His pleasure was immediately tarnished. He might have guessed! Swivelling in hungry pursuit of her gaze, he saw the slender back and pretty buttocks of her Virginian playboy artist, two of whose works, Elizabeth quietly indicated, were on display. One of them the vagina.

'Are you shocked? Christopher will be awfully pleased, he's terribly in awe of you.'

Wearing a see-through blouse in delicate white cotton with nothing underneath, she beckoned to the awful American – who mimed extravagant delight.

'Oh my God, how wonderful! Aren't we all coming together!'

Stern thought about this phrase: so mid-Atlantic was Christopher's accent that it seemed impossible he could ever utter a double-entendre in complete innocence. Stern appraised his student. On no two days did she enter the world wearing quite the same face – as if she was constantly engaged on her own portrait, revising a detail, responding to a new mood of nature, anticipating the human weather. Yet Elizabeth, once varnished for the day, went about her business without a trace of self-consciousness; when she glanced in a shop window it was to inspect the fashions, not her own reflection.

'I hate your vagina,' Stern told Christopher.

'Do I have one? Oh, I see where your delicate little finger is

15

pointing. Actually – though an artist should *never* translate his work into crude, instrumental categories – it's not a vagina. It's the Lincoln Tunnel.'

'Surrounded by pubic hair?'

'Oh my God, Elizabeth, what does one have to do? That, Richard, is the rush-hour crowd, desperate little people dwarfed by the megapolis, hurling themselves at the rim of the tunnel.'

'Are you serious?'

Mounted on monstrous platform heels, Christopher swivelled in his see-through shirt (cut, outrageously, of identical cloth to Elizabeth's) to survey the collages, kinetic artefacts, pop posters, works marked 'disposable' and the canvases threatening to eat the viewer if he stepped too close.

'This is a liberation, Richard. It's frankly experimental. It's aimed at the nerve endings.' Christopher emitted a long, theatrical sigh and ran delicate, glinting fingers through carefully streaked hair. (What *could* she admire in this charlatan?) 'I daresay the People's Police will arrive, sooner or later.'

'Isn't that part of the happening?' Stern asked. 'As my mother might say, "You wouldn't have so much trouble if you didn't put on such rubbish".'

Elizabeth Halliday laughed. Her nipples moved beneath her transparent blouse. Christopher's handsome features registered a hint of annoyance.

'Richard, politics will always elbow-wrestle art to the ground.'

'Is that original?'

'Oh my oh my, such *hostility*, Elizabeth. Let's say it's deeply felt. Richard, you simply must join us for dinner, there are a whole lot of wonderfully gifted people here who are longing to meet you and we have a table booked in the most gorgeous place twenty minutes out of town, quite the best cooking in Bohemia.'

Life in the presence of the desired one is a constant test and so it remained when the revolution in Paris brought Harry, Stern and Elizabeth (this time without Christopher but he was bound to show up) across the Channel on the last ferry before the CGT transport strike confined revolutionary perspectives to the pier at Calais. That Dean Ramsay, devoted Eltonian and expert on Tudor administrative law, would raise the matter of these constant absences in mid-term did not worry Stern, who could shelter behind Ramsay's great enemy, Harry.

They crossed the Channel on a gentle May swell, Elizabeth's flaxen hair folding round her face as they leant over the rail, studying the ability of seagulls to shadow a moving boat without a visible motion of the wings. It passed through Stern's head that he might be the seagull of the revolution; the previous day he had spent money on clothes for the first time in memory. London had become a continuous clothes horse, an orgy of narcissism. Herbert Marcuse was quite right about that, if not about everything else. The trousers he (Stern, not Marcuse) had bought, largely to impress Elizabeth, felt painfully tight – an absurd contrast to Harry's billowing clown's trousers worthy of a wartime allotment.

Harry didn't join them at the rail. He was drinking in the lounge, the sulking subject of a dissertation about to be retitled 'Harry Marquis: Theory and Praxis'. Loudly contemptuous of the infantile insurrection at the Sorbonne, he had relented when real men, the working class, began to occupy the factories, shut down essential services, and formulate 'mature demands rooted in historical experience' (as Harry told his students while rummaging for his passport).

On the train from Victoria Elizabeth had laid her notebook across a stretch of unskirted leg and taken notes in efficient shorthand while Harry, clouded in Gold Block, denounced the 'student fallacy':

'You can't overturn two thousands years of soci-economic development by building barricades in the Boul'Mich. The so-called *groupouscules* are merely baby anarchists wrapped in histrionic self-regard. Once they've kicked papa in the balls they'll settle down to being papa.'

Elizabeth let the rubber tip of her pencil rest lightly on her lower lip:

'Professor Marquis, why are your collective categories always male categories?'

Harry turned to Stern in bewilderment. They inspected the sterilized glass-and-concrete university annexe of Nanterre, where it had all begun, Elizabeth noting down both the slogans and Harry's considered reactions to them (which were not always very considered). 'Vive le FLN' was fine but 'Professors, you are old' drew a contemptuous snort and a rattle of Swan Vesta matches as he dug into the pockets of his corduroy jacket for his dummy.

'You're as old as you feel.'

Stern saw him wink at Elizabeth: a most peculiar moment worth protracted analysis.

'A mausoleum for 12,000 students,' Stern said. 'As the slogan says, "Here freedom stops".' A week earlier, soon after their return from Prague, he had told his third-year political theory seminar that 'the essence of bourgeois empiricism is fragmentation. This and this and this – they show us the trees. We have to make connections, we have to see the wood.'

17

Walking up the Boul Mich from the Place Saint-Michel towards the Luxembourg Gardens, Harry was reading *l'Humanité*. Seven million on strike. He gestured towards the embattled Sorbonne with a dismissive flick of his smouldering pipe:

'Revolutions require desperation. None of these *fils à papa* is desperate: just bad-tempered.'

Whenever Harry's street thoughts threatened to assume magisterial dimensions, Elizabeth quickly closed to his side, her little Japanese tape recorder discreetly raised. She was rich. In an age of legs she had legs. Even in the King's Road, where leather and suede competed to swathe gorgeous bodies in delight and desire, Elizabeth Halliday could make heads turn. Scorning the new chrome-plated boutiques, she ordered her clothes from small couturiers whose low profiles rested easily behind the windscreens of Porsches and old Rolls knocked into art nouveau.

Painted on a wall: 'Revolutions are the ecstasy of history.'

Harry snorted.

Sipping *citron pressé* at a pavement café table, Elizabeth asked whether style, aesthetics, were not crucial indicators of a revolution's humanity.

Stern nodded. 'I agree.' Earlier, when Harry's attention had been diverted by a bookstore window, she had playfully slipped her hand between Stern's belt and stomach. 'Not bad.' Pleasure and confusion beset him in equal proportions.

At the Lycée Condorcet they found more slogans. 'When the last capitalist will be hanged with the guts of the last reformist, humanity will be happy.' Over lunch Harry explained his attitude to violence and in the evening took himself off to the 16th arrondissement home of his colleague Mangin while Stern and Elizabeth braved the occupied Théâtre de France, half-sleeping together on the floor while revolutionaries plundered the theatre's wardrobes and sallied forth to confront the CRS dressed as medieval knights, Crusaders, Ottomans and Roman centurions, their mouths and noses wrapped in handkerchiefs soaked in lemon juice. Delighted by this spectacle, Elizabeth allowed her head to rest on Stern's shoulder.

'Any minute and your Virginian will manifest himself in a fig leaf,' he said.

In the morning his head ached; the steady thud of tear gas canisters and the wail of ambulances throughout the night had been almost as disturbing as Elizabeth's body stretched noncommittally beside his own. After a breakfast of coffee and croissant (he had entered a permanent hunger), Elizabeth dutifully suggested they go in search of the living subject of her dissertation. Stern responded that she might find it more illuminating to meet the young anarchists whom Harry scorned.

'It's time we stopped behaving like tourists.'

'Fine.' She took her unreconstructed face off to the toilet, re-emerging with darker eyelashes and lips in silvery pink.

Searching for Cohn-Bendit, they were informed by anarchist militants manning the barricades that Danny was in Germany, or being interviewed by Sartre, or negotiating with '*La Chienlit*', an esoteric reference to de Gaulle.

Not all reactions were friendly:

'Danny's cultivating his personality'

'Cohn-Bendit's on sale at the Beaux-Arts'

were two of the sardonic reactions which left Stern humiliated in front of his pupil. Sulking, he allowed her to drag him to the Ecole des Beaux-Arts, where she began shamelessly to buy posters.

'Collecting for Christopher's Bond Street gallery?' he muttered. He was beginning to wonder where they would spend the coming night. After months of thwarted desire this cool, level-headed woman was finally offering herself to him in the city of love and revolution; if he faltered now she would despise him. A man must do, he told himself, tight-lipped, gazing abstractedly at the rows of satirical posters, what a man must do.

Gloomily he found himself trailing behind her through the Louvre and the Jeu de Paume. It was she who now regulated their itinerary: as if to say, well, if we are only tourists, let us be tourists. He scowled at the Mona Lisa, his long neck stretching over the thick crowd of revolution-shocked tourists gawping at the painting. Elizabeth skirted the crowd: the obvious did not engage her. He monitored the easy motions of her hips and shoulders until, in the Jeu de Paume, she came to rest at Degas.

Gently she took his arm: '*Tu t'inquiètes?*'

'A scene out of Sartre.'

'What is – Degas?'

'No, us.'

'Remind me. I should know.' A hint of exasperation in her tone – must he always live his life at second-hand, through books?

'In *The Age of Reason* Mathieu takes Ivich to see Gauguin. He sees the paintings, she sees the painter.'

'It's in your book.'

'Yes.'

'But Mathieu was an old man of thirty-eight. Doesn't that console you?'

Leaving the Jeu de Paume, she ventured to inform him that her father owned a Degas.

'That's hardly the point about Degas,' he said.

'Sorry?'

'That Daddy owns him.'

They tried a succession of Left Bank hotels, each of them full. Bored and a little impatient, Elizabeth allowed him to argue and haggle with receptionists and concierges, her blue eyes frosted, her back turned – each failure a nail in the proverbial coffin. And then, under a night sky, they saw the red and black flags in the rue Saint-Jacques, a huge banner proclaiming 'The general will against the will of the general', heard the battle renewing itself out of sight, the thud of paving stones, the roar of burning vehicles, and pitched themselves into the crowd, wrapping handkerchiefs round their noses and yelling '*à bas les flics*!' Later, at about two in the morning, covered in honour, the pair presented themselves at the apartment of Harry's colleague Mangin, begging a floor for the night. They were given a huge omelette and a soft bourgeois sofa.

The following day belonged to Harry. With several thousand others they marched to the great Renault works at Boulogne-Billancourt, Elizabeth's little tape recorder turning attentively as Harry analysed the paralysis of the PCF and the CGT, reminiscing about Waldeck Rochet, Séguy and Fachon, the waning stars of a Communist firmament familiar to him. Harry's mane flowed, his loping strides were huge, his turned-up trousers flapped like the wings of an ungainly goose striving for lift-off. History (history fulfilled or history betrayed, it barely mattered such was the pulse-beat of the encounter) lay ahead of them in the huge, barricaded factory where the working class, bemused by prosperity and the consumer goods derided by the students, was conducting a cautious, disciplined ritual owing more to memories of Robespierre and Jules Guesde, the ghost of Lenin, then to any urgent revolutionary imperative.

The march came to a halt at the factory gates. Communist shop stewards greeted students and intellectuals with respect while warning against 'provocations' in gravel voices.

'A party of sergeants,' Harry grunted.

Clearly he was horribly torn; here, in front of his prize pupil and his pupil's pupil, he had come to the final cul de sac: a juvenile pseudo-revolution he couldn't stomach and a proletariat betrayed by men of his own generation. This, at least, was the analysis that Elizabeth Halliday's tutor offered her on the returning cross-Channel ferry – a rougher sea, more in tune with the *zeitgeist*, kept Harry off the deck – but Stern knew it wouldn't sound quite like that when Harry reported to a packed meeting of students in the LSE's largest lecture theatre. Harry would speak of renewal, tossing the challenge of theory at his audience:

'You, the custodians of the future, must fill the gap between (1)

20

passive acceptance of man reified by the market and (2) man intoxicated by the new pantomime of extravagant gestures.'

All three were exhausted, depleted, as they climbed into the train at Dover. Like a shroud to cover the coffin of the Paris revolution, Elizabeth had put on a long black skirt; she had obliquely offered herself and not been taken. Stern, grabbing the last (or perhaps the only) copy of the *Times Literary Supplement* at the station bookstall, curled his long, thin frame grimly into his seat and began to read the front-page review, anonymous of course, of the book to which he had devoted three years as graduate student and lecturer, *Freedom and Responsibility in Sartre*.

She watched his dark, hawk's eye devouring the paragraphs, hunting for the verdict, his half-handsome features stiffening into a saturnine scowl. The train began to move.

'It's probably not so bad as you think,' Harry said, tamping his pipe. He half reached for the periodical but Stern clung to it, his eye fastened in loathing to the final paragraph. Eventually he tossed it at Harry, rudely, sprang from his seat and disappeared.

Harry lifted his bushy eyebrows at Elizabeth, then settled comfortably with his pipe to read the review. She closed her eyes, as if exhausted by these two gladiators of the global Colosseum.

'Could have been worse,' Harry concluded. 'Richard has written a few scathing reviews in his time, of course, I daresay they had it in for him.'

The hairy hand holding the review out to her was insistent. She took it. Her father had wanted her to read Modern Languages at Oxford, her mother thought she was cut out for art school. Neither could comprehend why she had chosen 'Government and Philosophy' at the LSE but she was clever, three passes at A level, two of them with distinction, strong-willed, mistress of her own destiny and it was really quite convenient to have a responsible daughter looking after the flat in South Kensington while they were living at Holmenkollen 88, Besserud, Oslo, commanding NATO's northern approaches. She had spent her first week at the LSE wondering whether she had made an awful mistake; the flesh of revolutionary ferment was less beguiling in those packed, drab utilitarian corridors than viewed from the desperate distance of a posh boarding school.

Even the slogans painted on the walls were ugly, slapdash, and sometimes mis-spelt; the female students treated Elizabeth's sharp vowels and expensive clothes with suspicion while the men raped her with their eyes or made crude, ridiculous passes. She told herself that she didn't dress to impress, or be different, she dressed to please herself. Alone in her parents' expensive flat, she wept for want of a single friend who would peel away her own inhibiting frost and be nice to her. Someone to go to the cinema and exhibitions with. Despite the London flat she had spent most of her childhood, the school holidays, in the seclusion of the country house near Banbury. You invited the best of the school bunch to stay, if they could play tennis and ride, and the rest was siblings and cousins, boring but not threatening.

She knew hardly anyone in London and this remained the case for most of her first, awful term at the LSE, until a beautiful, gentle, laconic American artist picked her up during a lonely Saturday afternoon at the Tate. He was wealthy, too, which made things easier; the radical seducers of the LSE were the sort who wanted to go straight to bed because it was free, and were wounded to the quick if she offered to pay her way to a decent restaurant or theatre. When Elizabeth flew to Oslo for the spring vacation, the Admiral and Lady Halliday noticed that their youngest daughter had noticeably cheered up since Christmas. She didn't seem to have fallen for the fashionable revolutionary jargon either.

—She's redeploying, Sir Walter told his wife.—I always said that girl's got her head screwed on.

A year later, however, he had to wonder. No sooner had the Norwegian servant brought the first course than their daughter remarked:—I suppose exploitation, like charity, begins at home. Worse was to follow. Something called 'authoritarian hierarchies' had flown to Oslo with Elizabeth, along with 'the nuclear war machine' and 'American genocide in Vietnam'. Even in front of guests, fellow officers and their wives. Sir Walter and Lady Halliday did not know – and were not informed – that the solace of a gentle, rich, innovative Virginian artist had been overtaken by the fiercer, hawk-like pursuit of the School's most brilliant junior lecturer: Honorary Treasurer of the International Marxist Group and with enough money in his own pocket to put her at ease.

Folding the *Times Literary Supplement*, she realised Professor Marquis had been observing her from behind the acrid cloud of pipe smoke that permanently irritated her throat and stung her eyes.

'Don't worry, Richard will bounce back. Hard as nails, that young man.'

She nodded politely. One passage in the review nagged at her throughout the journey: 'That Dr Stern is in every sense a disciple of Professor Marquis no attentive student of his work can doubt. One can therefore only regret that while borrowing the master's urgent polemical style, his flair for the iconoclastic image, the turn of phrase designed to shake us from our lamentable complacency, Dr Stern has not absorbed the profound learning and the subtlety of analysis which have distinguished Professor Marquis's own, increasingly influential publications.'

The third seat remained empty until the train slowed into Victoria.

At Victoria the three of them took three separate taxis. Harry first – a grunt, then gone. His dark eyes manic, Stern held open the door of the second taxi for Elizabeth, the *Times Literary Supplement* squeezed almost to pulp in his free hand.

'Shall I tell you who wrote this review?'

'Who?'

'You know him.'

The taxi driver restlessly turned the meter.

'Harry wrote it.'

TWO

A week after his return from Paris, Professor Harry Marquis delivered an unscheduled lecture on 'The Politics of Cultural Despair'. Notices went up on the boards announcing that it would be open to all departments, and indeed to members of the public, too.

It was a cool day and Elizabeth Halliday, whom comrades in the IMG called Beth, wore a thin Jaeger sweater above her jeans. Admired now, rather than distrusted, for her social background and expensive clothes, she sat in the company of comrades not quite sure what to expect from the maverick professor they affectionately dubbed 'old Harry'. A few of them would study Stern's impassive, hawk profile to gauge the proper ideological response.

It was common knowledge that Marquis had brought Stern to the LSE from Oxford. But they also knew that of late there had been a cooling between the veteran socialist and his closest disciple. Democratically as he conducted his classes, adamantly opposed as he was to the old, tired system of exams and grades designed to process labour into the market – Harry was known to have grown disenchanted with the student revolution storming the academic citadels, the exhausting cycle of demos, sit-ins, occupations and happenings by which the new generation had revived and revamped the old anarchist tradition of 'propaganda by deed'. Stern was making his own space.

The rows of gowned dons who had filled the front rows during Harry's inaugural lecture, two years earlier, were now conspicuous by their absence. No Director, no Dean Ramsay, no Dr Gough, no custodian of traditional 'academic values', no spokesman of the System.

Harry shuffled his notes, fiddled with his lectern, pulled his glasses low on his nose, then glowered over the half-moon lenses at his audience.

'What we witnessed in the 1950s,' he began, 'during the glacial era of the Cold War, when Natapolitan culture dominated our shrunken mental landscape without challenge, was an unprecedented abdication of critical responsibility. The specific failures of the Stalinist system were presented as evidence not only of the myth of revolution, but also as proof of man's inability to transcend the capitalist system without descending into barbarism and psychopathology. Schools of sociologists, historians, economists and psychologists' – he glanced up with a look of wicked innocence – 'some of whom may still be lurking not many miles from this platform, set themselves the remunerative task of explaining, and thus explaining away, our desire to change the world and surmount our chronic alienation. They told us we were neurotics infected by guilt of pathological proportions. Those of us who retained the vision of an economic order not based on the exploitation of man by man were advised to scan our childhood and search family photograph albums for evidence of maladjustment.'

He paused for laughter and got it. Stern sat motionless, his eye fixed on Harry like a detective searching a smoking gun for fingerprints. Elizabeth had been writing steadily in her efficient, economical shorthand.

Harry's voice rose. 'It was all a protracted nursery tantrum, you see! Well, I must confess to be still wearing my nappies a half century later. Very soiled, too.'

The students laughed again. A handful of older Labour leftists, invited by Harry for the occasion, chuckled merrily.

Stern, unsmiling, expected the kick-back: the 'nursery' image would be projected forward into the present day, given a ferocious twist, and turned against the juvenile revolution itself. It was an old dialectical trick which Harry could perform in his sleep but it threatened to open up a frightful wound on the Left.

For a moment Harry's fluency deserted him. Rummaging through his notes, he stuttered, prodded his glasses around his flushed nose – and then hurled himself sideways into a diatribe against contemporary American culture.

'I used to admire the American populist tradition: Whitman, Mark Twain, Jack London, John Reed, Sinclair Lewis, Dreiser, Sherwood Anderson, Dos Passos . . . mm. But then came the capitulation. Hemingway fell into meretricious posturing; Farrell embraced the crudest anti-Sovietism; Dos Passos embraced *Life* magazine. Howard Fast sold his soul to Hollywood. Steinbeck became script writer to James Dean . . . Mm?'

A faint titter of laughter in the packed hall. Where was Harry going? Stern was still brooding on a nuance: in Harry's lexicon was not the word 'populist' faintly demeaning, suggesting a raw gush of breath from Hicksville?

'And these new ones, these "Beats": what do they stand for? *Beats* me.'

A groan from the audience, half affectionate, half exasperated. Harry responded to the challenge:

'Hoboes, bums on the road muttering into their beads about nirvana, spiritual vegetarians – drugs, kicks, escapism, total regression. Just the kind of "radical" art favoured by General Motors.'

Silence. Harry now desperately groping for a come-back:

'By General Motors, Boeing, MacDonald and Lockheed in the era of America's genocidal attack on the people of Vietnam.'

But there was no way back. The audience sensed, though perhaps with less precision than Stern, that Harry had somehow ducked the challenge he had set himself when he announced the lecture. He barely mentioned Prague or Paris, Berkeley or Columbia. He said nothing of the raging confrontations within the LSE itself. He plucked Camus out of obscurity to damn him, savaged Orwell, declared himself ashamed to be a member of the Labour Party, and stumped out of the hall fifteen minutes early with a final quote from Blake about Love.

Harry had blown it.

The comrades studied Stern's saturnine, expressionless features then rose and filed from the hall.

The following day Stern faced his third-year Political Science seminar. The notional subject was Locke and Hobbes but the universal preoccupation was Harry's lecture.

Stern sat down and lifted his long legs on to the second chair he kept for that purpose and shrugged, as if reluctant to embark on an autopsy. Glancing at Elizabeth's faintly frosted smile, he experienced a moment's sharp disequilibrium, then stretched his legs and studied his size-ten jungle boots as if puzzled by them.

'Perhaps a small anecdote may illuminate. As you know, I studied under Harry at Oxford. In my second graduate year I put in for a one-year fellowship at Harvard. When I told Harry he declared himself wounded and betrayed. "The wound may be subjective, Richard, but the betrayal is objective." Had I forgotten Harvard's "disgraceful" record during the McCarthy era? (Actually, by prevailing American standards it hadn't been all that disgraceful.) I said, well, yes, yes, but that was all more than a decade ago. Banging his pipe furiously, he gazed out through the mullioned windows overlooking Broad Street and held me captive in one of his long, crucifying silences while I stared at the worn carpet. "And who would be your supervisor at Harvard?" he snapped. I said I didn't know . . . maybe Kleinmann. Harry erupted: "Exactly, Kleinmann! Star of the Congress for Cultural Freedom. Or maybe you'd prefer Ushinsky, a Catholic fascist from the Ukraine via the Hoover Institute? Or Andrews, an effete pseudo-WASP who has ten fastidious objections to monopoly capitalism and ten fastidious reasons for living with it?" '

Stern surveyed his fascinated seminar, allowing his eyes to rest momentarily on Elizabeth's. They all knew, of course, that he had been in pursuit of her for months, but the doctrine of the age permitted no condemnation and such was his intellectual integrity that no one suspected he might favour her with higher grades than she deserved. Not that they believed in grades anyway, so it didn't matter.

'It was an odd episode, but a revealing one. I suppose Harry must have felt guilty about it, because not long afterwards he waylaid me in the quadrangle, announced that he had been given a chair here, as head of a new department – and promptly offered me a job.'

Stern studied his hands thoughtfully; he saw that Elizabeth's finger nails, today, were a deeper shade of red than usual, as if dipped in Harry's fiasco. Tomorrow evening there was to be a reception at the Institute of Contemporary Arts – a new exhibition of avant-garde collages and silkscreens, including Christopher's. 'Do come if you can,' she had said, the scent of her brushing him in the crowded corridor, her small body hurrying off, always busy. And Hattie, Elizabeth's most devoted admirer in the IMG, dear dogged devoted Hattie, now raised her hand in pained confusion:

'Richard, I really don't understand.'

He lifted an eyebrow. He was gentle with Hattie. Usually he graded her essays up a few points, from the mid–50s, where they belonged, worthy but obtuse, just as he kept Elizabeth hovering on the vital 69/70 frontier even when her icecube logic and austerely tailored analyses clearly merited more. Her essays read like the Chairman's report. She pretended to share the fashionable scorn for grades but he relished the quick flutter of her eyelids as she glanced at the mark, she couldn't help it, the Admiral's daughter whom a certain Miss Tavistock, one of those teachers who bring distinction to the most conformist school, had wooed and inducted into the new-fangled, suspect subject of political studies.

—Of course, Miss Tavistock mused, as the final, autumn term began, —you'll be applying to Somerville, like your mother?

—I suppose so, said the girl, fascinated by the enigmatic buddha-face, lined beyond its years by some catastrophe, which breathed alphas on to and into Elizabeth's essays with benign regularity. —Shouldn't I?

Miss Tavistock smiled as if in resigned anticipation of the Halliday family instinct.

—If you're *really* interested in the . . . shall we say 'collision' between politics and philsophy . . . are you, Elizabeth?

—Yes, Miss Tavistock. Blue eyes steady.

—Then the LSE is the place. Harry Marquis has just moved there from Oxford.

Eighteen months later Elizabeth had visited the school one Sunday to take tea and cucumber sandwiches with Miss Tavistock. The lady fussed with her two cats while Elizabeth conscientiously described every detail of her curriculum, every dramatic event in the ongoing student revolution; fussed with her cats and the teapot, interrupting Elizabeth in mid-sentence with trivia about more milk and more butter, as if defraying an excitement, or a nervousness, that the young woman couldn't quite explain. Only when Miss Tavistock lit one of her naughty Turkish cigarettes (as a boy Stern bought his mother a packet of Balkan Sobranies for her every birthday) did buddha also light up:

—Fascinating. And you hated the place to begin with, you poor thing? Sweet of you not to have written and told me. I was entirely irresponsible when I sent a girl of your background into such a jungle. Do you want my confession?

—Confession, Miss Tavistock?

—Hm. I hope this doesn't sound too much like dialogue in a modern novel but, well, Professor Marquis and I were both undergraduates at Oxford when the war began. I remember he joined the University Flying Corps, he knew Richard Hillary, oh he was such a dashing young man and so brilliant. Oh yes oh yes.

Elizabeth inferred the rest but Miss Tavistock had applied the brakes: self-control and fortitude invaded the tea trolley as if it were one of the Spitfires flown by Hillary and Marquis.

—He never speaks of the war, Elizabeth said.

Miss Tavistock smiled, inclining her head as buddhas sometimes do.

—Harry wouldn't. None of them would. Did you ever read his inaugural lecture, dear?

—Why, yes, you kindly gave me a copy while I was still here.

—Oh did I?

—I hope I now understand it better than I did.

Miss Tavistock had always enjoyed Elizabeth's asperity, the flicker of damaging mischief in her nature, so different from the other Daddy this and Daddy that daughters in the sixth form – a mischief which would one day do to some young man what Harry Marquis had done to Virginia Tavistock.

—I've always felt the most remarkable passage in that inaugural

28

lecture concerned the diminishing value of love in our time. Miss Tavistock kept her folded eyes steadily on her guest, noting that the girl still dressed expensively – she had rather expected some concession to the populism of the zeitgeist.—Do you remember it, dear?

—Oh certainly.

—Not many political scientists dare venture into that terrain. Mm. 'To Mercy, Pity, Peace and Love,' wrote Blake. 'For mighty were the auxiliars which then stood/Upon our side, who were strong in love!' wrote Wordsworth.

—'Wait without Love/For love would be love of the wrong thing,' wrote Eliot.

—So you do remember. Not just politeness to a silly old woman. And *he* feels that decline in the coinage of love so acutely. The meaning of history, he teaches us, lies in the quarrel between 'ought' and 'is'. Human nature is *potential*. I think that's . . . so true. So true.

Miss Tavistock produced a small handkerchief then thought better of it and put it away again.

—And this Dr Stern . . . Is he nice?

Elizabeth laughed, forgetting that Miss Tavistock was not to be treated like her mother, then hastily apologised.

—Oh it's quite all right, Elizabeth, the clever ones never are very nice, are they? Harry wasn't very nice either. Which wife is he on now? Is bed part of the curriculum for the prettier girls? You must know.

Hattie was raising her hand in consternation. 'I just don't understand, Richard. I mean, when Harry first came here he seemed, I mean, so full of optimism. Isn't that right, Beth?' Hattie's eyes squirmed in confusion behind her glasses, her unwashed hair lank with resignation to never quite understanding. Somewhere in the building the voice of Joan Baez rose to proclaim a new provocation, a new protest, a new linking of arms against the pigs. Stern stood in the vast exhibition room of the Institute of Contemporary Arts confronting a sculpted pair of hands, palms open, fending off invasion, punctured by a row of machine-gun bullets.

'He doesn't trust his initial reaction,' Christopher said sadly. 'He wants to think it through, cerebralise it.'

'Go away, Christopher,' Elizabeth chided the Virginian. 'You're breathing down his neck, it isn't fair.'

Stern passed through the crowd to the next masterpiece, still shadowed by Christopher, who had now grown a Jesus beard and wore the plain white robe of the messiah. Erotic female bodies had been collaged on to the silkscreened heads of famous astronauts, statesmen, generals.

'Well, yes,' Stern said.

'He means, "Well, no," ' Christopher sighed.

Elizabeth had discreetly wandered away.

The afternoon had been wasted in a raging Faculty meeting, the corridor beyond the door jammed with students demanding the right to formulate their own courses and grade their own dissertations on a scale from X to X. Dean Ramsay's Tudor features were fixed on Harry, as if he held him uniquely responsible for the collapse of civilization.

'So it's to be cafeteria education from now on? Women's Studies, Black Studies, Relevant Studies, Alternative Studies, Liberation Studies.'

At Ramsay's right hand Dr Gough looked suitably outraged. His massive forehead seemed to stretch with re-heated moral capacity. Harry doodled Spitfires.

'Heaven forbid,' continued Ramsay, 'that we should impose the authoritarian constraints of chronology on these children of the apocalypse. Isn't history bunk, after all?' He smiled sourly at Stern. 'We must be "relevant", mustn't we, Richard? I gather that knowledge is no longer "relevant" – only "making connnections" is relevant. Bursting the "bourgeois categories", is not that the urgent task? Ah yes, I forgot "situations". And "structures", mustn't leave that out, Richard. I gather your students now hop about merrily from one half-digested lettuce leaf to the next, like contented rabbits.'

'And I gather that your current course on "Main Factors in Tudor and Stuart Government" is currently supported by a devoted audience of three.'

The Dean blew his fuse-box.

'Should we hire Trafalgar Square for Dr Stern's overflowing course on "Comparative Imperialism"?' Trembling, he turned to Harry. 'Forgive me if I misunderstood your inaugural lecture, Marquis, but my antique, fuddled mind told me you were denouncing consumerism as the inhuman touchstone of the rotten, bourgeois society currently binding us in subtle slavery. Yet now your protégé, whom you so kindly brought us from Oxford, is heard measuring the intrinsic value of a course by the size of its audience.'

Harry continued doodling.

Hubbub in the corridor. A renewed thumping on the locked door. On Ramsay's instructions locks had been fitted to the administrative offices and the Senior Common Room (the students were demanding integrated meals) following scenes in which teaching staff had been manhandled, taken hostage in their offices, held overnight, and subjected to various indignities.

'Won't you call off your dogs?' Ramsay asked Harry.

Harry looked up from a burning Heinkel. 'Rabbits? Dogs? This isn't Animal Farm, John.' But he spoke without conviction.

'I rather thought it was,' said Dr Gough. 'Ever since I found the papers on my desk smeared with excrement.'

Stern studied Harry sidelong. Clearly he had no stomach for the fight today. Walking down Houghton Street from the Economist Bookshop, Stern had seen Elizabeth quickening her step to keep pace with Harry's loping strides. They had turned the corner into Aldwych.

'May I speak?' Stern asked Ramsay.

'I would have thought that was inevitable.'

'We are creating something called "access". We are trying to relate learning to life.'

'Access? Is it a credit card?' Dr Gough's laugh came in a thin trickle. 'You mean universal illiteracy, sloppy hedonism and idleness decked out as "dialogue".'

Again Stern glanced at Harry. No reaction. The rumpled mane of hair declined to lift. For the first time Stern experienced a twinge of alarm. The forces of progress and reaction round the table were evenly balanced; strength of personality had hitherto resolved each clash, with Ramsay in permanent retreat before Harry's luminous wit and slow, burning stare. If Harry now abandoned ship Thermidor would come swiftly: Stern held his post on probation, without tenure. An exultant premonition of martyrdom gripped him. He turned on Gough:

'Like all revolutions, this is a messy, uncomfortable affair. But sarcasm won't solve it. I move that we unlock the door and listen to what they have to say.'

'You will personally guarantee our safety?' Gough asked sarcastically.

Harry did, then, look up. 'Yours, maybe, but not mine. Danton knows Saint-Just too well.' So saying he was on his feet, shovelling a disordered pile of papers under his arm, then out into the corridor, yelling 'Passage! Right of passage! Thank you, thank you, most kind.' Stern followed and was immediately confronted by Hattie's owl eyes, wide with bafflement. The students had fallen back for Harry but his loud remonstrances continued as he threaded his way, bulky and round-shouldered in his baggy corduroy jacket, through the packed throng. 'You don't combat fascism by practising it, thank you, thank you.'

Tall and self-assured, hemmed in by student union officials who closed round him like secret service bodyguards, trailed by pretty girls in miniskirts, Stern beckoned his constituents towards the nearest lecture room.

No sign of Elizabeth; she was doubtless decking herself out for the Virginian's apotheosis at the ICA.

'Harry isn't well,' he told the students. 'It's an old war wound he doesn't talk about. Perhaps not many of you know that Harry served as a fighter pilot during the Battle of Britain. He flew almost forty missions and was shot down twice. You may have noticed the slight limp.'

Now, bored and jealous, Stern drifted through the fashionable crowd at the ICA, deserted by the wounded Christopher.

'He's easily hurt,' Elizabeth explained in the taxi.

'By you, not by me.'

'It's you he's jealous of.'

'My dear girl—'

'I'm not a girl, Richard, I'm a woman. Would I address you as "my dear boy"?'

He looked stunned. 'It's just a convention of language.'

'Are you so devoted to convention?'

'No, but . . . Doesn't "my dear woman" sound rather rude?'

'Only the "my dear" bit. Why should "woman" be rude? And why, may I also ask, do you address Hattie as "love" when you want to be condescending to her? "You haven't quite grasped the point, love." Would you say such a thing to a male student?'

'Anything else?'

'Yes. I've decided to abandon my dissertation about Harry.'

Silence in the taxi as they passed down the Cromwell Road.

'I thought you might,' Stern said, though it hadn't occurred to him. 'Was that before or after Harry took you home to help his shy, reclusive wife type his new book?'

'He did nothing of the sort!'

'I didn't imagine he did. Maybe it was *you* who took *him* home to help type your dissertation?'

Her long mascaraed lashes dipped. 'Don't be silly, Richard.'

The taxi drew up outside her parents' South Kensington flat. Stiffly Stern alighted, holding the door for her.

'Goodnight, Elizabeth.' He poked his long neck at the driver: 'Notting Hill Gate, please.'

She laid a hand on his arm. 'Won't you come in?'

'To sip cognac with Christopher? I assume he'll be showing up when the sulks wear off.'

She stepped close to him, tilting up her chin. 'No, he won't. I told him I was spending the night with you.'

Stern followed her thigh-high suede boots up to the second floor, armouring himself against the oppressive opulence of the flat with its single, tiny masterpiece riveted, behind unbreakable glass, to the wall.

'So Daddy does own a Degas.'

His remark to her on leaving the Jeu de Paume had been forgiven. Repeated, its offence revived.

What depressed him about the Halliday town residence was not its large, unused rooms, its idling, casual reflection of inexhaustible wealth rooted, layer upon layer, in accumulated profit; what depressed him was its quiet self-assurance. This was the grand effect that his mother and Monty had aspired to as they plastered their walls and floors with marked-down flash and filigree, everything a 'bargain', everything 'genuine', everything 'a wonderful investment'. Everything hideous.

'A drink? There's some cold hock in the fridge.'

He shook his head.

'I think I might,' she said.

He drifted after her into the kitchen. A lush and lazy cat eyed him from its cushioned basket. Sipping the wine she perched on the edge of the big pine table, her leather skirt a mere pelmet to the two priceless limbs swinging before him. Her voice tinkled, the admiral's daughter, as whenever she felt nervous.

'Richard, I showed Harry thirty pages of my dissertation. All right, all right, I knew you'd disapprove, it's against the rules, I grovel. "My dear girl" grovels before sir. But I had to.'

He nodded. 'Guilt?'

'Well, yes! By the time we came back from Paris I knew it was your thesis not mine.'

'I don't think that's true at all.'

'Yes, you do. I could never have written anything half so clever. Or half so critical. And then when we got back from Paris I realised . . . well, that I'm caught in a war between you and Harry. I'm out of my depth. I remember that awful look in your face, quite terrifying, as you stuck your head into the taxi at Victoria station. The idea that Harry could have written that foul review.'

'Paranoia, you conclude?'

She refilled her glass. Normally one glass would last her a whole evening.

'Perhaps I will have one,' he said, 'if there's any left.'

'Oh, bottles and bottles. Daddy has Degas, Daddy has bottles.'

He repressed a fleeting impulse to apologise for that. A desire such as his could not accommodate apologies. It was to her acolyte Hattie that he regularly said sorry. 'Sorry I'm late. Sorry I missed yesterday's tutorial. Sorry I didn't have time to find that book for you in the London Library. Sorry I walked past you in Aldwych without saying hello, too many ridiculous things on my mind.' In this life you had to be at war with what you wanted. If it wasn't worth fighting it wasn't worth conquering.

'And what did Harry say when you told him?'

'Told him what?'

'That I knew he'd written that review.'

Her lashes dipped demurely. 'He admitted it. He also claimed to have written the eulogy of your book in the *Observer*, the handsome tribute to your talent in the *Guardian*, not to mention the forthcoming diatribe in *New Left Review*, nicely offset by a rave review in his own, your own, our own, *Thought and Action*.

Her neat buttocks slid off the pine table. As her hand inserted itself between his belt and his abdomen her silvered mouth curved into an enchanting smile.

'Richard's not still a secret virgin, is he?'

His long, brittle body trembled.

'Christopher believes your appreciation of contemporary art, not least of his own, won't improve until you lose your monk's cowl. Aren't I a bitch?'

She left the kitchen. When she came back she was carrying her dissertation.

'Dr Stern, do sit down, please make yourself more comfortable. Just a few readings, one or two key passages which particularly incensed your *maître* and my *grandmaître*, to quote an old joke of Miss Tavistock's. Please feel free to use this other chair for your legs, I know you like to have them up when you're apologising to Hattie and countless other insect pupils you happen to have stepped on. Ready? Introduction, page seven.

' "There can be little doubt that Marquis's service in the Royal Air Force in 1940 was, in his own estimation, a poor substitute for the 'real thing': Spain. Born in 1921, Marquis was too young to join the International Brigades. By the accident of his birth, the ferment of the brilliant Thirties generation of intellectuals and poets passed him by. To Harry Marquis belongs the unique distinction of having joined the Communist Party a few weeks after the Nazi-Soviet Pact. This, however, did not prevent him serving King and country in the skies over southern England. A year after the end of the war he wrote an undergraduate review denouncing Orwell as a saboteur of Anglo-Soviet friendship, an enemy of socialism, and the harbinger of a new, fashionable pessimism. Not until 1956, following Russia's suppression of the Hungarian revolution, does he seem to have noticed the Gulag archipelago, the persecution of the Jews in the USSR, or the need for socialism with a human face. In short, Harry Marquis has consistently missed the boat: not until 1968 did he witness and experience a genuinely radical "moment" in his own society – and that, he concluded, belonged to others." '

'You wrote all that down?'

34

'Why, yes. If it's true, it's true. And this – oh, Harry was *most* interested by this passage:

' "The main flaw in Marquis's *Reason and Revolution* is its failure to offer a theory of human psychology. Every manifestation of human alienation is attributed to class society. Infantile anxiety, sexuality and the role of the family are all ignored. History with a capital 'H' consumes all human activity like a dialectical boa-constrictor swallowing a cow it can neither digest nor cough up. As a consequence Marquis offers no insight into the problem of *power*, no analysis of elites beyond superficial complaints about 'betrayals' and 'distortions' which belong more properly to polemic than to philosophy." '

Elizabeth tossed the corkscrew to Stern. 'Open more wine, Dr Stern.'

Harry's mane lifting: Danton understands Saint-Just.

Stern said, 'I really don't know whether to believe you.'

'Daddy and Degas insist a "dear girl" must never tell lies.'

'Elizabeth, you're drunk.'

Dropping the dying dissertation on the floor, she sauntered across to him almost sluttishly and fastened her arms round his neck. 'A teeny bit drunk.' As her silvered lips fastened on his mouth her small, perfect body bent into his like an archer's prize bow.

'Know when I first loved you? It was when we chased around Paris and couldn't find your great *copain* Cohn-Bendit. And why? Because you were down and stayed on your feet. Because you were dreadfully humiliated and didn't show it. As my Daddy always says, know a man not by the battles he wins but by the ones he loses. Daddy and Degas.'

'It was a disgraceful remark.'

'You are forgiven – provisionally.' Taking his hand she led him to her bedroom. The chest of drawers and bedside tables were strewn with a young girl's childhood mascots, little china birds, fluffy things, a cuckoo clock, embroidered baskets, a Japanese singing doll, more dolls, a wooden owl, pretty bottles, a Swiss barometer, tinted portraits of her family. A huge golden teddy bear lay on the brocade bedspread over her pillow.

'That's Herbert. He velly jealous. Bite you.'

She cuddled Herbert then kissed him. 'Go on, you kiss Herbert. Love me, love Herbert. *Poor* Herbert.'

This banter continued. She introduced him to virtually every little mascot and china creature in the room. 'This is Emily. What's her name? The silly man can't remember already, what shall we do with him, Emily? This hippo is Horace. From the Congo basin, he says, though I've never been sure whether he's making it up. I

35

think he likes you. Do you like Richard, Horace? Is he nice enough to go beddies with? Mm? Not sure?'

She was waiting. He felt like a large, ungainly grey moth fastened by the sharp, bright pin of her impatience – if only her body belonged to someone he didn't know. If only women's bodies didn't have people attached to them. But, even as he balked at this final subversion of his status, he succumbed. Herbert and Horace watched impassively – no novelty, perhaps – as the long stranger sank on to the bed with their mistress. They observed her fluttering beneath his brittle, angular limbs with the quick, vibrant motions of an exotic bird courting captivity, her impertinent hand unceremoniously goading him into an admission of need. The man now began to grab, fondle and squeeze, laying a prospector's claim to breasts, thighs, buttocks, yet uncertain of their most remunerative point of claim. He had begun to moan.

'Let's undress,' she whispered. 'I want you to make love to me properly. Like a gentleman.'

Naked, it was the best thing he'd ever experienced. But he didn't say so and afterwards she cradled his head, as if to console him.

THREE

'Do you eat bacon, Richard?' Lady Halliday asked.

'Just a boiled egg, thank you.'

'Christopher?'

'You know I only eat an apple, Cressida,' drawled the Virginian, leafing through the *Telegraph*. She regarded him indulgently, a handsome woman whose regular features, Stern had noted, predestined Elizabeth's.

'One can see you don't eat,' she rebuked him affectionately. 'I'm sure Richard is more sensible.'

'Oh he is, Cressida, he is.'

Lady Halliday tinkled a silver bell and gave the breakfast orders to a comfortable woman called Edith.

'What about Miss Elizabeth, m'um?' Edith asked.

'I rather think she's given up breakfast, Edith.'

When the woman had gone Lady Halliday pointed her china chin at Stern.

'Edith rather thoughtlessly bought pork chops for lunch . . .'

'Fine.'

Lady Halliday looked rather disappointed. 'Are you quite sure?'

'I'll even drink milk in my coffee afterwards.'

The eyes that blanked over were not quite as frost-sharp as Elizabeth's. 'Milk, don't you drink milk?'

She struck Stern as over-dressed for breakfast; to see 'English' country clothes nowadays you had to move among the Italian and Spanish upper classes. Of course it had been a mistake to come. Lady Halliday could perfectly well have questioned Elizabeth about his dietary habits, and indeed probably had – but this needling was as nothing to the fury he'd felt when, reaching the Georgian mansion a quarter of a mile from the boundary gate, he had seen the Virginian's silver Porsche gleaming snugly in the gravel courtyard.

Elizabeth had read his expression. 'I hope you don't mind. Christopher said he might look in on his way to an exhibition in Oxford. I could hardly say no.'

'Of course it's all pure Constable out here,' Christopher drawled, refilling his breakfast cup from the silver coffee pot. 'It completely throws me, Cressida. I may have to do your portrait *après* Gainsborough.'

Lady Halliday giggled. Perhaps she fancied Christopher. Perhaps she felt her daughter was safe with him.

The Admiral came in for breakfast dressed in jodhpurs. He had the pinched moustache of a worried stockbroker.

'Rodney says Thumper is lame in his right foreleg. That boy has been over-riding him but won't admit it.'

'Christopher is threatening to do my portrait,' Lady Halliday said.

'Heaven help you. How much will I have to pay?'

'Much less than a million,' Christopher said. 'You need only sell your Degas.'

The Admiral grunted, loading his plate with bacon, sausages, kidneys and mushrooms. 'Do you ride, Dr Stern?'

'Only a bicycle. But never in traffic.'

'Hope you won't be bored here.'

'And how is little Oslo?' Christopher asked.

'Even more boring since your last visit,' Lady Halliday said. 'The town is still quaking, you know.'

'My dear Cressida, I had no idea the liberated Norwegians are so puritan.'

'If you saw the sun only twice a year, you'd be puritan,' the Admiral said. 'Do you play tennis, Dr Stern?'

'I could try.'

'We'll need you for a mixed doubles this afternoon,' Lady Halliday said. 'I've forbidden Walter to play. He tries to serve aces, won't acknowledge his age, then seizes up.'

'*That's* worth seeing,' Christopher said.

'Don't be impertinent,' the Admiral said. 'Elizabeth still in bed?'

'She's been working hard, dear.'

The Admiral shot a look at Stern. 'Has she?'

'Oh yes.'

'I gather you're now the custodian of her intellectual development?'

'That cap fits no one but Elizabeth herself.'

'Hm. Sounds to me like a continuous riot. Rent-a-mob stuff. A miracle anyone learns anything.'

'They learn how to riot,' Christopher said. 'The University of Life.'

The Admiral ignored him. He was intent on Stern. 'You're a philosopher?'

'Political theory is a debased form of philosophy. Not unlike the relationship of accounting to maths. The analogy may indicate the necessity of the debasement.'

'No, I don't understand. That's too clever for me,' Lady Halliday said.

'What's this International Marxist Group thing?' the Admiral persisted.

'Elizabeth insists we call her Beth,' Lady Halliday explained.

'Beth?'

'There's a Tudor validation,' Christopher said.

This comment seemed to ease the Admiral into temporary affability. 'Of course this is Civil War country here. In my view the Levellers were an interesting bunch – unlike the Fifth Monarchists, whose spiritual descendants now control our universities, minus God. Take Lilburne – widen the franchise but one step at a time. Lilburne had his head screwed on.'

'Yes,' said Stern. 'He was arraigned by the Star Chamber and variously flogged through the streets of London, committed to Newgate and the Fleet, thrown into the Tower . . .'

The Admiral winked at his wife. 'We're a tolerant people.'

Elizabeth came in wearing jeans.

'Oh God, she's not in jodhpurs,' Christopher sighed. 'Some fateful decision has been taken.'

'I've got work to do,' Elizabeth said.

'But surely you can take an hour off, dear,' protested Lady Halliday.

'Do your spirits good,' said the Admiral. 'You're looking peaky, washed out.'

Everyone except Elizabeth turned accusingly to Stern.

'Couldn't you spare her for an hour?' Lady Halliday pleaded.

He shook his head. 'Greek verbs till ten. French unseen till eleven. Latin prose till noon. A five-minute break before she recites the whole of "Paradise Lost". After lunch her serious education begins: Karate, molotov cocktails, barricade building – can we use the stables?'

'Daddy's library would be better,' Elizabeth said, taking the Chippendale chair next to Stern's. 'For the book burning.'

The rage in Christopher's delicate, doctored features made Stern happy.

'The joke,' roared the Admiral, 'is evidently on us.'

Lady Halliday tucked her folded napkin into its ring. 'I'm sure

39

Richard wouldn't fall off Soldier. No one falls off Soldier. We could find a hat.'

'Thumper would be better,' Christopher said, 'if he's truly lame.'

They all went riding, Elizabeth included, without Stern. 'Are you sure you don't mind?' she whispered to him. At lunch Lady Halliday repeated her act about pork chops and the Admiral was soon back on the warpath:

'Surprised you tolerate weekends with your warmongering father, Elizabeth.'

'Daddy, don't start.'

'Just trying to make conversation. Wouldn't want to bore you and Dr Stern with talk of cows, pigs and broken fences.'

'Make love, not war, Daddy.'

'Is that what you do?'

'Walter!' Lady Halliday had flushed.

'I suppose the Russians will expropriate this place into a collective once you people have thrown our nuclear weapons in the sea.'

'The Russians are very keen horsemen,' Stern said easily. 'The commissars would take over the stables. Within a week most of the local gentry would be riding with them.'

'Ooooo . . .' crooned Christopher. 'Blood is being drawn at last.'

The Admiral's anger was such that he couldn't speak; he could barely eat. Lady Halliday and Elizabeth hurried to pour oil into the void, both speaking at once. When the Admiral got down his morsel of pork he turned blindly on his daughter.

'I gather we now have to call you "Beth".'

Surprised, she lifted her chin. 'It's optional for you, Daddy.'

'Was the International Marxist Group responsible for amputating half your name?'

On a wall of the Sorbonne: 'Genocidal generals are genitally deprived.' Stern slowly wiped his stiletto:

'It's part of the initiation ceremony, you see. Later we renounce our own names entirely and adopt a number, as in *Brave New World*. But that's merely a prelude to disowning God, country and Daddy. Only when we are thoroughly conditioned and tested are we given back the deceptive appurtenances of our original persona and sent out into the world by Control to do our deadly work.'

Elizabeth was breathing fast, flushed like her mother, possibly close to tears, Stern wasn't sure. Even Christopher had fallen prudently silent, no doubt hoping to regain lost ground on the rebound. Lady Halliday wore white for tennis but Elizabeth wore jeans and the only problem was to find a pair of soft-soled shoes large enough to fit Stern. The new-mown grass smelt lovely. Christopher gallantly begged Lady Halliday to partner him. 'We have the brawn even if you have the brains,' he called across the net

40

and Lady Halliday giggled, hopping up to the net when the Virginian began to unleash his cannonball serves. Elizabeth played with tutored style, sometimes with flourish, patient and unflustered by Stern's inability to make contact with a single ball throughout the set – even when serving.

'Don't drive so fast.'

'I'm not.'

'You must be driving as fast as you are driving.'

'Any other offences to be taken into account?'

'And please don't let's have a post-mortem. I can see one brewing in those lovely sulky eyes. Did you know that your nose palpably grows when it's indignant?'

'I'm indebted to your vast tolerance on the tennis court.' She pinched his leg. 'Stop it.' Studying his solemn profile she tried not to laugh but her mouth twitched. She had always wanted to look like Garbo and secretly felt she was a passable, off-the-peg version; defrosting and collapsing into helpless laughter as Commissar Ninotchka had done was a histrionic catharsis that Elizabeth had practised in front of the mirror ever since she'd first seen the film in the summer of '62, with Mummy and Daddy at Cannes. Stern even reminded her of Melvyn Douglas if she closed her eyes.

'Daddy really admires intellectuals,' she reassured him. 'Well, not exactly. I mean, he likes cocky, ambitious people who put him down. It's because he despises Christopher that he's polite to him. Next time he'll eat out of your hand and admit his passion for Degas. You're still driving too fast.'

Abruptly the Halliday family receded from his angry horizon, to be instantly replaced, as the M40 carried them towards the western outskirts of London, by an alternative ogre, Harry. The sardonic reserve with which Harry had initially treated Elizabeth and her dissertation – as if his life was plagued by juvenile thesis-writers from all over the world – had now yielded to a fussy badgering. Notes constantly summoned her to his office. Or to local pubs. Her handbag was stuffed with scraps of paper on which Harry had 'clarified' or 'reappraised' this question and that. A chance comment about an avant-garde play she had seen with Richard precipitated a barrage of notes, abrupt and elliptical, tossed into the enemy citadel like grenades.

—Do try to distinguish between the drama of history and the history of drama. I'm not sure Richard can.

—Don't forget that live performances are merely social occasions, usually pretexts for posturing and [illegible] prostitution. To penetrate Euripides, Racine or Shakespeare, you need only read the text.

—He who is *au courant* is usually a current bun.

—Any one novel by Balzac or Dickens is worth the whole modernist charlatan [illegible]. Life is neither a dustbin nor a cracked mirror.

—In the Roundhouse and the Royal Court they now murder language and with it reason. Everything is now defaced, from lecture halls to human dignity.

—Try to keep your feet on the ground even when spending the night in a smart high-rise flat in Notting Hill. (In that connection, don't under-estimate Ramsay and his gang. If they can pin any discredit on me they will – even if they have to do it via your irregular relationship with your tutor.)

When this last note passed into his hand the normal sardonic smile was wiped from Stern's features. Despite Elizabeth's furious protests, he took it straight to Harry. Compounding the injury, he afterwards refused to disclose to Elizabeth what had transpired.

For the next few weeks tutor and pupil lost their appetite for London's flourishing avant-garde theatre. Harry's bulky shadow, replete with a pain which was both eloquent and inarticulate, lay across them. They even avoided one another in the corridors of the LSE. When the subtly obtuse Hattie's owl eyes poked round Stern's office door in search of 'Beth', the stinging rejoinder sent her into confused retreat.

Beth did confide to Hattie that she would give her right arm to abandon her dissertation, but it was too late to begin another one. Either she completed it or she flunked her degree.

'But we don't care about degrees, do we, Beth? Integrity is what it's all about.' She gazed hopefully at her adored heroine. 'And defeating the men?'

Beth fixed her with the frost-blue eyes and luminous skin that invariably caused a commotion within Hattie.

'Yes. But we can only do that from a position of strength and don't you forget it.'

Trembling, Hattie awaited the appearance of the dreaded diamond ring on Beth's pretty hand. It was awful: everyone was getting married.

Elizabeth couldn't report all this faithfully to Stern without mentioning marriage and diamond rings.

FOUR

Rhodesia House occupied. Stern drifted into this minor event almost by accident. Three years had passed since Ian Smith unilaterally declared white Rhodesia independent of Britain. Despite demonstrations of protest at the LSE (where, for some reason, occupying Dr Gough's office was felt to be the proper response to UDI) Stern hadn't allowed southern Africa to intrude on more urgent priorities – the area had yielded to his uncertain knowledge no revolutionary theory and no Che Guevara. Fanon was included in his curriculum, of course, but Fanon was from the Antilles and Fanon was dead.

By some oversight, Richard Stern did not even figure on Anti-Apartheid's mailing list. The regular demos outside South Africa House, only five minutes' brisk walk from the LSE, passed him by. He had hurried past Rhodesia House, an imposing building in the Strand, graced by an Epstein carving, with barely a glance, and was quite unaware, on this brisk morning in the New Year, that it had been occupied by a glittering company of writers, intellectuals and actors, all squatting on the floor in protest at the illegal Smith régime's continuing occupation of the High Commission in whose windows seductive colour photographs of the Victoria Falls and copulating lions flagrantly beckoned to tourists, while leaflets within, lauding the low levels of taxation in this 'land of opportunity', brazenly solicited white settlers. When politely invited to leave, the intellectuals refused – all according to plan so far! – and were soon pleasantly engaged in gossip about new poetry magazines and recent productions at the Court, the RSC and the fringe theatres. So it goes.

The bemused skeleton staff of Rhodesia House summoned the police, as they were intended to do. An Inspector arrived and was treated to a short lecture on régimes engaged in illegal rebellion against the Crown. He was unmoved. 'I'm asking you to leave now,' he said and withdrew. Within half an hour two bus-loads of police had parked round the corner; the Labour Home Secretary was reportedly in conference with the same constitutional advisers who, the previous year, had found a formula for excluding from British soil British passport holders of Asian descent.

In due course the National Front showed up, magnetized by the provocative posters now plastered over the large plate-glass windows of Rhodesia House. A certain unease beset the occupiers. They hadn't bargained for so much realism. Shortly before lunch a radiant playwright and a Trotskyist actress burst into Richard Stern's utilitarian office at the LSE and ten minutes later Stern was standing on a table in the main refectory, flanked by the President of the Students' Union, urging the comrades to abandon their shepherd's pies. Long of stride and nose, Dr Stern led his contingent down the Strand, past the charabancs disgorging stupid old people outside the commercial theatres, exchanged insults and a few shoves with the skinheads chanting their hideous hatred outside the building, then pressed inside, exchanging greetings and kisses with the beleaguered company of saints within.

He had not press-ganged Elizabeth, or even gone in search of her. He had never involved her in violent confrontations.

'Congratulations on your book, Richard. Wonderful reviews.'

'Not all of them.' He took the upstretched hand of the *New Statesman*'s gnomish correspondent, Tree. Finding no space on the floor in which to fold his long limbs, Stern remained upright, awkwardly placing his feet between friendly legs.

'Have a good "Paris"?' asked Tree. 'I got to within ten feet of your *maître* Sartre before an acolyte elbowed me in the stomach.'

A black bloke in a beret was reading aloud messages of greetings from nationalist leaders detained south of the Zambezi. The assembly hushed itself, applauding politely. Then, raising the temperature, one of Stern's own students, Oscar Mucheche, a member of the IMG and known for his quotations from Frantz Fanon and his rare attendance at classes, launched into a strident attack on racism, imperialism and 'white liberals who fight apartheid by going to the theatre'. Stern's long neck swivelled slowly until his attention was arrested by a young woman standing almost next to him. Her gentle, composed smile, fixed affectionately on Oscar Mucheche, immediately tied a knot in Stern's chest. Her oval face, exquisite in every detail, was framed in rich, chestnut hair, and even as he stared at her, hypnotized, Oscar beckoned to her to speak. Shyly she shook her head.

'Come on, Esther,' Oscar insisted.

'Well,' she began diffidently, almost inaudibly, 'I'm white, I'm liberal and I never go to the theatre.' The quiet ripple of answering laughter lifted her voice to a stronger cadence, a voice as sweet and soft as crushed demerara.

'I'd just like to say that the men in Smith's detention camps will truly appreciate this gesture of solidarity you have made today. I know many of them, I've visited them, I've seen the appalling conditions under which they live. They are the future leaders of *my* country – Zimbabwe. Thank you.'

Warm applause. Stern gazed at her transfixed, momentarily plucked out of the compelling enterprise called Richard Stern.

Friendly hands reached out to her. She moved away.

'Who is she?' he asked Tree.

Tree offered a gnomish shrug. 'Some born-again Jacaranda Queen.'

Stern felt a hand on his shoulder. He turned.

'We've met,' the man said. 'Stockholm. Last year. You were with Marquis and a pretty girl.'

'Ah . . .'

'Leonard Tanner.'

'Yes, I remember.'

'Come to join the party, have you? Usual rent-a-mob. How's your Professor Marquis? Is it true that he's fallen out with the militants?'

'Am I being interviewed?'

Leonard Tanner's crumpled face of wax and leather suddenly set. 'Frankly, I don't give a bugger. This charade's worth five lines at the bottom of page five.'

'Hardly worth spoiling your lunch hour.'

Stern saw his words etched, in acid, into the wax. He watched Tanner force his way to the main door and disappear, only seconds before the police Inspector returned at the head of a platoon of constables to issue a final warning:

'I now have instructions to remove you. No, sir, no arguments. Kindly leave now in an orderly fashion, otherwise my men will clear the building.'

On his feet with commendable speed, Tree pushed past Stern.

'Urgent deadline,' he winked. 'There are some events worth reporting before they happen.' Stern watched the *New Statesman*'s correspondent, famous for his reports of the first Aldermaston marches, rutting and barging his way out.

Those remaining all sat down. Stern tucked his knees awkwardly under his chin. The police studied the squatters with the professional objectivity of dockers about to unload carcasses, then began to lift and carry, working in pairs. It seemed a decorous exercise from inside the building and Stern relaxed slightly; only when the constable fastening his hands under Stern's armpits muttered in his ear, 'You long string of shit', and dropped him on the pavement outside from a height of three feet did he remember, with a flush of fury, that the IMG disowned all forms of passive resistance.

He heard a high cry of pain the moment after his spine struck the ground. Behind him the young woman with chestnut hair lay clutching her back, fighting off tears. His own wounded pride forgotten, he bent over her and gently, solicitously, eased her to her feet.

'You should be ashamed!' he shouted at the police in general.

'Oh they don't know shame,' she said, slowly smoothing out her skirt. Looking up at him, she smiled shyly. 'I saw you on television.'

A moment later a score of privileged hands plucked Esther Meyer from him. Among them he recognised Oscar Mucheche's dirt-packed fingernails.

With Bow Street magistrates' court he was familiar enough: standing bail for students or testifying (perjuriously) to their good character was now a routine motion in a radical lecturer's cycle of duties. Dressed in an enchanting cotton frock, Esther Meyer was carrying a bunch of lilies of the valley presented to her outside the court by waiting admirers as she arrived chaperoned by Amy Brand, the fighting general secretary of Anti-Apartheid, and their solicitor. Stern was proud to have been called as a defence witness, though rather humiliated not to be facing the same charge as Esther – when Elizabeth wanted to put him down she inquired innocently why his telephone wasn't tapped.

They waited while the usual parade of drunks and dossers shuffled before the magistrate, cheerfully mumbling their guilt in the hope of a warm night in the cells. A policeman tonelessly read out the previous convictions and a woman clerk with a crystal voice repeated, liturgically: 'Have you anything further to say?' The magistrate benignly tossed routine warnings to ruined faces he knew well:

'Ten pounds or seven days, when can you pay it?'

The veteran offenders boiled 'no fixed address' (or was it 'abode'? Stern wondered) down to 'NFA', saving their breath for the fifty-yard haul to the nearest pub.

'Are you in work? Yes? No? Persistent soliciting in Piccadilly Circus. Fined three pounds.'

For stealing a magazine worth six shillings.

Esther's turn. 'Not guilty,' she said, grave and beautiful. The magistrate pretended not to look at her. Stern itched as he watched Oscar and other defendants step into the dock beside her.

Stern's vision of Africa lacked focus. Latin verbs and the Common Entrance examination which his father imposed upon him by remote control from Syria or Paraguay subsumed the early stages of the Algerian revolution; he had been only thirteen, and preoccupied by the horrors of fagging, when the Osagyefo Kwame Nkrumah proclaimed pan-Africa's new dawn; only sixteen, and embroiled in 'O' levels, when Nkrumah began to throw his colleagues in gaol alongside his opponents; totally absorbed in preparing for an Oxford scholarship when Lumumba was murdered by Tshombe's mercenaries in Katanga. The grim birth pangs of black Africa were lost in the pain of a groin flicked by wet towels after the weekly cross-country runs he dreaded to the point of feigned illness.

When the police sergeant had finished droning his evidence the magistrate turned impatiently to the defence solicitor, cupping his hand over his ear as if he expected absurd legal arguments to be inaudible. The magistrate's mind was already settled:

'Whether or not I am a legal tenant of my home doesn't give you the right to squat in it. Nor to obstruct police officers acting in accordance with their duty.'

The solicitor said the defendants had offered no such obstruction. Stern took the witness stand.

'You were also carried from Rhodesia House by the police?'

'Yes.'

'Did you resist ejection?'

'No.'

'Describe the behaviour of the police officers.'

'The one lifting me by the arms told me I was a "string of shit". Once outside, the two officers dropped me on my spine from a height of three feet.'

'Did you observe Miss Meyer receiving the same treatment?'

'A leading question,' snapped the magistrate.

Defence counsel re-phrased himself. 'Tell the court how Miss Meyer was ejected.'

'As I was. Horizontally on to her spine. From a height of three feet. She cried out in pain. One of the officers responsible then stamped on her hand and called her a "nigger's bitch".'

Everyone, including defence counsel, looked rather startled. Amy Brand beamed. Esther Meyer's gaze was steady.

Police counsel casually took up the questioning.

'You say you didn't resist eviction?'

'Yes.'

'Yes you did or yes you didn't?'

'I did not resist.'

'Had the police ordered everyone to leave the building?'

'Yes.'

'Yet you didn't comply? Isn't that resistance?'

'No. When they lifted me from the floor I offered no resistance. It was the general pattern.'

'The officers dropped you on the pavement from a height of three feet, you claim?'

'Yes.'

'Did you produce a tape measure?'

'Without a tape measure I would put you, sir, at five feet ten inches in your socks.'

Outside the court, in Bow Street, Esther gravely took his hand.

'You were wonderful. I loved the remark about the socks and my hand has begun to ache since I learned that they stamped on it. If only we'd had a jury.'

A devoted admirer of Stendhal, he stood speechless. 'Courtiers of all ages feel one great need: to speak in such a way that they do not say anything.' To which he could add: 'And lovers of all ages feel one great need: to be silent in such a way that they say everything.'

Her almond eyes reminded him of *'Bread, Love and Dreams'* – Lollobrigida on a bicycle, storming his puberty. Encircled by friends and courtiers, Esther passed from one to another with regal modesty, receiving tributes, offering compliments and kissing favoured faces. His mother had always ignored Bow Street and the orange set when playing game after game of Monopoly, her smoke-screwed eyes fastening on the yellows and the royal blue of Mayfair, Stern waiting for the long ash of her Balkan Sobranie to fall on the carpet. The priceless carpet. How could he know, as Esther Meyer drifted away with her entourage, raising her hand to him in a last, lazy salute, wincing teasingly at her 'crushed' fingers, that her father, hounded out of America in the age of McCarthy, had carried with him into exile an addiction to Scrabble? There was no hint of America in her accent, only the exotic mystery of the land north of the Limpopo.

He dithered over the telephone for a couple of days, seething with passion, then braced himself to call Amy Brand. Her sergeant's voice rasped back guardedly:

'I didn't catch your name.'

'Richard Stern.'

A blank silence. She had either forgotten or his utility had expired.

'I gave evidence in court for you.'

'Oh yes. For a moment I thought you were the one from Granada Television.'

'We want to invite Esther to address our group at the LSE. I

48

can't promise television cameras, though you never know.' He tried a laugh, it came out as a honk.

'Which group is that? The same as Oscar Mucheche's? He's a nice boy, of course, but full of wild nonsense about Fanon. Esther's much too level-headed for all that.'

Stern swallowed. He had in fact twice dialled Amy's number and twice replaced the receiver when male voices answered.

'I'd like to speak to Esther if that's possible.'

'Everyone does, dear. Give me your number and I'll leave a message.'

When Esther telephoned his flat in Notting Hill two days later Elizabeth was in the bath. As soon as he heard the soft, silky voice he stretched a long leg to prod the open door of his study.

'I'm so sorry, Richard. I seem to be living out of a suitcase. And now they've invited me to do a lecture tour of America and I'm both exhausted and delighted. Tell me, Richard, it can't be healthy to become a celebrity, can it? Do you think it might turn my head?'

He groaned with love. It choked him.

'We wanted you to speak to our group at the LSE.'

'I'd so like to,' she said dreamily. 'Such an honour.' His pulse hammered. 'Let me call you when I get back from America.'

Elizabeth walked in, wrapped in a big green Habitat towel, brushing out her wet hair.

'Darling, what have you done with my blow dryer?'

Ice-and-lemon in a cold glass.

'Is that a promise?' he murmured into the phone.

'I'm writing it down at this very moment: "Call Richard Stern on return." '

Rum-and-pineapple in a warm coconut shell.

'Have a wonderful trip,' he said. 'I love America.'

'Thank you, Richard. Goodbye.' Snapping the padlock on his uncertain heart.

'Who was that?' Elizabeth asked.

'A beautiful woman who attends great indabas in the open veld north of the Limpopo. When the winter wind signals the jacquerie, hers is the only hair that stirs.' He touched Beth's cheek. 'Tell me, am I capable of love?'

'Other than self-love, you mean? Clearly she's someone you want to impress, since you've never set foot in America. Where's my blow dryer? We're due at the Royal Court in half an hour.'

'Does not Harry forbid you to go the theatre with me?'

'Couldn't we forget your tedious quarrel with Harry for a couple of hours?'

Stern took down the bottle from his dictionary shelf, poured

49

himself a thick whisky, then flopped into the steel-framed leather rocking chair he had bought for seventy-five pounds in the King's Road to impress Elizabeth. He stretched his long legs.

'Forget Harry, she tells me! And how do I forget him as I work here alone, long into the night, knowing that my mistress is not asleep in South Kensington, with Daddy's Degas and teddy bear Herbert and Horace the Hippo, oh no, she's dining *à deux*, by candlelight, with Harry. No longer does he conduct her to seedy transport cafés with formica tables, or pubs pooled in Watney's, nowadays it's chic little bistros in Hampstead, *très sympathique*, *tête à tête*, with red tablecloths, ingratiating waiters and candles with phoney drips. How her golden hair gleams – no wonder she has mislaid her dryer! How attentively she listens in her low neckline as the old warrior unfolds his dramatic, contentious life to her. The struggles and the crusades. Ostracised on high table during the Korean War, attempts to deprive him of tenure, cold-shouldered by comrades after the traumatic Party congress of fifty-six, the wife who died in childbirth, the second wife so clamped in shyness that she never ventures out of the house but devotes all her energies, like Mrs Tolstoy, to typing manuscripts she cannot comprehend. Now his hairy paw reaches across the red tablecloth; out of pity her fingers close on his. "An old man can lose his head," he murmurs, "confronted with such . . . " "Such what?" she asks innocently. "Elizabeth," he warns her, unflinching in his invidious duty, "you will not be happy with Richard." Harry pauses and curtly summons the waiter: another carafe. "Stop me if I must stop, Elizabeth. Richard needs a bitch. You're not a bitch. Look what he's done to this damned dissertation. I scarcely recognise myself in these pages. The idea that I, of all people, ignore psychology! That I've never confronted the problematic of power! Lies! Power! That young man whom we both love, yes I love him as a father, how *he* wants power, how ruthlessly he bends truth and those of us, like you and me, who humbly pursue and serve it, in pursuit of his demonic ambition! Save yourself before it's too late, my girl; listen to a battered old priest of the human condition, hate me if you must but only pay heed! And if you won't listen to me, listen to Blake, to Wordsworth. Elizabeth, you have fallen into the grip of a ruthless ventriloquist." Hearing this, Elizabeth lowers her long eyelashes to the required angle. In the car he places one hairy, trembling hand on her thigh while fumbling at his flies with the other. "Your gentle hand would do, my dear, though a groaning heart could dream of more." '

'Clearly we're not going to the theatre tonight,' Elizabeth yawned. 'Who was that woman on the phone?'

'You don't deny it?'

'Deny what, my darling?'

'What I've just reported.'

'Denials are futile – when tutored by so many experts in philosophy and truth.'

'My mother has invited us to dinner.' Stern refilled his glass, more expansively this time. 'Should we take Harry along?'

Lifting her small, light body he peeled off the Habitat towel and carried her to the bedroom. Throwing her face-down across the bed, he began to sting her firm little buttocks with light slaps and, stirred by her fluttering, birdlike protests, thrust himself to the quivering hilt – 'Did Harry point out to you that physical sensations, including pain, terror and copulation, can be described only by inadequate analogy and metaphor? Primary sense data, as he must have told you, is pre-verbal.'

Her face was pressed into the pillow, eyes shut; in later years, when her eyes never closed, he would remember the late sixties with a fogged sense of loss.

He held back his climax; he was never sure whether hers were feigned, or whether Christopher had done better.

'So, as Harry must have reminded you, our vocabulary is at its most assured when labelling what we can neither experience nor logically imagine: God, death, free will, reincarnation, infinity, the immortal soul – and the ego. What we cannot describe is a woman's voice on the telephone.'

'Richard,' she whispered.

FIVE

He took the longest possible route from Notting Hill to St John's Wood but his mother's house came into sight on his own back projection even before he turned from Ladbroke Grove into Harrow Road. Elizabeth had dressed for the occasion in a simple blue frock and a Victorian diamond brooch, bequeathed by an ancestor who had gone 'into partnership' (as Lady Halliday put it) with Cecil Rhodes in Kimberley's 'big hole'.

'The last girl I took home was wearing something from Biba.'

'Oh?' (Elizabeth had never inquired into his past, for which he was grateful, having none to conceal.)

'My mother grabbed a handful of it. "When I was a girl," she said, "this sort of fabric was known as shoddy." Mother, I should warn you, invariably dresses like a gift parcel.'

'And who was the last girl you took home?'

'It was long ago, in the time of Richard Coeur de Lion. What you have now is Richard III.'

Elizabeth Halliday smiled. ' "But since you teach me how to flatter you, imagine I have said farewell already." '

'There: look, to your right – the liberal synagogue. The last time I was in there was Uncle Shimon's memorial service. "May God grant abundant peace and life to us and to the whole house of Israel, and let us say: Amen." Afterwards we went to the Clarendon Court Hotel for sandwiches and sat round the table in our sub-clans, each Momma clutching her own brood. Aunt Orna leant across the table towards me and said in a loud voice intended for my mother's ears: "I remember when you were a baby living in Park Rise. None of us was allowed within three yards of the cot in case we breathed on you." '

Elizabeth studied his hawkish profile.

'I'd better get it straight: you were how old when your parents separated?'

'Nine.'

'And you have one younger sister, Rachel, currently reading anthropology at Oxford?'

'Are we in a novel? Are we priming the reader? Yes, yes, I am fond of Rachel, so much nicer than her hunchback brother.'

With a low groan he turned into Wellington Place.

'Perhaps I should warn you about Monty.'

'Your mother's companion?'

'And business partner. He wears two-tone shoes and whines. He may kiss you on the mouth.'

'Richard, you're too old to feel ashamed of your family.'

'Wait and see.' But it stung. 'One shouldn't fake these things,' he said. 'Not even orgasms.'

He turned into the gravel forecourt of a neglected front garden, applying the handbrake with a long sigh. The house was solid Edwardian, with peeling window frames and curtains drawn on the upper floors. He read her upward glance.

'In case the afternoon sun gets at the Hepplewhite.'

He climbed the steps and tortured the bell.

'I have a key for emergencies,' he murmured. 'Is this an emergency?'

'Ssh.'

The door eventually opened, but cautiously, on a chain, as if no one was expected.

'Good evening, mother.'

'Oh, it's you.' The chain rattled. 'I thought it was another of those Jehovah's Witnesses.'

Tall like her son, Mrs Stern tottered on very high heels, towering over Elizabeth and lifting one leg like a flamingo as she bent to plant red lips on Beth's porcelain cheek.

'My dear, I've heard so much about you.'

Sheathed in a tight-fitting gown of shot silk tattooed with huge orchids, her steps confined by its tight skirt, Mrs Stern led them on swollen ankles into the drawing room where she swivelled dramatically and clasped Elizabeth's unadorned hand in fingers flashing with huge stones.

'My dear, I'm so delighted. I've been urging Richard to produce you for months, but you know what he's like. Now, Richard darling, you do the drinks, I've no idea what young people drink nowadays.'

Stern detected his mother's half-empty glass of gin concealed behind a vase of artificial flowers. He refilled it with tonic water from the tray and poured Elizabeth a glass of white wine; touching the bottle, he was relieved to find it had been chilled.

He handed his mother her glass, rimmed in lipstick.

'Have "the other half",' he said.

'How *does* one put up with him, Elizabeth? Thank God that's now your problem, dear, not mine.'

'I'm working on it, Mrs Stern,' Elizabeth said lightly.

'And that brooch, my dear – so pretty.'

'It's from the big hole,' Stern said.

Mrs Stern shot an alarmed, almost pleading, glance at him with eyes already glazed. And then, out of nervous reflex, retreated into her own tribulations, crooks whose cheques bounced from one end of the Grosvenor House Antique Dealers' fair to the other, corrupt officials (Kensington & Chelsea) who blocked her plans to extend her shop – 'Because I won't pay baksheesh' – and young people who walked the streets with transistor radios blaring. Motorcyclists without silencers. Refuse collectors who tossed your dustbins around like frisbees unless you greased their palms.

'I hate noise because I'm musical, dear. Richard has the ear for it too, it runs in my side of the family, but he let his fiddle lapse and once it goes it goes for ever. Doesn't it, Richard?'

Stern observed Elizabeth's slow, cautious assessment of his mother's Chinese vases, Persian rugs and large, gilded mirrors. Yes, it ran, how it ran, in his mother's side of the family, those loud, brash aunts trumpeting the talents of their offspring, cousins arriving Sundays loaded with violins and cellos, their eyes luminous with praise and ambition:

—His teacher says he could be another Horovitz – if he works. Did you hear that, Micah: *if* you work at it.

—They say she's almost too gifted for the Royal College.

—I keep telling him: the world needs and honours great brain surgeons, not football fans. 'Yes, mama,' he says and turns straight back to the television.

—Dorah, do any of them of this generation ever listen like we did? (This is Aunt Orna, whom Mother alternately loved and hated, embraced and fought.)—Now, Richard, you have all these brilliant brains, your mother says, why don't you become a famous professor like Mr Laski or a famous QC like Mr Montagu?

Every child destined for greatness or fame. And when he shrugged diffidently Orna would turn to Deborah:

—You see that, Dorah? He thinks the world will wait for him but you and I know the world doesn't wait.

Rich North London voices, Highgate, Finsbury Park, Golders Green, voices coarse and honest with love of this world, flowing rich like oil round his own limpid, watery vowels – the Anglican public school, cavalry twill and Harris tweed, where his father had despatched him with remote but unchallengeable authority.

'Monty not at home, mother?'

She lifted her chin, focusing on Elizabeth. 'Monty called from Edinburgh to offer his most profuse apologies. He *so* wanted to meet you. Monty is my business partner, Elizabeth – did Richard tell you about the family business? No? So like him. Frankly, my dear, I think he's secretly rather ashamed of it, even though it bought him his education and all those long, ruinously expensive trips to Europe every summer.'

'My father paid my school fees,' Richard said to Elizabeth.

'When he remembered,' Mrs Stern snapped. 'I started from nothing, you see, I had to fend for myself, I slaved for Richard and Rachel, but Richard resents any kind of debt, you'll find that out, dear. He despises commerce – though he is gracious enough to live off its profits. I daresay you're familiar with the flat in Notting Hill Gate, dear?'

Elizabeth smiled faintly. 'It's more than he deserves.'

'Oh no, dear, he deserves *everything*. And what about your family? Richard tells me so little.'

'My parents are living in Norway but our home is in Oxfordshire. Daddy's a sailor.'

Stern watched.

His mother's mascaraed eyelashes fluttered. 'A sailor? I thought he was an officer.'

'Oh – yes.'

It hadn't occurred to Stern that his mother would dine with them alone: Monty apart, she invariably imported one or two uncles for such occasions, a 'brilliant' cousin on the verge of international acclaim as cellist or barrister. He glanced back at the cold shoulders in the Clarendon Court Hotel after Uncle Shimon's funeral; his mother had bequeathed him her tongue, her asperity, her fated isolation.

Elizabeth was detected politely admiring Mrs Stern's furniture.

'You must call me Deborah, dear. I have never been one to stand on ceremony. Richard, I think I'll have just the ghost of another gin.'

'On an empty stomach?'

'Heavens, do you get it or do I get it?'

His fear was that she would sink into insensibility before dinner but she rose to the occasion, producing an elaborate meal – artichokes, veal, strawberries – and chattering to Elizabeth with mounting good humour, clearly relieved by the young woman's easy, relaxing attention.

'One dare not say it in his presence, but Richard was always a brilliant child. And he knew it! Oh, how he knew it! I wanted him to be an architect, he has a wonderful eye, something creative, to make the world a little less ugly than it is, but his head was always full of theories, abstractions, I'm sure *you* understand them, dear, but I don't want to, I read the papers, I see ugliness everywhere, violence, no standards. Why must girls walk about looking like cats out of a dustbin? Why can't they wash their hair? And all this filthy lesbianism we're getting, quite repellent.'

Stern noticed that the pause was deliberate.

'Don't you think?' His mother's eye was fastened on Elizabeth.

'About noise and violence? Oh, certainly.'

'And this filthy lesbianism.' Repeated, it sounded manic.

'Well . . . I wouldn't quite put it like that. More often than not it's just friendship painted in sensational colours by the press . . .'

Stern watched his mother etching a note on the deepest of her tablets.

'I do hope,' she resumed with an air of tact, 'that Richard's acne spots have gone away. His back was covered with them during adolescence, I tried everything, sun-ray lamps, diets, the poor boy would never take off his shirt at the seaside. I don't suppose he's a passionate man, dear – is it tactless to ask a fiancée such a question? – too much of his father in him.'

'Mother,' Stern said gently.

'I didn't know I was his fiancée,' Elizabeth said with a smile.

'I certainly see no ring, dear. But don't you let him off the hook. Too many silly girls chasing after him. Tall, handsome and irresistible, my Richard.' She reached across the polished mahogany table, between the silver candlesticks, and took Elizabeth's slender wrist in her bejewelled claw. 'My dear, I don't want my grandchildren to suffer a broken home. These things are passed on, you know: like father, like son. When Richard's father abandoned him it left a terrible scar and you will have to live with that scar, Elizabeth, till death do you part.'

Stern remembered the freezing day at his Norfolk prep school when her letter arrived, its adult phrases written in a large, violent, disintegrating script numbing his imagination – the sort of letter she might have written to Uncle Shimon or Aunt Orna, perhaps thrust into the wrong envelope. 'The basest adultery . . . innocent party . . . a decade of deception . . .' The lines widening and slanting up the page like unwashed linen caught in a gale. He waited for a letter from his father but none came and when he went home at the end of term there was no alternative but to accept and assimilate his mother's diatribes.

—I suppose you think it was *my* fault that he chased after that bitch?

—No, mother.

—Do you imagine he loves you and Rachel? Wouldn't he write to you more often, wouldn't he come and see you? Don't forget the efforts poor Uncle Shimon made after Sarah ran off with that remittance man from Golders Green.

The boy's silent shrugs were not evidence enough of loyalty. She would scrutinise his fast-growing beanstalk frame as if marking down the veins that carried the poisoned blood.

—You know what *she* is now plotting?

Ah, *she*, the never-seen 'she'. He waited. There were two standard versions of this plot: to snatch himself and Rachel and carry them away to Bolivia, where his father was serving as Consul; and to push Deborah herself 'under a taxi' (for some reason it was never a bus or tube train – perhaps his mother intuited she might survive the taxi, if the driver was a friendly member of the Reformed Synagogue).

Then Deborah would return to first base.—I suppose you think it was *my* fault that he chased after that bitch?

—I have never said that.

—But you think it. You get that habit from your father – masking your thoughts.

Elizabeth's cool, indulgent tolerance of his mother's monologues reminded him of her behaviour in bed: noblesse oblige, as if enduring a bizarre interlude in her education, picking up a foreign language, before returning to her destiny: horses, houses, tennis and marriage to a stockbroker with a flair for buying unknown painters cheap and selling them dear. A well-hung sportsman who would take her twice a month to the National Theatre or the Royal Shakespeare Company and give her a genuine orgasm afterwards. A considerate, slow-tempered man with the confidence of a landlord who already knows which key fits the difficult lock.

'Mother, you mustn't bore Elizabeth.'

Elizabeth blushed and he felt ashamed. By way of atonement and escape he offered to make the coffee. When he carried the silver tray into the drawing room his mother was telling Elizabeth how her relatives had for years been urging her to marry Monty because he was such a fine man but she wouldn't, couldn't, because 'I wanted Richard and Rachel to know who their father was'.

'They all despised Monty because he wore flashy suits and bet on the races instead of pretending he was enjoying lunch-hour concerts in the Wigmore Hall,' Stern told Elizabeth, placing the tray in front of his mother.

'That's a lie!' Mrs Stern screamed, her precious, transitory happiness stolen. '*You* despised him!'

He sat down and spread his long legs. 'Mother, you know Monty's a crook.'

'You're not worthy to shine that man's shoes!'

'I'd need polish in at least two tones.'

'Oh you're so smart! Such a smart man you're marrying, Elizabeth.'

He remembered her arriving with Monty on the first school prize-giving day after his father's letter, her high heels wobbling across the summer turf, handbag and shoes of crocodile, her hair swept up in a great beehive, the red stain on her teacup, Monty shuffling behind in his sideburns, Richard's friends watching sidelong as she lowered herself into a deck chair on the boundary of the cricket field and took out her compact and mirror. That evening they 'treated' Richard in a stuffy hotel and she made up her face between every course – for Monty. Monty paid the bill out of a beautiful flash wallet but Richard knew his mother gave Monty the money afterwards.

At family gatherings his father was never mentioned. Conrad Stern. Stern went through his entire childhood without ever hearing the word 'Conrad'. The Jew who pretended he wasn't a Jew because his grandfather had converted to the Catholic Church to save his carpet business in Galicia. A 'Catholic' who'd joined the Foreign Service and sent his boy to an Anglican public school – Dorah had married that kind of a man and no one, least of all Orna, was rubbing it in, much better to say nothing and close the book.

'With or without milk?' Deborah asked Elizabeth, fighting back her tears.

'Black, please. Is that a Stubbs?'

'That's a genuine Stubbs, Monty found it in a country-house sale.'

'Isn't it odd how long it took painters to discover how horses really run?'

'There's nothing Monty doesn't know about horses. He yet owns two.'

Years passed before he rebelled against his mother's refusal to grant his father a divorce, her rigid, obsessive determination that *she* would never become the second Mrs Stern. It was Rachel who, tumbling into adolescence, sparked the rebellion by launching a regular correspondence with their father and threatening to run away from home when Deborah tried to intercept his letters. Behind Rachel's locked bedroom door the two children would study every phrase in quest of a man who wrote as if they were two 'young friends' who had joined his ornithologists' club.

'Yesterday I photographed a Cape Vulture so disgusted with the empty plain that he was clearly considering becoming a vegetarian . . . The brilliant red Bishop Bird is not, contrary to rumour, permitted to administer the sacraments . . . The Weaver bird has solved the problem of overcrowded accommodation, so vexatious to us humans. He simply likes it. Clever fellow.'

Brother and sister divined that their father judged every diplomatic posting in terms of the available bird-life. References to themselves, his children, were always friendly: well done for achievements, better luck next time for set-backs. Never a rebuke; and never a mention of 'she', the scarlet woman at his elbow. It did not dawn on them that a British diplomat may not set up home with a lady not his wife; nor that their mother had inflicted on their father years of loneliness and pain. What did dawn on Rachel was that if her father couldn't inspect her small, sprouting breasts, her brother could. Notes were slipped under his door in dead of night:

'You'll never get a girl with those foul spots. It's worse than B.O. If you want it come to my door at 10.42 *exactly* and tap twice, then twice again. It will cost you every penny in your Post Office account. Love, R.
PS. Can you do it?
PPS. Mummy does it with Monty. I saw them.'

Stern saw Elizabeth's discreet glance at her watch.
At the door Deborah again fastened on Elizabeth's hand.
'My dear, I do hope I didn't say the wrong thing.'
Elizabeth, uncertain, responded swiftly. 'It was lovely, Mrs Stern.'
' "Deborah", please.'
'And such a wonderful dinner. No wonder he doesn't admire my cooking.'
Stern grinned. 'I might admire it if I ever tasted it.'
'I do hope I didn't say the wrong thing,' Deborah repeated, her words noticeably slurred. 'About lesbianism, I mean.'
They drove in silence past St John's Wood synagogue.
'Well,' he said, 'you now know the worst – almost.'
'I think your mother's a woman of great spirit.'
'Shall I tell you a tale? Careless of the "fiddle" and blind to my mission as an architect, I won a History Scholarship to Oxford. Mother insisted on throwing a party in celebration – all my school friends must attend, she wouldn't heed my protests.'
'Is your will so easily overcome? I hadn't noticed.'

'Mother turned out in a low-cut dress with a slit most of the way up one side and began to flirt outrageously: "You young men are all animals at heart." Downing neat gins she announced that she had "embraced Eros" because "an old woman must lead her life to the full until she goes out like a light – phut!" '

'My father isn't above pinching girls' bottoms when he's had a drink or two. But that, of course, is acceptable.'

'Wait. Announcing that her long legs would have destined her for a brilliant stage career had she not foolishly married a rotter – the aforesaid legs being very much on display – she then embarked on a description of my conception in Buenos Aires at five on a very hot afternoon. "I only remember that we had to be at a diplomatic reception by six," she said, "and all I could think about was what I would wear." '

'Why are men so humiliated by their mothers' sexuality? Why must women, even in a mind as "progressive" as yours, always maintain a decorous tongue, while men proudly exchange lewd jokes and dirty stories? You're driving too fast, Richard.'

'And then, much inspired by this line of thought, Mother grabbed he who was temporarily my best friend and asked him what he really thought about when he was "doing it".'

' "Doing it, Mrs Stern?" '

Stern was shouting now, gripping the wheel.

' "Yes, my dear handsome Frank, don't pretend, what do you *think about* when you're shooting your load?" '

Elizabeth's resistance softened. She touched his arm.

'Oh God, how awful for you. Is drink a serious problem?'

'I don't know whether it's cause or effect. Periodically she retires to a health farm to dry out, usually when Monty has made a killing at the races, and for a time she won't allow a drop in the house. But then something snaps, there are half-empty bottles secreted under every chair, and it's "Go Directly to Jail. Do Not Pass Go." She loves playing Monopoly, by the way. She and Monty play for hours, each trying to steal money from the bank, listening to Mozart.'

'Richard, you frighten me,' Elizabeth whispered. 'I'm not sure I can cope.'

'That usually means you want to spend the night in South Kensington with Herbert and Horace.'

'Actually – yes.'

'Should we add Christopher?'

'Christopher is in America.'

He lay awake for over an hour, seething and tossing in remembrance. Ten years after his father's abrupt departure, when breakdown had still not replaced guilt as the legal rationale of divorce, he and his father had walked across the Oxford Meadows, two strangers, striding between the cowpats in silence.

—I suppose, Richard had ventured, —you could have cited Monty.

Silence. Then his father raised his stick to the distant sky.

—Buzzard.

The following morning the telephone rang at eight-thirty. Even as he lifted the receiver he knew it was his mother.

'Richard, I want to speak to Elizabeth and don't argue.'

'Mother, please.'

'It really won't take long. I know how busy you both are.'

He knew the latent hysteria behind that hyper-control. Always the violent kick-back after the artificial affability.

'Perhaps I can help?'

'No, I must speak to Elizabeth.'

'She isn't here.'

'You're lying.'

'Either way, she isn't here.'

'Give me her number then.'

'No.'

'Richard, do you imagine I slept a wink last night? How can you believe that girl could ever make you happy? Can't you see what she's really like beneath that . . . that . . . She despises us, Richard, we're not her class . . . Calling her father a "sailor"! With that permanent smirk on her face and—'

'I've never seen Elizabeth "smirk". I think she coped magnificently.'

'Coped! How condescending of her.' A pause, heavy breathing. 'And what about bed?'

'Bed?' (But he already knew.)

'Drop the pretence, Richard, she doesn't sleep with you and if she does she doesn't mean it. Can't you spot a lesbian right under your nose?'

He laughed with relief. 'Oh I see. I see. It's all because she resisted your denunciation of "filthy lesbians".' He laughed again.

Hysteria no longer latent: 'Richard, did I give birth to a complete fool? I know the signs, I'm a woman, I haven't led such a sheltered life as you think and don't contradict everything I say.'

He glanced at the clock and began to read the front page of the *Guardian*, his mother's voice increasingly remote as he removed the receiver from his ear. Finally, with a gentle click, he laid it to rest.

SIX

'We decided to see the two of you together.' The Dean brought the tips of his fingers into delicate contact, like his Tudor hero Thomas Cromwell weighing a monastery for closure.

Stern waited. A consummate committee man, Ramsay had abandoned the delights of scholarship for the burdens of administration the day he was appointed to his Chair. Compounding the sacrifice, he now headed the finance committee of the British Academy, served as a trustee of the Leverhulme Foundation, and not infrequently dined at White's with the Shadow Minister of Education. Stern was in no doubt that Ramsay would spin out the ordeal.

'Hm. Dr Gough and I, er, thought it more appropriate to speak to each of you separately, but Professor Marquis—'

'—insisted on seeing you together,' Harry cut in, rummaging for Swan Vestas.

Elizabeth crossed her legs with a light swish of nylon and continued sketching on her small pad.

'This isn't going to be easy,' Ramsay said.

'Or pleasant,' Dr Gough said. 'Believe me, Stern, Miss Halliday, all of us would have avoided this if we could.'

Gough, though hunting the country for a Chair, was at that time Senior Lecturer in Applied Economics and author of a little-read work, out-of-print but still found on library shelves, demolishing the interventionist, 'inflationary' theories of John Maynard Keynes. His head was graced with a high, almost extraterrestrial, brow; the weight of it constantly seemed to threaten him with sudden sleep. He had even been known to fall asleep for a second or two during his own lectures, resuming in a deadly monotone, forged out of slow granite in the Edinburgh of Burke and Hare. (As Stern told his students.)

'You're having the time of your life,' Stern said.

'We'd like to minimise acrimony,' Ramsay said.

'As Cardinal Wolsey said to the poet Skelton, showing him the block.'

Ramsay bridled. 'Oh – did Wolsey say that?'

'He might have done.'

'What we are discussing is the relationship of a male member of staff and one of his female pupils,' said Ramsay.

'I dissent,' Harry said.

Ramsay nodded. 'Dissent noted.' His gaze had fixed on Elizabeth, who was severely tailored in black skirt and white blouse, her face lightly powdered to increase its pallor.

'Miss Halliday, tradition dictates that I direct my first question to the lady: what is the nature of your relationship with Dr Stern?'

Harry's growl came up like green phlegm.

'Elizabeth, you need not answer. This inquisition is obscene. It offends human dignity and natural justice. If the Dean has accusations let him make them. Let him support them. Let him define his own mind. Do not be intimidated. Remember that the Student Union exists to defend your rights. I sometimes think our academic potentates will not shed their arrogance until confronted by lawyers.'

Ramsay lifted his gaze to the ceiling.

'It is my duty to remind you both that legal rights are not here involved. The Court of Governors enjoys absolute discretion as to student status and academic tenure. And I must make it clear that, given the evidence before me—'

'You employ informers?' Stern cut in.

'I have informants, Dr Stern, not informers.'

'Who?'

'That is something we need not explore.'

'As your hero Thomas Cromwell said, "I do not cease to give thanks that it hath pleased God's goodness to use me as an instrument and to work somewhat by me." '

Ramsay sighed. 'Dr Stern, given the evidence before me, I would be failing in my office if I did not require an explanation from Miss Halliday and yourself.'

'Evidence of an engagement might be taken as a mitigating factor,' Gough said helpfully.

'Miss Halliday's private life is no one's business but her own,' Harry said.

Stern noted that he was not included in this indulgence.

Ramsay slowly swivelled his gaze from Stern to the young woman. 'Will one of you answer, or both – or perhaps neither?'

'Offer a question which can be answered yes or no,' Stern demanded.

'Very well. Do you co-habit?'

Fresh from the American lecture circuit, Esther had arrived at the LSE with her little retinue, radiantly greeting fellow-Zimbabweans with the triple handshake of the liberation struggle – thumb, palm, thumb. Though he had arranged the lunchtime meeting, Stern found himself competing for the role of host with Oscar Mucheche, whose incandescent eyes mirrored the same exotic landscape as Esther's, running from the rain-washed mountains of Manicaland down to the great, dry veld north of the Limpopo – the romantic bond of suffering and insurgency from which Stern felt painfully excluded.

Esther didn't attempt a formal lecture, she simply 'spoke from the heart, as one who can do little enough to lift oppression from the shoulders of my black brothers and sisters'. In the soft, melodious voice which enchanted Stern, she recalled her own burden, 'the guilt I have carried ever since my Headmistress took me aside and asked whether I was really wise to invite two black girls home to tea'.

Her rich chestnut hair flowed down to her shoulders, touching a blouse in palest pink; occasionally she would tuck her hair behind her ears but it soon broke free and so the enchanting little war continued between Esther and her hair.

—I belong to a tribe which insists on conquering and subjugating all other tribes. When I suggest to members of my tribe that we are guilty of arrogance, they remind me that I am young, naive and sentimental. And, when I ask them why the black nannies to whom we entrust our children may not legally bring their husbands and children to the servants' quarters we build at the bottom of our large gardens, they reply: 'Esther, you don't realise where it would all lead.'

The packed lecture theatre broke into sympathetic laughter.

—And when I innocently ask, 'Where would it all lead?', the ladies of my tribe whisper the unspeakable and imagine the unimaginable. I honestly don't understand this terrible fear of inter-marriage – we aren't pedigree dogs, are we?

Stern's long, sundial nose morosely monitored the answering laughter. What could her words mean except that she was sleeping with Oscar Mucheche? Oscar's jungle features were plainly wrapped in conquest. Stern was appalled (as often) by calculations so mean and shallow as his own – what use writing about good

64

and evil if one does not (like Esther Meyer) make a selfless commitment to virtue? He told himself that it was not her Lollobrigida eyes he had fallen sickeningly in love with, nor the curves of a body even riper in promise than Elizabeth's, but a virtue so intense as to require its own subversion. Stern had wondered what it must be like to be good: did the enchanted spirit soar from its fleshly envelope and nest in every neighbouring soul? Did Esther sip water only when she divined her companions' thirst?

Stern had occasionally imagined he could be good if he trained for it. Perhaps he should meditate and listen to music. But suppose Esther's virtue surrendered only to villains? One had to heed Strindberg as well as Stendhal.

—I confess I have never read Mao, or Fanon or Che Guevara, Esther said in answer to a question from the packed hall.—But I do read letters from men torn from their families and incarcerated in Gonakudzingwa, men condemned without trial to rot in a scorching wilderness among wild animals and tsetse fly. These men are the future leaders of my country and they enjoy only one diversion – I wonder if you know what it is? It's watching the railway wagons from South Africa pass by, loaded with oil, despite the economic sanctions which Mr Wilson boasted, four years ago, would bring down the Smith régime in a 'matter of days'.

Thunderous applause.

Elbowing Oscar Mucheche aside, Stern guided Esther to the bar through the throng of courtiers and admiring students. Her progress was regal, her cheeks slightly flushed, her every word considerate and tender, to friend and stranger alike.

—What will you drink, Esther?

—A fruit juice, thank you, Richard.

—Something stronger?

She looked at Stern as if he were the only man in the world.

—It's a disease among exiles, you know, drink. So I make it a rule never to start until seven in the evening.

Oscar laughed knowingly and ordered scotches for himself and other guerrillas to hand.

—This is on me, Stern said, reaching for his wallet. No one demurred.

Amy Brand was pointing to her watch.—Esther, we are due at the BBC at three-thirty.

—Will you forgive us, Richard? It has been such a pleasure and an enormous privilege. I was quite frightened before I came but you were all so kind to a very under-educated woman and I'm immensely grateful. Richard, you must come to dinner when I get myself sorted out. Do you perhaps have a wife? If so, I'd like to meet her.

65

Oscar was grinning. He gave Stern a knowing wink.

Stern broke out in a light sweat of despair, frustration, anger. She was slipping away, smiling, shaking hands – thumb, palm, thumb – through the throng.

'Yes,' Elizabeth told Ramsay. 'We do co-habit.' She shot a contemptuous glance at Dr Gough. 'To answer *your* question: no, we are not engaged.'

'I am grateful,' Ramsay addressed Elizabeth, 'for your candour. To be blunt with you both: a member of the academic staff who makes a student his mistress cannot assess her work impartially. The grades she receives are suspect; the dissertation she writes is also suspect; it may be less – or more – than entirely her own work.'

'I deny that,' Stern said. 'Indignantly.'

'Indignation is always a help,' Dr Gough said.

'Your hands sweat upon your Bible, Gough,' Harry said.

'Have you read Miss Halliday's dissertation?' Stern asked Ramsay.

'No.'

'You are thus engaged in pure conjecture?'

Ramsay lifted his brows high at Harry. And waited.

'I have read it,' Harry said. 'I have read it because I was asked to read it. Honesty compels me to tell you, Elizabeth, that I cannot regard it as your own work. It is either Richard's work or it is a work implicitly about Richard's work – not mine.'

Stern saw that his pupil and mistress was trembling beneath her white satin skin. Fury contracted his gut. Only the radicalised working class could destroy the Ramsays and Goughs; in the meantime he would make it his personal mission to take out Harry Marquis. (That he had long ago embarked on precisely that project didn't occur to him.)

Harry continued to address Elizabeth alone: 'Unlike Professor Ramsay and Dr Gough, I am not the least bit interested in your private life. Had you been a male student my reaction to your dissertation would have been identical.'

'I would like to ask a question,' Stern said.

'Of course,' said Ramsay, leaning back in his chair.

'Since you are so preoccupied by propriety and conflict of interest, I presume you would not assign Professor Marquis to examine a thesis about his own life and work?'

Ramsay's back straightened. 'That is not at issue.'

'You wouldn't, would you? And why wouldn't you?'

'Because justice must not only be done but be seen to be done.'

'Ah. In public, you mean. Private inquisitions, by contrast, may safely dispense with justice altogether. Prejudice and base passion suffice.'

'Passion, you say?' Gough lifted his huge forehead.

Harry silent.

It was almost as if Stern felt Elizabeth's beseeching foot under the table. Ramsay, registering his hesitation, pounced.

'The entire project has been wrapped in impropriety from the outset. It is my unfortunate duty to try and clean up the mess. To that end I have a proposal to make. If Miss Halliday will agree to withdraw her dissertation, then we can arrange for her to elect a new subject, under alternative supervision, deferring her degree by one year.'

'That's not ungenerous,' Gough said.

'And if she refuses?' Stern asked.

Ramsay gazed up at the ceiling. 'In that event I would have to refer the whole matter to the Academic Board – with what repercussions I cannot predict.'

Stern laughed coldly. 'I can.'

'Do I detect some kind of threat, Dr Stern? Another chapter in the heroic saga of rent-a-mob?'

'The threats come from you, Ramsay. It's my head you want – since Professor Marquis has now taken the long walk to Canossa.'

'No need for all that,' Harry growled. 'The thesis itself is potentially viable – given an immediate change of supervisor. I see no alternative but to take it on myself. But we may need the extra year.'

'That would make for a furious scandal!' protested Gough.

Stern was staring at Harry, who finally met his eye.

'Even God does not supervise classes in the Old Testament.'

Harry nodded sardonically. 'And even Judas did not imagine himself the founder of Christianity.'

'Marquis, it's out of the question,' Ramsay said.

Harry turned his ravaged countenance, in a final entreaty, to Elizabeth. Watching him fold like an unpegged tent, Stern had a distinct premonition of the nervous collapse which was to follow.

Elizabeth stood up abruptly, hoisting her Mexican leather bag to her small, soft shoulder.

'I have decided to abandon the dissertation entirely.'

'Miss Halliday, please take time to think it over,' Ramsay said, victory perched on his arm like a falcon.

'And my degree.' She was trembling.

Ramsay looked genuinely distressed. 'We all appreciate what an ordeal this has been for you. Please take time to consider – your work here has been, er, quite highly regarded.'

She shook her head. 'Frankly, I've had enough.' Hair swinging, she strode with short, angry steps to the door. 'Congratulations, Dr Gough – you're the only one here present who hasn't asked me to go to bed with him.'

She handed Gough a sheet of caricatures from her drawing pad. The door banged behind her. Then re-opened.

'I'd just like to say that all of Richard's students have complete faith in him.'

Stern stood up to follow. Yet lingered, blood in his eyes.

'And Saint-Just also knows Danton,' he stood over Harry. 'Beware, old man, beware.'

In the hallways and corridors below he fancied he heard the thundering feet of the *sans-culottes*, the creak of the tumbrils, the hiss of the guillotine. What Stern did not hear as he hurried in pursuit of Elizabeth, passing the lecture hall which Esther Meyer had packed only the previous day, was the steady click of a plain young woman with owl eyes, knitting.

That evening Stern asked Elizabeth to marry him.

SEVEN

Hand in hand they sat in the yellow cabs bounding up the switch-back avenues, agents, publishers, interviews, Lexington and Madison, a working honeymoon. The generosity of the Hallidays put them in the Algonquin. The adventurous squalor of the IRT, the trains covered in graffiti taking them to the Met. or up to Columbus Circle to look at the moderns, tall black youths, street-wise and menacing. Guggenheim, Whitney, weekends with friends in Connecticut. Basement bookstores in the Village, steam rising through the sidewalk grilles, hazardous drunks along 8th Street. WALK DONT WALK. Elizabeth remarked that the iron fire hydrants were sculpted like fluted penises. Her sketchbook was full of them. Man and wife competed to excavate penises in the urban landscape; gazing up the long uptown avenues on a cloudy, sullen day, he found the grey sky falling vertically between the highest buildings like God's member.

He hoped that Esther Meyer had taken note of his marriage.

The marriage ceremony itself was a topic they buried by tacit agreement. Elizabeth's parents had taken a church wedding for granted but Stern had dragged Elizabeth to the local vicar and forced the man, over tea and toast, to admit, most reluctantly, that a Jewish atheist who wouldn't believe a word of the ceremony could not, in good faith, be married in Banbury parish church. And when they stood in Banbury registry office, her parents and his mother in sulking attendance, each gazing down their own avenues of disappointment, bride and groom had repeated their solemn promises in voices ghostly with disbelief.

Elizabeth had lied to her parents about leaving the LSE, claiming that she and Richard were agreed that her dissertation needed an extra year. Interrogated by the Admiral, Stern had no alternative but to subscribe to the same tissue of lies. The Admiral clearly smelt a rat; Stern feared he would write to Ramsay. Perhaps he did.

His mother was on her best behaviour, telephoning him every day before the wedding to warn him he was making a fatal mistake. Invited by Lady Halliday to tea at the flat in South Kensington, Deborah twice altered the appointment to demonstrate that she couldn't be 'taken for granted'.

—You don't want me to bring Monty to your wedding, do you? You're ashamed of him.

—He might sell the Admiral a lame horse. Otherwise – fine.

Deborah had arrived with Aunt Orna and a brace of cousins. Stern dispensed with a best man: he didn't have one. Rachel came with her husband, smiling and relaxed, bridging the families.

—I hope you'll both be very happy, she told Elizabeth. —Mind you, happiness isn't exactly Richard's thing.

Driving together to the Halliday country estate after the ceremony, Dr and Mrs Richard Stern had seen an old, shambling man, perhaps a tramp, it was all over in a flash, hit by a lorry and knocked half-way across the road. Through his mirror Stern could see the inert sack in the gutter: massive internal injuries, haemorrhage. The lorry didn't stop and Richard didn't stop either, they had to be on the receiving line at the reception and check-in time for their flight to America was six-fifteen. Dressed in pink and a gorgeous hat to break the Admiral's heart, Elizabeth Stern had greeted each guest with perfect grace and faintly exaggerated professions of delight, her vowels like finely ground glass. Beside her Stern bobbed awkwardly, a camel among horses, his voice loud with goodwill, regressing into heartiness.

No sign of his father. Just the memory of a walking stick raised to the sky over the Oxford meadows:—Buzzard.

It was not until they were high above the Atlantic and Bogart had finally consented to embrace Hepburn that Stern laced his hand through his wife's and mentioned the road accident, the awful, sickening thump as the old man took the impact of the onrushing lorry.

—I thought of Harry, he said.

—So did I.

—But I was driving the lorry that didn't stop.

The seductive throb of the New York telephone. 'Richard, WCBV just called and they're crazy to interview you.'

Out of her monogrammed cream suitcases Elizabeth produced, every day, a new outfit. Or so it seemed. They didn't quarrel or even argue. They flirted. They went shopping. They bought things. They talked and thought – and heard themselves think and talk – in this brisk, jumpy Manhattan patter: his favourite performance was as an urgent, dramatic newscaster, while she specialised in baby-doll innocence hotting up, after a bottle of wine, to licentiousness.

'I want to be a kept woman,' she announced. 'I don't want a degree, I don't want a job, and I don't want babies either. I just want to travel the world with my handsome man.'

In taxis, buses, planes he let his hand rest on her ornamental thigh. Everything they did carried the vulgar complicity of lovers. They giggled incessantly.

She: 'Oh Richard your body really works for me have a nice day.'

He: 'I'm into your body baby thank you for calling.'

Both of them had always known it would be a mistake to marry. Grabbing at air. Her sketchbook filled up steadily. They never mentioned Harry.

They visited friends, stayed with friends, inspecting the early marriages made by the American graduates he had known at Oxford, alumni of Princeton and Harvard who had carried off bright girls from Somerville and Lady Margaret Hall. The Petersens, he an economist, she a linguist, were living in a small house in New Haven and toiling with second and third degrees, nappies everywhere. Elizabeth pretended to love the baby but Stern registered her suppressed recoil. At Amherst the Kleins greeted them with a party in the middle of which Gerry Klein went to bed and after which Diana Klein told Elizabeth he was having an affair with one of his students and she wanted a divorce despite the two young children.

There were also Elizabeth's friends, who tended to be her parents' friends, intelligent naval officers who read Samuel Eliot Morison and bookclub editions of Barbara Tuchman and urged Stern to keep the British flag flying for the good of the planet.

'It's the fashion to denigrate the British Empire,' they told him. 'The forces for order and decency in the world are on the retreat.'

The ladies asked him how he found America: wasn't this his first visit? His reply grew nastier the more he worked on it.

'It's odd, isn't it – I have two visas in my passport, one "for the sole purpose of carrying out the programs stated in item 8 of the form DSP–66", the other more indulgent: "Admit to the United States indefinitely." Because I'm British.'

'That's a proud heritage, Richard.'

'In the Middle East, India and points East men line up outside US Consulates, filling in humiliating forms, treated like beggars, eating their hearts out for a toe-hold in this wonderful country of enterprise and opportunity. And what does one find when one arrives? Poverty, ghettoes, garbage strikes, fear of mugging, an unbeatable homicide rate, corruption, the Mafia, burning cities, young men fleeing into exile to avoid the draft, Vietnamese villages burning on the television screens, preachers denouncing "materialism" even as they exalt the profit motive.'

Lady Halliday also had a scattering of well-appointed female cousins who were neatly logged in Elizabeth's address book as Aunt This and Aunt That. Calling them collect was legitimate. These aunts tended to live in houses of striking elegance, not least Aunt Di in Charleston, whose walls were hung with miniatures in gold frames, Corot, Ingres, Boudin.

Everyone seemed to praise everyone. Stern was disconcerted by the prevailing politeness. Travelling and travelling, he sometimes wondered whether Esther had trodden these sidewalks, cast her lovely Lollobrigida eyes on these landscapes, eaten the same cream cakes, scallops, clams and broiled lobsters. Eating at Max's Kansas City or the Hamburger Heaven, he might glimpse her across the room, beautiful, serene, her voice like crushed fruit soaked in honey.

Elizabeth received many letters from home, he very few. One day in Charleston when Elizabeth was in the bathroom staunching a bad attack of the curse with Kotex he found a re-addressed envelope poking out of her bag. The large, solemn handwriting, familiar from so many boring essays, drew him:

'Dearest Beth,

You promised to write but I suppose you are too busy. The IMG women's group passed a resolution condemning your decision to abandon your dissertation and degree under authoritarian patriarchal pressure. It was unanimously agreed that you had betrayed the Movement. I tried to stick up for you, of course, but the sisters are very angry and regard your conduct as a stab in the back. Resolutions were passed condemning the chauvinists Ramsay and Marquis. A motion expelling R. Stern from the IMG for his manipulative and conformist behaviour was deferred until his return. Beth, you were an inspiration to all of us but now you have betrayed yourself through selfishness and false pride. You will never be truly happy until you purge yourself into humility and service. When will you see the light, my darling Beth, when will you rip the gold and diamonds from your finger? Beth, there is only one enemy: MEN. They are slaves to domination and competition. He doesn't love you, he merely wants to possess you, own you, control you. To him you are not a real person with a mind, heart and soul of your own, just an object, part of his fantasy for power. Men are incapable

72

of love. Only rape. You will learn the hard way. I grieve for you and I miss you, what you did was so horrible that I sometimes want to kill myself but I won't. I still believe in you. Your weakness will pass. You will come back to us, I know it.

Your adoring
Hattie.'

Boarding the flight for London they both felt drained and depressed. The pilot announced an hour's delay in take-off. The businessman in the next seat slowly went mad, fretting about his connecting flight from London to Brussels. 'Come on, come on!' he cried.

Gradually (yet swiftly) Elizabeth refurnished the flat in Notting Hill Gate, replacing the heavy Maples gloss and shimmering velveteens chosen by his mother with simple, elegant pieces, canvas and chrome, natural colours, cane lampshades, rush matting from Vietnam.

'When am I going to be invited to dinner?' his mother asked.

'As soon as we've sorted ourselves out.'

'With so many lovely wedding presents is that a problem? What makes you think I'm against new ideas? One's never too old to learn.'

The tide ran for him. Commissions poured in by telephone and letter, invitations to lecture from Copenhagen to Montreal, an international conference in Havana: collective farms, a visit to the Sierra Maestra. Elizabeth brought Herbert and Horace from South Kensington and redid the shower in an engaging pattern of blue, curly-tailed fish leaping across frothing waves. It amused him to take her in the shower, lifting her by the waist, impaling her slight, willowy body under a blast of warm water until his stick-legs buckled and he slithered down the cool tiles, among the leaping fish, groaning, mocked by her china-blue eyes. The pleasures which had eluded him now came with the service.

The bombs falling in Vietnam seemed far away. So, too, Esther Meyer's Zimbabwean nationalists languishing in captivity at Gonakudzingwa, watching the oil trains pass. Afterwards, wrapped in the flashy silk dressing gown his mother had given him as one of her many wedding presents, lightly dusted in talcum powder

73

and guilt, he would sip whisky and chart his own corruption, calling himself a colour-supplement stud, berating his own collapse into 'one-dimensional materialism'.

Elizabeth would listen attentively.

'All very flattering.'

He looked at her in surprise. 'Oh my God, I've offended you.'

'You don't consider these post-coital monologues the least bit offensive? Isn't it really the old Genesis story – Eve and the apple?'

She spoke mildly.

'The best prose is post-coital,' he told her.

Elizabeth read everything he wrote, in draft. He begged her to be critical, even harsh: 'I'm a professional,' he told her. He wasn't sure what she did with her days and decided it would be tactless to ask. They rarely spoke of the LSE, or of Harry. If Elizabeth was applying for jobs she didn't mention it; when Stern tentatively broached the subject of her resuming her degree course she shook her flaxen hair and he felt relieved.

He and Harry stood shoulder to shoulder as comrades on one further occasion before Harry was deported to a certain institution. This latest demonstration was reported in several newspapers:

'Classes and lectures were disrupted at the LSE yesterday when five hundred students attended meetings to protest against the Government's decision to deport the German student leader, Rudi Dutschke, from Britain. Several members of staff displayed solidarity by cancelling their classes. Dr Richard Stern, Chairman of the International Marxist Group, told a packed assembly hall that the Home Secretary's decision posed a clear threat to civil liberties. Dr Stern, a close friend of the German revolutionary intellectual, warned that the ruling class was now developing a concerted strategy to repress dissent.

'In a further demonstration of protest, two dozen scholars and writers demonstrated on the steps of the British Museum, demanding permanent resident status for Mr Dutschke, whose health has never recovered from an attempt on his life in Berlin four years ago. Speaking through a loud hailer, Professor Harry Marquis, of the LSE, read passages of English literature illustrating Britain's tradition of hospitality towards political refugees. Mentioning, among others, Garibaldi and Mazzini, Professor Marquis reminded a small audience of somewhat bemused tourists that Karl Marx had been granted asylum from persecution more than a century ago.

' "Need we be less tolerant than the Victorians?" Professor Marquis asked, pointing out that Karl Marx had been allowed to work undisturbed in the Reading Room of the British Museum while writing his famous book, *Capital*. In a challenge to the Home Secretary, Professor Marquis, who left the Communist Party in 1956, demanded; "Is Rudi Dutschke really a more serious threat to captialism than Karl Marx?" Hearing this, one American lady turned back from the entrance to the Museum, loudly remarking to her husband: "If Karl Marx is in there, I'm not going in."

'Professor Marquis and Dr Stern then led the protesting intellectuals inside, accompanied by a Deputy Director of the Museum, where a token occupation lasting twenty minutes was allowed by the Museum authorities. The police were not called and there were no arrests.'

Some of those taking part in the demonstration on the front steps of the British Museum noted sadly that exchanges between Marquis and Stern were noticeably brief and lacking in affability. Indeed the Professor appeared to give the cold shoulder to other young intellectuals of the Left, including several members of the editorial board of *Thought and Action*, the journal he had founded after his expulsion from the Communist Party. In particular he avoided even eye contact with Stern's wife, who now wrote under the name Beth Halliday and was widely regarded as the rising voice of the new feminism. None of this was lost on the *New Statesman*'s observant columnist, J. R. Tree.

A dedicated Gaitskellite and close confidant of Anthony Crosland, Tree regarded the Marxists of the New Left as frivolous dilettantes who merely discredited the Labour movement. 'You can't argue with them, you can only expose them, genitalia and all,' he told the many dinner parties to which he was invited on account of his unfailing supply of embellished and frequently salacious gossip – a quality which made up not only for his lack of elegance with a knife and fork but also for the dullness of his columns (as if the act of writing stifled his natural wit, dredging up a sludge of solemn statistics and Fabian tedium).

Once a month, however, he was given the diary to write under the Puckish byline 'Acorn': four weeks of wine and oysters duly spilled out.

Singing for his suppers during the week following the Museum demo, Tree elaborated on a sub-plot unnoticed by the other hacks in attendance. While prose and poetry reverberated through loud hailers from the steps of the Museum, and visitors searching for the Elgin Marbles paused nervously in the forecourt, a young woman with oval features of striking beauty had threaded a passage through the throng until, finding the person she sought (her 'prey', said Tree), she had gently touched the other woman's arm. 'Two not unbeautiful women, one dark-haired and ripe with sunshine, a peach, the other blonde, a glacier mint, frosted in thoughts only a novelist could excavate.' Closing on them with the zeal of a Hobbit, Tree had stationed himself within earshot while gazing thoughtfully at the sky 'as if to discover whether God wanted Rudi Dutschke deported or not'.

(Here Tree would pause tantalisingly until it was realised that his glass was empty. Watered, his legendary memory performed prodigious feats of total recall. Thus:)

—Excuse me, you must be Elizabeth Stern.

—Yes, I am.

—I just wanted to say how kind your husband was to me.

—I'm sorry, I don't know your—

—No reason at all why you should. I'm Esther Meyer.

—Oh yes . . . of course. Richard did speak of you . . . Weren't you both involved in the occupation of Rhodesia House?

—We were. In fact your husband picked me off the pavement.

—And gave evidence for you in court?

—He did. He was wonderful. He later invited me to speak at the LSE about the liberation of my country.

—Really? I must have missed that.

—I can't tell you how nervous I felt even though I'd been lecturing in America, but your husband was wonderful, so kind and considerate, he put me completely at ease.

—Richard can be nice when he tries.

—I don't think you were married at the time because I remember saying he must come to dinner and bring his wife and he said, 'Oh no, I'm a confirmed bachelor.'

—Did he? Richard normally avoids clichés. I'm sure you'll be able to find him today if you try hard enough.

—Really I just came to support the demonstration. I do think liberty is indivisible, don't you? It's terribly tempting for people like myself to remain blinkered about things happening outside Africa.

—I wish I knew more about Africa. Are you from South Africa?

—From Zimbabwe.

—Oh yes, of course – occupying Rhodesia House and all that, silly of me. Come and meet Richard.

—No, really, he's much too busy. I'm just a simple colonial, you see, and I'm still not sure of the customs here.

—Customs?

—Some of the local tribal dances are rather complicated.

76

—Oh . . . yes, I see.

—In Zimbabwe we try to keep politics and . . . personal relationships . . . separate. But in London it's all rather different. A man rings up to ask for an interview, or expresses concern about the continuing oppression of my people, and then . . .

—Then wants to sleep with you?

—I didn't mean Richard.

—Male chauvinism is rampant here. It would be easier to fight it if so many women didn't encourage it.

—Why do they? That puzzles me.

—I've no doubt Richard would have screwed you if you'd given him an amber light followed by green plus a road map to your flat and a pair of roller skates.

—I'm sorry, I had no idea you felt like that . . .

—Like what?

—I didn't intend to offend you. I just felt awfully guilty that I'd never kept my promise to invite him to dinner. I did mean to, but then I had to go to Nigeria, and after that it was Kenya, we're so dreadfully in need of support . . .

—*A luta continua*.

—Exactly. Then when I came back someone told me Richard had married one of his most brilliant pupils and I really felt rather shy about the whole thing.

—Look, do talk to Richard and then come and have dinner with us.

—You're so very kind, Elizabeth. But I have to go now and I just wondered whether you could give Richard a message . . . It's rather confidential, actually.

—In that case, should I know it?

—Oh certainly. I'm sure he tells you everything. Just to say to him that despite threats to arrest me, I've decided to return to Zimbabwe. The real struggle is there, you see.

—I think you're very brave.

—Oh no. You should meet the freedom fighters. Those are truly brave men. And how they've paid for their courage! One day, perhaps, Richard will find time to come to Zimbabwe and write about them. Will you tell him that? Goodbye, Elizabeth, it's been such a pleasure meeting you. And I'll remember what you said about 'male chauvinism'. Goodbye.

—Good luck!

Tree leant back in his chair and gazed at his empty glass. As guest of honour, he had been seated at the head of the table.

'Beyond that . . . one could only speculate.'

The decanter was hurried in his direction. Tree offered his impish grin while his hostess and several other women competed to remind him that he would (easily) have been a novelist if his copious talents had not diverted him to the heavier end of literature.

The gnome beamed and plucked up one of his host's circulating cigars.

'Turning to appearances,' he teased the ladies, 'one might aver that Miss Meyer was rather fancily turned out for a demo on behalf of our cut-down version of Garibaldi, Herr Dutschke. Esther does tend to look as if she's on her way to Wimbledon. Don't forget she was brought up in Rhodesia, where every white girl dreams of becoming a jacaranda queen.'

'But isn't Esther Meyer rather different?'

'She is and she isn't. That's one reason why white women in Rhodesia hate and revile her. If she scrubbed her face and dressed as a nun they might tolerate her eccentric loyalties – as it is, her act is to knock the white blokes over like ninepins and then run off with a bunch of coons and munts – I'm using the local parlance.'

'And Mrs Stern?'

Tree grinned even more impishly. 'Ah. La Halliday, who was once the best – and most expensively – dressed student at the LSE, has now cut her hair short and adopted the uniform of the new sisterhood: unisex jeans and floppy sweaters. But the mutation is not yet stable. Confronted with the honey-voiced colonial beauty . . .'

'She would like to display her abandoned wardrobe?'

'Camilla, you must not steal my best lines.'

'But what of the brilliant Richard? Where does he stand in all this? Has he been pursuing the jacaranda queen? It's simply ages since we had him to dinner.'

'His wife will not inform him that Esther is returning to Rhodesia – if she is.'

A correspondent rarely, if ever, invited to dinner parties was Leonard Tanner. He, too, had attended the demo in support of the kraut terrorist. Gloomily plodding back to *The Times*, Tanner had composed his usual five hundred words, mostly dead reporting but enlivened by a viperous little paragraph concerning rising tension on the editorial board of *Thought and Action* – to which Beth Halliday had recently been co-opted out of deference to the *zeitgeist:* 'Tampax has apparently replaced tear gas as the holy odour of the Left' (not that Tanner's flair for such imagery was given much scope by *The Times*). Tanner's paragraph hinted at past scandals involving 'prominent members of the teaching staff and the daughter of a senior British naval officer'. The sub-editor duly applied his blue pencil. Tanner was not surprised, indeed he would have done the same. But there was still some kick in him.

'Fuck you, Arthur, that's news.' A crumpled face of wax and leather, but still capable of animation.

'It's gossip, Leonard. It could be libellous.'

'Sir Walter Halliday happens to be Officer Commanding, Northern Group, NATO. That makes his Marxist son-in-law, a prominent member of the Campaign for Nuclear Disarmament, potentially privy to every bloody nuclear code now in operation.'

The sub reached for his Gold Block. 'Insinuations don't make a story.'

'Fuck you, Arthur. I was in Korea when you were still reporting the Cheltenham Gold Cup. A big story breaks day by day. The smell flushes out the inside sources: they begin to sing.'

'Leonard, go and see the editor. This is too big for me.'

But Tanner didn't; on reflection it might be better to cache the gun under a tree until he was certain of his ammunition.

From the notebook of Richard Stern:

Catching sight of Esther at the demo I immediately felt sick with longing. Why didn't she speak to me? What did she say to Beth? Esther is a virus I can't expel or suppress. I am haunted. When I lecture I see her in the audience. When I write I imagine her reading over my shoulder. When I pour wine I pretend the glass is hers. When I go to the theatre the next seat in the stalls is occupied by Esther. Thank God I never transplant Esther into Elizabeth's body when fucking. Am I deceiving myself when I insist that the one thing I don't feel for Esther is carnal lust? Possibly this is the delusion traditionally suffered by women when first in love.

Harry has been carted away to the bin.

Thought and Action have invited me to write a reply to his polemic. It's not easy. Harry has fired a blast of scattershot against pseudo-revolutionaries admiring themselves in gilded mirrors, emissaries of the latest Paris jargon, hysterical females revelling in their self-assumed slavery, disciples who betrayed the master. Harry has re-incarnated himself as the spokesman of romantic moralism and old-fashioned British common sense. This merely means that the old lecher looks back on our visit to Paris in May '68 as the moment Beth was stolen from him.

When she went down to the bin in Sussex, Harry pretended not to recognise her, rather a waste of a rail ticket. The psychiatrist told her they might administer electric shocks. She could have explained: 'A night in bed with me would cure him'.

Foolishly I showed her a first draft of my 'Reply to Harry Marquis'. She said it was too harsh, and also misdirected. I suspect that the 'collective' (i.e. the scheming Hattie) is/are considering a 'statement' of its/their own. One can guess the line: 'History has been written, but not made, by men. It is no coincidence that "hysteria" and "uterus" spring from a common Greek root . . .' Beth is slipping away from me. Discord surfaces too often for peace of mind. Physically she is almost (sometimes) unrecognisable.

Whatever Beth may say about polemic being the male substitute for genuine debate, I am determined to include this sentence: 'Those of us who have learned from Harry Marquis himself the poverty of empiricism can hardly have anticipated that he would now be teaching us the utter poverty of theory.'

Beth gazes at me reproachfully from beneath her new, *pétroleuse* (pudding basin) haircut: —Richard, your target is presently incapable of reading the message on a packet of cornflakes. But if you prick him with his own spear, does he not bleed?

She no longer wears a trace of make-up during the day. She vanishes for increasingly long, unexplained periods. I try to suppress my curiosity – she *wants* me to ask. That Hattie creature is in constant attendance, smugly monitoring me through her owl-glasses. She wears a tall, pointed hat, that one: a coven called a 'collective' is audibly chopping up newts and toads somewhere in the North. Beth returns with morsels of the Pennines lodged in her crystal vowels.

Elizabeth's body is still available on demand but it now belongs to Beth Halliday. Beth's body. One is serviced like a car with a faulty carburettor and a flat battery. She does it like a busy nurse placing a bed-pan under an incontinent old invalid, then bustles away down the ward, starched in a hundred pressing duties. That's two metaphors and I'm working on others.

Thank God we have never been so naive as to try and resolve our differences in bed – the most shop-soiled of white flags.

Nasty diary piece by Tree in the *New Statesman*. He clearly rejoices in the fact that despite two well-acclaimed books I have still been denied tenure at the LSE. Who's his source? One could suspect Harry, or Ramsay, or Gough. We were waiting for our flight home from Kennedy Airport when I finally asked my bride what she had meant when she congratulated Dr Gough on being the only man in the room who had not asked her to sleep with him.

Elizabeth re-crossed her legs, a swish of nylon.

—Darling, it wasn't true. I wanted to frighten Ramsay – for your sake.

Even the cat familiar with proverbs will expend eight of its lives on curiosity. When we returned from our honeymoon we were both determined to respect each other's privacy. Neither of us looked at the other's mail, unless invited. One didn't listen to the other's telephone conversations, unless unavoidable. But now the flat is often empty, silent, and I am already gazing, like Bunuel's disenchanted, down the long grove of poplars to the cemetery where minuscule figures angrily gesticulate out of earshot. I have begun to riffle through her notebooks, diaries, desk drawers and filing cabinet. I am shattered but no shock deters me from returning my fingers to the live wire. Each lover is accorded his own folder, courtesy Rymans the stationers. I am catalogued as conscientiously as any other – the stage buffoon who has just discovered that he is not the only one who enjoys champagne and caviar. Sweating thumb-prints: not only Christopher but also his cousin Simon (whose existence is news to me), about half of the IMG – my own pupils! laughing at me over their seminar papers! – and a good proportion of the editorial board of *Thought and Action*. No wonder she has been co-opted.

The letters from Harry go back and back – clearly he was on to Elizabeth even before I was. Pleas for love and understanding, pitifully humble, are gradually replaced by vulgar remonstrances: 'whore', 'harlot', 'bitch', and 'tart' lead the league. Worse are the sentimental literary allusions, lines from Blake, lessons from Machiavelli, and Harry's own attempts at poetry:

'When I think
of all the wars
in which I have not fallen.'

Most eloquent is a note of congratulations on our engagement:

'And now you will join in a ceremony of mutual obliteration, your project a solipsistic society of two. Richard will readily succumb to the bourgeois destiny you offer him. His pen will shed none of its radicalism, merely its sense of life. You will smother and petrify him in a lava of babies and mortgages – your female revenge on us both.'

Postcards, lined sheets torn from exercise books, the backs of unpaid electricity bills. I gape, my jaw slack with disbelief, my brow knitted and furrowed like the village idiot:

'So you told him that it was I who reviled his book in the *TLS*!

81

Bitch! And what serpentine lies, I wonder, do you feed his innocent maw about me? Oh, I can hear the dinner bell of your tinkling laughter, the Admiral's daughter: "I made old Harry ejaculate while forcing him to write down the meaning of the world on my garter." '

These archives require a bottle of something, if only Cyprus sherry. Normally I hurl only soft things, cushions, or my brain, at the lampshades, but one night when Beth was away I destroyed her entire wardrobe, fell across the bed in a stupor, and awoke next morning to find a large stain on the carpet. Beside it my sodden trousers.

Why, why, why did Esther choose not to talk to me at the demo? Why does she torture me? Whenever I screw myself up to dial her number I'm forced to replace the receiver when I hear her voice: *mauvaise foi*. I hear that Sartre is very ill, incontinent, unlikely ever to write again. Castor says he cannot dictate, the act of thinking being inseparable, by habit and reflex, from the motion of his writing hand across the page. If a fairy granted me one wish – that Sartre should recover and write again, or that Esther should offer herself to me – which would I choose?

Stern made a pot of coffee with slow deliberation, like a rock climber short of a ledge. Unfolding the morning paper, he rapidly worked his way towards the dark recesses of the centre-fold, hoping, or hoping not, to find news of the schismatic exchanges which had sent the circulation of *Thought and Action* rocketing from 6,500 to 6,750. Less than a week had passed since the *Observer*'s diary column had informed him that his wife had marched with other women to Leeds City Hall to protest against sexual harassment in the recreation and leisure department – they had then moved on to the local magistrates' court to 'picket' a stipendiary magistrate who regarded any woman who hitched a lift on the M1 as 'asking for it'.

The headline leapt out of page six and slowly coiled round his throat: ESTHER MEYER ARRESTED IN RHODESIA.

EIGHT

Supporting the story was an old agency photograph of Esther picketing the South African Embassy in Trafalgar Square, her hair tossing in the wind, the placard in her hand demanding 'Free Nelson Mandela'.

Grabbing the telephone, he dialled Amy Brand and by mid-morning found himself in a sparsely filled committee room of the House of Commons hastily reserved by a Labour MP who had been given the bum's rush out of Rhodesia shortly after UDI. Pale, long-nosed and aloof, Stern obliquely examined the scattering of concerned faces around him: Amy's professional exiles; ancient churchmen obscurely celebrated for the stands they had taken, deportation orders tucked under their dog collars; a few left-wing politicians with half-familiar, front-page faces disconcertingly well-fleshed in repose; and a token presence of journalists who kept glancing at their watches.

Tree of the *New Statesman* lifted his brow in greeting and moved to the chair next to Stern's.

'What brings you here?'

Stern had prepared a dignified rebuke for Tree when next he saw him: or several. But Tree's question, in its awful, piercing simplicity, left him dumb.

'She's a lovely girl, of course – Esther.' Tree winked.

Stern flushed. His passion for Esther had remained padlocked. He never mentioned her and never responded when he heard her discussed. But Tree's casual thrust went to the marrow.

'What news of the great Harry?' Tree asked.

'I thought you were the expert on that.'

Tree affected an expression of mock contrition. '*Mea culpa.*'

Amy Brand marched to the front on legs of oak, her armpits stuffed with press releases, and announced in her down-to-business

83

rasp that Rhodesian Special Branch had raided the homes and offices of at least forty people suspected of assisting the banned nationalist parties. According to her information, twenty-five had been arrested under the Law and Order Maintenance Act. Esther Meyer had been dragged from her bed during a dawn raid on her parents' home in the Avondale district of Salisbury.

Stern thought: she's sleeping at home.

'Any charges?' demanded a voice of familiar grit and gravel from behind Stern's shoulder. He glanced over his shoulder.

'No charge is required,' Amy snapped. 'The Minister of Justice merely signs an indefinite detention order.'

'Where is she held?' Tanner's ravaged features were fastened on Amy Brand in folds of scepticism.

'We don't know. At the time of her arrest she was working for Geoff Cowans, whose law firm represents a large number of detainees held in Wha Wha, Khami, Gatooma and Chikurubi. So far his enquiries have been unsuccessful.'

'Have you spoken to the Foreign Office?' Tanner was gnawing away at Amy.

She laughed coldly. 'You speak to them, Mr Tanner.'

Stern wondered whether Tanner had been to Rhodesia – he carried the air of a man who has seen it all.

When Amy raised the prospect of torture there was a detectable hint of relish in her throat. As with other professional exiles, the worse the better.

'The strategy of Special Branch 2 is to provide access to lawyers only after the interrogations are completed.'

Stern trembling. At this very moment . . .

'Sheer balls,' Tanner was muttering to anyone who would listen. 'They'd never torture a white woman down there.'

'Shut up, Leonard,' Tree said.

Suddenly a high voice was raised in ironic protest: 'No problem, Amy! No problem at all!'

Heads swivelled in guarded alarm: of late there had been several bomb scares in the Palace of Westminster, rowdy demos in the public gallery of the Commons, and a Turk arrested with a meat cleaver secreted in a laundry bag.

It was Oscar Mucheche. Stern had lost contact with Oscar after the Zimbabwean patriot was tossed out of the LSE for repeated acts of insurrection, including an attempt to set fire to the senior common room. With Harry gone to the bin, Stern denied tenure for another year, the IMG in disarray, and Ramsay's counter-Reformation in the ascendant, the Law and Order Maintenance Act also prevailed at the LSE. Oscar had accepted his fate with surprising equanimity. —I've had enough of phoney wars, he told

Stern, leaving the lecturer with the impression that he was now heading for the base camps of Mozambique or Zambia, the bandoliers already clinking round his waist. Oscar, it now transpired, hadn't got that far. 'No problem for our dear Esther!' he cried from a seat in the back row. 'Rest assured the white lady sleeps on a Category A bed in a Category A cell with access to a nice toilet and maybe a nice bowl of fruit, too. The black leaders of my country and two thousand freedom fighters have been detained without trial for ten years! They sleep on the floor! They eat slops! One blanket in winter! Executions in Chikurubi every Monday morning! Why do we all rush to the Whorehouse of Commons as soon as one white woman is detained by her fellow tribesmen of the ruling race, tell me that, Amy?'

Stern heard Tanner chuckle grimly. The grizzled old warrior even took out his notebook.

'Esther would be the first to agree with you, Oscar,' Amy said.

'Don't patronise me, Amy!' Oscar cried.

'Oscar, we're all comrades in the struggle.'

'I used to believe that, Amy. I came to this country as an exiled freedom fighter fleeing fascist racism. Then people abused me in the street, yes here in London. "Black bastard," they said. "Nigger, go home," they said. Then I was expelled from the LSE for singing a freedom song in the toilet! So I decided to write a book for a well-known publisher, exposing all this hypocrisy and deceit. And when the police picked me up for walking the streets of London and wearing out the paving stones in search of work I went to this famous liberal publisher for protection. And what did he do, that noble fellow? He accused me of stealing one ream of typing paper, six sheets of carbon paper, one typewriter ribbon and four paper clips. So I said to him, "What kind of shit is this, man?" and he called the police and told them to detain me indefinitely in any cell in Wormwood Scrubs where regular gang rape was practised on black boys. So then—'

'Shut up and sit down, Oscar,' Amy said.

'How can I sit down, Amy, when my bum is lacerated by beatings? Who wants to see my black bum?'

Oscar suddenly strode from the room. The feeling was general that he might soon be back with reinforcements.

An elderly cleric raised his hand. 'I believe all of us feel that some form of direct action is called for. We must bear witness with body and spirit.'

'We too must suffer imprisonment,' said a lady, 'until Esther and her black brothers and sisters are released.'

Tanner groaned loudly.

Stern felt sick: even at this moment real fascists were wrapping

Esther's head in a plastic bag and forcing it under water while she sobbed and choked and here were these pensioned milk puddings engaged in fantasies of martyrdom within a hundred yards of Westminster Abbey. Yet such irritation was quickly buried under the landslide of self-contempt: he who had cultivated his passion for Esther to the point of obsession had not even known she had returned to Rhodesia. In truth, my boy, you only love yourself! Unable to offer any alternative course of action, he found himself trailing out into the warm sunshine with Amy Brand and the former Bishop of the Upper Nile, crossing the square, passing Clive and Churchill, and then into the front hall of the Foreign Office, two by two, like animals entering the ark, the gnomish Tree a limpet at his side, and then they all squatted down decorously on the great marble staircase under the surprised gaze of Palmerston and Curzon, waiting.

They waited. Nothing happened. Pinstriped mandarins hurried past, puzzled. Finally a Deputy Under Secretary (perhaps?) paused in mid-stride, carefully weighed the danger, found none, and cast a wolfish smile on the former Bishop of the Upper Nile, squatting at the foot of the marble staircase, bearing his invisible Cross:

'Why, Henry! Didn't we last meet in Zambia? Or was it the Sudan? You want to present a petition to the Secretary of State? About what? Angola? The Falklands? Ah, yes, the new wave of arrests in Rhodesia! – pity it's all out of our hands now. Yours is rather an unorthodox approach, Henry, but I recall we've covered that ground on previous occasions. I'll see what I can do.'

Off he hurried to break his promise and five minutes later police began dropping from the ceiling like blue bats. Lifted by his armpits and legs, Stern recalled Esther's cry as they dropped her on the pavement outside Rhodesia House. This time they were more gently treated. The police even supported the former Bishop of the Upper Nile while he regained his balance and ascertained in which diocese he had been set down.

'Could have been worse,' Tree grinned.

'Brave of you to have lasted the course,' Stern said.

'Want to be interviewed, Richard? Just one question: when did you last sleep with Esther? I hear she's married a freedom fighter.'

Stern walked away. An old lady tugged at his sleeve.

'I think we made our point, don't you?'

'Oh yes,' he murmured.

Tanner was barring his passage. The journalist had chosen to wait outside during the 'occupation' of the Foreign Office.

'Hardly your scene?' Tanner inquired. 'All these bourgeois liberals and milksop Prods.'

'I get the impression you don't like me,' Stern said, slackening his long stride but keeping moving so that the older man was forced to follow. Tanner emitted a short laugh, a snort, and let him go. Stern strode up Whitehall, crossed Trafalgar Square, turned into Piccadilly, and burst into the offices of British Airways.

'When's the next flight to Rhodesia?' he asked a girl in a crisp blue suit.

'We no longer fly to Rhodesia, sir. It's a Government regulation.'

'Really? What do you advise? Camel? Hot-air balloon?'

She gave him a faintly indulgent smile.

'Try South African Airways.'

As he opened the front door he heard water running in the shower and wondered what mood to adopt – with a wife you could select a feeling from the kaleidoscope of possibilities and let it hang out. He remembered that this had been a day of torment and grief; on the other hand the splashing water evoked an itch in his groin. He was of course aware of these contradictions, and of others besides: he was a writer, after all.

'Not much hot water up North?' he called.

Her answering laugh surprised him. A rare commodity these days. It quickened his lust. He knew what had brought her to town: notice of an emergency meeting of the editorial board of *Thought and Action* from Tom McAllisty, who had been deputising as editor since Harry was wheeled away. It transpired that the journal had received two replies to Harry's polemic, one Stern's, the other from Beth and the women's collective.

McAllisty, a courageous libertarian with charm to match his good looks, wanted to know whether he should publish them both.

Stern had traced Beth, via Leeds and Bradford, to a flat in Manchester. The exercise had earned him several strip-searches by female voices clearly on guard against the Pig. He recognised the stretched vowels which Beth herself was beginning to adopt – the slow, dreary, monotone voices of English radicalism, purged of emphasis, flat as the silted Fenlands. Roundheads, rendered artless by an overdose of virtue.

Now he pulled back the Habitat shower curtain with its tile-matching design in blue and white of fishes leaping across frivolous waves.

'You look nice,' he said. 'I've missed you.'

'You only miss me when I go away, eh?'

'I suppose that's logical. Shall I join you?'

'If you like. I won't be long.'

'What does that mean?'

The upwards motions of her arms stretched her small breasts.

'It means I won't be long.'

He turned away, schooled in wisdom by unhappiness. He went into the kitchen and put the kettle under the cold tap, barely covering the element. It was a way of living dangerously.

To have made love at such a time would have been a betrayal of Esther. Like the first meal after a death in the family. Or something like that. He slumped into a chair.

Beth emerged in a shapeless blue sweater, combing her short wet hair.

'What's the matter?' she asked.

'The matter?'

'You look awful. I see they've arrested your Miss Rhodesia.'

'Yes.'

'It's been on my conscience – she told me to inform you that she had decided to embrace martyrdom and then it slipped my mind.'

He nodded slowly. 'Isn't probity encouraged in the Movement?'

Beth went red. 'Manage your own bloody love affairs!' she shouted, seizing the wall phone and dialling with short, angry jabs. In the old days, when she cared about her nails, she had used a pencil.

He rose and poured hot water over a tea bag, barely pretending not to listen.

'Hattie? Yes, it's me. Yes, I'm in Notting Hill Gate.' [Ah, no longer 'at home'.] 'Listen, when I got here I found a letter from Jo.' [Or 'Joe'? Wait.] 'Her allegations against the EWP' [Equality Working Party?] 'are complete fabrications and she knows it. I mean we made it clear last month by Conference resolution that policy is to be determined by the AGM' [easy] 'and not by the NEC' [National Executive Committee]. 'She then goes behind our backs and starts freelancing her own negotiations with the Joint Council' [?] 'and the AWP' [Amalgamation Working Party? Absent Without Permission?]. '*Then* she has the absolute effrontery to demand a debate with the EWP! No way – not unless she first agrees that her actions have been in violation of the Code of Conduct. Now she comes out with a diabolical diatribe in the newsletter, a whole load of typical liberal shit about censorship, Gestapo tactics, you know, the usual line of the accommodationists who can't distinguish between job-sharing and part-time work . . .'

He poured himself a cup out of the teapot and took it into his study. His hand shook as he laid the cup carefully between piled books and manuscripts: what causes tears, Harry had once remarked, are tears themselves. The bleeding knee, the sudden bump, may precipitate the child's initial cry, but it is that cry, that sound of panic, not the injury, which produces five minutes of hysteria.

He heard, finally (he still paid the bills), the angry click of the telephone. He dabbed his eyes with a fairly clean handkerchief. Beth pushed the door of his study ajar with her foot. She appraised him guardedly.

'Sorry,' she said.

He managed a smile. 'This flat is now sown with semantic boobytraps. Alternative pronouns fly like torn-up paving stones. Our bed is haunted by stereotypes.'

'Richard, whenever you're upset you try to be clever.'

'But also when I'm not upset.'

She leant against the door-jamb, cradling a hot cup, watching him with what seemed to him a mixture of pity, distaste and regret. He had to admit that she had not hurled her new culture at him in private; on the contrary it was he who constantly endeavoured to provoke her, to tease (or flush) her out of her cool, aloof self-sufficiency. She had adopted a religion which could not, by the laws of nature, be his – it was as simple as that. The roles had been reversed; he now behaved like a homebound wife determined to penetrate the captivating mysteries of the Masonic lodge.

'Actually,' she said, 'I really am sorry about Esther. She's not exactly my type but I admire her guts.'

'Nice of you to say so.'

'I gather she once invited you to dinner and asked if you were married. You told her you were a confirmed bachelor.'

'So indeed I was.'

'We were already living together, actually. But that's not the main point.' Beth took a cigarette from his desk – she had begun smoking when she joined the Northern collective and when, as she put it, 'I decided not to have children'.

'What is "the main point"?'

She still blew smoke amateurishly, like a child pursing her lips to inflate a balloon.

'The main point is that when I mentioned that long-ago dinner invitation you instantly remembered it, and with awful clarity. You answered like a lawyer – lawyers trade in guilt.'

'Tell me about Christopher's cousin. Robin, wasn't it?'

'Richard, I'm perfectly content for you to spend your life in my desk drawers and filing cabinet. That's why I leave them unlocked.' She drew on her cigarette in quick, nervous pecks, as if weighing something. 'Have you any money?'

'My wallet's on the desk.'

'I don't mean that sort of money. The thing is, we've got to raise nine and a half thousand.'

'We?'

'Not just the collective. The new women's section of the union. They're trying to break us before we've begun.'

'Who's "they"?'

Beth said calmly, 'The men. In fact they're taking out an injunction. We're going to have to fight it in court.'

'Will you win?'

He saw her suppress her irritation. 'It would be a loan. In case it's relevant, I've already committed everything I possess.'

'Everything!'

'Twenty-two thousand.'

He leapt up. 'Holy cow! Now I see why those witches have been courting you!'

He spent the night on the Habitat sofa – the first time they had shared a roof but not a bed. He didn't sleep. He waited for the cautious motion of the door, the soft footfall of peace, the tender embrace of reconciliation, and wondered whether she was doing the same. Anger, grief and self-pity alternated with alarming rapidity. His penis pressed hard and swollen against the cushions, aching for Elizabeth, aching for Esther, aching finally, in the exhausted small hours before dawn, for himself. Walking to the bathroom he saw the bedroom door ajar. He stopped beside it in a final agony of hesitation, then locked the bathroom door behind him. It took only a few seconds.

NINE

The telephone plucked him from the nightmarish sleep into which he had sunk some time after the birds began celebrating their carefree destiny. The wall clock said 7.45 and his watch said 7.45 – he was reminded of the philosopher's joke about the definition of a duck.

He lifted the receiver. 'Then it's a duck,' he said. At such an hour it could only be a wrong number – unless it was one of Beth's harridans putting in a cheap call before 8 a.m. He also had a number similar to a local nursery school; mothers would frequently wake him to explain about Tom's tummy or Miranda's measles. He had developed an unsympathetic response:

'Miranda is malingering again? Our patience is exhausted, Mummy. Send her to a state school.'

But the voice at the other end was neither harridan nor Mummy. It was high-pitched, sinusitic and discernibly originated in those outlandish concrete deserts of greater New York he had glimpsed with apprehension from the Kennedy Airport bus.

'Am I speaking to Richard Stern?'

'Yes.'

'*The* Richard Stern?'

This sounded like a challenge to the three criteria for a duck. It needed thought.

'Paul Meyer,' the man announced himself. 'Canya make lunch? Say twelve-fifteen?'

'Lunch or breakfast? Where?'

'Jane and I are staying at the Connaught.'

'I might make it by one.'

'Earlier ifya can. We never eat that late.'

It was past one when Stern stumbled down the narrow staircase littered with unsold copies of *Thought and Action* and began to

91

search for a taxi in Soho's web of one-way, wrong-way streets. He saw the blue light of Harry's ambulance flashing before it turned the corner into Wardour Street, wailing. He had no idea where the Connaught was – his publishers invariably booked a table somewhere Greek or Croat where the food was 'excellent', i.e. cheap.

The taxi dumped him outside the Connaught at half-past one, sweating and dishevelled. The uniformed doorman smartly barred his path.

'Yes, sir?'

'I've come to plant a bomb. But I'll have lunch first. I assume you do take Albanian credit cards?'

The doorman conducted him inside; the young man's accent and tone were authority enough. They belonged. And such juvenile humour was not altogether unfamiliar, either.

Stern appraised the rich, elderly people sitting in antique chairs round the lobby like waxworks in Madame Tussaud's. After a moment's hesitation a man in a yachting blazer and a goatee beard approached him.

'Dick Stern?'

'Richard. Yes.'

'This is Jane.'

'Delighted to meet you, Dick,' she said.

'We thought ya'd stood us up,' the man said, brandishing a large, waterproof Seiko. 'Boy, am I hungry. Let's go in there.'

Stern began to follow them across the priceless carpet but a morning-coated figure stepped forward discreetly, hands clasped behind his back:

'The gentleman will need a tie, sir. Several are available at the reception desk.'

Stern suppressed the inclination to walk out. He knew that if his mother survived a serious heart bypass operation, he would start quarrelling with her as soon as she came out of 'intensive care'.

'Old Etonian or Grenadier Guards,' he told the morning-coat.

'You may mean Brigade of Guards, sir.'

Paul Meyer led the way into a mahogany-panelled restaurant of palatial proportions where they were engulfed by waiters drawing back chairs, hovering with huge menu cards, murmuring attentively. Meyer ordered a double scotch for himself and a vodka-and-tonic for his shy wife.

'What's yours, Dick?'

'Richard. I usually drink champagne at this time of day but the vintages here are suspect so I'll settle for Perrier water. At least you know what you're getting.'

Paul Meyer glanced nervously up at the hovering maître d'hôtel, whose face had come apart at the seams.

'If the gentleman—'

Stern winked at him. 'I vos only choking.'

Paul and Jane Meyer were buried in huge, ornate menu cards, fighting with the French words as if their lives depended on it. Paul asked the waiter what this 'rendez-vous' thing was.

'Is it some kind of speciality?'

'Certainly, sir. Rendez-vous du pêcheur sauce légère aux asperges de Mexique. White fish, scallops, fresh salmon, lobsters, and crab's legs.'

'I'll have it,' Paul Meyer said, seizing a roll from the bread basket and reaching for the butter.

'Is it fattening?' Jane asked the maître d'hôtel.

Paul Meyer was already eating his bread like a dredger pump, slurp, smack, clearly short of molars. He wolfed like a refugee, driven not so much by hunger as by the idea of hunger, past and future, a man grabbing at the material universe before it slid from his grasp. Stern searched each parent in vain for the source of Esther's faultless beauty. The father's puffy features, split by fast, calculating eyes, were like a dog's – they could never smile. But when Jane Meyer smiled a familiar sunshine passed across the cratered landscape and Stern abruptly experienced a vast tenderness. He took her hand:

'What are they doing to Esther?'

Her hand slowly withdrew. 'We don't know.'

Beth had come up that narrow, littered staircase, passing the unsold copies of the magazine in flat heels, shadowed by Hattie's slow, aggrieved owl eyes. She and Stern had made their separate ways to Soho – what he had said the previous evening would not be forgiven. The atmosphere in the editor's cramped office was grim, comrades seated shoulder to shoulder but exchanging not a word. Tom McAllisty tried a few jokes. They fell flat. Stern, light-headed from sleeplessness, anxiety and what he diagnosed as 'sexual trauma, grade 2', tried to support the gallant editor, who had inherited an ugly storm not of his own making.

'We could discuss "over-determination",' Stern suggested.

Gratefully McAllisty rose to the bait. 'Headmaster's report on the boy who keeps breaking his bones because he tries too hard.'

'And we must come to a decision about Goldmann's "nonconscious". Does anybody here have a "nonconscious"?'

'Ha ha,' said Hattie.

'Is parody a legitimate metaphor for "things fall apart"?' Stern asked. 'Divide content by form and the revenge quotient is high.'

'Coffee everyone?' inquired the charming McAllisty.

Four years ago the women would have made the coffee while the men talked the higher politics, but now Eros had fled and Stern saw Hattie's restraining hand on Beth's arm, the two women maintaining the stony faces of *tricoteuses* beneath the guillotine. McAllisty produced paper cups and a large tin of instant coffee.

'Cheapest brand in London,' he boasted.

Stern caught the fleeting hook of Tom's eye on the eye of her eye, which remained in neutral, armoured for battle. Why had her body become so tormentingly attractive, Stern wondered, since it passed out of his proprietorial domain?

Playing for time, McAllisty raised various minor items on the agenda. It was agreed that they should run an article exposing the centrist leadership in the Labour Party, which was – yet again – abandoning principle in pursuit of electoral expediency. Stern reminded McAllisty about Clement Attlee's response when asked whether he was an agnostic. Attlee had said he didn't know.

McAllisty's grin was on its own.

'Brendan has sent us a piece on schizophrenia,' the good-looking editor announced, searching among the chair legs and human legs for Brendan Hogg, who often chose to squat on the floor, melancholy as one of his patients. (And what were Tom's recollections of Beth's legs?) Finally located, the diminutive but lecherous psychiatrist (another casual inhabitant of Beth's filing cabinet) then explained that society conditioned its members to regard total immersion in outer space and time as normal, as healthy; thus penalising and marginalising those whose equally valid self-discovery took place within inner time and space.

No one demurred, no one cared.

The conversation turned to the crisis in Cyprus. The women continued to say nothing: Cyprus was not a feminist issue. Rigid with apprehension at the prospect of his first public confrontation with his own wife, Stern proposed a useful title: 'The Cyprus of the Colonels – from Humous to Hubris.'

'I thought this was an emergency meeting,' Beth snapped.

Tom McAllisty flushed and began to stutter. Stern glanced pityingly at the young man who had erected barricades, braved tear gas and baton charges, published helpful diagrams of molotov cocktails, been imprisoned in Franco's Spain for a week, and amassed the finest collection of police helmets in revolutionary London. Tom quaking before those clear blue eyes.

'I came down from Leeds,' Beth said icily. 'Hattie came from

Manchester. If we'd been men we might have hitch-hiked without fear of being raped.'

McAllisty flushed. 'Sorry, Elizabeth.'

'Beth,' said Hattie flatly.

'Sorry?'

'Her name is Beth.'

'Shouldn't we vote on that?' Stern said. But his heart was hammering. Two pairs of eyes settled on him like tarantulas.

'The fact is,' Tom McAllisty said, 'er, I mean, Harry rang up this morning and said, well, he'd like to join in the main discussion. So I thought . . .'

No one spoke. So Harry himself was about to erupt from the bin. Their mentor and their masthead. Harry in person, mad. On his way at this very moment, like a hurricane predicted by the weather bureau. In the only concerted motion of the morning, they all turned towards the door.

'You're the ideas man, Dick,' Paul Meyer said, his rendez-vous demolished, his stomach at ease. 'You have the contacts, the top media people here, prime-time television, *The Times* of London, MPs . . .'

He laid a silver pencil on the crisp tablecloth beside a notebook with his monogram in tooled leather.

'We have to dramatise Esther's plight,' Jane said, close to tears.

'Frankly, I'm a lifelong opponent of capitalism,' Paul said. 'We're all Marxists round this table. So we all know what we have to do, right? The philosophers have only interpreted the world, the point is to change it.'

'Esther's never been a theoretical person,' Jane said.

'Esther's a nurse rather than a physician, let's put it that way. But she admires your work, Dick, she sent us your book on Sartre.'

'Did she?'

'Sure. Her own, autographed copy. "Dad," she wrote, "I feel so proud. This was given me by the cleverest man in London." '

'Anything you write in the press, she clips and sends,' Jane added. 'She wouldn't want me to tell you this, but when you got married she was heartbroken.'

'Jane, she wasn't heartbroken,' Paul growled, picking slithers of rendez-vous from his teeth. 'I haven't seen that girl in tears since she was seven years old. She's a chip off the old block, Dick, and her parents have seen it all.'

'History certainly repeats itself,' Jane said, tears welling again.

'Jane was teaching at PS3, Brooklyn, when the purge hit Local

555 of the New York Teachers' Union. That was in forty-nine. You were – '

'Five.'

'OK. Esther was two. The spooks got to everyone, the Head, the staff, even the kids. Those Catholic red-baiters on the Board of Education wanted Jane's head and they got it, oh boy.'

'Dick doesn't want to hear all that, Paul.'

'Who says he doesn't?' Paul resumed chomping a cucumber salad. He had made some fuss about the dressing but sugar had been brought and his slurping palate was now content. 'Cardinal Spellman's cronies. They twisted Superintendent Jansen's arm until it broke. Yeah.'

'I'll never forget that day,' Jane said.

'Oh, what a day, that!'

'I'd taken my eleven-year-olds up to the Botanical Gardens and – '

'What a lousy teacher to want her kids to know about nature!'

' – when I was summoned to the school office. I was handed a note from Jansen, right there, suspending me without pay.'

'It was ten years before we ever told Esther about these things, Dick.' Paul leant intently across the table, forking cucumber.

'Twelve or thirteen years,' Jane corrected him.

'Article 5, section 6, of the New York State constitution makes merit and fitness the sole tests for civil service employment. Sole test, yeah.'

'It was a witch hunt, Dick.'

'We were slaughtered. Ninety-nine per cent of the teachers purged were Jews. Now ya figure that out and imagine what we felt when our own daughter started dressing up as a Catholic nun.'

Stern's long features registered incredulity. Coffee arrived. Paul Meyer lit a cigar.

'Then the FBI began poking in our garbage.'

'Dick, when Paul and I graduated it was straight into the dole line.'

'No use talking to Esther about her roots. She doesn't want to know.'

'Paul, that's not fair. Esther was only seven when we fled to Mexico.'

'Jane, when ya went underground in Michigan ya changed names so often ya couldn't remember whoya were.'

'That's true, Dick. Paul and I met twice a year at the most. Never at home, that was too dangerous.'

'Dick, when we were kids we took the world seriously. We didn't chase after Beatles. At City College we had the alcoves – '

'Paul, Dick doesn't want to hear about the alcoves. He wants to know about Esther. Can't you see he's crazy about her even though he's a married man?'

'Why doesn't he? A Marxist should know his history, no matter where he was born. In Alcove One you'd find the saboteurs, the Trotskyites, Lovestoneites and sectarians. In Alcove Two, the YCL – that's us. We kept strict discipline and controlled the student newspaper. Jane, gimme one of those mint chocolates, eh?'

Stern cleared his throat. 'Would it help if I flew out to Rhodesia? You do live there, I assume?'

The Meyers exchanged glances. 'We could ask Geoff Cowans.'

'The lawyer she was working for?'

Paul Meyer nodded, glancing conspiratorially at the neighbouring tables. 'Yeah, Geoff crossed the Botswana border the night before last. He took the gap, as we say. Just in time. A contact in Special Branch tipped him off. No more defence lawyers. Just like when I was in the National Lawyers' Guild. McCarran, McCarthy, Eastland, they broke us one by one. Nowadays people talk as if the Un-American Activities Committee was the only one profiteering off the Cold War. That's shit. In Rhodesia, of course, things are that bit more physical. Africa is Africa. The Iron Heel has descended, Dick, and none of us may ever see Esther alive again.'

He spoke like a man who would always want to be proved right. His wife burst into the tears she had been saving up throughout lunch, throughout the overnight flight from Salisbury, throughout her life.

'Dick,' she sobbed, 'you were the first person we called. Apart from Amy Brand. When the Special Branch came to our house that Tuesday night and Esther began to pack her bag, so calmly, she slipped me a note of people to call in London, and you were right at the head of the list with a big star beside your name. A Star of David.'

Gently Stern took her hand. 'Please call me Richard. No one has ever called me "Dick".' (Tom, Dick and Harry –no!)

They heard Harry's footfall on the stairs, stumbling into the cardboard boxes and piles of unsold copies, a curse on them all, then a clumping, cloven hoof in the corridor, banging doors. After a long silence the unoiled crank of the toilet chain and a slum flush. Tom McAllisty, who had faced mace outside the Pentagon and fragmentation bombs in Haiphong, went to find him. Harry was on a stick. No one could look. Tom ushered him to a chair – to *the* chair.

'Coffee, Harry?'

No reply. His corduroy jacket hung loose from a wasted frame which had shed two or three stone. He dug into one pocket, then the other, then the first again, fumbling for reading glasses with vibrating hands that would not obey. Heaving his battered brown briefcase on to his lap, he rummaged while they waited, then drew out what he wanted, his own paper, not the replies. The search for his pipe, tobacco and Swan Vestas caused further delay – all quite deliberate – and then he forced a pipe-cleaner down the stem, the wire emerging twisted and stinking of nicotine.

Without invitation Harry Marquis began to read Harry Marquis. Everyone present had read all three papers, Harry's, Stern's, the women's, but Harry was instantly lost to his own magic, his voice gaining in power and authority with every phrase.

' . . . our infantile pseudo-revolutionaries . . . each outbidding the other in adopting ferocious verbal postures, each engaged in an imaginary psycho-drama, each embracing the most banal bourgeois elitism. . . . Life is too short to follow each of them into his meretricious theoreticism, but Dr Stern, so widely admired among the *fils à papa*, will have to stand for them all. I'm sure he won't mind; he is not shy. . . . He tells us that history does not exist, that history is a theoretical construct – oh what a giant epistemological leap is this, from darkness to day! And since history does not exist – bad news for the human race, but unflinchingly delivered! – Dr Stern is reduced to inter-rogating the words out of which (he reminds us) history is constructed and deconstructed. I fear that Dr Stern himself is no sooner constructed than he is deconstructed by rival prophets, not to mention ambitious heretics. . . . I had once believed Dr Stern to be a man possessed of free will, but he assures us that he is merely a kind of robot, a *träger* or vector of ulterior structural determinisms. In short, we can no more make history than a physicist can make the universe. Pure scholasticism, of course, intelligible only to the prophets themselves . . .'

At the half-way mark Harry produced a brandy flask from his briefcase with a hand that no longer shook. He did, then, for the first time study his audience – a long scrutiny, one by one, wrapped in a fatherly smile, as if to say, 'You won't forgive me, will you, but it doesn't matter. . . .' His gaze lingered on Beth.

'Meanwhile, Marxism suffers a second, simultaneous mutilation: enter the modern feminist. She has inflicted on herself a different kind of surgery – she has transplanted her brain to her womb. She and her sisters have resolved that the entire corpus of human

98

knowledge and historical experience shall be swallowed into the radioactive slit between her legs. . . . We used to believe that the cutting edge of every authentic liberation was to rescue an oppressed class, or race, or sex, from its specific subordination. To offer each person his or her full humanity and full potential from the cradle to the grave. We now stand corrected. The fashionable feminism, of which Ms Halliday has suddenly become so strident a spokesperson, insists that the sex war is rooted not merely in ignorance and prejudice – that is to say in history, the history that Dr Stern tells us we cannot understand – but in the innate biologial properties of male and female. The one barbarian, the other enlightened; the one chauvinist, the other tender; the one – let us face it bravely – inferior, the other superior. The sixpenny women's magazines offer us what? Woman reduced to her femininity. Ms Halliday's Movement offers us what? Woman vastly expanded – to her femininity.'

'That's shit,' Hattie said,
If Harry heard he did not register. He rode over her and on, sweat pouring down the gulleys of a rock face worn to the limit by excavation and explosion.

'A woman who takes an oath to have no dealings with men, no personal relationship with men, is no less a prisoner of sex than the beauty queen who spends her days under the hair dryer and her nights under a film producer. . . . It is a mutilation self-imposed . . . like that of the proverbial vegetarian philosopher who closes Plato, Descartes or Spinoza with only one question in his head: Did they eat meat? Likewise the militant feminist closes her Dickens (if she reads him) with a single inquiry: Did he beat his wife?'

Harry leant back in his chair and closed his eyes.

'I have concluded. Let the trial begin. Speak, Dr Stern. To play the gentleman is the last resort of a scoundrel.'

Stern's tongue had been roaming over dry lips. His lined pad was covered in small, tight, geometrical forms, triangles, cubes, octagons, equations demonstrating the ahistoricity of human experience. Harry's rheumy eyes were fastened on him.
'I have not quite lost my fondness for you, Richard.'
Beth stirred at this. 'You will publish our reply,' she told Tom McAllisty.
'I founded this journal,' Harry declared. 'It has certain achieve-

ments to its credit. Whatever I may think of Richard's polemical style, I still recognise a genuine intelligence at work. But I see no reason why *Thought and Action* should be debased by the semi-literate outpourings of hysterical women.'

Hattie leapt up, trembling. 'You pig!'

Harry smiled for the first time.

Beth turned to Stern. 'I see you're still his darling little boy – a "genuine intelligence", no less.'

Tom McAllisty cautiously raised his voice. 'I was going to propose that we publish all three articles, concurrently, in a single issue.'

'I second that,' Stern said.

'Agreed,' said Brendan Hogg, still squatting on the floor.

'No!' bellowed Harry, shuddering like a bomber hit by flak far from home, scanning the night for a friendly coastline. Alone of those present he had been in the sky, alone. But the generations come on, wave after wave of sperm, each claiming its meagre cube of time to be eternity.

'You're outvoted,' Beth told him.

He chuckled nastily, whipping his pipe from his mouth then jabbing it back between bared teeth.

'So the libido is now in disgrace, eh? Fucking is no longer freedom? The *pétroleuses* of the new puritanism make common cause with the Tory ladies in blue rinse. Banish porn – banish imagination.'

Beth's reply carried the chill of an ice cube hitting a steel sink on a winter day. 'The truth is, Harry, you're just a dirty old man.' As she spoke she reached for Harry's brimming briefcase, lifted it from the floor with a drastic effort of her small shoulders, and brought out, unhesitatingly, a brown paper package sealed with sellotape. As she slit the tape two glossy magazines spilled on to the table among the paper cups, each adorned by a naked lady with wide-open legs.

'That was why you were late,' Beth told Harry.

'That was a venomous thing to do,' Stern said to his wife. 'You know bloody well Harry isn't well.'

'I ought to know, Richard. I've visited the bin every month for over a year while you've stayed at home, polishing your ego.'

'And you know where it all led,' Paul Meyer told Stern.

Stern had closed his eyes. It had all led to Esther.

'To the execution of Julius and Ethel Rosenberg,' Jane Meyer said.

Paul Meyer cast a wistful glance at a trolley loaded with chocolate gâteaux, whipped cream, cold gooseberry pie – the meal was going to cost him a fortune anyway. But Jane intervened.

'We've already had coffee, Paul. You can't start again.'

'It's a free country, isn't it?' He winked, hopefully, at Stern.

'Paul, tell Dick why they arrested Esther.'

'Jane, we don't know for sure.'

'Paul, we know.'

Paul sighed. 'Well, this guy Zim is a leading figure in Zanu's central committee. Somehow he jumped out of jail: Wha Wha, I believe. That was when Esther flew home.'

'They first met at the University,' Jane said. 'Zim was later in detention for four years. They thought they'd catch Esther's man through her, but she was too smart for them. In the end they came for her alone.'

'They called her a "Kaffir's whore",' Paul whispered, glancing nervously around the palatial, almost-empty restaurant. 'Where didya get that long nose, Dick? Damn it, some of our closest comrades in the Party underground were Negroes.' He gestured for the bill. When it came he checked every item and queried a couple on principle, then limped out of the restaurant as if his loaded stomach had drained the blood from his legs.

'I'm a survivor, Dick. I never had time for existential despair or all that crap.' In the lobby Jane went off to the ladies' while the man in the morning-coat politely divested Stern of the hotel's necktie. 'I tell ya something, young fella: I'm in business and I mean to stay in business. If money could buy Esther's release I'd gladly give every cent. Gladly.'

Jane came heavily across the thick carpet with her huge, croco-dile-skin purse and clutched Stern's arm.

'If you love my daughter, Dick . . .'

'Let's go up to our suite and call those top media people,' Paul said. In the lift he offered his second wink. 'Strictly off the record, as they say, how far didya get with Esther?'

'Paul!' Jane had reddened. Stern saw that she both loved and despised the man.

'Listen,' Paul protested, 'if I was thirty years younger I'd chase that girl round the town myself.'

A stalactite of snot hung lime-green from Harry's nose. He swayed, a puzzled smile stiffening in plaster of Paris. Tom McAllisty, the only one trained in physical crisis, was the first to move.

Attempting to lift off the runway, Harry clutched at stars, spun and crumpled, smoke pouring from his fuselage. McAllisty was already behind his chair, to catch him. Beth was kneeling over Harry in a flash, tearing his collar open, pumping his heart. McAllisty pulled back Harry's head and Beth plunged her mouth into an indescribable mess of snot and foam. Stern was at the phone: 'Ambulance,' he said.

The ambulance men fastened an oxygen mask but they refused to carry Harry down stairs which they described as a health hazard and a fire hazard and 'diabolical'.

'Take a leg,' McAllisty instructed Stern. 'We'll have to carry him down without the stretcher.' But then the ambulance men relented and started fastening Harry to the stretcher with straps.

They all followed the stretcher down into the street. Beth climbed into the ambulance with Harry while Hattie stood trembling, her owl eyes awash. Stern glanced at his watch then scanned the street for a taxi half-aware of the blue light of Harry's ambulance flashing to the corner of Wardour Street.

'Anyone know where the Connaught is?' But no one answered, for he was already striding away from the stunned group gathered on the pavement.

TEN

Returning home late the following Friday, Stern found his wife curled on the sofa in a shot-silk dressing gown he hadn't seen for many moons and – he divined – nothing underneath. Her hair, though still cut to fit a steel helmet, curled engagingly round her ears. It had been done.

'Hullo,' she said.

He let drop his briefcase. His instant need crashed all barriers of dignity and shame and he came almost before he was inside her.

'Sorry.'

'No, *I'm* sorry about asking you for money. It was rotten.'

Her vowels were back to normal; Admiral Halliday's daughter once more. He almost offered her the money. Then he saw the large, rectangular parcel, thickly wrapped and resolutely secured with tape and string, leaning against the wall.

'What's that? Daddy's nuclear codes? I must tell you my masters and minders are growing impatient.'

She fondled his hair. 'Shut up.'

Catching up his trousers he hobbled to the bathroom.

'How's Harry?' he called.

'Tucked up.'

'Did you give him back his mags?'

'Make peace, not war, Richard.'

He soaped his penis. 'Agreed. But why?'

He found her in the kitchen, making an omelette with fast, flying fingers. Light-headed, he curled his arms round her from behind, pressed himself into her neat, perfect buttocks (by adroitly shortening his legs) and whispered into her ear, 'Unfinished business.'

'And what of Esther's parents? Were they a frightful disappointment to you?'

He released her. 'Good God! How did you know?'

'Vee haff oor spice. I happened to be in Great Turnstile, giving the grisly Tree an account of our struggle with the male chauvinists in the union, when the phone rang. It was you, grovelling for column inches from the Connaught. Mummy used to take me there for lunch at half-term. I hear the food isn't what it was.'

'Forget the omelette.'

'What?'

Turning off the gas ring, he lifted her and carried her to the bedroom. As the shot-silk dressing gown fell open to reveal her milky body she stretched herself across the bed, languidly, like Ingres's prostitute.

'Wish I was Esther?'

He flung himself upon her and stretched out her arms.

'I thought women were unworthy of crucifixion.'

'Oh my God,' he groaned, 'I am your slave now and for ever.'

'Esther's slave. I wish I could do the part but I just can't manage that sugary colonial accent, the coconut milk, and no man could straighten his tie in the reflection from my hair. But nothing venture . . . "Richard," she whispers, "you are more brilliant than any man in London, more handsome than any hunter huntin' south of the Zambezi and north of the Limpopo." Yum Yum? Ah, now you possess her – at last! "Richard," she moans, "I have always loved you . . . secretly . . . though I knew it was hopeless because I'm only an off-the-peg rum truffle." '

'No, Beth!'

'Call me Esther!'

'Elizabeth!'

'Esther!'

'Darling, I – '

'You what, eh?'

'Ah! Ah! Aaaagh!'

'Then up she pops, having fastened her hair and fixed her face, to gaze in awe at her brilliant cosmopolitan philosopher with his high-rise view of West London, though not high enough to glimpse the working-class Irish to the north, the black slums round Ladbroke Grove, or the squatters in derelict homes doomed to demolition by the new Westway along which Dr Stern speeds in his Triumph Herald. Look now, she leans over you, feigning domination, playing the arrogant jungle princess, her breasts teasing your glazed eyes, and begins to pump you into oblivion . . .'

He slept for less than a minute. When he woke Elizabeth was gazing at him thoughtfully. He reached for her.

'Ah, look, now he kisses and fondles her breasts, one by one

–like making conversation with two female cousins, each deserving consideration. And isn't it fascinating to recall that the most respectable lady novelists used to think that to "ejaculate" meant to speak?'

Beth slid out of bed and took her gown. 'I'm hungry. Two eggs in your omelette?'

He watched her familiar motions, his groin numb, fending off the process of understanding in a faint haze of self-congratulation. He felt vaguely flattered and wanted to leave it like that. They ate their omelettes, with a bottle of wine, on the Habitat sofa, idly scanning the television news. There was no mention of Rhodesia; merely the miners' strike and the three-day week, on and on. Beth's collective had been raising funds for the miners' families and it occurred to Stern that he ought to make a contribution himself. Everywhere he went people were rattling coin boxes. In the end you couldn't ignore it.

'About the parcel,' Elizabeth said.

'Mm?'

'Over there.'

'Ah. Daddy's nuclear codes.'

'Are you my friend, Richard?' She lit a cigarette.

'Friendship is a lot to ask from a husband.'

'I want to leave the parcel here. But hidden. Very hidden. Just for a while. *Comprends?*'

'What is it?'

'Never mind. And don't try and unwrap it.'

'Hidden from whom?'

'From burglars. Or from the police. But where does one hide it? This flat's like a series of matchboxes, no loft, no attic, no cellar. Richard, I want you to take up the carpet and hide it under the floorboards.'

'What is it?'

'It's better that you don't know. That way, you're not an accessory. You know nothing about it. If it comes to the pinch, it was I who took up the floorboards. Actually, I was going to, but I was afraid you'd notice and start sniffing around.'

The Pennines had crept back into her vowels. He noticed that her hair had stopped curling engagingly round her ears; it hung straight and severe, pudding-basin Roundhead.

'Given the delights of this evening, I can hardly say no.'

'That's up to you.'

She left early the following morning for Euston. He didn't stir and slept until ten. Sartre's Mathieu, after all, taught in a lycée but never once attended a class in the entire course of *The Age of Reason*. Brewing coffee, Stern glowered at the parcel, then at the carpet; he wondered what tools he would have to buy, and where. He saw things in shop windows but when he wanted something he could never remember where the shops were. Sinking on to the sofa with the morning paper, he was at once informed that a Degas valued at $400,000 had been stolen from the South Kensington flat of Sir Walter Halliday, Officer Commanding, Northern Group, NATO.

He leapt up. 'Woman, you're out of your mind!'

He glowered at the newspaper. Sir Walter and Lady Halliday were presently in Norway. The theft had been discovered by a cleaning lady. Despite multiple locks, the front door of the first-floor flat had been forced and a burglar alarm wired to the painting de-activated. An expert from Sotheby's was quoted as adamant that such a painting, if stolen, could not possibly be disposed of on the open market.

Stern jumped. It was the front door bell. In a panic he seized the painting and shoved it under the mattress in the bedroom. Then he said, 'Fool, that's the first place they'd look and fat lot of use you pleading you had no idea it was there!' The door bell rang again, more insistently, and he decided he wasn't in. He heard a thud against the door and broke into a sweat. Then retreating footsteps. After ten minutes he gingerly opened the door: a parcel of books. They weren't supposed to do that; they were supposed to leave a card for collection at the Post Office.

It made him quite angry.

He turned up his address book at 'H' and dialled Oslo. A maid answered (in Norwegian presumably): 'Hullo.' When Lady Halliday came to the phone she sounded frightfully calm.

'So kind of you to call, Richard.'

'About the painting . . .'

'Well, Walter is rather fond of it.'

'Did the police telephone you?'

'Well, obviously.'

'Actually, it's not stolen.'

'Oh good. Elizabeth borrowed it, did she? I thought she might. So nice of you to call, Richard.'

'What shall I do with it?'

'I'll call Walter's bank manager. Lloyds in Pall Mall, you know, near the Duke of York's statue. Just take it along and he'll put it in the vault or something.'

'Take it?'

'Well, yes.'

'What about the police?'

'Well, I'll have a word with them. Inspector Somebody. He sounded a nice man, I'm sure he'll understand.'

Stern put the painting on the front seat beside him, then got out and locked it in the filthy boot, then decided to take it by taxi. There were no taxis. He began to walk, ran after a bus, boarded it, changed at Oxford Circus, and finally reached the vast, imposing bank on the corner of Pall Mall and Lower Regent Street. He was shown straight to the manager's office, where he found Inspector Somebody and the expert from Sotheby's.

'Do you wish to unwrap the parcel or shall I?' the valuer asked him.

'Er, you.'

The man lifted the parcel delicately and eased it up and down, as if one could weigh a Degas, then produced a beautiful, ivory-handled knife, slitting string and tape with the utmost delicacy. Stern reflected that in a novel of 'suspense', a 'thriller', frame, backing and glass would all be discovered in immaculate condition – only the canvas would be missing. But what emerged was half a million dollars of Degas.

'I'll need to take a statement,' the Inspector told him.

'Why?'

The Inspector thought about this. Clearly he was too intelligent a man to find an answer. Then he bridled.

'We don't have one rule for the rich . . .'

'I quite agree. A working-class girl would never get away with lifting her Daddy's Degas.'

Filthy weather. The sky had settled low over the city, blotting out the descending Boeings, and the first snow lay on the pavements like laundered pigeon shit. Reaching the mansion block off Baker Street, Stern avoided the ancient lift and bounded up the uncar-peted stairs hoping he would be offered a cup of coffee. He pressed the bell twice before a shadow appeared behind the frosted glass panels. The door was opened on a chain.

The stranger who peered at Stern from a darkened hallway wore an overcoat round his shoulders; gaunt, unshaven, deathly pale, his eyes were dull with the fear of an actor whose performance has run out.

Stern said, 'Richard Stern,' but the man did not unfasten the chain until another figure warily appeared at his side, fingered his goatee beard, and said: 'S'okay, Geoff.' Stern stepped into a large, sullen flat, chill with winter and suspicion. The curtains were drawn. A television set flickered silently in the sitting room. Geoff Cowans slumped into a chair whose cover fabric had been rent by cat's claws, pulling the black overcoat round his shoulders and lighting a cigarette. The metal ashtray on the arm of his chair was overflowing with twisted filter tips savagely extinguished.

Empty beer cans, crushed flat, littered the floor round the chair.

'Anyone follow you here?' Paul Meyer asked Stern.

'Nobody has ever followed me anywhere.'

Geoff Cowans began to laugh but it turned into a smoker's hack, racking his sandpapered lungs.

'Don't go for an X-ray,' he told himself, opening another beer.

The two men had been playing Scrabble.

Ten days earlier Stern had been forced to play Scrabble with Paul Meyer in the Connaught, in between making despondent telephone calls to Amnesty International, Defence and Aid and, more humiliating, to J. R. Tree and Leonard Tanner. (Tree had not mentioned that he had Elizabeth in his office and Stern had never forgiven the gnome for damning the Russell-Sartre War Crimes Tribunal with faint praise.) Paul had a passion for Scrabble. Stern hated the game – the sterile divorce of words from language and context, the smug ivory pieces spreading across the board in grotesque copulations, breeding new wordlets out of one another's armpits. Paul, who had a special, leather-covered pad for recording the scores, played the game with a permanent smirk, placing the letter 'a' next to 'w' then smugly folding his hands.

—'Aw' isn't a word, Stern protested.

—It's a word, just like 'ah' is a word.

—You won't find it in the dictionary.

Slowly Paul opened the New York Rules Committee Scrabble Dictionary, plus a printed supplement of admissible two- and three-letter words.

—It's definitive, he announced. —No appeal.

—Why don't we play in Zulu? Stern suggested.

—I can see you hate losing. Great: I'm not a loser myself.

Stern stood up, about to walk out, then felt foolish.

—Why don't you call *The Times?* Paul said.

—It will do no good.

—Try. Try. Always try – the rule of life.

Stern got a direct line from the hotel operator and dialled 837 1234 with leaden fingers. At the third attempt he got through to Leonard Tanner.

—Tell me something new, Tanner said.

—Well—

—Fuck it, we can't announce every day that your sugar girl has been arrested.

Now, ten days later, Cowans lifted his beer can.

'So you want to help Esther?' he asked sardonically, his tongue wrapped round a hot light bulb.

108

Stern nodded. 'How is she?'

'That depends, Mr Stern. Mondays it could be Jan Snyder, family man, attended Mount Pleasant School, Dutch Reformed Church but sticks to the rules. But Wednesdays she could have Kepler, a maniac born in the Transvaal, obsessed by conspiracies, sees every interrogation as a personal challenge to his manhood. Then on Fridays you may have Roberston, straight out from Ulster and dead keen to win one holy war if not the other – the fact that Esther's a Catholic who loves a munt terrorist won't help her with Robertson. Nor with Kepler. Nothing will help her with Kepler.'

Stern couldn't control his hands.

'Esther's really a Catholic?'

Cowans sighed. 'Paul, does this fellow know anything?'

Paul's gaze was fixed on the television screen where a woman was giving a silent cookery class.

'She made a personal statement . . . some years back . . . like kicking her parents in the teeth.' He took a dead cigar butt out of his mouth, examined its wetness, then put it back in. 'Esther never met Cardinal Spellman or Senator Pat McCarran.'

Cowans lit another cigarette. 'Esther told me you once laid on a meeting for her at some college. If you did, Rhodesian Special Branch know it. They have the run of BOSS's computer in Pretoria. They have informers everywhere.'

Crunching the empty beer can, he tossed it to the floor.

Stern's thoughts fell on Oscar Mucheche.

'Geoff knows the score,' Paul Meyer grunted. 'This woman needs to use more butter. That pastry will be like rock.'

'You don't know the meaning of fear,' Cowans resumed, reaching for another beer. 'When those last-word bastards in Special Branch tip you off because maybe you were at the same school or grew up on a neighbouring farm, then you have to believe them. I was through Plumtree then on to dirt tracks, minefields, sweating like a pig, and over the Botswana border within four hours. We Rhodesians speak the same language you know and there isn't one of us who doesn't throw up at the idea of a girl like Esther in bed with a kaffir.'

'Take it easy, Geoff,' Paul murmured.

'Mr Stern is looking down his nose, I see. We raw colonials drink too much, yes? Go on, convince me you'd like to be on site when this educated munt, this *doctor*, is letting it all hang out to Esther – did you ever see a hard-on the size of Nelson's column?'

Paul Meyer was fiddling with Scrabble pieces. In the Connaught he had come up with 'na' (Brooklynese for 'no') and a series of etymological space-invaders: 'de', 'vox', 'lex' – all validated by the New York Dictionary and supplement. Dismissing Stern's weary protest over the word 'catched', Paul had gone below the belt to report that Esther used to say, 'Daddy, I catched a butterfly' when six years old.

—She used to tear their wings off, too. Does that shock you?

'Mr Stern,' said Cowans, 'I'm just a simple, bigoted farmer who became a lawyer by accident and never sat next to a kaffir in church until John XXIII spoke to me and told me to devote my life to the black people of Zimbabwe.'

'Geoff's a good man,' Paul said.

'So tell me what I do now, Mr Stern. Who gives a shit for Roman-Dutch law in London? Who'd put an accent like mine into the Queen's Bench Division?'

'Talking of accents,' Paul said, 'I read somewhere that this Queen's English is nothing but an east Midlands regional accent which kinda caught hold of the ruling class and after that yaall had to master those phonemes to prove ya were officers and gentlemen. Jesus, I pity anyone who lives in this country, absolute stasis, cold all day, cold all night.'

'Yees.' Cowans savagely ripped open another beer. 'Esther reckons they're all a bunch of pansies.' He drank. 'Anyway, who are you really, Mr Stern?'

Abruptly he sat up straight, tie loosened and grimy collar unfastened, arm pointing rigidly to Stern.

'Take it easy, Geoff,' Paul murmured.

'Now Esther's munt, I mean I have respect for that man, he's an intelligent bloke who got out of Wha Wha maximum security disguised as a wheelbarrow full of shit and that's never been done before. He also got Esther in the sack which you tried to do and I tried to do and which the best part of Special Branch 2 are trying to do at this very moment – '

Paul leapt up, trembling. 'Shut your fucking mouth, Geoff!'

Stern walked to the front door, Paul following, and began to unfasten the bolt and chain.

'Know something, Dick? Jane and I suffered hate mail for five years in the United States. So we quit. We got out. We made a new life. We tried Mexico City. My fellow exiles drove me out of business – no one understands the laws of capitalist competition better than a Communist. No sooner we arrived in Kenya than the goddam Brits began to scuttle. As soon as we moved down to Northern Rhodesia somebody called it Zambia. We settled in Southern Rhodesia *before Smith*, at a time of immense dialectical contradiction. We sent Esther to a progressive school with a dozen African kids and straightaway she invited a coupla black girls home for tea. That's Esther. We joined the struggle against white racism but she joined the saints. And now we have hate mail all over again. Esther's a wonderful daughter but I sometimes wonder why she has to be mine.'

Stern's mouth was a faint pencil line on wood.

ELEVEN

It was the bleakest winter he could remember. His sense of time collapsed. Beth came and went but mostly went. When she came it was usually in the company of the 'sisters'. He made an effort not to remember their names or even their faces – hostility seemed to secrete its own natural amnesia. Hattie would stare at him accusingly until, like an animal, he dropped his eyes. Haversacks, sleeping bags and dirty socks littered the flat. Tired of finding brown coffee rings on his manuscripts, he fitted a lock to his study door. This was noted and publicly analysed. The stolen Degas was never mentioned but the silent prosecution was relentless and observed no statute of limitations.

When he and Beth shared a bed Hattie sank into brooding melancholy or became hysterical. Beth adroitly played off their mutual jealousy.

'That girl, sorry, woman, is a stereotype of a stereotype,' he complained.

'She was your pupil, Doctor. Blame yourself.'

'I do blame myself.'

'She's my comrade.'

'I know how you could raise funds for the collective, the women's section of the union, and the Movement.'

She half turned her head. 'Yes?'

'Take Harriet and me and Harry and Tom and Brendan and all those Roundhead women to bed by turns and invite an audience. It's a new idea – a sponsored fuck.'

From the diary of Richard Stern:

Alone for much of the time, writing about Brecht, too lethargic to summon my few remaining friends (sic and ergo), I have plenty

112

of time to study the literature piled on Beth's table. Pamphlets, playscripts, manifestoes, polemics, they all 'struggle' to break the mould of male domination, to restore the authentic female union of reason and emotion ruptured and 'decimated' (oh God) by a patriarchal order determined to enslave women.

Determined to put women down. Beth's table is littered with 'putdowns'. The language employed suffers from the indigestion afflicting most radical movements. Transvestite nouns and verbs, hideous hybrid offspring. 'Discourses' are 'critiqued' and (hopefully) 'ruptured'. The male jargon of the social sciences alternates with the hippy cult of the inner life. Hattie is forever 'freaking out' and getting into 'hassles'; experiences 'touch' her or 'really touch' her or 'really totally touch' her. One film by a Swedish woman director about female circumcision in Africa not only 'really alienated' Hattie but also 'really totally incredibly' touched her. 'I really identified with that situation.' As for me, a Sartrean jealousy guarding the crucial notion of the 'situation', I can only fume when I read of Hattie being, or not being, 'into a reciprocal sex situation' with Beth – though 'not being' is better.

And the awful puns, taken seriously: 'No longer history, Beth, from now on its herstory.'

In grappling with this I sink into debasement. Mine, not theirs. My thoughts are mean, spiteful, jealous. *They* have taken Elizabeth from me – that's all I know.

Probably it's all Harry knows, too.

It is I who provoke open conflict, though not often. (Their stance is more cunning: leave the beast to his own lair. Leave him to plan wars, pollute the environment, and club baby seals to death.)

'Matriarchy is a historical fantasy, a myth, like Marx's primitive communism,' I announce to three or four pairs of eyes.

'Matriarchy,' Hattie says, 'is the way we feel.'

The cases they clip from the press are not typical. The ageing male magistrates who insist that when a woman says no she means yes unless she claws your eyes out to prove it. 'Judge tells rapist: "Better luck next time." ' How eagerly they seize on and typify the bizarre! Well, be fair, I'm not short of colleagues who sift the press for the words 'multinational' and 'monopoly', as they prepare to expose the 'final crisis' of capitalism.

And that of course is integral to radical psychology in the affluent bourgeois democracies. Things have never been worse. We are at the very limit.

It would take a novelist to chart Elizabeth's conversion.

But if I turned to fiction I would pan across the global panorama while methodically taking daguerreotypes of myself from beneath the black cloth draped over the camera. That male authors can empathise with female characters, producing portraits satisfactory to women readers, is as well established as the converse. But, as Clausewitz might have said, autobiographical fiction is a continuation of war by other means.

All right, Harry. All right, Tom. And all right, 'Dick'. Let us begin with the obvious: male chauvinism was rampant in the New Left of the late sixties. We wanted the girls to make coffee and display long stretches of thigh. But every imperialism requires its collaborators. At the time it seemed like 99 per cent of the female 'natives' were keen to serve as our askaris. And then there is this:

A proletarian who turns to revolution is clearly not a failed proletarian. A black who turns to revolution is not a failed black. But a woman who turns to revolution is quite likely to be a disappointed woman. Doffing cap or bobbing knee is not in the worker's genes; 'yess massah' is not in the black's; deferring to every patriarchal ruling is not in woman's. But. But woman needs man whereas the proletarian, though a product of Capital, can and must transcend Capital, just as the time of the White Man will soon almost be lost to the collective memory of the blacks. Woman's problem is woman's need. Not only love and children: but – despite 'SCUM' and a noisy urban élite – marriage too.

Yet isn't Elizabeth a failed woman? Or 'disappointed'? Her filing cabinet tells me she has run through the lot and a few more: how can I blame myself?

Even Beth does not deny that I have always been in favour of equal pay, equal education, equal job opportunities, equal legal status. But, as she puts it: 'What about the other half of the day?'

I don't think she means the shopping or the washing up (the syndrome now so familiar in 'liberated' Soviet Russia). The 'other half of the day' is not a segment of the clock, it is a second level of existence which runs right round the clock: inferred roles, inferred expectations – a sense of destiny.

Thank God she didn't want children.

But at least I have my work, do I not? My lectures and seminars no longer sustain their numbers: after the second week of term the rows of vacant chairs begin to yawn. It is Ramsay and Gough who now command the big lecture theatres. I feel myself declining into formless melancholy, supine doubt. Students drift away in irritable bewilderment, their notebooks empty. The telephone in my flat is silent. More than a year has passed since a television producer called. Piles of books no longer arrive from the newspapers and periodicals. The American lecture circuit has fallen silent, the conference firmament has found younger stars. (Yet, Momma, yet.) I have sent a synopsis of my book on Brecht to three publishers: all

114

have politely declined, professing interest in my work but blaming 'the state of the market'. Soon they will not bother to reply. Today a letter from my publisher arrived regretting that 444 copies of my *Freedom and Responsibility in Sartre* are to be remaindered – would I like to buy some at 15p a copy?

Every day I rise from my bed at a later hour. For a while excessive sleep swaddled my apathy, but now I just stare at the ceiling, counting my grievances and composing angry letters I shall never write. The flat is filthy.

Beth appeared one afternoon, alone, her small, lithe body supporting a painfully large haversack. She put her head round his study door.

'Hi.'

'Hullo.'

'I feel as filthy as this flat,' she said. 'Must bath.'

Bathed, she poured hot water over instant coffee, tucked her legs underneath her on the Habitat sofa, spread out her tented skirt, and told him she was pregnant. He took guard in the steel-framed rocking chair.

'Congratulations.'

'Why do you say that, Richard?'

'Tell me what to say.'

She shrugged. 'Anything honest. Anything real.'

'Does one ask who the father is?'

'I live with women.'

'Was it Harry in the ambulance – an elaborated kiss of life?'

'Hattie warned me you'd behave like a pig.'

'Degas, perhaps? Or maybe Christopher? The gallery columns inform me he's still *sur le champ*. No doubt it was through Christopher that the unsaleable masterpeice was to be flogged to a megalomaniac Saudi prince for a knock-down eighty thousand.'

'Listen, Richard. I want a child. I'm not getting any younger.'

'You're twenty-six.'

'And the baby's father will be thirty on 25 February. Does that satisfy you? Wouldn't you like a son? If it's a girl we can always put her out to die.'

'And will it be called Stern – or Halliday?'

'Christ, Richard, I'm not looking for a smug, bourgeois nuclear family. My baby and I are not asking to be supported, if that's what you imagine. If a woman wants a child, that's her business.'

He shrugged. 'Then why tell me?'

'Oh don't be so bloody . . . ridiculous.'

115

'You planned it of course. The night immortalised by Daddy's Degas.'

'Wouldn't you like to be a father?'

'Isn't "father" a bad word? Don't fathers alternately neglect their children while out boozing and playing golf, then treat their kids as symbols of proprietorial power?'

'You're going to be a father whether you like it or not.'

'So was Mathieu. But he never set eye on Marcelle's child.'

'You're not Mathieu. You're actually quite a decent man.'

'But not fit to be consulted before conceiving? You people talk about "sex objects" – yet you treat me like a breeding bull.'

'I'm not one of those women who will allow her nature to be crippled by male authoritarianism. I know how violence passes down the line, each victim slapping someone smaller.'

'Try slapping someone bigger.'

'Is that how you really visualise yourself – battered?'

'It is not *I* who have been unfaithful to *you*.'

'You're faithful to yourself. Always. And what about Esther?'

'I am not a Christian. He who lusts after another woman and yet refrains is a better husband than he who suffers no temptation.'

'I shan't "batter" you with the simple truth about your jacaranda queen.'

'Can't Hattie be your baby's father?'

'I've been waiting for that.'

'Doesn't it strike you how utterly repellent that relationship is to me? Why do you keep coming here? For the hot water?'

'Hattie and the sisters have offered me a kind of love, a tenderness, a sharing of things, that is simply beyond your comprehension.'

'A sharing of your money.'

'As you said on a previous occasion. Richard, you're a fool.'

'Answer a fool according to his folly. As a dog returneth to his vomit, so a fool returns to his folly. But thought's the slave of life, and life time's fool.'

'You haven't been watering that plant. I'm going to clean this flat.'

She jumped up. Morning sickness rooted him to his chair.

Esther Meyer returned to England on the nine o'clock news. Alone again, Stern had switched on the small, black-and-white Toshiba shortly after six and settled into his rocking chair, a bottle of wine to hand, to watch whatever rubbish was served up to him. By eight he was too blurred to put his TV dinner in the oven. Such a clean oven, such a clean flat. He gave the reviving potted plant a long, withering look, but to no effect.

At his first glimpse of Esther he began to tremble.

The Meyers had long since returned to Rhodesia but Stern could see Geoff Cowans at Esther's elbow, vying with Amy Brand and shouldering aside the tabloid journalists, murmuring in Esther's ear, protector, minder, adviser, lover, his gaunt features hatchet-sharp. Stern searched Esther's velvet skin and luminous brown eyes for scars but saw only saintly serenity. She faced the banked microphones with grave attentiveness.

How did she feel about her release?

'Just wonderful.'

Why had they released her?

'You'll have to ask Ian Smith.'

Why had she been arrested?

'Same answer.'

Why had no charge been brought against her?

'The only charges we bother with in Rhodesia are baton charges.'

But obviously she was regarded as subversive?

'As are all those who call for freedom in my country.'

How had she been treated in prison?

'I'm white. That helps a lot. You get a bed and food off a plate. I was allowed no visitor and no lawyer. I was kept in solitary and not allowed to communicate with any other prisoner. I was not permitted a radio. The newspapers I got had been clipped of any reference to my case.'

Had she been interrogated?

'Yes.'

What questions did they ask her?

'Fundamentally, why it is that the black people of Zimbabwe don't feel grateful for white rule. That does puzzle them. It also enrages them.'

Had she been accused of aiding and abetting armed guerrillas?

'I believe that did crop up.'

What was her reply?

'That the only terrorist organisation in Rhodesia is the Government.'

Was she a member of the banned party, Zanu?

'I'm very proud to be a member.'

Was she the only white member?

'No. There are others.'

The only white woman?

A slow smile. 'Possibly. But in our struggle gender isn't all that important. Comradeship breeds equality.'

Was it true that she had a close, personal relationship with a

117

prominent black nationalist who had escaped from prison and was now in hiding?

'Would you ask a man that question?'

Had she been tortured during interrogation?

'Oh yes. They can't help themselves, it's the only way they know of dealing with what they can't understand. One gentleman, Mr Robertson, with a strong Ulster accent, insisted it was hurting him more than it was hurting me – though I didn't agree. He told me he had a family and became quite confessional. Mr Kepler, however, never apologised when depriving me of food, sleep and even water. Mr Kepler even forced me to perform my natural functions in the most humiliating circumstances. Periodically he helped me to clear my memory by forcing my head into a plastic bag and then immersing it in water. Mr Kepler kept warning me I was going to die and I often believed him.'

Did she still carry physical evidence of torture?

'Oh yes. I shall be examined by a doctor on behalf of Amnesty International.'

Anything she could show the television viewers?

'Not decently.'

Her immediate plans?

'A good night's sleep. Maybe two.'

What of Rhodesia's immediate future?

'The British Government should stop the international oil companies brazenly flouting sanctions. Secondly, it should stop proposing phoney solutions and fancy franchises. Thirdly, it should give full support, moral and material, to those engaged in the armed struggle against tyranny. Excuse me, I really am rather tired now.'

But was she saying the British Government should send arms to the guerrillas?

'Yes. I am saying precisely that. Nine years ago the British Government should have responded to UDI by physically taking control of its colony. Instead Prime Minister Wilson assured Ian Smith he would never resort to armed intervention. It was a disgraceful capitulation and the full burden of it has been borne by the black population.'

Cut.

A colliery disaster in Belgium.

Stern stared at his telephone. The potted plant stared back.

Adrift in sleep, he felt Beth's small body beside him. He touched her stomach. A voice, his own, warned: London is at this moment full of couples shaking hands with their loins, in search of détente – broken plates in the kitchen, ecstatic groans in the bedroom. And in the morning? – broken plates in the kitchen. 'You've never enjoyed it?' he said. Wind and rain lashed the rattling window. Years ago she had said: 'You make love like an intellectual.'

She slipped down the rock face; his hands clung desperately then let go. Far down the gulley the dull thud of the baby's head splintering: no cry from either of them. Ramsay swept out of his packed lecture hall, gown flowing, Harry limping in his wake on a knotted stick, dead pipe fastened in his mouth like a dummy, his livid features quartered by a stroke. 'Tenure?' laughed Ramsay, hurrying on, pursued by devoted students, 'you must be joking. You had promise, that's all.' Stern fled to France. Seeking asylum in Sartre's apartment, he was immediately admitted, embraced, and given a neat whisky almost overflowing. 'He sleeps late,' Castor whispered. *'Il fait la grasse matinée.'* But Sartre shuffled out of the door almost immediately on the same knotted walking stick, his livid features quartered by the same stroke. 'You still have promise, Richard. What news of my old comrade, Harry Marquis?' Sartre listened attentively, solicitously, to news of Harry's long illness; when the two pornographic magazines were taken out of their brown wrapping and shown to him Sartre shook his head sadly. 'My own mind,' he said, 'now dwells exclusively on women. *Castor et quelques autres.* I remember your beautiful wife, Elizabeth, she came here once, alone. I slept with her. She said she loved me and I did not believe her. Then I said I loved her and she believed me. So I gave her a copy of *Erostrate* before handing her back to her husband. When she had gone I read a book about the German theories of value and then wrote a letter, recording the incident, to *mon cher Castor, mon épouse morganatique.* When I'm dead she will publish them. Perhaps you will take a hand in the English edition.'

He laughed, a cackle, dribbling. Castor wiped his mouth.

'Come and see me again tomorrow,' Sartre said.

Walking into the plate-glass door of a cheap hotel off the Boul Mich, he badly bruised his nose. The corridor lights switched off automatically when he was half-way up the stairs: entering the room number inscribed on the key, he found Elizabeth and Harry on the bed. Both were fully dressed. Stern said, *Prière de laisser ces lieux dans l'état de propriété où vous souhaitez les trouver en entrant.* Harry said, 'Each of your dreams is the same – you want a second chance.' A black student from Zimbabwe (not Oscar Mucheche) came out from behind the cheap curtain veiling the bidet: 'Dr Stern, are you giving the course you're supposed to be giving?' The black student's strong hands gripped him by the shoulders and began to shake him: 'Answer me! I pay my fees, I don't want to be cheated!'

Hands shaking him.

'You were shouting,' Beth said. 'Night after night, bellowing and shouting. I'm pregnant, remember, I want some sleep. Why don't you go back to your mother and shout at her?'

Again she slipped away down the rock face. The fingers to which he clung were now his mother's. He could hear his mother's voice from far down the gulley. 'I've always entrusted you with a key to the house. You let her use it. She came here with her lesbian friends when I was asleep, they tied me up and slapped me when I cried out, *she* slapped me, then they took my best silver and my Stubbs painting for their filthy commune. "Horses don't gallop with four legs outstretched," she sneered.'

Hands shaking him.

'Richard, please! Christ!'

The ventriloquist – my husband – is muttering again, a lock of black hair across his eyes, like Hitler. If one is going to end the night on the sofa one might as well begin there but I don't want to wound him, he's in such a state and Harry says a decision has already been made to refuse him tenure at the LSE and let him go. Does he know this? I daren't ask. Darling Hattie, you're so right: for years we kept things bottled up, as if the gift of tongues was *their* prerogative, each of us women choking on the cork cock in our throats. Look, he's smiling now, a moment of tranquillity, the fever abated, his long stick-limbs curled like a foetus – so innocent, so vulnerable! Baby, observe your father: will he be able to love you if he is incapable of love? Yes. Hattie, you're right, one does not discover oneself by teasing old men and jerking them off in cars. The reason his tongue has never ventured near my cunt is terror of silence. Ah, a new disturbance, he writhes and groans Esther's name, his smooth skin cruelly torn by jungle creepers. Look, baby, his arm is now raised, rigid, what does that mean? The little white mice are escaping from the cage, Richard, squealing happily. Mummy was very angry when I began to move out, she blamed Richard, then she blamed me, then our entire generation. That's because she's spent her whole life not knowing how to leave Daddy. All those girlfriends of his, a mistress in every port, nowadays he doesn't even bother to conceal them. Mummy said she quite understood that a relationship could never be based on gratitude alone. Gratitude? I thought she meant grateful to Richard but she meant grateful to herself: 'You just wipe the slate clean, Elizabeth, when it's convenient, and remember only the petty irritations . . .' My lifestyle horrifies her – if only she knew the half of it! Rats, sleeping in cold trains, drunken propositions, gropers . . . If only *he* knew the half of it! The endless financial crises, lawyers' fees, threats, unpaid printers' bills, betrayals, hitching half-way across the country to address ten women in a clothing factory . . .

Is this my voice, baby? Is it our voice? Look at him – dictator even in his sleep. The long unbroken paragraph, the elemental female stream of consciousness. No use telling *my* mother that *marriage is like being a female character in a novel written by a man*. After I took the Degas she arranged for me to see a Harley Street psychiatrist. A man, of course: I declined.

If you're a boy what shall we call you? Jimmy? Would you like that?

Oh, the miners: he did write one small cheque. But he's more at home in the Middle East, granting the Israelis the right to exist but also granting the Palestinians their right to a homeland – and all to annoy his mother. Never went near the coalfields but travelled, seeing yet not seeing, from Eilat to Galilee, from Haifa to Jerusalem, from kibbutz to moshav, from Ashkenazi to Sephardi, taking notes, thinking of Esther, firing off postcards, eyeless in Gaza. Baby, tell your father that liberation, like charity, begins at home. Not in Jerusalem or Zimbabwe. Harry: God I was scared in the ambulance. I felt like a girl who dangles her baby brother out of the window for fun, then drops him. I knew what Harry wanted six years ago when he took me to see Eisenstein at the National Film Theatre then told me to read Anna Kollontai – he wanted to be knocked out for the count, revived, and given a blow-job. But I was flattered. He worships Bresson too. Great man. I think he really fell in love with me. He offered to leave his wife if I'd marry him.

Compared to Harry, baby, your father's as tough as nails. Look at that long nose, poised to snort, to trumpet derision, even as his toes turn up in a last salute to his own genius. That arm still straight up in the air: *Sieg heil!* Maybe the only thing that keeps bringing me back is his passion for that jungle queen, though God I had to admire her when she said on television, 'Would you ask a man that question?' It's not jealousy, you're wrong about that, Hattie, just intense curiosity, the great gash of longing ripping his face apart, I quite like him when he's on the ropes because unlike Harry he never sinks to his knees. He's not much in bed but I did marry a real man.

Will you have his nose, Jimmy?

TWELVE

Crouching on the rim of the Round Pond, a light breeze blowing hair into his eyes, he gently lowered the tiny blue boat into the water. It bobbed nervously then headed straight back for shore, like a small child seeking comfort.

'Should you loosen the sails?' she suggested.

He fiddled with the strings and gave the boat an imperious shove. Though splashed with water, the sails filled and the boat headed out gallantly for the middle of the pond.

'First steps in fatherhood,' he said.

He took her hand. She pointed to a kite hovering high over the trees: a fat man was running backwards at the end of the string, tugging. In pointing, she released her hand. He didn't attempt to re-claim it.

'I wasn't sure where to find you,' he said.

His pride tensed like a bowstring against Cowans's sardonic contempt, Stern had finally telephoned the bleak flat off Baker Street where he'd met the exiled lawyer. The number seemed permanently engaged. Finally someone answered, a woman with an English voice, frigid: it was like talking to an answering machine programmed to filter love into the same condemned cell as intended murder. Finally he was given a number in Fulham. Dialling, he was answered by Cowans: when he asked for Esther there was no reply, just the bang of the receiver on a table and an angry voice calling:

'Another admirer. Yes or no?'

The little boat was becalmed. The fat man had stopped running and the kite was spiralling to the ground.

'I wish I knew what to say to you,' Stern said.

'So many people have been so kind,' she said dreamily.

'How are your parents?'

'Did you like them?'

'Oh, very much.'

'Mum said you'd been just wonderfully kind.'

He remembered Paul Meyer's last phone call from the Connaught before their return to Rhodesia.

—Hey, who's this guy Tanner ya fished out of the septic tank? He turns up here and tries the old FBI routine: what do I think of Alger Hiss, the Rosenbergs, the Hollywood Ten, the so-called Gulag archipelago, Solzhenitysn, the whole Cold War routine? I told him: I'm a businessman, not a politician. I have a nice garden with a swimming pool, a tennis court and coupla fine avocado trees – he's free to visit any time. Then he starts a probe into Esther's private life, wants a regular Who's Who on Zim.

—Zim?

—Esther's man. Christ, Dick, don't you know anything?

Esther took a thick lock of chestnut hair and curled it round her finger. He tried to imagine the same hair soaked in the prison bucket, matted with sweat, but his imagination was threadbare.

'Now they're threatening him with charges under the Exchange Control Act. Something to do with emeralds and Botswana. Poor Dad, I'm not the ideal daughter.'

'He's very proud of you.'

'Shall I tell you something, Richard? I was sixteen years old before I discovered that my parents had been persecuted in America. That was the first time I heard the name "McCarthy". Dad was suddenly subjected to a vicious attack in the *Rhodesia Herald* – he'd become involved in a very small way with a group of harmless white liberals called the Progressives. The article advised the liberals to purge their ranks of "proven Communists". Dad was shaken. I asked him what a Communist was. Mum took me aside as if she was teaching me the facts of life or showing me how to use a sanitary pad. "Communist", she explained, was just a dirty word for someone who was a "progressive". Or for anyone who had voted for Henry Wallace. I said, "Who's Henry Wallace?" She just looked at me sadly, sighed and then the lid came off the kettle: my head was buzzing with strange things called the Attorney General's list, the ALP, the Smith Act and the Subversive Actions Control Board.'

'Subversive Activities,' Stern gently corrected her.

'You're right. At first Dad used to scowl and sulk when Mum told me these things but in the end he decided to get in on the act and after that – ' she smiled, 'well, you've met him.'

'We played Scrabble. He won.'

'He even wins when he plays against himself. I remember the morning the police first came to our house – Dad built it himself and brought an architect up from Joburg – for the first of my three arrests.'

'Three?'

She smiled. 'Three so far. It was awful. I mean, he seemed so defenceless, as if a nightmare had leapt from behind the curtains. Mum was the strong one: she told the Inspector that whatever I had done, she was proud of me. Later the anonymous letters began to arrive.'

'Threats?'

'They called me a kaffir's whore. Always the same phrase. I knew who was behind it, a bloke I'd turned down at University and who later made a fine career in Special Branch.'

'So you took the letters to the police, who naturally promised to investigate?'

She shook her head. 'No. Dad was too ashamed. He asked Mum to find out from me whether it was true.'

He tried to concentrate but there were two tapes turning in his head, one on mono, the other vibrating with the stereophonic howl of unrequited passion. Alone with her at last, he wanted to blurt out his love, to throw himself at her feet, to stampede her with ardour, but he dreaded a definitive rebuff: even a muted confession of sexual desire might wipe either tape – or both.

Now he regretted having brought his unborn child, the boat, along as a chaperone; as a phoney emblem of honour; as pathetic proof that he still enjoyed an intimate relationship elsewhere.

'We occupied the Foreign Office, you know.'

She gave him a long appraisal. He felt himself being sliced into ragged cubes.

The little boat was now bobbing among some ducks, as if seeking playmates. A brace of big model yachts were creaming across the water, their passage assured by pre-set steering, pursued by middle-aged men carrying rubber-tipped poles who walked at first, then scampered.

'The diameter of a circle must be shorter than half the circumference. Two r is less than pi r.'

'Do you want a boy or a girl?'

'A girl. Then I won't mind so much.'

'Mind what?'

'Beth bringing her up to hate men.'

A graceful, long-limbed black youth glided past them on roller-skates, twisting and flipping, ecstatic in his skills, a heaven of heavy metal pouring through his earphones.

He waited for Esther to rise to the bait, poised to pitch himself into the perils of disloyalty. A faint smile hovered, a dimple danced in her cheek:

'I see,' she said slowly, shutting him down.

'One can only admire her. I also admire Rosa Luxemburg, but wouldn't necessarily want to be married to her.'

'Amy told me your wife is active in the trade union movement. And she writes, too? How I wish I could write.'

'She's very keen on sexual harassment at work.'

'You mean she's not keen on it?'

'She counts the number of female contributors to newspapers, magazines, and television current affairs programmes – then bombards editors with letters of protest.'

'How admirable.'

'It's called consciousness raising.'

'You should approve of that.'

'I do. But I'd like to be happy.'

She said gently, 'Then why the baby?'

'I wasn't consulted.'

'Was Elizabeth very different when you married her? Should I call her Beth? She's extremely beautiful, I think.'

Obliquely he audited her body, buried in the shallow grave of winter clothes. He hadn't asked about her hidden scars. If only she would touch him.

'Sometimes,' he said, 'after a very long journey, there is nothing to ask and nothing to report. The whole has subsumed the parts.'

'Richard, don't apologise – '

'To see you now, here, in this peaceful setting, sealed into your amazing serenity, and yet to imagine you in that cell . . .'

'They call it the VIP lounge. As Kepler said, "We'll make you throw up three courses instead of one." '

He gestured helplessly. The young black on roller skates came past again, pirouetting, gaudy as a peacock.

She said: 'At this moment, beyond those trees, people are dying in St George's Hospital. At this moment Kepler is beating someone else and Robertson is confiding to the victim that he's a family man.'

He touched her cheek. 'You're saintly. And brave.'

'Two versions of the same vanity.'

'You should write about it.'

'I can't write. I give interviews. When I read what I've said it seems accurate but not true. The truth may be too private. I don't mean the intimate physical details. I'm capable of hatred, you see, but I wouldn't want to erect a mausoleum to it. There is already too much hatred in Zimbabwe and it will be the blacks, not the whites, who finally reap the harvest.'

He felt Zim crawling on to his tongue like a fly on to adhesive paper. Once planted he would be immovable. All would be lost if he pushed her out of no-man's land, the only viable terrain for a no-man. He spat Zim out. For God's sake, cease moping and drooling, you're depressing her.

At a distance a man as tall as himself stood by the water's edge, huddled in a long coat of good cloth, shivering. A child on an expensive, latest-fashion, bicycle was pointing to Stern's little boat, trying to attract his father's attention, but the man, who was of Stern's age, was lost in adult torments, bored by the boy's infantile chatter, and quite possibly pondering the considerate way for a family man to do away with himself.

Stern touched Esther's elbow.

'That man there.'

'You know him?'

'I did. Let's wander in the opposite direction – I'm not sure he's in any condition for an encounter.'

She complied with the elastic grace of a dancing partner.

'His name is Giles Carpenter. We first met at New College and fell into a form of friendship: intense but not intimate.'

'I am fascinated by your distinction.'

'As editor of *Isis* he gained fame by satirising ambition. He accorded weekly star ratings to the television dons, always on a minus scale. He lampooned my mentor, Harry Marquis, without respite, explaining to me once that what an audience enjoyed in a satirical column was its obsessive quality, the ritual appearance of its regular victims, the predictability we associate with the comics' custard-pie routine. "Absurdly inevitable, inevitably absurd." '

'Is that his son?'

'The eldest of three. Giles won prizes for his first novel and a famous film was made out of his second – perhaps you saw *Taylor Made*, a satire about an ambitious don called Taylor who regularly got made and unmade in all main branches of life. Giles sent me a copy inscribed, "To Richard, who inspired it all – why not sue me for damages of one penny?" Then Giles turned out a pot-boiler about incest which became an international best-seller and married a pretty girl with acres of land in Scotland. He glittered and became a tax exile; the more he betrayed his talent the more seriously he took himself.

'But Giles remained loyal to one publishing house, though he exploited the numerous offers he received from elsewhere to up the bidding. In particular he valued his association with Henry Pitt, a gentleman scholar of the old school, widely read, a brilliant editor, a confirmed bachelor shielded from the rat race by a private income. Henry became godfather to the boy you see on the bicycle, Jack, and never forgot his birthday. Whenever Giles slipped in from tax exile to steal a few hours of home-grown oxygen, Henry would be a weekend guest at Penny's estate in Lanarkshire.'

'Penny is Giles's wife?'

'Penny is Giles's adoring wife – a Catholic and very keen on breeding. But I must watch my words with you on that.'

'No need.'

'Now came the big one: a multi-national project, with a New York publisher tied in, serial rights sold in advance, and discreet advance hype to the trade press. Giles Carpenter was writing a book on guess what? On "Loyalty". A wonderful subject which sent Giles off in pursuit not only of Wilde and Forster but also of MacLean and Philby in Moscow, Alger Hiss in New York, mothers loyal to murdering sons, priests loyal to the most appalling secrets of the confessional – do you confess, Esther? – '

'I do.'

'Daughters silently loyal to incestuous fathers (a throwback to his last book), and the bovine loyalty of large tribes of men to meaningless flags, figureheads and oaths of allegiance. Conflicts of value at every turn – wonderful!'

'Young Jack still wants your boat. He's telling Giles that it doesn't belong to anybody.'

'Yes. We're hardly dramatising our claim.'

'Perhaps you should. The boy is moved less by greed than by anxiety.'

' "Wonderful, wonderful, wonderful," said Henry Pitt and Giles's New York publisher, Berny Holzheimer, whenever they met Giles to discuss the ongoing project in Crete or the Antilles. There is nothing more "wonderful" to a publisher than a book that hasn't been written . . .'

Stern broke off. Brecht smiled at him from exile: 'Fleeing from my fellow-countrymen/I have now reached Finland.' The little boat cried for help from the middle of the Round Pond, like a kitten up its first tree. 'So too the games we invent/Are unfinished, we hope.'

Stern resumed his tale.

'After three years Giles turned in the typescript. He spent the weekend in Lanarkshire being a good father. On the Monday he and Penny flew down to their London flat, leaving the kids with nanny, arranged a series of dinner parties (I was flattered to receive a call, Giles wanted to know *everything*), and luxuriantly inspected a new Hockney exhibition, revelling in the insolent pleasure of not being at home when Henry and Berny called to congratulate him. Then he came home and turned on the answering machine. Nothing.'

Esther moaned in sympathy for Giles Carpenter, the gaunt, lost figure across the pond.

'Look – he hasn't moved for ten minutes.'

'The dinner parties the Carpenters gave that week became increasingly strained. By the time it was my turn, at the end of the week, Giles's anxieties were swarming like maggots over rotting meat. Should he telephone Henry? – Chamberlain's ultimatum to Hitler was not more agonisingly weighed. "Give it another day, darling," Penny kept saying, "after all it's a frightfully long book." I later learned that a further two weeks of silence followed until the letter arrived.'

'Ah, a letter. Don't tell me. I don't think I can bear it.'

And how can I bear my insupportable passion for you?

'The exact details of what followed are somewhat obscure. The advance payments Giles had received vary from $100,000 to $250,000, depending on one's informant and the time of day. Hating the book, the publishers now conspired to demand the return of the money – though in compassionate stages. Giles made his first suicide attempt, not entirely serious, people say, his pride gored to the gut.'

'Oh.'

'Some time later Giles rang me: would I read the typescript? Would I criticise it with merciless candour? – nothing else would be a service. He was on my doorstep half an hour later, clutching other copies for other friends: haggard. Seeing me, he said nothing more about merciless candour: "I hope you like it," he murmured, and fled, leaving behind him a strong odour of *honi soit qui mal y pense*. I read it all through the night. I think I wanted it to be good because, on balance, one's friends' failures are more threatening than their successes.'

'Ah. You are disarmingly frank. And was it good?'

'I don't know. As the night passed, that didn't seem the point. I saw only Giles at work, the journeys, the interviews, the serpentine manoeuvres with exiled traitors in Moscow, the patient penetration of reticent priests, the doorstep battles with working-class mums whose sons were on the run. As I turned the pages I found myself passing from the work itself, to Giles at work, and finally to Giles, bleak and blasted, on my doorstep. Having read four hundred pages on "Loyalty", it didn't seem to matter what I thought: only what I said.'

'You told him it was wonderful?'

'I told him that his editors had expected him to prostitute his talents – to put Loyalty on the Cross, hammer in the nails, then send it soaring from the Tomb on another thousand-year orbit.'

'He must have been delighted.'

'He was furious. He claimed that was precisely what he had done and who was I to look down my long, cynical nose at it. He also pointed out that I might not have sunk into impecunious obscurity and turgid scholasticism if I'd had the humility to recognise that people wanted to enjoy what they read. Two weeks later he made his second suicide attempt, from Waterloo Bridge, managing to splash down three feet from a patrol boat of the River Police. As a result of the ensuing publicity his publishers dropped their demand for the return of the money – unless he placed the book elsewhere.'

'Did he?'

'No. The splash had been too loud.'

'Nothing fails like failure?'

'You're right.'

'I'm not quite sure of the moral of the story.'

'There is none – simply a man staring at the water. A child demanding attention. Just as I stare at you and demand attention.'

'Your friend has gone now.'

'I've been in love with you for years.'

'Ever since they dropped me on the pavement?'

'Did you know?'

'Well, we all mean different things by "love". I've always been a bit frightened of you, Richard. Not just your intelligence, or your reputation . . . I often think that very clever people aren't sure who they are.'

'Homicidal maniacs share the same quality, I believe.'

She smiled. 'You said it.'

The boat bobbed in to a point of the pond rimmed in thick duck (no, migratory goose) shit, clusters of turds, as if a disease had struck. He bent and reached: the boat was wet in his hand.

'The boat would like to kiss you.'

'A she kiss or a he kiss? Boats are usually she.'

Stern looked so sad that she relented. She tilted up her oval face and brushed his lips with hers; he felt as if he was lying in an English rose garden on a summer's day. The black athlete on skates sped past with a salute to whitey passion and the first of the afternoon's Boeings passed low overhead, descending to Heathrow.

'The wind must have changed,' he said.

'Sorry?'

'They alter the flight path according to the wind. I can also mend a broken ballcock, change a flat tyre and mow a lawn. What about Geoff Cowans? Is there anything he can't do?'

'Richard. That was unworthy. Geoff's life is in ruins. His wife Fay can't leave, they have a farm at Wedza, the kids are in school, and Geoff can't find a job. He needs company. It's the least I can do.'

Her slender neck was as firm as a pedestal; her dark eyes challenged him to announce his disenchantment.

He experienced a sudden stab of longing for Elizabeth in her short leather skirt, nothing underneath, flashing her thighs, that cool, seductive, cynical laugh. Elizabeth was right: all this solemn colonial virtue was boring. The spell was broken. He looked hard at Esther to confirm it.

'Tea time?' he said.

She glanced at her watch. He knew she was not asking the time but the place.

'There's an Italian café in Notting Hill, open on Sundays.'

They walked in silence now, and he didn't feel able to take her hand. The silence filled him with apprehension. The Boeings growled across the sky, one a minute, landing lights flashing. A group of young men, Italians, were playing football between the trees, running hard, each calling eagerly for the ball. 'Alberto! Alberto!'

He wanted to say, 'I wish you'd let me write the story of your life' – so many hours closeted together, in his flat, a slow, intimate unfolding – but he knew she would refuse.

They left the park and turned into the Bayswater Road.

'I wish you'd let me write the story of your life.'

She tucked her arm through his.

'It might be simpler to go to bed with you, Richard.'

The Italian café was almost empty, a waiter he knew drying cups behind the espresso machine, a romantic song blaring from the juke box, just a man and a boy at a corner table, the man huddled in his overcoat of good cloth, the boy involved in a multi-tiered ice-cream whose crowning cherry he was jealously preserving for the end. Stern hadn't noticed the expensive, latest-fashion bicycle chained to a lamp post outside.

Stern guided Esther to a table by the window.

The boy pointed. 'Look, Dad, that's the boat, it's the same one. That man's got it.'

Esther saw the father's weary, appeasing glance. No hint of recognition invaded his deep-set grey eyes.

Stern had turned his back. Later she would tell Geoff Cowans the whole story and ask him what he thought about it.

'I'm afraid your lectures now lack conviction,' Ramsay said, 'your students complain of listless digging with a weary spade.' Gough nodded. 'Mechanical excavations. Exam results very poor.' Shields, recently appointed Professor of Economics, was studying the reports before him. 'Absence during office hours, querulous response to questions, short temper, physical and emotional unavailability.' 'One can defer tenure only so many times,' Ramsay said. 'We're letting you go. I'm really very sorry.' Stern glanced at Harry – no sign of life there. A meeting of mass protest was arranged by the International Marxist Group: seven students and two lecturers attended, one of them Stern. He went back to his GP, one of Socrates's wise men who know what they don't know. But he could sign his name to a prescription: valium, iron tablets, stop drinking if you can. Stern sat waiting in the outpatients' unit of St Mary's Hospital, feet planted on clean linoleum alongside the other silent losers, his mind furred, staring at the fat starched bums and bulging waistlines of the ancillary staff, hearing the world rush past in Praed Street – the winners.

He didn't tell anyone.

THIRTEEN

LEONARD TANNER on screen: reptilian grin of welcome.

'Good evening. Tonight, continuing our series, "Thinking Aloud", we discuss the frightening problem of political violence. What are the real issues behind the headlines? How should we describe the men and women who increasingly resort to the bomb and the gun to make their point? Murderers or fanatical idealists? Terrorists to some, the moderate majority, but "freedom fighters" to others. And can we ever draw a line between justified and unjustified violence?'

Sprawled in the Habitat sofa, a depleted bottle of vodka at his feet, Stern laughs. The potted plant is dead. But, as he told his wife on the phone to Leeds, 'its soul went to Heaven'. A frozen 'Ocean Pie' from Sainsbury's bubbles in the oven, forgotten; whether he did or didn't remember to remove the silver foil, he got it wrong.

And *solid, dependable LEONARD TANNER, monarch of the middle ground, is following the auto-cue above the camera.*

'To help me tackle these dilemmas, I have with me in the studio . . .' *Camera tracks to smooth fellow, glassy pop eyes, sloppy wet mouth, slack smile, not sure where to look* ' . . . the journalist and commentator, Patrick Warner, a noted expert on terrorist organisations.'

Stern burps.

Camera tracks. 'Esther Meyer, a noted proponent of guerrilla warfare in southern Africa, who last year spent four months in detention in Rhodesia.' *ESTHER, beautiful and serene in a bottle-green dress with a white lace collar.*

Camera tracks. 'And last, but by no means least, the distinguished political philosopher . . .' *HARRY, blasted oak, hair down to his shoulders now, eyes madly unfocused, Lear on the heath* . . . 'Professor Harry Marquis of the London School of Economics.'

Finding the bottle, Stern jams the neck into his mouth.

Camera on TANNER. 'If I may begin with you, Patrick Warner. Are you opposed to the use of violence in all circumstances?'

Camera on WARNER. 'We wouldn't be here, would we? Hitler would be here – or Stalin. Of course there are justifiable wars: this country has fought a few. But that, of course, has nothing to do with bombs in department stores, hijackings, knee-cappings, or murderous attacks on innocent civilians – the first resort, and the last resort, of ideological fanatics who enjoy no popular support.'

Stern: 'Arsehole.'

'Dresden!' *Voice of thunder, off. Camera pans frantically to HARRY.* 'Hiroshima! Nagasaki! Hanoi! Haiphong! How many innocent civilians?'

TANNER, determined to establish authority at the outset. 'Professor Marquis, we'll be hearing from you in a moment.'

'Good.'

'Esther Meyer, if I could put Patrick Warner's point to you – you may regard it as a challenge?'

ESTHER, cucumber cool. 'Obviously it's Mr Smith who has resisted peaceful change in my country. It's the illegal régime which resorts to the gun. The nationalists have always wanted—'

WARNER, cutting in. 'An alluring simplification, if I may say so. I'm sure we all find Miss Meyer alluring – with the possible exception of the hundred or so white farmers slaughtered in cold blood by her comrades.'

Camera to ESTHER. 'I didn't finish . . .'

Voice off, TANNER. 'Professor Marquis?'

Camera on HARRY, manic smile.

'The blood-dimmed tide is loosed, and everywhere
The ceremony of innocence is drowned;
The best lack all conviction, while the worst
Are full of passionate intensity.'

TANNER, nervous. 'Perhaps Yeats's famous lines echo your own change of heart, Professor Marquis?'

HARRY laughs, an upheaval of tented corduroy. 'If I may be forgiven for paraphrasing Camus, he's so much out of fashion: "The proper task of intellectuals is to excuse one campaign of violence from afar, while roundly condemning another, also from afar . . ."'

ESTHER, unhappy, out of her depth.

TANNER, uncertain.

WARNER, beaming pop-eyed. 'Beautifully put.'

HARRY'S voice, off. 'Shut your face, you fascist turd.'

TANNER. 'Now, gentlemen, please! This is a live programme.' Smoke from the kitchen.

ESTHER. 'I know that the women of Zimbabwe, who bear the cruellest hardships in the present war . . .'

WARNER. 'A young woman married to a prominent left-wing intellectual recently stole her own parents' Degas to finance terrorism. She claimed to have "liberated" the painting.' *Chuckles.* 'It's rather like "relieving" a man of his watch.'

HARRY, eyeless, now Lear, now Gloucester. 'Miss Meyer will weep for all the dead, black and white. Freud was right: "What does a woman want?" Does Miss Meyer subscribe to "The Bitch Manifesto" or the thing called "SCUM"? Don't forget the love life of spiders – the male services his partner until she decides to bite off his head – '

TANNER, desperate. 'I'm not sure any of this is – '

HARRY, mike coming adrift from his lapel. 'Relevant? Aren't we talking about the sources of violence? The female tarantula may live for thirty years, the male for only five. Jab! I ask myself: do nuclear weapons really originate in the fission of male chromosomes?'

An explosion in the kitchen, the metal plates of the oven coming down from the mountain in a lava of Ocean Pie. Stern raises his snout like a shocked dog as smoke obscures the corpse of the potted plant. He tries to rise but falls heavily, spilling the remains of the vodka on the carpet. He begins to lick and weep. Reaching the television set, he claws his way through the screen, *arms outstretched to ESTHER, radiant with relief.*

The sound which finally announced itself as the telephone began as an unidentified disturbance, in some other flat perhaps, gradually drilling through the walls, gaining in urgency until the summons was for him alone. Stern found himself stretched across the carpet beside a television set whose piercing, closed-down-for-the-night wail had failed to penetrate.

He peered at what ought to be his wrist watch, either the luminous paint on the dial had evaporated or he had gone blind.

Crawling past the bleating telephone, he found himself in a wardrobe, grappling with soft hanging garments, chiffon and silk, the Elizabeth Stern of 1970, pliant yet intractable, which he gradually identified as the chorus of women in the *Oresteia*. He giggled at the idea. Driven out of the wardrobe by a bladder swollen to the status of inner tube to the brain, he groped on automatic pilot to the bathroom, where he encountered problems. *Prière de laisser ces lieux dans l'état de propriété*. . . . On the bathroom door was crudely taped a note from his mother, a swastika, a ragged spider of scorn – Aunt Orna had considerately sent her an article he'd written, 'Israel and the Palestinians'.

He had decided to publicise this maternal stigma soon after Esther's note arrived on mauve paper: 'I really think it's for the best that we don't see each other again . . .' Eyeless in Gaza. She had cut him off with consummate tact a few days after their walk round the pond. She hadn't mentioned any other man or commitment; there was no hint of rejection, only of a wise, surgical severance of a rising passion subversive of duty.

The telephone had stopped ringing; he was holding the receiver.

'Mm?'

'Richard?'

'Mm?'

'Blind drunk?'

'Nnm.'

'Richard, get a grip. You're becoming pathetic.'

He could tell from the slant of her vowels that she was in Leeds not Manchester, sorry, Personchester.

'We've decided to get rid of the baby.'

'..gh.'

'Did you hear what I said?'

'We? We? We? Aren't you and me supposed to be we?'

'That's why I'm telling you.'

'Is it another reprisal raid? What the Americans call defoliation? Is the child a weed? First you conceive without consulting me then you abort in the same democratic spirit. I'm not a sperm bank. How would you like to have been aborted? And don't tell me the foetus is part of *your* body, enjoying no independent biological existence and therefore no moral rights. Does a baby lead an independent existence? Does a man in an iron lung? No – but that doesn't entitle you to finish him off. From the moment of conception human life is a continuum. Go on, tell me you're listening to a predictable printout of male proprietorship. The truth is, Elizabeth, the child means nothing to you. You switch it on and off in a display of biological dictatorship, deaf to its long, silent scream, proud to demonstrate your "freedom", your "emancipation", by murder. Oh, I can imagine the dramatic discussions in your witches' coven, a real life to play with, shall we, shan't we?, did Hattie weep a little while sharpening the blade? Tell me you will die in childbirth and you have my consent; tell me you will suffer a nervous breakdown and you have my consent; tell me your life will be an unbearable slavery and you have my consent. I listen to no cardinal and no priest. All I have is my imagination. Elizabeth, imagine that child. Give it a name, colour its eyes, see it at four tumbling down a slide, at six absorbed in a story, at eight painting pictures of the birds of the air, at eleven gravely crouched over geometry, at fourteen . . . I mean, we all suffer from diminished responsibility, you, me, Harry, the pilots over Vietnam . . .'

There was silence at the other end of the line but he knew she was there.

'Elizabeth, listen – can't you hear its plea, its promise? "Mummy, I promise I won't be any trouble. Daddy, please save me." '

A longer silence. Then she said, 'Go to bed, Richard. All you can hear is the slosh of booze in your ears.'

She might very well call again: 'Richard, did you mean what you said?'

'What did I say?'

Although the morning was warm, Stern ventured out wrapped in his own winter, huddled in an overcoat not unlike Giles Carpenter's, a balaclava helmet knitted long ago by Rachel pulled down over his ears. Some fifty yeards down the street from her front door, outside a pub, he spotted a telephone kiosk, filthy but unvandalized and subject to no great patronage at six a.m. on a Sunday morning. The debris, the litter, the overflowing binbags and cardboard boxes outside the pub lifted his barmy spirits. Given an air raid or two, it would be very Humphrey Jennings (whose documentary films Stern had encountered while meandering in pursuit of Brecht). Scanning the row of small, terraced houses, he wondered which window was hers.

A woman came by walking a repulsive little dog, which lifted its leg over the detritus piled outside the pub. Stern smiled gently: 'I know how he feels. One needs to leave one's mark.' The woman marched on with short, indignant steps. Stern entered the kiosk, gagged at the smell, lifted the receiver experimentally, studied the graffiti (much fucking in Fulham), then vaulted, rather to his surprise, the locked gate of a small public garden. The woman came back.

'That's a private garden,' she said.

'It's all right, I'm looking for my mother.'

The woman huffed round the corner and a white police car drew up, slowly disgorging a fat young constable without a hat.

Stern nodded affably: 'Good morning.'

'So what's the game?' The policeman spread himself, beyond

the railings, his chubby features pensive; according to the police manual there were twenty-one possible scenarios here, though not all of them came immediately to mind. The policeman beckoned, a slow curl of his forefinger – first rule, always make them come to you.

''Ad a few, 'ave you?'

Stern came to the railings, smiling. 'Officer, you're absolutely right.'

'There's been a complaint: loitering.'

'Terribly sorry.' He noticed that Harry and Beth had joined the policeman the other side of the railings, along with Hattie, Tom McAllisty and Brendan Hogg, drooling at the prospect of diagnosing schizophrenia and cure. Christopher flitted discreetly in the background, his drainpipe legs almost tap-dancing with pleasure, camera clicking. Mother's car turned the corner, Monty at the wheel; overhead, the Admiral's helicopter. On all their faces a single sentiment: about time, too. Only Rachel seemed to be reaching out to help him, but she was invisible, like her father. Stern's fart came up like a rebel nigger slave from below decks.

'Terribly sorry.'

'So what's your game?' The constable had planted his feet.

'Making a film, looking for locations, atmosphere, something a bit run down, litter, condoms, dog shit – you probably know my director, Humphrey Jennings . . .'

'Let's 'ave you out of that garden, for a start.'

Stern gripped the moulded spearheads of the iron railings and made a heroic effort. Reluctantly the young constable extended a clean hand. Stern landed, stumbled, lost his balaclava, scooped it up.

'What the film ideally needs is a folkloric figure in blue, a Jack Warner, calm, sagacious, a word of homely advice to young scamps, implacable in the face of real villainy.'

'That your car?'

Stern followed the young constable's gaze down the empty street to the Triumph Herald cowering behind the telephone kiosk, not wanting to get involved.

'I wouldn't want to see you attempting to drive that.'

'Oh, she just needs a wash.'

'You wouldn't be takin' the piss?'

Stern found himself backing across the road, miming peace. A door opened behind him and a gentle hand drew him in, her calm voice negotiating a truce with the smouldering policeman, who proceeded through a checklist of cautions and warnings, ending up not far from moral rearmament. Stern sat down on the stairs, a morse code of shame hammering against his aching skull.

'Richard, you look awful.'

'Wanted to see you. Couldn't help myself.'

In the darkened hallway he looked up and saw a pale, oval face still smothered by sleep. She lifted the balaclava from his matted hair:

'Have you got a fever?'

'Such is love.'

He followed her up the shabby staircase, absorbing everything and nothing, the faint odour of mildew and rot, expecting Cowans at the stairhead. Following her into the flat, he had an impression of cramped improvisation, of the exile's caravan; he longed to make her a prince's gift of his own smooth spaces in Notting Hill Gate. She lifted a pile of magazines and papers from a chair.

'Forgive the mess.'

'Look – I'm sorry.'

'Why are you sorry?'

She stood serenely before him, in a full, flowery dressing gown, arms folded across her breast.

'I shouldn't be here.'

'But you are here. Coffee?'

He began to focus, greedily absorbing detail, sniffing for Cowans. The walls were covered in posters -ZANU!- woodcuts of guerrillas with raised fists, the slow stoicism of suffering peasants, women behind wire, hungry children, *a luta continua*. The floor was heaped with pamphlets, more posters, the heat of a revolution, the long burn of history. A small kitchenette adjoined the sitting room. He heard her striking a match, then the flare of gas igniting, the soft metallic touchdown of a kettle. Stern's raven eyes took in two other doors, one of which had to be the bedroom. He could smell Cowans behind it, the ashtray on the floor beside the bed overflowing with twisted filter tips.

She came back with two mugs on a tin tray. 'Milk? Sugar? I ought to know.'

'Is one of those photographs your man Zim?'

She shook her head with a grateful smile.

'I saw you on television last night,' he said.

'I wish you'd been there. I couldn't cope.'

'You were marvellous.'

'It was a nightmare. When I got home my head felt like a calico bag stuffed with shapeless patching. I couldn't remember a thing I'd said – if I said anything at all.'

'Tanner, of course, is monarch of the middle ground. Any man who proclaims himself a "moderate" is axiomatically a scoundrel. But I really came to apologise for Harry.'

'Careful, the mug is rather hot. The professor? You know him?'

'Since Oxford. He was my graduate supervisor. Harry brought me to the LSE. We travelled the world together – do you remember the heroic events of the late sixties?'

'I do.'

'Then they carted him away to the bin – entirely my responsibility.'

'Oh? I'm out of my depth, as usual.'

'The academic life's not unlike the Thirty Years War. Petty jealousies, poisonous rivalries, embattled factions, calculated betrayals, shabby opportunism, rationality murdered by ambition. It was I who drove Harry round the bend.' He pulled a flap of lank hair from his forehead. 'Let's not talk about me.'

She lowered her eyes over her coffee.

'And your baby, do you hope it will be a boy or a girl?'

'It will be neither.' (But he didn't believe that Beth . . .)

Esther was fingering the rim of her mug: 'I'm sorry. What happened?'

'Elizabeth is a liberated woman.' (. . . could do it.)

His eye kept returning to the bedroom door.

'How complicated London is,' she said softly. 'I could never do that. But then . . . people are different, I suppose.'

His question pumped out like hot blood from a severed artery: 'Is Geoff asleep?'

She raised her beautiful eyes and regarded him. He remembered that look.

'Geoff isn't here,' she said.

He waited.

She picked a speck off her dressing gown and let it drop to the floor, like a woman waiting to be alone.

'How was it that you opened the door for me – at this hour?'

'I never sleep late. It wasn't the woman with the little dog who called the police, Richard. I've had two break-ins here in the last four months, and several threatening phone calls.'

'How grim.'

'There's also the man who replaces the receiver as soon as I answer. It was only when your strange balaclava helmet fell to the ground that I recognised you. Won't you take your coat off?'

'Why did you decide not to see me again?'

'I'd be grateful if you wouldn't ask me that.'

A pale sunlight filtered through the grimy window panes. He stood up. 'I'll go.'

'Please don't. You must sleep. I'm going to put you to bed.'

He sat down again.

She said: 'It was Geoff who advised me not to see you again. He thinks you work for the British Secret Service. Which, as you know, operates hand-in-glove with Rhodesian Special Branch – despite UDI and "sanctions".'

'The academic market place being divided between the bent and the bendable? So Cowans has promoted me to the pivotal cliché of the modern pseudo-drama, yet still a distant figure to you and him, out of focus, one of a crowd at Wimbledon or Henley regatta, blobbed in with a casual daub of Dufy's brush.'

'I wish I were clever.'

'There's lemon in your honey.'

'You *did* ask me. Now you're angry.'

'When you were in prison your father insisted that I meet Cowans. I found him in that flat off Baker Street surrounded by empty beer cans and paranoia – '

'He'd just fled from his own country, his family, his job.'

'It was the way he talked about you.'

She flushed. 'He's not really like that . . . He was probably trying to provoke you.'

'So he told you I was a spy and that was enough?'

The pale, filtered light played on her chestnut hair as she gravely shook her head.

'No, Richard, it was that story you told me in the park, the day we took your boat to the Round Pond: the story about "Loyalty".'

'Giles Carpenter, you mean?'

She nodded. 'I told Geoff. Every detail stuck in my mind – and all the time we were looking at that gaunt, haggard, emaciated man across the water – are you sure you won't take your coat off? You do look feverish, Richard.'

'I'm cold.'

'I'll turn on the gas fire.'

'Gas fires give me a headache. The headache I've already got will do. So you reported every detail to the sneering Roman-Dutch lawyer while he crunched beer cans in his huge, trembling paws?'

'Geoff is certain that Giles Carpenter is a fiction. He said your ego and alter ego had been involved in a noisy collision as soon as the black boy on roller skates came past. In Geoff's opinion the whole fable about loyalty was a kind of tortured warning to me that you were not what you seemed; out of love for me you were offering me the truth in the only way you knew how.'

'Balls. What had the black boy on roller skates got to do with it?'

'According to Geoff, your subconscious signalled that the black boy was Zim.'

Stern placed an elbow on each knee and cupped his head in his hands. The name and notion of Zim infuriated him.

'My dear Esther, was it for this that you brought down a curtain of blackest misery on my life? Was this the fantasy that finally exposed me as an agent of British intelligence?'

'To be honest, Richard – should one be honest? – I was never quite sure about you. Not from the moment you gave false evidence on my behalf in Bow Street magistrates' Court.'

He looked at his watch; the morning had progressed to 7.15. He dragged himself to the door with the shuffle of a condemned man. His despair was total: he must kill himself without delay and make a better job of it than Giles. Yet a whining, lawyer's voice travelled up his tube.

'And if we drove the short distance to Notting Hill now, and I showed you Giles's typescript, which he never bothered to collect, would that make any difference?'

She picked his flattened balaclava off the chair and took it to him. As he reached for it she provocatively tucked it behind her back.

'Your Controller wouldn't want you to leave this behind.'

He looked down, his nose the sun dial of a private night. An extraordinary radiance possessed her, like the dawn sun claiming the sky. A split second passed before he realised that the source of her joy had nothing to do with himself.

'Tell your Controller that Esther Meyer has been invited to attend the Geneva Conference next month as a member of the Zanu delegation, at the personal invitation of Comrade Robert Mugabe. Tell him she wouldn't give you back your balaclava.'

'I arrive, you depart yet again.'

A dimple surfaced in her cheek. 'Want to come?'

'To Geneva?'

She nodded slowly, but said: 'To bed.'

He seized her, pulling her close and burying his mouth in hers. The answering kiss was real. He ascended rapidly to heaven. Gently she detached herself, pulled off his overcoat and led him to the bathroom, where she presented him with a clean towel from the linen cupboard.

'The water should be hot.'

'Mother to the world, I love you.'

She withdrew. He ran hot water from the bad-tempered Ascot and climbed into the small tub, awkwardly tucking up his long limbs, still colonised by vodka and gloomily observing his penis floating like a stranger on the increasingly scummy surface of the water. It occurred to him that those parts of the body we regard as 'innocent' are precisely the ones we cannot regulate on a signal from the brain: eyes may be sinister, the mouth may sneer, hands are threatening – but it would be absurd to refer to ears as calculating, buttocks as angry, the chest as cunning. Which brought

141

him to the paradoxical case of the penis, Harry: the guiltiest party of all yet unable to respond to any command – merely the pathetically passive creature of stimulus. Was it the filthy Denning who'd informed him in the lower fourth that no two women's vaginas were located in precisely the same place? Stern heard Esther's telephone ring and listened, through the bathroom door, to her soft, dreamy responses, the urgency of Africa born out of the weary womb of the American dream, mbira music rising from the black hills of Dakota, 'God Save Africa' rising from the dying strains of 'We shall overcome' – Esther's mysterious affinity to Eartha Kitt and Joan Baez, the magic carpet carrying her from the chromium age of Harley Earl and the tail fin to Martin Luther King and the great pilgrimage through the Old South.

Exhausted by so much magic, Stern climbed out of the tub and warily examined his unshaven features, his mean red eyes. The cabinet yielded no razor. 'I'd horse-whip you,' said Paul Meyer, 'if I had a horse.' Stern identified the facetious fragments flowing through his head as neurotic fall-out. 'I'm afraid,' he thought. He lingered in the sanctuary of the bathroom.

With Elizabeth – that first occasion in South Kensington – he had wished that a woman's body was not attached to a person. He had wanted the body but not the knowledge, the incriminating diary entry, that followed. Now he wished that Esther was pure spirit – no corporality from the neck down. Could comradeship, respect – dignity even – survive a grinding transaction between triangles of hair and strips of flesh dripping with alien fluids?

He was sure Esther didn't want him; time and devotion had merely earned him a colonial courtesy; constrained to offer the battered refugee a bed, she had not known how not to be in it.

He opened the bathroom door, the towel round his waist, his damp feet leaving large clues on the carpet. The bedroom door was ajar, the makeshift, unlined curtains drawn. She lay with the covers pulled up to her neck, her chestnut hair fanning across the pillow.

'Better?' she said.

'Better.'

He approached the other side of the bed, turned his back, let the towel drop and reversed into the empty half, pulling the sheet up to his own neck. He assumed Esther was naked but felt it was an imposition to find out. She lay very still, as if under a pre-med anaesthetic; he did the same, the two of them side by side, on their backs, toes up, like sculptured knight and lady on a medieval tomb, miming death.

'I'm afraid I'm not very good at this,' she said.

Presently his eyes closed and he felt himself drifting back down the river of his own life towards the lock gates of the womb.

'Love gets in the way,' he said.

He turned on his side, propping himself on his left elbow, leaning over her, but leaving his body behind.

'I'm in awe of you,' he said.

She smiled, lifted an arm lazily from under the sheet, then let it rest, an offering. He took her hand.

'I'd like to see you,' she said.

'There's not a lot to see.'

'Then it won't take long.'

He pulled back the sheet, a bit, and they buried their eyes in a kiss.

'I couldn't find a razor,' he said.

'Oh, I know. I can feel. It's quite frightening.'

His gaze fell to her shoulders and breasts. She was beautiful. If her satin skin still bore the scars of Kepler's electrodes or Robinson's crocodile tears, there was no evidence of them. Esther lifted a leg and kicked back the rest of the sheet, then ran her toes down his calf.

'You're beautiful.'

'Do you really think so?'

His long neck bent to kiss her breasts.

'Could you make me happy, Esther? It's never been done.'

She rolled her dark eyes. 'I can do anything to a man, once I've got his balaclava.'

With intense, almost hysterical, relief, he felt the answering swelling below. Perhaps reading the voltage in the new urgency of his hands, she folded her soft body into his and took him between delicate fingers: a bloated wind-sock now. As he lifted her body her fragrant hair cascaded across his face and shoulders and she made him a gift of her tongue – a pledge of silence – and the two bodies began to perform without the people, like children breaking off to play as their parents converse.

But the final negotiation was difficult.

'Am I hurting you?'

Waiting and waiting in the outpatients' department of St Mary's Hospital, he had flipped through the magazines. —If he hurts me, should I tell him? You certainly should (a Doctor writes). But remember that men are vulnerable and easily offended. Whatever you say, don't remind him of his mother, his nanny or the woman teacher who kept him late in school because he couldn't spell 'sorry'.

'I'm sorry,' she whispered.

He slid his forefinger into wet velvet. She shuddered but he

143

persevered, keeping himself hard by thinking of Beth, and soon he was in and away, galloping across open savannah, a great warm wind of love in his face, triumphant. It was she who sank into sleep afterwards. He studied her face with wonder. Twice she murmured a word – 'Zim'.

But Stern was happy to sink into the long, yawning Sunday which stretched before them: Sunday with Esther.

FOURTEEN

After a Chinese lunch – do you remember the Chinese lunch we had? – he drove her to Oxford to look at the river, the colleges, the topography of his distinction. They held hands, she talking like a champagne cork about the coming Geneva Conference (was *that* why you slept with me?), he telling her about Dr Clausewitz, the two narratives rarely merging but happily running on parallel courses.

Strolling through Tom Quad, he reported how St Mary's had finally passed him up to the Tavistock clinic, where he was invited to fill in a new set of forms ('I'll soon know my date of birth by heart') and to grade himself against a new set of intelligence (sorry, 'aptitude') tests by grouping silly shapes and blobs of colour. Two weeks later he had actually met the consultant psychiatrist, an elderly, scowling Viennese called Dr Clausewitz. After ten minutes' absolute silence, during which Dr Clausewitz stared gloomily at Stern's forms, tests and charts, Stern had said,—Why am I here?

—That is for you to tell me.

—Very well. I'm here because I'm not functioning. Now explain to me why I'm not functioning.

—That is for you to tell me.

—Very well. I'm not functioning because I want something and can't get it.

—Yah?

—Yah. Aren't you going to ask me what it is I want?

—If you ask me to ask you, I ask.

—But do you care?

—You care, that is what is important.

—Are you with me in this room or am I alone?

—I am clearly with you but you feel alone. That is your problem.

—What I want but can't get is a woman. I mean – a particular woman.

—Yah?

—Yah.

—Anything else you want but can't get?

—I am incapable of love.

—Yah?

—In my view a man can't love another unless he can love himself.

—Continue.

—Are you a Freudian, a Jungian, an Adlerian, a Reichian, or a follower of Brendan Hogg?

—It's important to you?

—My father walks out, yah? To accommodate his rejection I assimilate it; likewise I reject my mother because my father did. Too complicated for you? Whatever bubbles and spills I reject; I eat watercress for the bitter taste of iron and gag at the sight of a cream cake. I love my father for neglecting me. Please ask me a searching question.

—What question you want me to ask?

—One that starts in *your* head, Doctor.

—You ever see your father naked?

—No. Wait – no.

Dr Clausewitz waited patiently.

—It's still no, Stern said.

—You hide your own genitalia?

—Hide them? Shall I take my trousers down now?

—No need. Am I your father?

—Yes. No.

—Was Harry your father?

—How do you know about Harry?

—Harry smells, eh? He smells of tobacco, of body odours, of man, yah? His gestures are expressive, expansive, bold – he exposes himself? Answer yah or no.

—Maybe.

—Too much affection? Harry wanted to meet your mother, but you avoided such encounter? He used to buy you little presents? Obscure poets from second-hand bookstores, yah, lovingly delivered, etchings, generosity – suffocating, yah?

Stern nodded.

—Harry too much alive, Harry too much warm, Harry too much heart-beat, Harry too much women, yah?

Stern shrugged.

—So revenge on Harry?

—It's possible.

—Richard ashamed of Richard? Richard punish Richard? Then Richard rush to Dr Clausewitz and declare, 'Richard cannot love Richard'? When Dr Clausewitz silent, bored maybe, other things on his mind maybe, Richard see his father across desk and want very much to kill father? Richard ask Dr Clausewitz if he Freudian, Jungian *und so weiter* – meaning what? Don't think, answer.

—Meaning are you a true doctor or a charlatan?

—Yah yah yah. Try again. Don't think.

Stern couldn't.

—Meaning: are you true father or not father at all?

—So?

—If father not true father then Richard not true man. Just boy, still. For the first time Dr Clausewitz did not end on a question mark.—You want five-year analysis? – only way.

A Sunday in early spring with Esther, a slow mellow day which kept renewing itself, refusing to relinquish its charmed life. Strolling across quadrangles, fingers twined, her chestnut hair lapping his shoulder, a kiss outside the Sheldonian. 'I don't believe a word of it,' she said. He tried to persuade her to spend the night with him in Notting Hill Gate, but she declined. In mid-week they both had lunch with Leonard Tanner at Rowley's in Jermyn Street, Esther wearing a two-piece affair in beige, the waist nipped and the bodice flared at the hips, a beautiful creature whose radiance caused every head to turn as she entered the restaurant. Tanner rose heavily to greet her, hoisting his stomach between table and chair, his flushed features already oiled by alcohol. Seeing Stern, his half-lecherous smile waned; Stern was willing to bet the old bugger had wiped his afternoon free of engagements.

Tanner had made his move in the hospitality room after the television disaster, capitalising on Esther's distress, guiding her to a stiff drink, praising her performance, offering fatherly wisdom, expressing keen interest in her forthcoming impressions of the Geneva Conference.

—Just what we need, the inside track.

By 'we' (he explained) he meant the major national newspaper of which he was now the foreign editor.

—I enjoy full power of commission. I'm my own master – made damn sure of that when negotiating the contract with Selwyn.

—Selwyn?

—Selwyn Foyle. My editor. He was given his job over my head because he had strings to pull, connections, clubmen, the same old bloody story the novelists satirise but it makes no damned difference, the clubmen either don't read the novels or they don't care.

—Or they enjoy being satirised? Esther suggested.

147

Tanner appraised her hungrily.—How about lunch at Rowley's next Wednesday? Make it 12.30, I'll book a table.

Now Esther offered Tanner her most beguiling smile.

'Please understand it was I who insisted that Richard come too. He really needs your help and advice – we both do.'

Tanner grunted gracelessly, busying himself ordering the wine and food, already flushed on several dutch-courage cocktails, an overweight man hanging on to the tail end of his prime and not pleased to have been outwitted. He wanted – all three knew what he really wanted – Esther to report the Geneva Conference, an inside view from the guerrilla camp. He lit one cigarette after another with a silver lighter; when the steaks and salads arrived he left one smouldering in the ashtray. He told some stories. He had been places. Famous names. 'Before your time, eh?' A chuckle. A mature man very much of this world but not without ideals. 'Fashion's something else.' He shot a look at Stern. Esther listened gravely, with respect, dispensing admiration, surprise and ignorance in perfect womanly doses – not a flicker when Stern pressed his foot against hers.

Tanner ordered a second carafe.

'Now let's talk about you, Miss Meyer.'

'Well,' said Esther, coiling the ends of her hair round her finger, her long lashes pensive, her voice as soft as molten chocolate, 'I'm afraid the British press has made very little effort to understand the nationalist movement in my country.'

'Time we did,' Tanner said. 'You're not drinking.' He replenished her glass, affording a trickle into Stern's.

'But I can't write,' Esther said.

'Don't bother your pretty head about that. Just put it down, I'll knock it into shape.'

'Richard can write.'

Tanner slowly wiped his mouth with a starched napkin. Then he took the measure of Stern.

'Ever been closer to Rhodesia than Rhodesia House in the Strand?'

'No.'

'Any corner of Africa?'

'No.'

'Rule one: go. Book knowledge no use.'

Esther said that no one disputed that, least of all Richard, but she had the utmost confidence in him and guaranteed to make him the best-informed correspondent attending the Geneva Conference.

'You see, Mr Tanner, we in the Zanu delegation are at war and must bind ourselves to the strictest code of confidence. We can only deal with journalists we fully trust.'

Tanner grunted, fingering a clean knife which lay on the table-cloth amid the debris of the meal, his dragon's eye sullen with the knowledge that this opinionated prick, once Harry Marquis's darling, but latterly reputed to be on the skids, had made it in the sack – and made it good, evidently – with the famous kaffir's whore.

'You academics all think journalism's easy.'

'I don't. As a matter of fact, I've done some.' Stern reached down to the soft attaché case beside his chair and handed Tanner a large manilla envelope. 'Czechoslovakia, France, Cuba, Israel.'

Tanner handed the envelope straight back.

'Heavy on theory, light on facts.'

'That's not my impression,' Esther said. 'Won't you at least read his pieces?'

'I have. But ours is a daily newspaper – that's a different ball game. A deadline tonight doesn't mean any time tomorrow.'

Stern nodded gravely. 'Understood.'

'Six hundreds words – if you're lucky – doesn't mean two thousand if you feel like it.'

'Also understood.'

'Our paper isn't edited by Jean-Paul Sartre.'

Esther leaned across the table and gently took Tanner's hand.

'Mr Tanner, I ought to tell you in the strictest confidence that Richard has made a very important and, I believe, very brave decision. Few men have the courage and the vision to change course in mid-career, but Richard is resolved to become a journalist. Indeed he has already given in his notice at the LSE. They were quite shaken, I can tell you. They warned him that the academic profession is contracting – not the milky sixties anymore, as the Dean put it – and virtually promised him promotion if he would re-consider. And then, I think this will interest you, Mr Tanner, the Dean asked Richard whether he really regarded journalism as a profession. Richard said it was a profession he would be proud of, citing Walter Lippmann, James Cameron, James Reston, and, though he wouldn't want me to tell you this – yourself.'

Tanner flushed. Esther still had his hand.

'Whatever happens,' she went on, 'Richard is launching his new career in Geneva and I shall be his source – though no doubt one of his many sources. I wouldn't be honest with you if I pretended we won't be talking to other newspapers . . . though you're the first.'

'Does he ever speak for himself?' Tanner growled. Then relented, collapsed, under her reproachful gaze.

'You're a ruthless woman.'

'Is it a deal, Mr Tanner?'

'Please call me Leonard. I suppose I must seem on the edge of the grave to you. But I reckon I can still give certain gentlemen a run for their money – my arsehole of an editor for a start.'

Esther's beautiful eyes opened wide with wonder.

'Oh do tell me, Leonard, I love Fleet Street gossip.'

Flattered in defeat, Tanner shook his head.

'Mustn't. How about a brandy?'

Esther declined and presently the two young people took their leave, most grateful for the lunch, most grateful for everything, leaving the old warrior to drink his way through an empty afternoon before shuffling off to a peep show in Old Compton Street, his aching skull bombarded by the thunder of young loins.

FIFTEEN

From the notebook of Richard Stern:

Geneva is one city I never want to go back to. I don't mean Geneva 'in the heart of Europe', nor Geneva the Gallic town, the Roman city, the Burgundian capital; nor the Geneva of Jean Calvin and Jean-Jacques Rousseau; nor Geneva 'the gateway to the mountains'. I don't mean secret bank accounts, Longine watches or the flea market in the Plaine de Plainpalais. What I do mean is my Geneva during that autumn of 1976, the long corridors of the Palais des Nations echoing with sterile rumour and jaded cynicism, the killing of time. I mean waiting for Esther.

The initiation ceremony lasted two months, bordering on three. I used to wait for her outside the conference room of the Palais where four Rhodesian delegations, one of them white, faced each other in rectangular deadlock; wait for her in the lobby of the Intercontinental Hotel with its 400 bedrooms on sixteen floors and permanently jammed switchboard: telephone 34 60 91. Platoons of black delegates, fresh from the jungles of Mozambique or Rhodesian detention cells, bustled in and out with their brief-cases, basking in their sudden promotion to the world's headlines, snapping 'No comment' at the waiting hacks and television crews.

As Tanner had warned me, I learned humility (though I didn't), pushing, jostling, begging for a word, scampering after Comrade No Comment. The best apprenticeship for a reporter, Tanner had remarked when I went to collect my letter of accreditation, was to grow up as a child beggar in Calcutta: 'Keep dogging their heels until they toss you a rupee out of exhaustion.' He warned me I wouldn't make it: too proud, too used to commanding the centre of the stage. He threw me his harsh, smoker's laugh: 'You'll expect the story to come to you.'

In the Palais, during the long hours of fruitless procedural bickering, one hung around the news-vending machines, scavenging for scraps: Reuters (33 38 31), UPI (34 17 40), even Agence France-Presse (32 11 20). I spent fragmented hours reading other hacks' columns to discover what I'd missed; it was then that I discovered, with an eye sharpened by praxis, that most daily journalism is simply the re-cycling of stale paragraphs and tatty card indexes. If nothing happens, begin with Smith's declaration of UDI in 1965; if Mugabe has no comment to offer, regurgitate his biography and his supposed aspirations. When you know nothing, write down 'According to informed sources . . .' and go for a drink.

The white Rhodesians ran a slicker operation. Installed in the five-star Hotel du Rhône on the Quai Turretini (telephone 31 98 31 and always an answer), they dispensed free drinks and copious literature detailing the latest guerrilla atrocities and the abysmal economic performance of neighbouring black states. Their press spokesman, a muscular rugger played called Mike Gilson, took care to memorise every journalist's name and fielded difficult questions with such desperate sincerity that it was hard, as another frustrating day evaporated, not to wish him and his cause good luck.

The Intercontinental, where Esther was staying with the Zanla guerrillas at the expense of the British Government, swarmed with bodyguards, hangers-on, an electric animosity. I ran into Oscar Mucheche and asked him what he was doing; his eyes swivelled like ball bearings: his future was up for grabs. I soon ran short of money. Tanner had refused even minimal expenses – 'Sleep under the bridges of the Rhône, there are plenty of them' –and this was a city where you had to sell a Degas to buy a sandwich. To eat cheaply in the evening was virtually impossible; the self-service places, the Migros, closed after lunch, a meal my stomach was accustomed to skip. Avoiding my silent boarding-house room in the Avenue de Bude, I hung around the bars, lonely and aloof, a fringe figure listening in to the cynical banter and dirty jokes of the old professionals whose paths had crossed from Singapore to Stockholm, from Palestine to 'Nam'. I soon learned that you were nothing if you hadn't been in 'Nam'.

What had I expected of Esther? A privileged, nay pivotal, place in her daily timetable? Tête à tête dinners by candlelight, intimate de-briefings between scented sheets from midnight to dawn? I don't know: I'd let my comfortable assumptions ride on a cushion of warm air. Many of the salacious conversations in the bars turned on Esther: which gook commander had her last night. Patrick Warner announced that to his certain knowledge four Rhodesian Special Branch operatives had shot each other in a drunken brawl over the privilege of kidnapping her. The austere, scholastic Zanu leader, Robert Mugabe, was said to be biding his time, a prison graduate schooled in patience and with a notably jealous wife. An affable American reporter who was decent enough to buy me a drink told me that 'the Meyer woman' was just a groupie on a trip – 'But it's quite some trip'. Parting, he handed me his card: 'Bernard Holzheimer, *New York Times*'.

Yet their tone became respectful, even deferential, when Esther walked past in the lobby of the Intercontinental or the gleaming corridors of the Palais des Nations. Those who had defamed her in the bars now oozed unction: 'Esther, tell me this, Esther tell me that.' Invariably she stopped, the soul of courtesy, playing a dead bat but without a trace of self-importance.

'You really must ask Eddison Zvobgo.'

She was even polite to the ineffable, wet-lipped Patrick Warner, who had so grossly insulted her in the television studio. Invariably I hung back from the panting pack and she did me the honour of pretending I wasn't there – a signal of intimacy, surely? Or so I tried to convince my empty bed in the Avenue de Bude.

I was 'befriended' by a very short, tubular woman, apparently constructed out of Michelin tyres, who presented herself as a correspondent for the Rhodesian press agency. Learning that I was a mere stringer, paid by the word, Frieda Hersh gave me an unctuous leer and downgraded herself to stringer also – but immediately upped the odds with a second identity: wife to General Hendrik Hersh. The name meant nothing to me. Frieda winked: 'Naughty boy, you haven't done your homework.' I told her that now was as good a time as any but all I got was a painfully conspiratorial grin: 'Ask Mr Tanner, Leonard will know.' Digging into her camera bag – she carried many cameras – for the price of two more doubles, Frieda inquired about my reported relationship with 'the gorgeous Esther'. This was the first probe of that kind I'd handled since coming to Geneva and I was quite pleased: listening to others snapping 'no comment' had got to my soul. 'Yes,' I said, 'I know her.' Frieda leered: 'In the Biblical sense, Richard?' I said no. And did I know about Esther's black lover, the famous doctor, a powerful but enigmatic figure in Zanu's central committee? I nodded. Was I aware that Dr Zimunya was in reality working under deep cover for 'certain other interests' – here Frieda cautiously scanned the neighbouring tables – 'including Bishop Muzorewa and the British Secret Service'?

I allowed myself what I hoped was a smile enigmatic enough to deserve another double. You approach rock bottom when you discover that any company is better than none. I was very lonely and Frieda Hersh was a human being, just.

Abruptly she looked up at a man standing over our table, then tried a smile for size, like a hat.

'Why, Geoff! Long time, no see.'

'Two of a kind,' Geoff Cowans said, one eye screwed against the cigarette smoke trailing up from his pencil mouth. He went his way, nursing the badge of his bitterness.

'You know what that means,' whispered Hersh, her frog-features uncomfortably close to mine.

Presently Patrick Warner joined us, wet-lipped and knowing in a faded white suit and empty wine glass.

'My dear boy, rumour abounds that you know more than you divulge. My trade is to divulge more than I know.'

J.R. Tree of the *New Statesman* followed like a gnome on a lead, elbowing aside hacks longing to be home by Christmas, Noël and Weihnachten.

Tree was more direct than Warner: 'They say you had Esther in the sack. Did she cry "Zim!" as she went past the finishing post?'

These thrusts eroded what was left of my morale – the conclusion was ultimately inescapable that Esther herself must be the source of the entire Restoration comedy. When Esther's summons finally arrived it was delivered to my antiseptic lodgings at six in the morning by a sardonic Zimbabwean wearing smoked glasses and a tiger-dappled uniform of his own invention. 'Cubans Urimbo,' he drawled, giving the triple handshake, thumb, palm, thumb. 'You are instructed to present yourself at Room 719, Intercontinental, at 2145 local time. Don't be late, Mr Stern, the Comrade President is very hot on punctuality.'

Wouldn't I need some form of pass?

He shrugged. 'No problem. Just identify yourself.'

At the door he paused with an elaborate display of unconcern: 'Seen Cowans?'

I shrugged. 'Once or twice.'

'Yeah . . . know where he's staying?'

'Surely Esther knows.'

He threw me a look, which broadened into a wolfish grin, then slapped my hand three times. Pulling back the lace curtains, I saw a Mercedes speed away, blaring its horn up an empty residential street to flout the law and infuriate the natives. Geneva is littered with the headquarters of international organisations. The Swiss like the money but not, on the whole, the pockets it comes in.

'No problem' is the subtle Zimbabwean euphemism for every kind of hassle and delay. Arriving at the Intercontinental early, I was interrogated by paranoid bodyguards whose English extended to a '*a luta continua*' and frisked for concealed pencils until my balls felt as if they'd been through a roller-derby. It was not unlike the madness that had swept through Addis Ababa (Tanner reminiscing with his feet on his desk) the previous year after the fall of Haile Selassie. Neither press card nor passport impressed the Comrade President's security men: it looked as if I wasn't going to get nearer room 719 than the front lobby unless I produced credentials signed by the Party's Press and Public Relations Secretariat. The only thing that divided the several comrades who squeezed me was whether the said credentials required two or three accompanying photographs – one guerrilla very high on dagga wanted twelve. Finally their walkie-talkies crackling on expiring batteries produced Cubans Urimbo who approached me at a slow slouch, stared at his very new Swiss watch and said, 'You're late.'

Not that it mattered. A further hour-and-a-half elapsed before I was finally pushed through a door numbered 611 (not 719) like an unregistered parcel splitting at the seams. The smoke in the room would have done honour to the Battle of the Somme; the dozen or so black men bent over a table littered with beer bottles and overflowing ashtrays were either playing poker with British pound notes or studying the tea leaves round the Queen's head for a clue as to the future. Esther, whose combat fatigues appeared to have been cut from the same tiger as Cubans Urimbo's, took me by the arm, smiling very sweetly, and introduced me to each impossible name – Mhalalanga, Munangagwa, Chichawana, Makanganise, Kaparepare, Nzarayebani, Sanyangare – without conspicuously commanding the attention of the aforenamed.

'Richard, I'm sure you have some questions for the comrades,' she purred but the only question I could think of was 'Who are these men?' and that didn't seem to meet the moment. I therefore resorted, stammering, to general Marxist perspectives about the 'struggle' and the 'inner contradictions of the racist-settler régime', but this produced no noticeable deflection of attention from the poker game since I obviously knew all the answers anyway. When Cubans Urimbo lit a cigar and warned me that 'This is all off the record, comrade', I was granted the only quotable comment of the evening.

'I was hoping to meet the Comrade President and General Tongo,' I said to Esther, my eyes bleeding with love and reproach for the weeks of neglect, the betrayal of our bond, the erasure of our Sunday from the calendar.

'And they wanted to meet you, Richard,' she said, with the conviction of a machine dispensing fruit drops. 'But we have just heard that Smith is pulling out of the conference, confident of a new deal with the British involving Muzorewa and . . .' she hesitated, 'possibly one other party.'

She offered me her cool hand: thumb, palm, thumb. The hand that on the third of our three journeys to heaven (yes, I counted) had stroked my penis to white heat. Descending the stairs to avoid the bodyguards (whose sense of security did not extend beyond the lifts), all I could think of was the same hand bringing another member to black heat. In the lobby I ran into the nonchalant Holzheimer and begged a lift in his nice car to the Reuters office in the Palais des Nations. The big question, as I mentally composed my report to Tanner, a scoop at last, exclusive too, Esther's parting gift, was whether I dared push my luck to interpret 'possibly one other party' as Joshua Nkomo – Zanu's uneasy and distrusted ally within the hastily patched-together 'Patriotic Front'.

'Get anything?' Holzheimer asked casually, one hand on the wheel as we glided up Petit-Saconnex and into Ferney.

'Just the usual.'

'Jesus, do I need a story,' he sighed. 'One of these nights I'll close my eyes and peddle Comrade Esther's latest, dime-a-dozen fantasy.'

Esther came to my lodging house in the Avenue de Bude on a freezing winter morning to say goodbye. The grumbling concierge awakened me from a deep sleep in which – my dreams invariably grow more vivid towards dawn, as the periscope begins to surface – I had been pursuing Esther around the Round Pond, indignantly demanding that she give me back my little blue boat. Wrapped in fur, Esther waited on the landing with the fretting concierge while I climbed into long thermal underpants and glanced down at the street below where Cubans Urimbo sat at the wheel of the Mercedes, smoked lenses shielding him from the snow-glare, his engine impatiently ticking over, his exhaust emitting the toxic cloud in which the citizens of Geneva adore to eat their breakfast muesli.

Esther gently kissed me on the mouth: thumb, palm, thumb.

'Goodbye, Richard.'

'But – '

'The conference has been sabotaged by the imperialists and we have therefore taken a principled decision to continue the armed struggle while making it clear to all progressive nations that we seek a peaceful solution to the conflict.'

I searched her beautiful, tranquil eyes for a trace of irony but found only sincerity. She perched provisionally on the edge of my unmade bed.

'Perhaps,' I said, 'You've attended too many public meetings during the past two months.'

'Richard, this is war. People are dying. There are now ten thousand Zimbabwean refugees in Zambia and another ten thousand in Mozambique.'

'You're returning to London?'

'To Mozambique.'

'No!' I clutched her by the wrist.

'And then, God willing, back into Zimbabwe – underground.'

My dry tongue was caked in misery.

'Richard, I do want to explain one thing. If I had been seen alone with you here in Geneva, Special Branch would have got hold of it and you would never be admitted to Rhodesia. I'm assuming that's where you want to go?'

'Can you get me into Mozambique?'

Her hand tenderly rested on my arm. 'No way.'

'The comrades didn't approve of my reports?'

'The comrades did approve. They regard you as an ally. We don't have many. Go back to Tanner and twist his arm – we want you in Rhodesia during the final phase of the struggle.'

'I could start in Mozambique.'

'Richard, this is off the record. There have been serious . . . troubles in our guerrilla camps. A group of young Turks calling themselves Zipa are denouncing the comrades who took part in the conference as sell-outs. Foreign journalists are not welcome. You're not to repeat a word of that.'

Beautiful, she shimmered before me in the cold, grey Swiss dawn, her large eyes luminous with fixed purpose. I tried not to look at the high leather boots sheathing her legs.

She rose and handed me a letter out of her new fur bag. It was addressed to Geoff Cowans.

'Do you ever see Geoff?' She sounded as 'casual' as Cubans had done.

I silted up in anguish. 'No.' I gave her the letter straight back and the look she threw me seemed to say, 'Either serve me or . . .' In a panic of contrition I clung to her.

'Please write to me, my darling. Please find a way. I shall never forget you.'

At the door she said: 'Richard, take care, you're very special.'

I pulled back the curtains. The Mercedes gunned away as in a spy film, its snow-tyres gnashing the civic grit, horn blaring. I took myself to the spotless Swiss toilet and abused myself for the first time since Esther wrote to me on mauve paper: 'I really think it's for the best that we don't see each other again . . .' That had been Cowans's influence, of course – or had it? When I came out of the toilet, red-eyed, I saw her note to Cowans lying on my table. The envelope wasn't mauve this time, but white as driven snow. It was still lying there, unmoved and unopened, when I left Geneva.

Tanner affably nodded Stern to a chair, easing his Royal Artillery tie, unbuttoning his collar, instructing his secretary to put through no further calls for the 'next ten minutes'.

'So you want me to send you to Salisbury? The life of a freelance stringer is pure hell – and you won't have Lady Meyer to hold your hand. It's humiliating work. You have to crawl. It has to be in your blood. It has to be the only damned thing you can do. If you have options you won't last six months. We'll spike half your pieces, invariably the ones you're most proud of. Others we'll cut to shreds. You'll find paragraphs appended that you never wrote. What we don't print we don't pay for. We don't even have to fire you, we just let you go.'

'I was hoping for something . . . more permanent.'

Tanner lit a cigarette with brown fingers.

'You want to become a staff correspondent overnight, with full pension rights? Appointments like that involve weeks of manoeuvre and lobbying: Foreign Editor, Managing Editor, News Editor, Features Editor, they all have their fangs in the budget. We had a fine reporter thrown out of Amin's Uganda, he was lucky to escape with his life. When he got home I couldn't offer him a thing. He just looked at me – he'd been stripped and beaten at an army road block and forced to swim a croc-infested river to reach Tanzania. "What about Cairo?" he said. "You haven't had anyone in Cairo since Alan died." I told him we're sending someone to Damascus instead. He looked hopeful: "I know Syria pretty well." I said to him, "I can give you a month as sub-editor along the corridor." '

'What did you think of my pieces?'

'I ran them, didn't I?'

'Four out of eight.'

'There you go: prima donna. You were lucky.'

'It didn't cover my air fare and accommodation.'

'Then hire a bicycle. A camel. I told you to sleep under the bridges of the Rhône. Christ, man, no stringer can survive on one paper's patronage alone. Syndicate yourself. Peddle your muck to the *Cape Times*, the *Sydney Argus*, the *Vancouver Examiner*. You write fluent French, don't you? – well, cut the throat of the man from *Le Monde* on a dark night and don't forget that some dirty rag from Grenoble may want squalid stories about local heroes serving as mercenaries up at Bindura. It's the rags that pay.'

'What did you think of my pieces?'

'Not bad. Not good either.'

'Oh?'

'Lower your nose. Seems to me you went overboard to jettison your academic cargo. To write good copy you don't need to pretend you're Raymond Chandler. Been reading Hemingway, have you? Sometimes you sound like Bugsy Malone or *The Front Page*. Try Evelyn Waugh's *Scoop*, you'll never recover.'

Stern flushed and bridled at the blatant injustice; Tanner had clearly spent his working life rubbing his nose against a whetstone; you could bounce a sixteen-pound shot off it. He was as likely to insert an ambivalent sentiment or subtle metaphor in his prose as Rocky Marciano to throw a kiss in round three. Trapping these images, Stern groaned: he had hurried to imitate the man as eagerly as he had once embraced Harry's born-again Marxist humanism.

Tanner was warming to it. When the secretary rang through with the first call at the end of the ten minutes he growled her off.

'A reporter up a woman's skirt is a loser.'

'Go fuck yourself.'

Tanner seemed quite pleased with this.

'Lucky for you, and lucky for us, we didn't print that kite you flew about Nkomo and the Brits. Can't guess your source.'

Tanner chuckling, smoker's cough, Stern sullen.

'Liars don't make good reporters, by the way. You didn't resign from the LSE, you were given the boot. It took me three minutes to check out your story. Very well, it was *her* story, not yours. Tell me one thing: did she believe it or not?'

'She believed it.'

'You peddled that one on your way into bed or on the way out?'

Stern stood up. 'I don't suppose you talk to your editor or your proprietor in quite this engaging manner.'

'Nor to my dog.'

'Is there nothing in your life you've ever kept silent about – or lied about out of shame and misery?'

Tanner watched the tears coursing down Stern's long nose, the heaving of the sharp, bony shoulders, the rapid bellows-motion of the flat chest, and he felt, as Hemingway would say, good.

'We'll put up two hundred quid towards your fare to Salisbury. I think you've got talent. One day you may be a Lippmann, a Cameron, a Reston, a . . . Now get out and good hunting. Don't take unnecessary risks. Send my secretary your next of kin just in case – still married? I won't show you out, it's bad luck.'

PART TWO

SIXTEEN

'I was amazed how many people over there support Rhodesia.'

'It's the least you expect from your kith and kin.'

'But the racist remarks you hear on the London underground! You'd never get that in Salisbury.'

'It's the welfare state, if you ask me.'

The two women, strangers until they boarded the aircraft at Johannesburg and found themselves in adjoining seats, fell temporarily silent.

Pressing his forehead against the window, Tanner studied the flat brown savannah 30,000 feet below, searching for the Limpopo. He was bored with eavesdropping on these two Rhodesian ladies with their incessant 'if you ask me' – invariably prefix or suffix to the most universal cliché of the hour. In his time he had gazed down on the North Pole, the Amazon, the Arabian Gulf with its super-tankers riding at anchor in still blue waters like toys. The stewardess came past and he ordered another double scotch, hastily sculpting an engaging smile: 36–23–37 (he guessed) and that wasn't her telephone number.

'I don't suppose you could serve it in a real glass?'

'I'm sorry, sir, we only carry plastic ones for reasons of safety.'

He glanced at her legs: disappointing. On the whole he rated South African women highly: they took trouble, as if aware they were living on borrowed time. In less than an hour he would be able to cross Rhodesia off the shortening list of countries he had never visited and towards which, ergo, he felt a faint resentment, as if their presence on the map was a personal insult.

One thought darkened the prospect: Stern would be waiting at the airport. 'We're letting you go.' Or: 'I'm letting you go.' Or: 'My editor has reached his limit.' Or . . . Tanner had been weighing the *mot juste* – and the *moment juste* – intermittently since leaving

163

London. Occasionally he felt sad about it. When this happened he summoned indignation to the rescue. The vanity of a prima donna, the arrogance of a milord, the objectivity of a brooding swan: twenty-seven months of Richard Stern had been enough.

Tanner closed his eyes and set his features in an Economy Class scowl of discomfort. He thought of the gleaming swimming pools he'd seen as the plane gained height over the suburbs of Joburg, then the black townships further out, rows of matchboxes packed with the dynamite of racial fury. How many had died in the Soweto riots, and when? Bloody memory going. Stern would know, his nose lengthening as he reeled off the damning statistics. Tanner permitted himself a small grunt of satisfaction – in one 'short' week he had pulled off interviews with Harry Oppenheimer, General van den Bergh and Prime Minister Botha, the three great magnates of white South Africa. In this business you had to get to the top. In Rhodesia he'd talk to Prime Minister Smith, General Walls and Bishop Muzorewa. And Hersh – Hersh would be the big one, a scoop. Tanner had been probing the Rhodesia desk of the Foreign Office in London for months, but they remained evasive and noncommittal about Hersh and his role in 'Option B'.

—As far as we're concerned, Leonard, he's just another rebel general.

Like hell. At least that was one story Stern could never get. Too much ideology, too little common sense, the arrogant bastard. Yes, fire him.

A gentle hand touched his arm.

'Your whisky, sir. One Rand, please.'

Then fear also touched him. The captain had come on the intercom with the soft, clipped vowels, the guttural roll in the throat, that Tanner associated with the beleaguered Afrikaner laager under stress.

'Ladies and gentlemen, we have now crossed the Limpopo and are entering an officially designated war zone. There is no cause for concern but you are advised to keep your safety belt fastened. In the event of an emergency extinguish cigarettes, bring your seat to the upright position, and lean well forward with your hands clasped over your head. Our descent into Salisbury will follow standard practice and should you suffer pain in your ears from the severe loss of altitude you are advised to swallow rapidly. We are due to land at Salisbury in forty minutes and hope you enjoy the rest of your flight.'

Tanner could detect no change in the landscape: more parched brown veld, clusters of thorn trees, occasional lakes, no they must be cloud shadows. Tanner had met few men more impressive than Harry Oppenheimer: progressive, even visionary, dedicated to promoting the living standards of the African. When Oppenheimer's napkin had slipped to the floor during luncheon, the head of the Anglo-American Corporation had himself bent to retrieve it, even though two black waiters were hurrying forward. Now that was something Stern could never understand, a genuinely benevolent paternalism. Then Tanner was afraid again. Doubtless the captain had taken them above the operational ceiling of the Sam 7 Strela missile but the thought of a heat-seeking projectile closing on the Boeing's jet engines like a hound pursuing a bitch in heat made Tanner's anus contract. He stuck his little finger in his ear, burrowed intently, inspected the result.

'The white man accepts a challenge,' one of the women in the row behind had begun again. Tanner cocked an ear: her nephew Rick had been wounded in the shoulder and 'somewhere very private' while out in the bush fighting the terrs. Tanner almost reached for his notebook and bifocals but the effort was too much; nowadays he reserved such energies for the Harry Oppenheimers, the van den Berghs and the P. W. Bothas. Never for women; cock and cunt speak different languages.

—Fire him, Selwyn Foyle had said. —I'm sick of running reports which flagrantly contradict our own leader columns. Tanner pondered who was the greater shit, his editor or his Salisbury stringer. The impending general election in Britain had wonderfully sharpened Foyle's political ambitions. Rhodesia had become an election issue, raw, emotive, symbolic, and someone was leaning on Foyle from the distaff side of the party. Week after week Stern's reports had denigrated the internal settlement, the moderate, gradualist solution which would keep Rhodesia in civilised hands and exclude the terrorists. Week after week Stern emerged from the tribal trust lands, the heart of darkness, infuriating Foyle (and the lady in blue) with reports of overwhelming peasant support for the 'freedom fighters'. Finally Foyle had taken Tanner out to lunch, avocado and crabmeat, a bottle of Muscadet, a pink face radiating last-chance ambition.

—Frankly, Leonard, this can't go on. You'll have to fire him.

He tossed a sheet of telex across the table. Tanner had already read it:

'Despite the régime's claims that the coming election will be free and fair, the parties of the Patriotic Front, Zanu and Zapu, remain banned. More than a hundred Zapu supporters were arrested on Tuesday in Bulawayo. Only the whites, four per cent of Rhodesia's population, were offered a referendum on the new constitution, whose entrenched clauses guarantee continuing white control of the army, the police, the civil service and the judiciary. So long as his main enemy is the Patriotic Front, Bishop Muzorewa must perch on the lap of Ian Smith, a pawn decked out as a king. According to plan, after the elections Muzorewa will assume responsibility for the air attacks on neighbouring black states.'

—That's not a report, Foyle said, —it's a bloody sermon.

Tanner had nodded, wondering whether to show him Stern's account of a flight to Nyamaraopa and Mangula with Muzorewa's 'internal' rival for power, Ndabaningi Sithole. Stern had described a vast plain of rotting maize, cotton and tobacco deserted by its inhabitants on orders from Zanla. An armoured truck had carried Sithole to a beleaguered police post where the young white conscripts had pinned up a message from Zanla scribbled on carton cardboard: 'Smith is a dog down with dogs and running dogs. We want bloodshed to Smiths dogs down with you dogs and running dogs. Zanla Forces.' The Reverend Sithole had cast a mournful, marble eye at the message then walked out of the mess, without a word. Two hours later, as Sithole's plane touched down at Mangula on a runway heavily guarded by white police reservists, the Special Branch pilot pulled off his radio earphones and turned to Sithole with a grin. 'We took out Nkomo in Lusaka last night, Reverend.' Sithole looked stunned. Although a member of the supreme, four-man Executive Council, he had known nothing about it. 'Did they kill Joshua?' he asked in a whisper. The pilot threw him another grin: 'No definite confirmation of that – yet.' Descending from the plane, Stern had taped Sithole's immediate response. 'Well . . . well . . . it's very difficult for me to react rationally, so to speak . . . There is nothing we can do about it, one accepts it.'

—Drop him, Foyle insisted, picking at duck with orange sauce.

—He's not without talent.

—You mean he's your man. You made a mistake, Leonard. You don't make many.

Tanner studied his editor's pinched, baby face: it seemed to belong to a prep school photo. Tanner had attended a working-class elementary school, then taken a job as a messenger boy at fifteen shillings a week, but backgrounds such as his were still a rarity in the upper reaches of Fleet Street and he had become a keen, if embittered, student of the fast track. Foyle was the sort of boy you bullied; a sneak, a petty thief who quite probably got himself expelled for selling tatty versions of 'Eskimo Nell' in the lavatories. Eyes pale and watery with ambition. Sniffing the Tory wind, he'd changed tack, sleekly detaching himself from the 'wet' end of the party, the country squires with a social conscience, the Macmillanites, the technocrats who believed in Europe and the

United Nations. A harder-faced shopkeeping élite was now in the ascendant and Foyle had hurried to embrace the new chauvinism.

Tanner closed his eyes again, the plastic SAA 'glass' dribbling whisky on to his trousers, bracing himself for the fearful corkscrew descent foreshadowed by the captain's laconic announcement over the intercom. He slapped at a sudden itch on his nose but the itch was too quick: a fly at 30,000 feet. Tanner's own politics, as he frequently reminded the staff on the foreign desk, had barely shifted during forty years 'on the job': to the right of left-of-centre, the pragmatic middle ground. Voted Labour in 1945 and again in 1950; followed the *Manchester Guardian*'s advice in 1951 and voted Liberal. The same in 1955. Back to Labour in 1964, after thirteen years of Tory rule. Labour in 1966. Liberal in 1970. Torn between Labour and Liberal in both elections of 1974, voted Conservative on each occasion. Would do so again in May, though with profound misgivings: still believed in a pragmatic socialism, provided it took account of realities: impose wage restraint; curb the excessive power of the trade unions; encourage managerial expertise and business enterprise by means of tax cuts.

Whatever job Foyle was after in the next Tory administration he wouldn't get it; they'd hustle him into the Lords and entrust him with a commission of inquiry into doctored baby foods. Mrs Thatcher was said to favour men with balls: Foyle had none.

—Pudding?

—Just coffee. Unless they've got a good Brie.

—Time's not on our side, Leonard. The Socialist Government's refusal to send observers to cover the Rhodesian election is simply criminal pandering to Marxist terrorism.

The terrorists had brought down two Viscount airliners, the most recent only six weeks ago. Stern had driven up to Kariba and filed a long despatch proving that the female survivors had not as reported been raped before they were murdered. Stern had taken the trouble to track down the consultant doctor who'd examined the corpses. Tanner had been grudgingly impressed but Foyle's indignation boiled over yet again: the white women *had* been savagely raped by Communist terrorists and that was that. A strained, paper-thin sleep crept under Tanner's aching skull. Gravity, thirty-two feet per second per second, masking its lazy smile beneath the mute brown skin of Africa, master of all living things and dead ones too, fallen trees, raped women, foreign editors, sucking them down into manure, coal, oil. Swinging from the msasa trees, the baboons watch the sunlight glinting on the falling metal wings, waiting for the Boer stewardess with her long white legs.

Tanner could hear the priest's funeral oration. 'God is not angry with us. Sometimes He is exasperated. Sometimes He blames himself. But really God is saying to us, whatever you do, you can count on me. In death as in life, in the life after life. God is always saying, "I'm your Best Friend." ' Tanner wasn't sure which he despised more: the evangelicals who made God up day by day, or the new liberation theology peddled by Stern's contacts in the Catholic Church. People couldn't utter any banality without prefacing it, 'Speaking as a Christian . . .' Selwyn Foyle was always doing it. And, of course, Tanner's brother Gerald, well, a priest was entitled to his pretensions as well as his pittance.

'Nobody works in Britain unless they have to,' one of the women said.

'There isn't a single white doctor left in the National Health Service.'

Such talk irritated Tanner. Well, everything did. He had a mind to snap round and unload two sharp sentences on these bigoted colonial memsahibs but his neck declined. Hold your fire for Dr Stern, you'll need it. Tanner studied the rectangle of greyish cardboard, form IF.IA, he was required to present to immigration. All non-African adult males were obliged to indicate their security force commitment (Army, Police, Internal Security or Other), together with their service number, unit and station. Tanner put a line through the lot. Four boxes, one of which had to be ticked, demanded to know how long he had been away from Rhodesia and for what reason. He scrawled 'non-resident'.

The two women moved on to black servants.

'They'll always mistake too much kindness for weakness.'

'That's just it. Double their wages and who'll have a job?'

'My cookboy lost his hut in a fire. I fished around in some cupboards and fitted him out, you know, clothes for his wife and kids. Then he comes and "meddems" me: he wants a loan as well. He needs this, his wife needs that. I told him, "Go to hell, Benjamin." '

The captain came on the intercom to announce their imminent descent into Salisbury. Tanner experienced a flush of panic and looked about him shiftily, reading the tense faces of his fellow-passengers, including three black businessmen whose thoughts and allegiances you could never fathom. Muzorewa men, Nkomo men, Mugabe men? – they'd probably back whichever horse came in first. Gloomily Tanner watched the two long-legged stewardesses strap themselves in, knees pressed together, folding their fascinating bodies forward in an exemplary safety posture (did the dark one carry a touch of the tar brush or just sun tan? which of them would he most like to upend?). The question had no sooner begun to bend into familiar cravings when –

–he parted company with his stomach. The plane plummeted like a stone. His well-travelled ears screamed with pain and he tried to swallow rapidly, aware that the corkscrewing airliner was now descending through the most dangerous altitude, and there was Stern on the airport observation platform, his eyes hungry for the flash, the explosion, already composing his report about unidentified bodies charred beyond recognition, burying Tanner, the man who'd given him his job and shielded him against intolerable pressures, in a short, sarcastic sentence.

The plane levelled. Tanner's screaming ears eased. He could see Salisbury now – the same swimming pools, rectangular and kidney-shaped, and the same matchbox townships, as Joburg. From the air the city looked like an architect's model of Basingstoke dropped at random into the African plain.

'Home!' cried the two women behind him simultaneously as the wheels touched the runway with a white pilot's competence. The passengers began to clap, like Israelis. Tanner didn't clap. He loathed new countries.

SEVENTEEN

Richard Stern parked his battered Volkswagen in the front driveway of a large house in the Salisbury suburb of Avondale. Extracting his long, awkward limbs from the cramped beetle, his damp shirt clinging to his back, he cast a wary glance at the Special Branch car parked across the road in the shade of a flame tree, then took out his notebook and noted down its registration number. Futile games for boys, Dr Clausewitz, but it eased him. Yah.

His large feet crunching on the gravel, Stern approached the house with the air of one for whom it is no comfort to find the world ready-made. He could hear lunchtime laughter from the stoep at the back, a splash and shout from the swimming pool – every evening Paul Meyer lovingly scattered chemicals across the water, every morning his 'garden boy' spent half an hour scraping away nascent algae. When Stern walked through the french windows of the living room, ignoring the precious collection of Shona sculptures, he would find his host half-naked in a Sundowner easy chair, his goatee beard lifted in greeting, his mouth crammed with chicken salad.

'Dick! I was telling Berny that white Salisbury has a higher ratio of swimming pools per home than any place outside of Florida and California.'

On disclosing revelatory information – how the goons broke the Detroit automobile strike, how a 'stoolie' called Roy Brewer smashed union resistance to the studio moguls in Hollywood – Paul tended to clinch his point by thumping his right fist into his cupped left hand: smack. But somehow Stern never quite heard the smack.

Bernard Holzheimer winked at Stern behind his John Lennon spectacles.

'Paul's proud of all those swimming pools – and he tells us he's a Marxist.'

'I am.' Paul stuffed pastrami in his mouth, dabbing at his goatee beard with a paper napkin. A thick mat of sodden hair clinging to his chest and back like seaweed indicated that he had only recently emerged from the pool. Jane Meyer bustled forward, her heavy sun-braised limbs overspilling her swimsuit, to kiss Stern on the mouth.

'I know you'd rather it was my daughter.'

As usual the stoep was overcrowded. Guests would come and go throughout a Meyer Sunday, exchanging gossip, sharpening knives, servicing escape hatches and monitoring the smallest vibrations in the political weather. Stern nodded to a couple of black journalists he knew, devious cats soft-treading the hot tin roof, the younger of whom was Oscar Mucheche, once the best mixer of molotov cocktails in the London School of Economics. Grinning, Oscar took Stern by the elbow, drawing him aside:

'Did you hear, Richard?'

'Did I hear?'

'This afternoon Bishop Muzorewa will inform a rally of ten million people in Highfield that Ian Smith is a reliable sort of bloke with no funny ideas any more.'

Holzheimer sidled in on the game. 'President Jimmy Carter today told newsmen in Washington that his policy on Rhodesia would continue to be guided by double standards, hypocrisy and whatever the Kremlin told him to do next.'

Oscar Mucheche chuckled, eyes swivelling.

Stern didn't understand the many faces of Oscar Mucheche, who could crack jokes about 'the organ grinder's monkey' one day and publish an article in the *Herald* predicting an immense election victory for the Bishop on the next.

Stern's jaundiced eye travelled to the regular platoon of white liberals stuffing themselves on Jane's canapés and vol au vents while lamenting malnutrition and bilharzia in the squatter camps ringing the city. Scattered around the stoep was a token African presence, black 'internals', businessmen, lawyers, politicians, all perspiring for a puppet's portion of power. Their presence was Paul's insurance against the vagaries of history (—Though you and I are Marxists enough, Dick, to know where it all must end.)

Jane was fussing. 'Eat, Dick.'

Stern helped himself to a spoonful of rice salad.

'I said eat!'

'Be human for an hour,' Holzheimer said.

Paul regarded Stern with the slow sad gaze of a St Bernard.

'Have yaself a drink, Dick, it's all on the trolley. Didya see the SB car across the road?'

Stern nodded.

'This can't go on. It's pure Kafka. They won't track down Esther by sitting outside my house. I'll tell ya something. I first read Kafka when I began to take on Federal loyalty-security cases, furtive, shrunken men who crept into my office begging me to tell them what they'd done wrong. But how could I tell them? "I'm not a shrink." I said, "*You* tell *me*." Then I started to read *The Trial* and began to offload my lawyer's training. "Just talk," I advised them, "go back to the beginning, the womb if possible. Try to remember whoya beat up whenya was eight years old, whoya dated in High School, who was jealous, every club ya joined, didya ever write an essay about Russia, didya collect negro jazz records or foreign clothes? – everything." I became a shrink.'

'Bad times,' Holzheimer murmured politely. 'Still siphoning funds into Botswana, Paul?

'Hey, Berny, what kinda thing is that to say – on my own stoep?'

'Berny stoops to conquer,' Stern murmured.

'I never made a cent out of those loyalty-security cases. A man dismissed under Executive Order 9835 was dead and buried – no one would touch him. My normal fee was forty an hour but those poor sods got me for twenty.'

Reluctantly Stern appraised the guests he detested. He nodded in response to Frieda Hersh's effusive frog-smile. He nodded to Professor Vishnu Desai. He almost nodded to Patrick Warner's permanently empty wine glass.

'And when does the great Tanner arrive?' Warner inquired.

'Tomorrow.'

'Tomorrow may never come,' Berny Holzheimer said.

'Richard is at odds with the spirit of the age,' Vishnu Desai announced, refolding his sharply creased legs. Stern turned eyes like chestnuts fresh from the husk on the 'Ayshun' professor, Muzorewa's controller of the privy purse, who exuded a hot odour of nascent power, as pungent as garlic.

'So was Thomas Mann.'

'Was what?'

'At odds with the spirit of the age.'

'But he could write,' Warner said. 'Sorry, that was unforgivable.'

'Naughty boys,' said Frieda Hersh, tented in her khaki jumpsuit, poised to fly to a cull in the tribal trust lands at a moment's notice.

'And how is your naughty husband, the naughty general?' Warner asked her. 'Still plotting to lock himself in the loo when they come for him?'

'Look at Dick,' Paul said, suddenly aggressive. 'Like a clam in an icebox. Generous only with contempt. He despises us all.'

'That's right,' said Holzheimer. 'He should be like me. I smile a lot. I crack jokes. I never put a man down. I agree with everyone.'

'How's life up the Bishop's rectum?' Stern asked Desai.

Desai leapt up, quivering. 'You will not speak like that! I will not be insulted!'

'It was intended as a compliment,' Holzheimer said. 'Richard can't like a man unless he's covered in shit.'

Alarmed, Paul pulled himself out of the Sundowner.

'Boys, boys, ya guests in my house! I have a Special Branch car parked permanently outside my front gate. Whatya trying to do to me?'

Stern had long wondered why the Meyers entertained people like Desai and Frieda Hersh, Esther's mortal enemies.

'You wait,' Desai jabbed a finger at Stern. 'The US Senate will support us. The OAU will support us. And, when Mrs Thatcher comes to power in your country, she too will support our fight against terrorism.'

'You left South Africa out of your supporters' club.'

'Don't be clever with me. The South Africans are pragmatists, they understand the realities of black Africa.'

Clearly Professor Vishnu Desai did not yet know what had happened in Bulawayo the previous week. His insults were merely routine. Stern wondered whether Desai would be able to identify Cubans Urimbo.

Who was Cubans Urimbo?

Although Stern kept the door of his Baines Avenue flat locked, Cubans was leaning over his bed, shaking him, shortly before dawn. Isaac must have let him in – Isaac who combined servility, truculence and idleness in equal proportions; Isaac who said 'Yes, master,' as if about to cut your throat, yet stayed up all night, fretting, if Stern returned late: 'I think those Special Branch get you, Richard.' Normally it was via Isaac that Cubans Urimbo conveyed his cryptic messages.

'How the hell did you get in?'

'Let's go, Stern, we're not keeping African time today.'

'Go where?'

'Somebody wants to see you in Bulawayo. We'll take your car, I'm short of a wagon.'

Stern's car was parked peacefully between the trees of Baines Avenue, but as usual he began the day by checking the boot and looking under the bonnet. Cubans observed this ritual with disdain, despite the bombs that had killed Herbert Chitepo and Jason Moyo.

'If they have your number, they'll dial it.'

Fifty minutes later, as they passed through the European farming land round Hartley, Stern was reflecting on the peculiar sense of security he enjoyed when travelling with Cubans. They would not be ambushed on the road, surely Cubans could not be mau-maued by his own guerrilla comrades. Irrational, of course, like hanging a monkey's tail in the rear window, but potent.

'Who are we meeting, Cubans? Who is "somebody" today?'

'Need to know.' he drawled, his favourite phrase, though challenged by 'no problem'. They both recognised that there was only one 'somebody' in Stern's imagination just as they both knew that a wild goose must continue to fly so long as its arching throat was fed with scraps of paper showing a child's sailing boat bobbing across a pond. The foresail of the boat was invariably inscribed 'E' but there was no indication of the goose-shit ringing the pond. When Stern, exasperated by another futile and fuel-expensive chase, accused Cubans of forgery, the African shrugged on his cigar and came back a week later with a drawing showing a stick-like man holding a book called *Loyalty*.

Cubans was not known in Salisbury. He had surfaced in Stern's life, both dolphin and shark, like a personal message which declined to de-code itself. He vanished for long periods, his purposes unknown. He was Stern's secret – even from Holzheimer. One evening Stern believed he had seen Cubans slipping away through the Meyers' garden but it might have been an illusion of twilight.

Normally he dressed in civilian clothes but occasionally he sported plain brown camouflage fatigues – not the tigerish version he'd worn while chauffeuring Esther and accumulating traffic offences in Geneva. Cubans seemed surprised, even disconcerted, when Stern recalled having met him in that ghastly city.

'I thought a black man was invisible,' he murmured.

A man of many faces, he carried a perfect identity document, the dreaded 'situpa', and a small business card announcing himself as a 'representative' of a catering firm. A man of many contradictions. Bursts of energy alternated with drifting lethargy, revolutionary passion with chilling cynicism. On one occasion he casually claimed credit for having destroyed Salisbury's oil storage depots in December 1978, but when Stern asked him for details of the operation he withdrew into his shell: 'Man, don't believe everything I tell you.' His only point of insistence with Stern was that he came on Esther's behalf. Yet he rarely spoke of her; only under pressure did she surface in his conversation at all.

Cubans had been at Chimoio, in Mozambique, during the devastating Rhodesian air raids. He also claimed to have been in prison but immediately became vague about the details. Born in Sakubva township, Umtali, the son of a railway worker, Category E, a paid-up member of the black Associated Workers' Union, Cubans bitterly recalled that his father had made all the grades – stoker, fireman, even shunter – except mainline engine driver: that honour was reserved for 'whiteys from Rugby and Crewe'. And that, Cubans explained, was one reason why he had regularly blown up the Umtali line north of Melsetter.

—You didn't read about it? Man, Rhodesian censorship is efficient.

Cubans himself had never had much education, 'just Grade 7 then out', yet his conversation often seemed that of a highly educated man and when he recalled his trips abroad to Prague, Berlin and Moscow there were oddly assured references to Pushkin and Kafka. His physical competence was beyond doubt. During one trip together they came across an ugly accident – a bus had overturned, spilling injured passengers across the road. Cubans immediately took command, classifying injuries, shouting instructions, ripping clothes into bandages and makeshift tourniquets. But when the first police car came on the scene Cubans skilfully receded into the African landscape. 'Let's go', he murmured. Stern complimented him on his medical skills. He shrugged: 'Guerrilla training.' When Stern mentioned Esther's letter to her parents with its appalling description of field surgery without anaesthetics in the camps of Mozambique, Cubans gave him a look on a slow burn.

Did he know Esther's parents? Cubans nodded. 'They're being squeezed at both ends,' was his only comment. He despised the Bishop from the gut and was corrosive about the 'Uncle Toms shining Smith's shoes'. Desai and Frieda Hersh, he growled, would both 'hang on the same day'.

When bored, as on a long car journey, he would try to explain Zimbabwe to the ignorant British journalist.

—We're not a rational people, Stern. We don't want to be rational.

—Oh?

—Listen, man, many years ago the spirit of Mbuya Nehanda spoke to me personally through a great medium in Mazoe. My father took me there to hear that voice.

—What did Nehanda tell you?

—Aaah . . . rational again. That spirit cannot speak to white people.

175

Stern often probed further: was he married?

—Yes.

—Where does your wife live?

—With me.

—Which prison were you in?

—One of your prisons. He chuckled malevolently.

Approaching Que Que, Stern announced that he was hungry. Cubans shrugged: he had the stomach of a camel, he had fought the Rhodesians at Chimoio, in Mozambique, where rats were a luxury and a baboon a feast. Stern drove into a modern shopping precinct, scraped the VW's entrails on a speed ramp, and came to a halt outside a smart little café with a Hans Christian Andersen tiled roof and Tudor window panes.

Cubans groaned. 'Oh whitey. All I need is to see a picture of snow-capped mountains or Eskimos fishing through holes in the ice.'

Cubans had seen plenty if you believed only a quarter of it. Prague, East Berlin, Stockholm. He had stood on the promontory of Havana harbour watching the daily Soviet supply ship slip past the fortress of La Punta. The Cubans had wanted to know why he was called Cubans; he had asked them why Che was called Che. But now Cubans recoiled before a quaint little Que Que café called 'The Elizabeth'.

Swatting his inhibitions, Cubans climbed out of the car, stretched his muscular limbs, stuck a cigar in his mouth, and entered the café like an outlaw stepping into a saloon full of sheriffs, scanning each table slowly through mirrored glasses.

'Door didn't tinkle,' he said loudly to Stern who followed behind, tense as a telegraph pole, dark hair drifting in lank strands round his pale, suspicious face.

'The Elizabeth' fell quiet. The young housewives enjoying morning coffee stared. Two travelling salesmen began to wipe their mouths with paper napkins.

'No man likes to defend civilisation with crumbs in his moustache,' Cubans said.

Behind the counter stood a middle-aged woman, worn and probably widowed, lines of drudgery etched into poor-white gentility, the sort of woman whose good-time daughter dumped an illegitimate baby on her before taking off for Salisbury or Durban. Behind her an old black with the cropped head and dungarees of a racial convict was slowly mopping the formica counter-top and keeping the chrome tea express steaming. Hands in pockets, Cubans examined the sad selection of sandwiches and salads displayed, in plastic wraps, beneath a glass lid.

'Oh man,' he sighed.

The woman's pencil mouth tightened. From under the counter she produced a rectangular card: Right of Admission Reserved. Gently Cubans lifted the card from the woman's numbed hand and tore it in two, letting the pieces fall to the floor.

'Did your granny give you this, meddem? Pity I don't read English. How about you cook me a nice plate of sadza with some relish hot out of the pot?'

The young housewives with time on their hands drew their children to them. Beyond their flower-bordered lawns and neatly trimmed hedges they had at last glimpsed the spears. Their husbands had warned them. A baby perched on its mother knee also stared, a pink dummy wedged into her pink mouth, her tiny future at stake.

'The law has been changed,' Stern told the woman.

'Not in Que Que,' she said. 'If you're together I'm telling you both to leave.'

'Public Premises Act, 1978.'

One of the travelling salesman was on his feet; Stern saw Cubans's muscular body relax, a bad sign.

'Beat it.' The salesman's tanned face was blood-pulsing under a thatch of copper hair. The lady with the baby hastily gathered her shopping and hurried out. Holzheimer wandered into Stern's conscience, invisible but clearly in search of coffee. 'You set this up. Richard: defoliation of the middle ground: napalm on a village called consensus. It's called zapping the moderates. For Tanner's benefit? Why not bring in the Klan Wizard of the Rhodesian Action Party and the Prince of Parody?'

'Call the police, Betty,' one of the housewives advised the proprietress.

Cubans had wandered close to the travelling salesman.

'That moustache, boy, don't lose it.'

Stern turned his back and found himself outside 'The Elizabeth', glowering at the empty supermarket trolleys by the parking lot, ear cocked for police sirens. His cowardice had found wing in indignation – didn't Cubans appreciate that it was Stern who was the more vulnerable to reprisal?

They drove out of Que Que in silence. Stern was no longer hungry.

As they entered the avenues of Bulawayo, wide enough to turn the proverbial ox-wagon, Cubans tensed. This was a foreign city to him, more foreign than London, Prague or Berlin. Every black face on the sidewalk carried the same secret: Nkomo.

'Watch your tail,' he murmured.

'I can do that any day in Salisbury. I've driven four hundred kilometres, remember, and spent a fortune on petrol.'

Even so he glanced in his mirror. For fifteen minutes, at Cubans's insistence, they prowled the city aimlessly, waiting for a tail, Stern's temper rising, his shirt glued to his back, the blood gone from his legs. But he knew that what stretched his temper was not fatigue, hunger or danger: it was the little boat bobbing on the lake and the book marked 'Loyalty' – a choking love grown all-consuming on two years' deprivation.

It came out, somewhere between Main Street and Lobengula.

'You know I love her. You're a bastard to trade on that.'

Cubans needed time to think about this; he had grown accustomed to the tall Englishman's suffocating inhibition and self-denial. And he rather despised Stern's patient cultivation of Esther's parents; you don't sniff a woman's heat under her daddy's armpits.

'OK,' he said eventually, with a hint of contrition.

At the corner of Sixth and Fort they parked, entering the first floor of a modern concrete building by an outside staircase. The reception area was piled with identical parcels, neatly labelled. Stern stooped to look: political prisoners.

'Khami and Wha Wha,' Cubans murmured. 'I was in Wha Wha.'

Stern didn't make the connection; he had grown professionally sceptical of the man's casual claims. Cubans even repeated it, as if tired of the charade, but he couldn't bring himself to fry a fish which refused to bite. An electronically controlled door swung open before them: waiting in a windowless corridor was a small, hunched figure nodding and nodding, as if his exaggerated head was on a spring. The man had no neck.

'So you came,' he said.

He led them into a well-furnished office, leather and chrome, bare of papers, gleaming. The man sat behind his desk, his weighted head lolling to one side, his carefully folded hands vibrating.

'Obviously you are interested in our work here,' he said politely to Stern. 'But I must be cautious, you understand. Only last week our chairman was deported. Thrown out, yes. I can, however, inform you that we currently supply food, blankets and correspondence courses to 720 political prisoners. And legal advice, when possible.'

Cubans was looking out of the window, dreaming.

'All detained without trial?' Stern asked.

'Not all. In Khami they keep one thousand men convicted of

178

"terrorism" by the courts. We cannot reach those men – no food parcels, no jerseys or blankets for the winter months, no visits from relatives.'

'May I take notes?' Stern asked. His stomach ached for food.

The misshapen man didn't seem to hear. Slowly he rose from behind his desk, limb by limb, wrestling with gravity, to pluck a handsomely bound volume from the shelf above his locked filing cabinet. Ceremonially he placed it in Stern's lap, open at a centre-spread of old photographs showing white Pioneers in broad-brimmed hats standing beneath high, spreading trees, arms akimbo. From the lower branches, limp as hung game, swung the last of the Ndebele rebels of 1896, naked except for their loincloths.

'You're looking at my father's father,' the man said. 'My father, now eighty-six years old, was four when they hanged my grand-father. He was allowed to watch – he can still describe the photographer's grave expression.'

'These things still happen,' Stern said. 'I've seen it.'

Cubans turned from the window as if coming out of hibernation.

'That was the story your boss in London spiked?'

'One of them, yes.'

'Stern, you work for the wrong newspaper. We're wasting our time on you.'

But their host demurred. 'The central committee prefers to get one story out of three into a national newspaper than three out of three in some progressive periodical.'

Stern bridled. 'Which central committee?'

'In my case, Zapu. I am of course proud to belong to the Ndebele nation which has been pillaged, denuded and raped by the white man.' He glanced cautiously at Cubans. 'But of course,' he added, 'under Lobengula we were great raiders and thieves ourselves – Comrade Urimbo will tell you that. Now the liberation struggle has brought Shona and Ndebele together – is that not so, Cubans?'

'Yeah.'

'So you want to meet Esther?'

The remark was directed at Stern but without audible shift of pace or emphasis; the man was pacing the interview with the irritating metronomic control of a doctor.

'Yes.' Stern's fingers were rigidly interlocked.

'She was here.' A hint of reproach.

'When?'

'Yesterday pee emm. She thought you were coming yesterday.' The tone was now curt, accusatory. The code of hospitality had dictated the initial courtesies.

Cubans nodded in grudging admission.

'There were problems.'

179

'I think you may be able to locate Esther,' said the man without a neck, 'it is just possible.' He murmured an indecipherable name to Cubans: a person? a place? Hot air blasted off the streets and buildings as they descended the outside staircase. A blue Renault was double-parked, fifty yards away, beside Stern's exhausted VW. Cubans read the scenario through mirrored glasses; he wasn't at home in Matabeleland.

'I'll take a walk,' he said. 'You'll find me in Desai's shoe store at the corner of Main and Eighth. If they tail you, forget it.'

Cubans could cover a lot of ground in a few seconds without seeming to hurry. Two pairs of eyes watched Stern's approach, one white, one black. Neither man moved. Both were smoking. A secret policeman's day is in no hurry. The white one was of skeletal leanness, as if suffering from a wasting disease, with petals of hair plastered forward over his blotchy forehead. A livid scar ran across his cheek, ten stitches long. Call him Cassius. For a foolhardy fraction of a second Stern rested his hands on the roof of their car – the blisters later gave him trouble for a week – and politely asked them to move.

'Mr Richard Stern?' Cassius asked.

The sound of his name activated a familiar twinge of guilt – even an illegal régime asserts its own twisted moral authority.

Cassius tossed a cigarette end out of the window. 'What is the purpose of your journey to Bulawayo?'

'Identify yourself,' Stern said.

Cassius didn't like that, they never do. It threatens to shrink indiscriminate power to the vexatious paragraphs of the rule book. A name strips Authority down to a mortgage and a rotting marriage. It diminishes. The journalist walked to the front of the Renault and noted down the registration number, taking care to memorise it. One can lose notebooks in such company. A night in the cells of Stops Camp under interrogation would certainly be a story although – as Holzheimer liked to point out – a week would be rather a long story and after a month it might never get written.

Cassius lit a new cigarette. The hands that cradled the flame were not steady.

'Frankly, I'm doing you a favour,' he said. 'Isn't that right, Ciphas?' (The black one nodded gravely.) 'Know what I reckon, Mr Stern? Every fucking Brit reporter in this country is worth a thousand terrs to Nkomo and Mugabe.'

Stern waited.

'What did Nyathi tell you?'

'Who?'

'You've just spent an hour in there with the fucking Reverend fucking Elias fucking Nyathi, the great charity front man – if he's a Baptist I'm a baboon.'

Cassius casually lent out of his car like a man-eating plant and grabbed Stern by the shirt.

'Where is she?'

'Paws off, shitface.'

'This is a lovely city we have here, Mr Stern, and we don't like bad language – or motherfucking cunt-chasers consorting with terrorists.'

No point in complimenting him on his breath, the afternoon was ticking away. After more small talk, during which Cassius unfolded the world conspiracy against Rhodesia – not overlooking the tie-in between the Rockefellers and the Kremlin – Stern was free to drive to the Desai shoe store without even a tin can tied to his tail. Maybe they didn't need new shoes today. As soon as he entered a tall, leggy Coloured girl gestured towards a back doorway curtained in beads, beyond which he found Cubans slouched in a chair, feet up on Mr Desai's invoice-littered desk, counting huge piles of money while Vishnu's uncle stammered protests with the confidence of a Ugandan Asian honoured by a visit from Idi Amin. In plain English, the afternoon was beginning to resemble a clover-leaf flyover designed by Dr Caligari.

Uncle Desai's expression told Stern that where there is a white man there is hope.

'Good afternoon to you, sir, I believe you are acquainted with my nephew, Professor Vishnu Desai. To be perfectly frank, sir, all this is highly irregular. Of course the Desais give generously to the Beeshop's campaign fund. No stinting! One wears one's elbows out through thick and thin and one does stint at the end of the day. Now I must ask you, sir, this gentleman here, is he really authorised by my nephew to empty my safe? I only ask. These are troubled times for all of us. Frankly, I'm in no hurry to kick the bucket. We Desais have always supported the liberation struggle – I assume, sir, you are not averse to the liberation struggle? We are not Jew-boys. But a businessman has expenses. Downtown I paid rent of forty dollars a month – here I must pay ten times that amount. Big outlay, you see. My worries not your problem, understood. I could offer you some tea but these Coloured girls, when I ask them to make it, tell me they're not my bloody wife.'

Mr Desai trembled. Cubans glanced at him like a panther astride its goat. Anxiety continued to propel Mr Desai's tongue.

'I tell them, "That is hardly the spirit of the internal settlement," but they don't listen, too busy painting their faces in the mirror.'

'That's three thousand,' Cubans growled, dropping cigar ash on the linoleum.

'Yes, yes, three thousand.'

'Vishnu wants five.'

'Five!' Mr Desai looked appealingly to Stern. 'Of course Vishnu was always a brilliant boy. We have to be proud of him, so close to the Beeshop. You are acquainted with my nephew?' he asked Stern again, aware that this question had never been answered.

'I'm writing a feature article about him for a London newspaper,' Stern said.

Mr Desai sighed. 'Well, of course, in that case . . .'

Cubans stirred restlessly. 'The Bishop will hold a rally in this city on Monday week. Nkomo's boys will try to break it up. They'll also try to break every Ayshun shop window in town. You'll need protection – we're bussing in three hundred Pfumo reVanhu. That costs money. I spoke to the Bishop and your nephew yesterday.'

'But . . . but my nephew would telephone me!' wailed Mr Desai, his words travelling up the narrowing funnel of his solvency.

Cubans shook his head. 'Security.'

Mr Desai opened his safe again and they drove out of town past the great railway marshalling yards, through the western industrial suburbs, tail clean. Cubans, still jumpy, demanded a full report of Stern's interlude with Cassius and Ciphas. 'These Ndebeles. Thick.' He snorted disparagingly. 'A white Rhodesian is either a Shona or a Ndebele. We have a word: *"machuwachuwa"* for the way these bastard sons of Lobengula walk along, chuh-chug-chug. Not educated. They all think Nkomo will be king of Zimbabwe. No way. *Pasi nevanematumbu!* You understand?'

'Down with big stomachs?'

Delighted, he slapped Stern on the shoulder. 'Man, you're learning. There's hope for you yet.'

'I don't, of course, inquire where we're going?'

'To see Esther. Like Nyathi said. Not that I trust Nyathi. Esther trusts him. I have bad vibes when she comes down here. She'll give Desai's five thousand to the sisters looking after Ndebele war orphans. We have our own war orphans. Take the first right.'

They had been drifting through the black townships, watching the mirror, Mpopma, Mabutweni, Njube, and now Entumbane, rows of identical dwellings set out like army barracks with set-square and ruler in streets so finely meshed that there was no space to name them on the Surveyor-General's largest maps, scale 1:33,333. They passed the police station, walled and wired against insurrection, its high radio mast passing messages siphoned out of the city's intricate network of black informers. The Superintendent's building bore the same grim aspect: a fortress, every official vehicle corralled behind bolted gates. The helmeted guard ambled

182

forward, saw the colour of Stern's skin, and opened the gate with a lazy salute.

The Superintendent greeted them in a bare office smelling of carbolic, its windows covered in anti-grenade mesh. The wall behind his desk was bare – someone had removed the statutory photograph of Ian Smith.

'So how do you find Bulawayo?' the Superintendent asked Stern.

'It's a fine city.'

'It was a fine city in Lobengula's time and one day it will again be a fine city. Are you aware these townships receive no funds from the white ratepayers of Bulawayo? Did anyone inform you that the industrial areas pay their rents and rates to the white City Treasury? But who works in those factories? Who provides the labour power?'

'May I take notes?' Stern was already familiar with the municipal system and the last thing pressing on his heart now was rents and rates. The camel envied the rich man ascending to heaven.

The Superintendent shrugged. 'I don't care. I've always spoken my mind.' He turned to Cubans: 'Do *they* know you're here?'

Cubans jerked his dead cigar. 'We lost them.'

'In Bulawayo you never lose them, Comrade.'

Stern felt the tension rising between the two blacks – the comment about Lobengula had been a provocation and Cubans was not at his best when provoked.

'You're a journalist?' the Superintendent asked Stern.

'Yes.'

'You're looking for Esther?'

'Yes.'

'So are the Special Branch. They come here to the townships offering money for information, sometimes five hundred dollars, sometimes more – it depends whether their wives gave them a hard time in bed the previous night. We have one white character called Symonds. He carries a long scar on his cheek from a bar brawl in Joburg. His wife ran off to London with an airline pilot – I wouldn't want Esther to fall into the hands of that man.'

'I don't work for Special Branch.'

But the Superintendent was implacable. A column of soldier ants paraded across the polished ebony of his handsome features.

'They abducted my wife up at Tsholotsho to put the screws on me. I lodged a complaint with the Commissioner of Police. He promised to find my wife. That was four months ago. If I give them Esther, they'll give me back my wife.'

Cubans stirred uneasily. At that moment it came inescapably to Stern that Cubans didn't want him to find Esther – neither today nor any other day.

'You're white,' the Superintendent told Stern. 'Don't tell me Esther is white. In our churches you will nowadays find many paintings of a black Jesus.'

Stern said. 'I'm deeply moved by what you say. I wouldn't want to add to her dangers. And I'm sorry about your poor wife. I hope she's a brave woman.'

The Superintendent assessed him. 'Are you a Christian?'

'No.'

'But you speak like a Christian. The afternoon is late, it's almost dark, we'll make you an honorary Christian for the rest of this day.'

They followed the Superintendent's car through Entumbane and across the city as the great glowing fireball of the sun slid down the western sky, and the packed buses and 'emergency taxis' ran their human cargoes from the city centre and the industrial estates back to the townships in thick clouds of diesel fumes. In a darkened street the Superintendent had squeezed his car into the tiny back-yard of a two-room dwelling. A dog barked angrily, as if chained; the night air smelt of woodsmoke and frying chicken. Stern's pulse began to race.

'This is my house,' the Superintendent murmured. 'We will walk from here. Follow me at a distance of twenty yards. No closer. If I stop and bend to re-tie my shoe, turn back.'

They walked under a vast sky bejewelled by the Southern Cross, shadowed only by slow, sniffing dogs and the soft crunch of their own feet on gravel and dried mud, until they saw the Superintendent enter a humble brick building which turned out to have a crucifix above the door. A single electric bulb, unshaded, hung from the tin roof. There was no ceiling and no altar, no pulpit, just three prayer pews at the front and the rest clean-swept floor.

The Superintendent knelt in the front pew and closed his eyes. His heavy lips moved soundlessly through a long prayer until he said aloud, 'O Lord, have mercy upon these your children,' and rose to his feet. They waited in silence for half an hour until there was a scratching on the church door and a small boy, identical in age and frail, stubborn energy to the one Stern had seen hanged from a tree, entered timidly, the single light bulb reflected in his wide saucer eyes. The boy whispered in rapid, urgent Ndebele to the Superintendent, then vanished into the night.

So ghastly was the Superintendent's expression that for a moment Stern was convinced the boy had brought him terrible news of his kidnapped wife from Tsholotsho.

'They have been at my house – the Special Branch. Now they're on their way here. We have been betrayed.'

'Shit,' Cubans said.

184

'This is a house of God!' protested the handsome Ndebele Superintendent, close to tears. Stern gently took his arm, wishing now that he knew the man's name.

'Where is Esther?'

'Coming here, here, here!'

A public schoolboy despite himself, Stern was probably sick of being led. He was acquainted with Che's Bolivian diaries and knew that life in bad places often approaches bad art. 'Faced with this serious matter, I called Inti and Rolando. They confirmed that bad feeling existed in the advance party due to Marcos's temper, but they also reported some of Pacho's indiscretions.' So Stern now issued the orders.

'Then wait outside, both of you. Conceal yourselves. Intercept Esther, get her away from here, without fail. I'll entertain Symonds. Go, go!'

Cubans and the Superintendent looked at him, then ran.

Heart thudding, he found a prayer book on the seat of the front pew and tried to read, to concentrate, but he hated every sententious phrase – how could she embrace such mystification, such mumbo-jumbo? He heard a car skid to a halt outside and rather reluctantly turned to face the door.

Cassius strolled in followed by Ciphas.

'Alone?' he asked Stern.

'Yes . . . no.'

'In Bulawayo, Mr Stern, it's either yes or no.'

'I wasn't alone but I am now.'

'Waiting for Esther?'

Stern shrugged.

In the silence that followed he heard the distant approach of another vehicle. The Special Branch men glanced at one another and drew their revolvers, flattening themselves against the wall either side of the door. The oncoming vehicle's engine, still at some distance from the church, abruptly sank to a low throb. Cassius hesitated, then moved for the door.

'I hear your wife ran off with an airline pilot,' Stern said. 'Drinking yourself to death, are you, Symonds? In your shoes I'd gap it back to Joburg and get yourself a matching scar – it's called turning the other cheek.'

The petals of hair plastered forward over Cassius's forehead now looked like transparencies woven into his sun-drugged skin by *découpage*. Stern heard the vehicle backing hastily, turning, then the skidding tyres of a rapid acceleration. Cassius and Ciphas were gone now, their own car back in the movies, leaving Stern in the empty church alone with the knowledge that after ten years Esther was at last in his debt. This sense of exaltation only gradually yielded to ravenous hunger and fear of being mugged or killed if he left the church on foot. He therefore sat down on the prayer pew and waited.

EIGHTEEN

'The British have been trying to bring one rebel farmer to heel for fourteen years,' Holzheimer was telling Professor Vishnu Desai and anyone who would listen as the guests slowly circulated on the Meyers' verandah. 'You really think they'll easily abandon sanctions and so much fun? Not everyone realises that the British are surrealists. I did time in San Francisco. I saw relief workers, Tom Wolfe's flak-catchers, begging to be mau-maued by gang leaders, acid-heads, and revolutionary studs who could hardly cross their legs for muscle. I thought: this is *it!* I was wrong. The British are an ancient civilisation, way ahead of us, more devious and fun-loving than the Egyptians. I was on this plane from Salisbury to London, right? I started talking to the guy in the next seat. With no inhibition at all he told me all about his work: Rhodesian Special Branch. I thought, this man's crazy, doesn't he know the British have a blacklist, he'll be arrested on arrival. Anyway, down we came, threading our way into Heathrow through rows of cowering semi-detached dwellings. At immigration I was put in a line stretching back to the Mediterranean: a foreigner. And my friend, the Rhodesian rebel, through he sails on a UK passport. They did ask him one question: "Where have you been, sir?" "South Africa," he said. "Thank you, sir." He threw me a last salute. "Have luck!" he called.'

'That guy's probably sitting outside this house right now,' Paul Meyer said. Listening to Holzheimer he had been pulling on a cheroot, nervously fingering his goatee beard – the man who poured the drinks.

Patrick Warner's damp eye was back on Stern. He wore his slackest smile.

'Richard, do tell us where Esther is today.'

'You're talking of my daughter,' Jane said.

187

'Warner's like a gramophone record with a single scratch from beginning to end,' Stern said. 'Anyone can buy him at a discount.'

'I fear the morrow weighs on you, dear boy. The day of reckoning. I hear that Selwyn Foyle actually took old Leonard out to lunch before his departure and handed him a pistol loaded with a single bullet.'

'You wouldn't be after Richard's job?' Holzheimer asked Warner with an uncharacteristic hint of belligerence.

'My dear Bernard, I didn't know it was a "job" – more a fanatical vocation, one gathered.'

'You two share one thing in common,' said Holzheimer. 'You both live on sufferance, demeaning yourselves by haggling over expenses, forging invoices, bumming rides off the staff correspondents. Contrast your lot to mine – Holzheimer the prince of the bottomless expense account, bouncing his pictures off satellites.'

Stern said: 'Unlike me, Warner doesn't have to beg Mike Gilson to renew his work permit every twenty-nine days. Warner never describes terrorists as guerrillas, and almost every week Combined Operations come up with a facility trip or, more happily for him, a bottle of real whisky.'

Warner retaliated:

'My dear friend Tree – who knows everything – once confided that when Richard was a boy his Momma instructed him to learn and master the piano "like Horowitz". The boy frowned, then drove his tone-deaf fingers like ten plucky oxen, determined to wrench art out of endeavour. And here he is, still frowning.'

Stern laughed to muffle the sting. He hated anyone to know about his childhood or family: he had been re-born the day he went to New College; only those of his school friends who actively pursued him were granted an audience, but they, too, eventually fell away, discouraged. Freedom is to have no friends, Nietzsche might have said, and the poetry of the 'will' had always outgunned the panting, plebeian voices of reform in Stern's imagination. But in the mid-sixties the Left held all the ladders and Stern knew it. Or so he had once confided to Holzheimer. Who had demurred:

—The Richard Stern I know and love despises opportunists.

Warner came again, irritably dangling his empty wine glass before his obtuse host.

'And tell us about your, er, wife, Richard. It must be a relief no longer to be kicked in the groin or half-nelsoned in the liberated manner of BBC–2, Wednesdays.'

'You've lost me,' Holzheimer said. 'I don't like to be lost. Nor does West 43rd Street. Explain "BBC–2, Wednesdays".'

'Self-defence for lesbians,' Warner said.

Frieda Hersh's features were set in a rictus of livid curiosity.

Her husband, the General, hated Mugabe but despised Muzorewa and planned to ride to the top of the army on the broad back of Nkomo, with British help. Desai, Muzorewa's party Treasurer, smirked: he, too, had heard the rumours about Stern's wife. Jane looked embarrassed. Paul changed the subject:

'Just look at Ronald Reagan.'

'I'm looking,' Holzheimer said. 'I see an old man with several face lifts.'

'You know, during the McCarthy era—'

'Paul, spare us,' moaned Holzheimer. 'And please don't remind me of the shameful performance of my own paper when the chips were down. I was in diapers.'

'Reagan will be the next President, Berny.'

'I stand a better chance myself.'

Jane was paddling among her guests, holding a large jug of orange juice. 'Dick, I may as well tell you – last week I came home to find a stranger in this house fiddling with the phone. He said he'd been sent to repair a fault. There was no fault.'

Paul sank into melancholy. 'This surveillance is no longer so funny. It's round the clock. I thought we'd finished with this kinda thing twenty-five years ago.'

'They want your lovely daughter,' Frieda Hersh said.

Presently Paul took Stern up to his study for the regular half-hour in the confessional. As usual, his transistor radio was murmuring in the background. Stern had once assumed that this was Paul's answer to the Special Branch, like the proverbial running bath tap, but Paul found reassurance in radio voices.

'Dick, would it astonish you to learn that Jane and I don't even share a bank account? I've never been good at sharing. Call it primal insecurity. That's why I joined the Party. For thirty years my father stood all day over a steaming iron in a West Side factory. His body was covered in blisters and he brought home twelve, fifteen dollars a week. He always gave a dollar or two to the Party. My mother would say, "Feed your children first and save the world afterwards." '

Paul's insistent voice had the same effect on Stern as popcorn in a cinema.

Morosely Paul began fingering his treasured library of 'classics', his archive of old newspapers.

'Ever notice the smell of newsprint, Dick? Sugarsweet in America, acidic here. Here History soon stiffens, yellows and flakes like dry pastry. Heat and dust, eh? Thank God for the microfilm.'

Paul loved culture and he loved history, but the only way he could express his polymathic passion was the memory game. He was a collector; rarity was his yardstick. The early history of

Rhodesia fascinated him. Any book 'debunking' Cecil Rhodes or Dr Jameson was greeted as a masterpiece. 'That's real research.' He kept his first edition of Olive Schreiner's *Trooper Peter Haklet of Mashonaland* wrapped in oilskin – the same honour was accorded Dalton Trumbo's *The Time of the Toad*. Stern had grown to like the man; he no longer shuddered at the thought of Esther's genesis in these loins and gradually developed a respect for the qualities in Paul and Jane which had given Zimbabwe its white Joan of Arc. Paul, he recognised, was in pursuit of both happiness and virtue: in renouncing Stalinism for 'the democratic Sparticism of Rosa Luxemburg' he had also turned a lawyer's talents to the import-export trade of southern Africa. Well, why not? He could be generous, too: from time to time he lent Stern one of his cars; by some fiddle he found him a new typewriter and refused even nominal payment; when Stern's 'best' pieces on the 'struggle' were spiked by Tanner or Foyle in London, without payment, Paul considered it to be his revolutionary duty to cushion the blow: 'Just a loan, Dick, but it's open ended.'

Paul's blood bond with Esther had initially thrown Stern on the defensive, but now they intermittently offered each other solace, though their voices were raised more in part-song than duet. They agreed that Esther loved people, not ideology, that she possessed a rare capacity to absorb and incarnate the sufferings of others. Talking of her, both men often came close to tears – Jane was never party to these reverential conversations behind the locked door of Paul's study. It was a three-lever lock.

Furtively Paul took down an old book from his shelves, shielding the spine from Stern's scrutiny.

'Hey, Dick, who wrote this?: "I am sick of shooting pheasants and partridges, and want to have a go at some large game again. I am dead tired of doing nothing except playing the squire in a country that is sick of squires." ' Paul looked up with an expression of intense, almost trembling, expectation 'That's the whole colonial syndrome.'

'Minus the economics.'

'Oh sure. Minus the economics. You're playing for time. You pass?'

'It was Rider Haggard.'

Paul's features broke like an egg. 'Yeah.' He sniffed. 'Now I'm quoting from memory. Who wrote: "A wise man is he who knows what he doesn't know"?'

'Plato. Paraphrased.'

Paul guffawed. 'Plato! It was the old master, Socrates.'

'I'm not aware that Socrates ever wrote a word. Hence his unrivalled reputation.'

Paul blinked suspiciously. 'Wanna play Scrabble?'

'You have guests downstairs.'

Paul looked crestfallen, his Sunday ruined. One by one his guests had been inveigled into his first-floor study, with its shelf of soapstone birds of Zimbabwe, its Karanga carvings, its collection of mbiras, its beautiful view of the swimming pool, the tennis court and the two avocado trees: inveigled into playing Scrabble, New York Rules, screaming.

But now Stern, like the performing seal, wanted to be fed. Paul read his gaze and nodded.

The centrepiece of the study was not a work of art but a safe of solid steel. Here Paul kept Esther's letters, lovingly filed and even cross-indexed, letters invariably posted by a comrade from some other country or continent and then opened in transit by Special Branch, sometimes discreetly with a Swiss precision instrument, sometimes truculently torn from its envelope. Paul unlocked the safe.

Clutching the latest letter, Stern was forced to sit down. If left alone, free of Paul's fussy attention, he might even have knelt and kissed the cheap airmail paper: a sacrament.

'I have been working with the comrades in a field hospital. The wounds are so dreadful and we are pitifully short of medical supplies, antibiotics, surgical instruments, anaesthetics and even bandages and gauze. Amputations are a ghastly experience – the poor victims have to be held down as in an eighteenth-century man o' war.'

But where? Of that there was never any hint. Nor any reference to himself.

'Mum, Dad, please remind all dear friends who would like to hear from me that I really cannot write without fatally compromising them.'

And passages of whiplash:

'Give my love to all white liberals who would embrace black majority rule if only it wasn't so black and so majority. They know, of course, that although "our" security forces regularly display the corpses of freedom fighters to school-children, real barbarism begins north of the Zambezi, in Caliban's kingdoms, where the bodies of enemies (and friends too popular) are tossed from the backs of trucks, their penises stuffed into their mouths, to be consumed by jackals. All very true, no doubt – but not of overwhelming relevance to the half-million Zimbabweans that Smith has put in concentration camps, or the thousands killed in refugee camps during his air-raids.'

'Right now, dearest Mum and Dad, I don't imagine I have many white friends. In the event of my sudden funeral, some would no doubt surface. In the event of a victory for the Patriotic Front – many more.'

Stern glanced, yet again, with a terrible yearning, at the two large framed photographs of Esther on Paul's wall: one on graduation day at the University, a proud parent at each shoulder, all smiles; the other, ten years later, sent from a base camp in Mozambique – Esther in camouflage fatigues, coiled in bandoliers, and sporting an AK 47 rifle. No smile. Whenever Paul caught Stern's gaze on that one he would say,—You can bet she knows how to use that gun.

The most recent letters were clearly written from inside Rhodesia. Stern was lost in longing.

Paul placed a hand on his shoulder, almost ceremoniously.

'One day you'll know what it is to be a father.'

'Don't forget your guests.'

Paul sighed and re-locked the safe. 'How's your divorce?'

'Er . . . it's off and on . . . a way of life.'

'They'll browbeat you if you let them.'

'They?'

'Listen, Dick, I was born a fighter. In my Bronx you were either a gangster or you fought the hoods; either a trade unionist or a scab; either a socialist or a fixer, a pimp. I grew up fighting. Every Sunday my father sold the *Daily Worker* down at the bus terminal, never mind the weather, snow soaking through his cheap shoes.'

'Paul, you've told me all this.'

'You want to understand Esther, don't you? You love her, don't you? Can't you see where she gets her bundle of guts from? I remember when the Garment Workers' Union called out the entire dress trade. Anyone who crossed a picket line was beyond the pale. Boy, those battles! We won that strike, Dick. Winning's important.'

He locked the study door behind him. As they descended the open-plan staircase the mid-afternoon roar of well-watered guests hit them – the people who would attend Esther's sudden funeral.

'I'm not sure you're a winner, Dick,' Paul muttered.

Stern pushed through the throng until he found Holzheimer, who blinked amiably behind his John Lennons.

'How are Tom Paine, Andrew Jackson, "Abe" Lincoln and John

Reed – or was it the Rosenbergs today, "a passion play for our Christian masters performed exclusively by Jews"?'

'Oh well.'

' "Our great heritage: the hot soup kitchen." '

'Shut up, Holz.'

'Shall I tell you the most remarkable thing about those 1950s committee rooms with their klieg lights and acoustics like indoor swimming pools? Everyone – Senators, counsel, witnesses, spectators – all wore the same double-breasted suit and the same haircut. Honestly, I've seen pictures. Lots of them. But I've never seen a picture of Paul.'

From the notebook of Richard Stern:

I first met Holzheimer in Geneva, autumn of '76. I got to Salisbury a month later but Holz didn't show up for a further year. I was waiting (and waiting) in Linquenda House one Friday afternoon to renew my monthly work permit while pert white secretaries bustled along the corridor, back and forth, leaving me to speculate about their tumultuous affairs in the suburbs – adultery and hot showers, servants arriving at seven in the morning to change the sheets and dispose of the empty bottles. These pretty creatures minced past me with the worldwide eyes-ahead of women signalling their virtue under alien male scrutiny.

As I told Holz, Beth's letters – often affectionate, always interesting, as if our dead marriage might yet ripen into friendship – had a lot to say on that subject.

'Next time you take the underground, count the number of women who let their gaze rest on a man for more than a fraction of a second. We're like hunted animals. The veil we wear is inside the mind – at least the Moslem women can shield their faces from predatory male stares.'

The Rhodesian girls despised and distrusted foreign journalists. They believed in real men, the Rhodesians working for the *Herald* or RBC whom Mike Gilson slapped on the back and accredited to accompany the security forces into the operational zones and contact areas; the most favoured flew with the SAS and Selous Scouts on hot pursuit missions across the border into Zambia and Mozambique. Feminism was not an issue for Rhodesian girls. With black communism beating at the gates there was no time for that – just high heels and have a good time while the sun shines. Their painted faces lapsed into exasperation at the sight of an African. Blacks were for ever infiltrating Linquenda House, looking for work, saucer-eyed with apprehension, shuffling in a mime of deference.

'What are you doing here, boy? Didn't you see that notice downstairs – "*Hapana basa*"?'

'No, meddem.'

'Yes you did. Don't tell me lies. Now scram before I call the boss.'

Hapana basa, no work. The only two words of Shona the white girls knew. Further north it was '*Apana kazi*'.

I had been waiting to see Gilson for more than an hour when a man with ex-hippie hair and a nose like a ski jump came bouncing along the corridor with that air of ineffable optimism American reporters affect even when facing a firing squad. He carried a leather shoulder bag that had cost a fortune.

'This place is a maze,' he told me. 'Haven't we met? Geneva, wasn't it?'

I thought: this bastard will jump the queue like all the others who had offered me feeble, apologetic shrugs when Gilson called them into his office with a meaningful glance at his watch. The Ministry of Information closed at 4.30 sharp.

Holzheimer extended his hand. 'I'm a new boy. You look unhappy.' He examined me thoughtfully through wire-rimmed glasses.

I explained my problem.

'That's because you're so good,' he said. 'They don't like you.'

Rhodesia wasn't quite on his mind yet. He'd just come down from the Horn – Ethiopia, Eritrea, Somalia – where he'd been living rough with rebel guerrillas. He referred frequently to 'the Soviets' as if that word correctly referred to human beings rather than a form of elected council.

I said: 'You'll find Rhodesia dull by comparison. No "Soviets".'

Gilson's door opened and out came a Dutch TV crew clutching their work permits but still grumbling about having been refused access to the tribal trust lands. Sweat was pouring down Gilson's face and neck: his shirt had come open at collar, chest and stomach.

'Mr Holzheimer, isn't it?'

Noisily I cleared my throat.

'This man was here first,' Holzheimer said.

Gilson looked at his watch. 'I can take only one more today. Try me on Monday, Mr Stern.'

'The *New York Times* can wait,' Holzheimer said stubbornly.

Gilson hesitated then nodded in my direction and strode to his desk.

'Be my guest,' I said to Holzheimer, holding the door open for him. 'You may find it instructive.'

Joined at that instant in the conspiracy called friendship, we both sidled in and sprawled into chairs, he without invitation. From the wall behind Gilson's desk a photograph of Ian Smith observed us with bleak displeasure, one eye closed by the second world war.

'Frankly,' Gilson began, 'the Minister is currently reviewing your case, Mr Stern. I suppose you realise you've broken every rule in the book?'

For seven years Gilson had spent half of every year in the bush, eating out of rat packs, sleeping rough, chewed by mosquitoes and tsetse flies, fighting to preserve civilised standards, to protect the farms and industries which the white man had created. He now had my file open on his desk – always an interesting interlude, the moment when all the Special Branch shadows and bugged telephones translated themselves into an indictment:

'Entering tribal trust lands without authorisation, specifically Mutasa, Weya, Tande, Makoni, Buhera, Mtoko, Nyamaropa. Making contact with terrorist sympathisers. Filing copy by mail without submitting it to the censorship authorities. Entering black townships without authorisation, specifically Chitungwiza, Highfield, Sakubva and others. Describing terrorist-infiltrated areas as "semi-liberated zones". Attributing terrorist atrocities to the security forces, specifically the Selous Scouts. Need I continue?'

I had been writing it down with sardonic attention to detail and the habitual air of superiority upon which Holz was later to congratulate me. ('You're remarkably nasty, Stern.')

'We have a war here!' Gilson banged his clenched fist on the desk, a bellow compounded of bitter winter nights, tall elephant grass with nil visibility, dirt roads strewn with landmines, the long struggle with silent, know-nothing black villagers. Gilson had a house and wife in Greendale. His father, an engine driver, had emigrated from Barnsley when Mike was five years old and settled in Bulawayo. The last stand of Captain Allan Wilson on the Shangani river (1893) was all the history Gilson needed to know.

'I've no doubt you're a very sincere man, Mr Stern. You believe you're standing up for the poor, exploited African against the rapacious white man. But can you name one black country, just one, where the average wage matches ours? Can you give me one black country where the first free election wasn't also the last?'

Holzheimer had been listening with interest. He wore an innocuous, affable, almost timid air, but he had spent two months being innocuous and affable with Eritrean insurgents under Ethiopian air attack and now he leaned forward and said, very politely: 'There are always good reasons for censorship.'

The voice of the *New York Times*. Minister Prinsloo would have to be informed. Gilson mopped his face and offered the American reporter a placatory nod:

'I know how you feel. And believe me I respect your feelings. But what we have to remind people like Mr Stern is that no ways does your African want communism in this country. What your average tribesman wants is a quiet life and a chance to mind his own business in his own kraal with his wives and *mombes*. He wants a brood of barefoot piccaninns to prove his manhood and work his fields, and a nice shaded spot to eat his mealies and relish and fall asleep when the sun gets up a bit.'

'*Mombes?*' Holzheimer asked.

'Cows,' Stern said.

'Oh. Ah – I thought it might be some kind of sub-wife or concubine.'

'I'll be perfectly honest with you, Mr Holzheimer, war is never a pretty business. I've seen things done . . . things that shouldn't be done. But your Af mistakes too much kindness for weakness. You have to show him who's boss. Firm but fair. Our Western type of democracy . . . I mean our society is based on the individual, but your average kaffir doesn't want to think for himself, he wants to conform, to follow the tribe.'

'Is all this attributable?' Holzheimer asked innocently.

'Frankly, this is background.'

Gilson mopped his bull neck with a sodden handkerchief – he had played prop forward for Mashonaland before the kids came along. Again he glowered at Stern's open file.

'Another thing.'

'Yes?'

'On the fifth of March you filed a report indicating that the terrorists have ignored Bishop Muzorewa's offer of an amnesty. Now that's simply not true. I'll be plain with you – it's a damned lie.'

'How many Zanla and Zipra guerrillas have laid down their arms?'

'For security reasons, the figure is classified.'

Stern laughed. 'How many rogues in buckram did Falstaff slay?' Gilson looked at him with blackberry eyes stewed in rhubarb, then glanced up at the official portrait of his Prime Minister, as if half-expecting to find it supplanted by a chimpanzee in a dog collar.

Gilson's secretary came in on high heels.

'Half-past four, Mr Gilson.'

'I won't be long, Sharon.'

Stern picked up the note of appeal – so the rugger bugger was having an affair. Gilson's wife, he knew, had worked as a Health Visitor in Tafara township, feeding protein cereals to war refugees and treating women for VD. She wasn't happy about Mike having to spend half the year in the bush but she didn't hold it against the blacks because she knew the terrorist war would soon be won like the papers and television said. The first time Mike was hit by an AK 47 wasn't so bad, just a flesh wound, but then her brother came home without a leg, a paraplegic for life, and suddenly it came to her that all those patient, passive black 'nannies' waiting for their protein cereal and VD shots at the clinic were brimming with concealed enmity. She began to shout at them, to scream: then she quit. She aged. She even fired both their trusted servants because she'd seen them talking to a kaffir on a bicycle who she just knew was a terr, a gook. 'Mike, I could smell the man.' When Gilson came back from the bush for his six months as a civil servant she was no fun in bed, just cried all the time.

I knew all this because the despondent Gilson had begun to haunt the bars, Meikles and the Monomotapa, confiding to the reporters he believed he could trust. So now it was Friday evening with the lovely Sharon's quick, neat buttocks up on high heels and her permed hair flowing to her shoulders – but only if he shifted. Oh women, women, the smarter scouts of that terrain.

'Mr Holzheimer, if you'll just sign these forms . . . censorship regulations, mandatory I'm afraid.'

Holzheimer looked at the forms with the indignation of a traveller required to renounce his God in order to inhabit heathen terrain.

'Mr Stern was first – he wants his work permit renewed.' Delicately he shifted his glasses up the ski jump.

Gilson shook his head. 'I must make this very clear: the Minister has Mr Stern's case under review.'

Holzheimer understood. In his young life he had arrived naked in many foreign capitals and immediately understood.

'Well,' he announced with his maddening affability, some kind of khama as if he was on a battery-charged tranquilliser, 'I've got my first story without a shot fired. Couldn't happen in Ethiopia.'

In the corridor he touched Stern's arm. 'You'll get your work permit.'

'Pax Americana?'

On the stairs Holzheimer asked: 'Married?'

'Yes. No.'

He clasped my hand. 'I know what you mean! I'm on my third but am I?'

He suggested a drink then remembered he had an appointment

with Bishop Muzorewa's press secretary. He suggested dinner then remembered he was dining with 'some guy called Meyer – the famous Esther's Daddy. In Geneva I took her for a mendacious groupie but now they say she's masterminding the whole guerrilla campaign.'

'Who but a white could do it?'

'Do I detect a note of . . . ? Do you know this man Meyer?'

'Yes, I know him.'

'Then why don't you come along?'

I liked Holzheimer but I excused myself: 'Dinner with Ian Smith.'

The eyes widened innocently behind the John Lennon spectacles. 'Really? Without a work permit?'

Holzheimer, seated on the Meyers' verandah, was holding court to an audience of white liberals, mainly ladies. Standing aloof on the fringe of the cheerful gathering, Stern was counting the hours until Tanner's arrival. There would be recriminations, no doubt, a row, but surely, after twenty-seven months, Tanner wouldn't fire him.

'Well, I adore the exotic,' Holzheimer was declaring in his high, reedy voice. 'I'm really a creature of paradise. In the manicured suburbs of Salisbury I see only Surrey in the sun. The jungle does not press upon your gardens and golf courses as in old Malaya. Tigers do not stalk forth boldly to seize your dogs – I need tigers. Pythons do not strangle your garden boy in his sleep. Malarial mosquitoes with loaded hypodermics do not whine in like Japanese bombers. There is no port where you can dance with the prettiest girls in the world or get murdered in a rickshaw. How can I live without the aroma of meat cooked in coconut oil? Please tell me – when will someone kindly win this war of yours?'

The white ladies dipped their blue-green eyelids in muted delight. Berny made a diversion from discussing whether the Seychelles were better holiday value than pre-packaged Durban, 'so lacking in local character now'. Stern was another potential diversion. Though proud never to have voted for Ian Smith, these liberal women all had husbands or sons on reserve duty in the bush and it rescued a Sunday afternoon to encounter a journalist who openly supported Public Enemy Number One, the enigmatic and reputedly fanatical Robert Mugabe.

Besides: it was common knowledge that Richard Stern had been Esther Meyer's lover (though one of many) and knew where she was to be found.

As the afternoon cooled the guests gradually withdrew from the verandah and moved into the Meyers' drawing room. Here Vishnu Desai was holding court, perched on a sofa like a swami in sharply creased sky-blue trousers and a flowing, 'Ayshun' silk shirt – the Bishop's Treasurer. A power as fragrant as freshly ground coriander radiated from the expressive gestures of his delicate hands. Desai was addressing his hostess, Jane, and Stern was observed to be listening, tall, aloof, his hair straggling in lank tails down his neck. The ladies, and even those of their husbands present, rather hoped something might happen.

'My dear Jane, if we want to preserve standards, then for God's sake let us learn the lessons of history. And what *is* the Patriotic Front if not a pantomime horse?'

'They have the peasants on their side,' Jane said simply.

'How can we know? In Africa people are led – and misled.'

'With your help,' Stern said.

He saw Paul backing away and out on to the stoep.

'Ah, the white Moslem,' Desai said in Stern's direction. 'He kneels at sunset and bows his head not to Mecca but to Moscow – or is it Peking? All Indian Moslems were originally Hindus of the untouchable caste who weren't permitted to enter the temples. The Moslems thus found their natural constituency – just as the lumpen intellectuals of England were easy prey to the Communists.'

Jane looked at Stern, as if entreating him to go easy.

'How many free suits did the Johannesburg Chamber of Commerce present to Muzorewa during his recent visit?'

Professor Desai clasped his hands in despair. 'Doctor of Philosophy, Oxford – hard to believe.'

'How many OAU countries will recognise your dog's dinner?'

'Ten have already sent us private assurances, beginning with the Ivory Coast, Senegal, Zaire and Malawi.'

'That's news,' Holzheimer interjected.

'Then report it,' Desai snapped. 'A journalist's job is to report the news, not to invent it.' He beamed at his audience.

'Game and first set to Vishnu,' said Kitty Summerbee, a society hostess famous for her lavish parties.

'Mr Stern may not be aware that politics is the art of the possible,' Desai said, recrossing his creased legs with the help of his hand. 'We must not upset the whites – white skills and white confidence are our most precious assets.'

The white reservists scattered about the room grunted their agreement like hippos wallowing in friendly mud. Slowly they drifted away, talking of tobacco auction prices, farm subsidies, the cost of fertiliser. The party broke up, reassured.

'Maggie won't let us down,' Kitty Summerbee declared.

Holzheimer shrugged at Stern. 'There you are again, a stranded island of singular perception inhabited by a lone outcast.'

Frieda Hersh was tugging at Stern's sleeve, agitated.

'Someone wants to talk you, Richard. Please be a good boy, for Frieda's sake. Please go away, he wants to kill you.'

He had been observing the man for some time out of the corner of his eye; he remembered the short, sandy hair, the archipelago of freckles, the ice-blue stare somewhere beyond reason. They had met twice before – most recently six months earlier, in the Ministry of Information. On that occasion Gilson had not kept him standing in the corridor for his monthly work permit but had led him straight to the Minister's office. The freckled man had stationed himself beside the Minister.

—You had no authority to be in Buhera, Prinsloo snapped at Stern, —let's get that quite clear at the outset.

—I had a day permit from Combined Operations.

The Minister snorted.—Mrs Hersh, you mean? Frieda flings those things about like paper handkerchiefs.

Prinsloo rose from behind his desk and walked to the window overlooking Baker Avenue and the Old Shell Building, hands in pockets, statesmanlike.

—Did you write a report of that incident, Mr Stern? We haven't had anything pass through censorship.

Stern didn't answer. He had sent the report to Tanner by post. Tanner (or Foyle – Stern would eventually find out!) had spiked it.

—Good. What you saw, you didn't see. I hope I'm making myself very clear. I'm also speaking on Mr Chamberlain's behalf – aren't I, Chris?

—Yees, Minister. The freckled man had been staring at Stern since he entered Prinsloo's office.—We haven't taken out a foreign journalist yet. There's always a first time. He didn't tap the licensed revolver at his hip; there was no need.

Stern measured his rising fear but discovered that confronting Beth and Harry in the offices of *Thought and Action* was far more dreadful.

—How's the Edinburgh Academy appeal fund? he asked Chamberlain.—You were in Cockburn, weren't you, or was it Carmichael? I noticed your name on the list of donors.

Prinsloo was jingling coins in his trousers pockets.

Six months had passed. During the interval Berny had sent Stern's spiked report to the *New York Times* and they had – miracle! – published it. Now District Commissioner Chamberlain had come looking for him, here in the home of Paul, Jane and

Esther Meyer. The pistol he carried looked at least twice as big as the last one.

NINETEEN

'Only a woman,' Frieda had explained above the roar of the
Alouette that carried them down from New Sarum Air Force
base, 'can address the women. It's a Shona taboo, Richard, and
dreadfully important. You can't imagine how Frieda loves her
poor, terrorised people. I'm their mamma, you see.'

The helicopter skimmed low over the thatched heads of the
kraals, the parched earth and wilting maize.

'Look, baboons!' she cried, raising her Leica.

Stern noted that Frieda was having a good war, accredited as
translator and photographer to the military command, the unstopp-
able wife of the country's second-ranking general, an in-and-out
war, a contact zone in the morning, back to Salisbury for further
intrigues by sundowner time. She had cultivated Stern, winking
and leering and conspiring to circumnavigate the Ministry of Information's persistent vetoes on his movements. But why? The plot
emerged in ragged fragments, hints, innuendoes – a jigsaw in no
hurry to form a picture.

A posse of white police reservists ringed the Alouette as it
touched down on the edge of the kraal, shielding their eyes against
its dust storm: Frieda's fall-out. Clerks, fitters, electricians, shop-
keepers, they weren't having a good war and Stern could feel the
hostile charge of their frayed nerves as he followed Frieda's jumpsuit jump on to the powdered earth, ducking under the still rotating
blades. Another muckraker from Meikles.

The villagers had been assembled under the shade of thorn and
mopani trees, men and women in separate congregations. In all
probability they had been waiting since dawn for the Boss to leave
his footprint on their long-suffering hectare. Any day now they
might be cleared out of their huts at an hour's notice, 'uplifted'
into army trucks, parted from their fields and cattle, and driven

to one of the wired-in 'protected villages' now scattered across the tribal trust lands. Frieda pointed out an old man seated at the front, dressed in a shabby jacket, head bowed.

'The chief,' she whispered. 'Mutamba. He's in disgrace.'

District Commissioner Chamberlain hadn't showed up yet. He liked to keep the people waiting for three or four hours under the hot sun. It was a tradition extending back to the old Native Commissioners: never be in a hurry and show your authority by addressing every adult male, however advanced in years, as 'boy' or 'it'. 'Tell it to come back tomorrow with its birth certificate.' But the more modern-minded DCs no longer insisted on hearing petitions through a native interpreter or referring to supplicants as 'it'.

'He won't be pleased to see you,' she said, closely monitoring Stern's expression. 'Chris hates journalists. And he hates little Frieda, too.'

Her toad face was flushed with anticipation of something Stern could not divine. The Salisbury press corps was aware that Minister of Information Prinsloo now headed the Rhodesia Front caucus unreservedly committed to the 'internal settlement' (Muzorewa). Frieda's husband, the General, knew the world wouldn't wear that version of the internal settlement, it was too crude. The UN and the OAU could go fuck themselves but if the US Congress baulked and the Foreign Office twisted Mrs Thatcher's head towards Nigerian oil wells and the imminent disintegration of the Commonwealth, even she would have to curb her enthusiasm for the Smith-Muzorewa deal. Hersh had been working for a subtler formula since the Geneva Conference had aborted in December 1976. The name of the game was to split the twin-headed Patriotic Front by capitalising on the old rivalry between Zapu and Zanu, between Nkomo and Mugabe, between the Ndebele guerrillas of Zipra and the much more radical Shona forces of Zanla. Take Nkomo out of the war, neutralise the Western war zone in Matabeleland, appease the cunning old elephant's consuming power-hunger by offering him top spot in a new 'internal' formula, relegate the organ grinder's monkey Muzorewa to the role of prayer-leader, and then you stood a real chance of Anglo-American recognition and the lifting of economic sanctions. Bring Nkomo's Zipra 'on-sides', incorporate them in the security forces – then drive Mugabe's Marxists back into the bomb-shattered camps of Mozambique for the final reckoning.

For two years General Hendrik Hersh had been making unannounced, clandestine journeys to Lusaka, Malawi and London. That he was on Britain's payroll as well as Rhodesia's was the kind of 'common knowledge' that is too good not to be true (as

Holzheimer put it). Obviously Hersh wanted to 'save' his country by masking white power under a more sophisticated black mask than Muzorewa's; you didn't have to be Olympic champion for cynicism (Holz again) to penetrate Hersh's motive: Hersh, not Walls, would emerge as Field Marshal of the Zambezi and Limpopo.

—But where's the sub-plot? Holzheimer would muse. —Why does Momma Frieda cultivate the most widely disliked – and justly so – British reporter in Salisbury? Something to do with Esther, perhaps?

Stern told him to worry about his alimony payments and whether he was really married to his third wife. But, waiting to be uplifted by Alouette from New Sarum, Frieda grinned upon him wickedly:—*Cherchez la femme.*

—Are you the "fum", Frieda?

—Naughty boy! I mean the lovely Donna Prinsloo.

' Stern waited.

—Little Richard hasn't set eyes on the Minister's gorgeous gal?

—He hasn't. Where should he look?

—In the Anglican cathedral, where the heavenly Donna will soon marry District Commissioner Chris Chamberlain . . . Prinsloo's most dangerous henchman.

—A DC works for Internal Affairs not Information.

—Dear boy, everyone now works either for Prinsloo or my hubby. We are at five minutes to midnight.

—Oh? What about Smith and Walls?

—Yesterday's men.

Half an hour after they reached Buhera, District Commissioner Chamberlain showed up with a heavy escort of police and black auxiliaries, the Bishop's brown-shirted Pfumo reVanhu (whom Mike Gilson stubbornly identified, during the monthly hassle over Stern's re-accreditation, as Zanla guerrillas, Mugabe men, who had embraced the amnesty, but whom Stern knew to be unemployed victims of war recruited in the shanty towns of Salisbury and Umtali for eighty dollars a month). Chamberlain slowly surveyed the assembled villagers and then walked over to Frieda, his freckled features clouded by antipathy.

'Good morning, Mrs Hersh.'

'Lovely day, Chris. I've brought my bullhorn, I want to talk to the women.'

He nodded. 'No objection. Who's this?'

'My good friend Richard Stern.'

'Yees, but who is he? You know I can't accept just anyone here. I have to receive proper authorisation from the Ministry.'

From one of the big pockets covering her voluminous bosom,

Frieda extracted a document, leering. The archipelagoes of freckles on Chamberlain's sun-sensitive skin seemed to merge as he stared at the General's signature on the letter of accreditation – Frieda Hersh kept a supply of them, pre-signed and stamped, at her Glen Lorne home.

'I take no responsibility for this, Mrs Hersh.'

Frieda winked. 'Richard is a good boy. He knows the rules.'

'If he knew the rules he wouldn't be here. This man is not an accredited war correspondent.'

'He is today, Chris.'

Stern watched the DC swallow the price of martial law and eighteen-hour curfews: Hersh commanded the whole operational area from Mtoko to the Mozambique border with a touch as sensitive as a rhino's horn. Minister Prinsloo had been heard to extend the metaphor: Hersh's reputation went before him and behind him like a farting rhino charging downwind.

The Pfumo reVanhu auxiliaries were prowling among the mute villagers, lords of the day, black sheep reincarnated by their white shepherds as spotted collies, but the night round here belonged to the 'boys', the *vakomana:* not a single dip tank was operational within fifty miles, not a clinic still open, not a school functioning.

'Chris doesn't trust little Frieda,' she whispered, leading Stern into the shade where a small group of PsyAc men were lounging behind the concertinaed steel of a wide-axled, mine-proofed Ojay. He saw them recoil at her approach, gearing themselves to civility as she bubbled cheery greetings. Stern quartered his stride.

'Do show Richard our new leaflet, Bobby.'

The PsyAc captain produced a pile of strip cartoons, with captions in Shona and English, depicting snarling Communist Terrorists (CTs) callously massacring old men and kids before running their hands up the skirts of widows and wailing mothers. Frieda explained proudly that she had been responsible for the translations: 'The idiom has to be just right.' Frieda was for ever showing him bits and pieces. Penetrating the Hersh homestead in the vain expectation of interviewing the General, he had departed carrying glossy photos of dead terrs with shirts pulled up and entrails spilling. Frieda's Leica had been busy.

The PsyAc team distributed the leaflets among the villagers with the futile air of farmers tossing seed on to dry mud. Frieda followed, waddling forth with her bullhorn and a determined smile. 'I'm your friend Frieda,' she announced through the bullhorn and began reading aloud the captions to the women because the women couldn't read.

'Look, look,' she cried in Shona. 'You look at the pictures and don't forget these bad men are Communists, they want your land and your *mombes*.'

The women watched her, bemused. Stern inferred – the kind of cocksure inference that infuriated Leonard Tanner – that behind the crude drawings the village women saw their own sons, nephews and husbands, the *vakomana* who came at night to hold *pungwes* and promised them the neighbouring white farms. The *vakomana* were frightening because they used their guns freely on sell-outs and had stopped the buses running – but they were nevertheless 'the boys'. By day the white soldiers came cased in steel, peering through slits at knots of black women selling melons, at inscrutable villagers who harboured the secret knowledge of the countryside which the Special Branch pursued in their local detention centre with blows, beatings in the pig cage, immersion under water – a furious fumbling at the combination lock of an insurgent nation.

Stern noted the oval sweat stain under Frieda's armpit as she raised her bullhorn again to explain the evils of Communism. It looked like an avocado.

How she loved those glossy photos. —This is what the terrs did to my good and faithful friend, Headman Kayeesa. There had been a sob in her voice but her expression was ecstatic as she showed him the Headman's obliterated features. —Richard, Frieda sometimes wonders whether she can live through another day of this.

Panting and a bit flushed by the sun now, despite her floppy khaki bushhat, Frieda drew breath, resting her bullhorn on her heaving bosom, a single imperious curve from neck to waist. Only five days had passed since Stern came to this same village with the other hacks on a Government facility trip to hear Prinsloo and two black 'internals', a Muzorewa man and a Sithole man, both of them co-Ministers in the Provisional Government, explain the blessings of the 'moderate settlement' of 3 March 1978. The army and the police had been out, rounding up an audience from a radius of twenty miles, but the people had fled into the bush and when the meeting finally opened the politicians found themselves addressing twenty-five adults, twice as many kids, and one very moderate cow on its last legs.

Stern had observed Prinsloo's rage and humiliation on that day, District Commissioner Chamberlain tight-lipped at his side. The two black 'internals' took the rebuff more philosophically, as if they'd long since abandoned hope of the peasantry, but the white Minister treated the assembled reporters to a long diatribe about 'intimidation' and the West's myopic appeasement of the Kremlin – by the end of it District Commissioner Chamberlain was even tighter-lipped. Today the villagers were to answer for their defiance, behind closed doors. Frieda knew this well enough, she was in on the act, yet she had deliberately brought Stern with her and he couldn't fathom why.

The bullhorn was raised again. Stern's Shona was deficient despite long, solitary evenings with vocabulary, grammar and cassettes, but he could follow the central thread of Frieda's version of *Faust*. Behind the CTs came the Russians, men with snow on their boots which didn't melt even in Africa. They had no God but AntiChrist and their purpose was to dig up the graves of the people's ancestors, to kill their spirit mediums, to desecrate Mwari and defame Mbuya Nehanda, driving away the sacred spirits which bonded the people to their soil, the wisdom of their tribe, and planting the poisonous tree of materialism under the great baobab.

The PsyAc team were monitoring the reactions of the women as adults observe delinquent children.

District Commissioner Chamberlain did not listen to Frieda Hersh. He sat in his armoured Land Rover, airlocked in a capsule of rage.

The PsyAc captain, Bobby, was friendly.

'From London are you?'

'Yes.'

'I won't pretend British journalists are our favourite tourists – but I daresay you're only doing your job. We had a brace of politicians down here four or five days ago and a whole mob of reporters.'

'I was one of them.'

'Then you witnessed the shambles. The intelligence boys were dragged back to Salisbury and boiled in oil. A major Zanla unit under General Chimurenga had moved up from Gutu under cover of night and closed us down. And nobody knew! Prinsloo blew a gasket. He blamed Hersh . . . don't say anything to Mrs Hersh.'

Stern feigned lack of interest: he had perfected the weary shrug of the world-worn reporter who'd yawn through an earthquake.

'Can't win 'em all,' he said.

'I'll tell you something but we're off the record.'

Stern smiled gently. 'I never believe anything I hear – only what I see.'

'Several days before Prinsloo and the black ministers came down here a nun from St Hilda's mission, Rusape, turned up at the DC's office in a state of hysteria and told him that five hundred gooks had surrounded the mission, demanding food, blankets and medical supplies. The gooks had given the sisters forty-eight hours to produce the goods, chanted anti-Christian slogans, denounced Jesus as a white imperialist, and taken four of the sisters hostage.'

'Was this nun white or black?'

'She was white, of course. Sister Angelica of the Precious Blood.

207

You don't listen to black nuns, they're in business to lift their skirts and service the gooks.'

'Ah. I haven't been out here long.'

'So Chamberlain gave her a small brandy and decided to telephone the mission but Sister Angelica begged him not to do that. The Mother Superior, she pleaded, had a gun at her head and she herself had only managed to slip away under cover of night, taking her life and all their lives in her hands.'

'Ah.' Stern looked as grave as possible. At any moment the PsyAc captain might regret talking to him and switch off.

'So Chamberlain ordered her to return to the mission and tell the terrs they'd get their loot.'

'Poor Sister Angelica.'

'Wait. Spare your sympathy. Chamberlain got straight on to Comops and talked to Hersh though he hates his guts, but that's another story, I hope you're not *that* friendly with Frieda. Anyway, Hersh is hungry for a big cull and diverted—' (here the captain shot Stern a glance both wary and guilty) – 'well, I won't go into the SF units involved, let's say a helluva lot of manpower up to St Hilda's mission. Now that's to the north, isn't it?'

Stern nodded.

'They surrounded the mission and closed from all sides. What did they find?'

'Everyone raped? Bellies cut open – the usual?'

'They found fuck all if you'll excuse my language. The Mother Superior insisted she hadn't seen a terrorist for months. Four nuns taken hostage? – no ways.'

'And Sister Angelica?' Stern asked helpfully (well versed in the bemused time-traveller's traditional narrative role).

'Never heard of her!' The PsyAc captain looked almost triumphant, his pride in his story greatly outweighing his patriotism.

'Ah.'

'Meanwhile Chimurenga's gooks moved up from the south, encountered no resistance, closed down the district and turned Prinsloo's meeting into a shambles.'

Stern strove to suppress his love of Sister Angelica.

'Sorry. I can't make sense of it.'

The PsyAc men exchanged the masonic glances of a fraternity for whom mythology is the only antidote to stress, each waiting for the other to 'say it'. A young fellow barely out of school did say it, truculence coating his guilt.

'Ever heard of the "kaffir's whore"?'

'Sounds like a landmark,' Stern said. 'Stone or flesh?' London came down his long nose and posh vowels. The young fellow's adam's apple flushed aggression – you could never trust these types.

'One day we'll get her. And I want to be there.'

'Man, we've been hunting that bitch for years,' said another.

'Listen,' said the first youth, 'I respect a person who stands up for their own race. We cull the gooks but you have to respect them. I mean they're indoctrinated up to here, and crazy on dagga, but some of them are sincere. Maybe I'd do the same if I was in their place. I mean if the gooks ever take over here I'll be the first into the hills. But a white woman who betrays her own kith and kin, that's just sick . . . Jesus.'

The captain, Bobby, was watching Stern sceptically down a longer lens. Turning thirty and maybe in computers.

'Mrs Hersh didn't tell you any of this?'

'No.'

'I wonder why she brought you here today. I really do.'

Frieda had finished her peroration. Oiled in perspiration and accomplishment, she came on short legs and flopped down in the shade, her tyres of flesh refolding.

'You did a great job,' the PsyAc captain told her.

'I do my tiny best, Bobby.'

'Only a woman can talk to the women,' Stern said.

'Naughty! Big Richard is teasing little Frieda.'

From one of the huts of the kraal a dusty, barefoot boy, a mere child, was led by a rope looped round his neck and held by a sergeant of the black auxiliaries wearing a chocolate brown uniform. The child's face was covered in livid bruises, his eyes mere slits in swollen flesh. Too young to have abandoned hope, he wailed continuously, and this high lament was now taken up by the women of the village, rocking their heads and shoulders in unison, wailing and keening, flapping their hands on the ground.

'Now that naughty little boy's a *mujiba*,' Frieda explained. 'The eyes and ears of Zanla. How innocent he looks and how your heart bleeds, Richard.'

Chamberlain had taken up a judicial posture beneath the main tree of the village, where the elders customarily heard cases and sat in judgment. Haltered to the auxiliary sergeant, the battered boy was led in front of the District Commissioner, who now beckoned to the old chief to rise and stand beside the child – a double act of humiliation in a society where age and respect are synonymous. The sergeant planted out his gleaming boots behind them, a loyal askari, the pivot of every colonial enterprise. Stern noticed that his cheeks had been tattooed in distinctive quarter-moons, noticed that the fourth finger of the sergeant's left hand was missing – perhaps this one had served with Zanla after all.

In his right hand he gripped a sjambok which had clearly seen service on the boy; poised to please his master, the black sergeant wore the possessive air of a hound guarding a dying hare: he's mine.

Already kites were wheeling above the village. Perhaps their primitive computers had learnt to associate diesel fumes and the dust clouds raised by rotor blades with blood; and what are we all, Harry, if not bundles of conditioned reflexes?

'That is the boy's mother,' Frieda said, pointing.

Speaking in Shona with slow deliberation, Chamberlain had begun to catalogue the sins of the battered boy and of all the other *mujibas* who had aided and abetted him. And of all the sisters and girls who played camp follower to the terrorists. And of the parents who either connived or did nothing. And of the disloyal chief who had brought disgrace upon the entire region. The DC didn't mention the disastrous meeting addressed by Minister Prinsloo, it was beneath his dignity, but all was understood by all. The District Commissioner wanted to be an act of God, despite the freckled patches on his skin which suggested vulnerability and looked from a distance like iodine stains. Stern could imagine how those blue eyes had once been the delight of a missionary's wife raising babies under a tin roof in Nyasaland; how later they had gathered in fierce concentration as the boy scudded across the gravel yard of the Edinburgh Academy with clacken and ball after a thrashing with the tawse for carelessness about Latin past participles.

Stern looked from the mother of the boy to Chamberlain and back again. *Richard Stern reports from Salisbury:*

'I went to the woman and told her I wanted to help, explaining that though I was white I supported the people in their struggle against oppression. She regarded me with suspicion for a moment, but the other women urged her to speak, to testify, telling her she had nothing to lose. The woman said her name was Particia Mtende, wife of Samson Mtende, who had gone to work in Salisbury when her fourth child was due. (Possibly he is a guerrilla.) The woman explained that her eldest son, Kumbrai, had grown up wilful and ungovernable without a father, scornful of "woman's work" (drawing water, fetching firewood, fighting off the baboons at night) and swearing that he would join the struggle whenever the *vakomana* would accept him. One night the guerrillas came and took Kumbrai to Mozambique for training. The police questioned Mrs Mtende several times, warning her that if she ever heard from Kumbrai she must notify them immediately, otherwise they would confiscate her mealies and her *mombes* and fire her hut. "They fire people's houses very easy, they ever do it," she said in English, before reverting to Shona. Then one day her second son, Sorgachas, came to her when she was drawing water at the well, reporting that he had seen Kumbrai. She said to him, "What do you mean you have seen Kumbrai? Why come here and frighten your mother with such talk?" But Sorgachas insisted that Kumbrai was at some distance from the village carrying guns and landmines with certain other "boys". Kumbrai had sent a message: "Be well, mother." Then her son Sorgachas had begun running messages for these "boys", and reporting things to them, though only eleven years old. Though Patricia dared not inform the police she did tell the village Headman but he said, "Woman, don't tell me such things. I didn't hear you. Go away and hold your tongue." Then recently they had this important meeting here, some bosses from Salisbury came, including a white boss from Smith, and all the people ran away into the bush and the hills to sleep with the baboons and leopards rather than attend that meeting because the *vakomana* said they must not attend that meeting of sell-outs or they would be killed the following night. After the meeting the police came with the Pfumo reVanhu and started beating everyone and accusing everyone. They took her son Sorgachas away, saying he was a *mujiba* of the terrorists. All night she heard his cries. Now she was sure the District Commissioner boss would kill him because that one had killed many people.'

But Patricia Mtende didn't even notice the author of this report, who hadn't moved from the company of the white soldiers and the fat white woman in the shade of the tree. The village women called the white woman 'Talktalk'. She came often. Patricia Mtende did not see the biblical syntax passing through the tall stranger's head, nor did she imagine that he was surrendering both to a tradition of translation from the vernacular and to a romanticisation of peasant suffering.

The District Commissioner was yelling into the bullhorn, devising new collective punishments, more stringent curfews, closing more grinding mills and stores, threatening to shoot anyone riding a bicycle. The boy Sorgachas Mtende, he announced, was an 'accessory to murder' and must be punished under the full rigour of martial law.

A few of the younger men (there were not many, the majority having crossed the border or gone to the towns) nodded, eager to please the black auxiliary sergeant with his tattooed cheeks, just as they would nod to the guerrilla commander when he arrived that night or the one after. But the women paid no attention, their eyes fixed on the bleeding, haltered Sorgachas.

'Chris is a dangerous man,' Frieda whispered.

Stern noticed that the PsyAc captain had begun to sweat in anticipation. 'He's crazy,' he muttered.

The young conscript who had wanted to be on hand when the 'kaffir's whore' was caught, snorted, contemptuous of the captain's scruples.

'You can't get through to these kaffirs. It's the K-factor.'

'Watch,' Frieda nudged the journalist. 'Knowledge is power.'

The DC said something Stern couldn't hear, then nodded to the black sergeant. Three of the auxiliaries lifted the frail boy off his feet while the sergeant tossed the end of the rope over the stoutest branch of the tree – as casual as a woman hanging up washing to dry. A moment later Sorgachas hung from the tree, almost dead, but the knot round his neck had not been fastened correctly and his stick limbs thrashed in agony for most of a minute. A child, a mere child! Stern heard the discreet click of Frieda's Leica in the vast silence. There was no other sound until the sergeant's sjambok began to descend on the chief's bare back.

'Count,' Frieda whispered. 'Twenty is the limit.'

At thirty-three the chief keeled over into the dust.

'Naughty,' Frieda said.

Seated behind their disgraced chief, the village elders were nodding rhythmically, remembering how, in the 'other time', the other *chimurenga* as related by their fathers, the white soldiers 'without knees', the *vasina mabvi*, had dynamited the rebel chiefs of Mashonaland in their caves and cut off their heads as trophies and taken them to England for public display so that their spirits could never rest. In ninety-six. The elders could not read but they understood more English than their grandsons and were familiar with the relevant sections of the Gregorian calendar.

The District Commissioner was not satisfied. He prowled the rows of silent villagers like an actor demanding a more receptive audience. The evidence of life in them seemed to madden him; Africa would not achieve civilised standards until Africa ceased to breathe, eat and copulate.

Then, abruptly, he began speaking of guns, displaying an armoury of weapons which the auxiliaries scrambled to produce from the back of his Land Rover. Raising each in the air, he shouted its name, 'FN! G3! Uzi! LDP!,' finally holding aloft the famous AK47 with its distinctive magazine, curved like a shark's fin: 'The Communist gun!' Ballistics magic, he warned the villagers, was his window into their guilty souls and treacherous deeds. The security forces had plenty of 'ballistics ngangas' who could look at a bullet and know from which gun it had been fired. Unable to contain himself, breaking back into English, which he called 'God language', Chamberlain informed the quaking *povo* that a 'land' means not only earth but also the ridge between the grooves within the barrel – 'Do you get that?' – and then on, manically, to rifling, striations, linear scores, trajectories . . .

'Crazy,' muttered the PsyAc captain.

'Is Richard watching?' Frieda whispered, her oiled features opening into the toad's grin.

'Ballistics is white magic!' yelled Chamberlain. Initially Stern did not associate the sharp report with either the District Commissioner or the rifle he held in his hand. Stern jumped and Frieda sniggered, raising her camera. He saw the villagers sway like maize in a gale as the hail of bullets passed over their heads, then the women panicked and 'foolishly' (as Frieda later put it) began to scramble to their feet and run. The crowd of women broke and scattered like a bottle smashed on the ground, some with babies strapped to their backs, others clutching infants they had been suckling at the breast. Stern sat stock still, paralysed; on either side of him the PsyAc team had flattened themselves, faces down; only Frieda was on her feet, clicking.

The stampede seemed merely to madden Chamberlain. He had not been understood; the people's stupidity was wilful, part of a vast plot to resist and subvert reasonable authority; Stern saw him slam a fresh magazine into the rifle but the black auxiliary sergeant dared to grip the barrel, forcing it down, pointing with his four-fingered hand towards Frieda. The shooting stopped.

The dusty open space of the village was deserted now, except for five bodies, three of them women, one a child, the last a baby killed by the same bullet that had penetrated its young mother, a girl barely sixteen. The white police reservists converged on the bodies slowly, trapped in a shame they would never acknowledge, composing alibis, reminding themselves of all the colleagues and best friends they had seen blown apart by landmines or shot through the throat at a range of ten yards in the hills of Manicaland. District Commissioner Chamberlain strode through the dust shouting orders, fully in command, on top of every situation, then veered sharply towards Frieda, painted in rage.

'I want those bloody cameras, Mrs Hersh.'

But Frieda Hersh, unlike Richard Stern, was one of nature's marines.

'You're under arrest, Chris.' It was softly said – Stern had never known her raise her voice – but it brought clacken and ball to a halt on the gravel yard in front of the Academy's five Doric pillars.

'Now look, you've no authority to—'

213

'Nor have you, Chris. You're coming back to Salisbury with me.' She turned to the Member-in-Charge of the police reservists. 'Take his gun, Freddie.'

She knew them all, did General Hersh's wife. Chamberlain relinquished his FN rifle as if it was a stick he'd idly picked up in the bush, then strode away, barking new orders, reasserting authority, leaving the army men and police reservists adrift in the slow downbeat of another day, becalmed in the no-man's-land where nothing is done because nothing matters.

Five minutes later the Alouette climbed over the kraal, Frieda monitoring Stern's tense, drawn features with a momma's tenderness. She shouted above the roar of the engine.

'Does big Richard understand now?'

'Will Chamberlain be put under arrest?'

'What? Shout!'

'I said, will Chamberlain be put under arrest?'

'Silly boy. No ways.'

'But you'll report him?'

'What? Shout!'

'You'll report him?'

'To hubby. Nothing more. We Rhodesians must stand together.'

They flew in silence for a while; Frieda had succumbed to fatigue, her eyes closed and her head began to nod. In repose her face gained ten years, she was old. Neither spoke again until the high office blocks of central Salisbury came into view across the great, stretching plateau where the Pioneer Column had finally halted on a day in September 1890.

'Nothing about Frieda,' she said.

'Say again.'

'Whatever you write, clever boy, say nothing about little Frieda. She wasn't there.'

Later, driving past Cranbourne Barracks, Frieda said no: he couldn't use her 'pics' – not, that is, unless he was prepared to 'play winners'. Tiny behind the wheel of her Renault, barely able to see over the dashboard, she offered him the ultimate in lingering leers.

'It isn't Esther we want so badly, my dear, it's her chums. Hubby needs the gook commanders in a brown paper bag. Private delivery. Yes? You can have Esther, silly Richard, just lead us to her.'

TWENTY

Chamberlain was staring at him across the room. 'Dubious vibes,' Holzheimer murmured. 'Who is that repulsive-looking guy? Whatever he wants of you, it isn't the next dance.'

'Shall we go and ask him?'

'*We!* you say. You want me to drive the hearse? I've never seen a revolver like that.'

But now Professor Vishnu Desai materialised, plucking at Stern's arm and brandishing a carving knife under his nose.

'Marxist scum!' he yelled. 'Thief! Gangster!'

Holzheimer wrapped a friendly, but skinny, arm round the trembling wrist holding the carving knife.

'What would the Bishop think, Vishnu?'

'This "friend" of yours has robbed my uncle Amrit of five thousand dollars! A message had just reached me from Bulawayo. By telephone!'

Holzheimer looked impressed. 'By telephone, eh? Listen, Vishnu, there are several people in this room waiting to kill Richard, would you mind standing in line?'

District Commissioner Chamberlain turned away and strode out through the french windows.

'Thief!'

The guests had by now emerged from their late-afternoon lethargy. Paul was tugging nervously at his beard.

'You have been reported to the police, you petty swindler!'

Holzheimer sighed. 'I call upon the Right Honourable Member to withdraw the last remark.' He turned to Stern. 'What divides us, Richard, is that the *New York Times* believes in "law and order", a Platonic stabilising force, whereas you traduce the great tradition of Hobbes and Locke as the humbug by which rich

215

thieves put poor thieves out of business – the code by which this country was cynically wrested from its occupants.'

Holzheimer turned back to Desai and gently extracted the carving knife from his furiously clenched hand.

'Vishnu, what more can I say? I hope I've explained it all.'

Desai subsided into mere contempt.

'This lumpen-Marxist scum has a chip on his shoulder, to be honest. I've put his nose out of joint.'

'Does Richard wear his nose on his shoulder?' Holzheimer asked mildly.

'Wait a minute,' moaned Paul, gaining courage as the threat of violence subsided, 'you guys are my guests, you've eaten my food.'

But Stern's bored expression infuriated Desai.

'You swollen-headed, cancerous, fork-tongued, double-dealing Marxist scum! Thief!'

'That's a wide range of disabilities,' Holzheimer said. 'Why don't you throw him in Paul's swimming pool, Vishnu? I need a story, and what better than the bizarre death of a colleague in three feet of chlorinated water?'

Desai abruptly sat down, regarding Holzheimer uneasily: it was not expedient to quarrel with the *New York Times* when the Bishop was striving to gather support in Congress and short-circuit the Carter Administration's boycott of the internal settlement.

'Take no offence, Vishnu,' Holzheimer smiled easily. 'Like you, I'm only practising my English.'

Stern laughed. Desai's rage returned. He leapt up: 'Pimp! Chasing after a whore who –' He checked himself and sat down again, balletically.

'What goes up must come down,' Stern said.

'Shut up, Dick,' Jane said. 'Vishnu, I must ask you to apologise for that remark about my daughter or leave this house.'

Desai stared at her insolently. 'You may be forgetting certain things, Jane.' Stern saw Paul flinch. 'Nevertheless, as a gentleman, I apologise to you – though not to this gangster who practises armed robbery with an African henchman in the middle of Bulawayo.'

'Is anyone acquainted with the plot?' Patrick Warner asked. No one was. Desai sank into a brooding sulk, muttering.

'Does he deny it, that's what I ask everybody, you're all witnesses to this perfidy, have we heard a single jot of denial?'

'As with Rembrandt's "Anatomy Lesson",' said Stern, 'the corpse merits less attention than the audience.'

Desai leapt to his feet again. 'You think the Desais have no culture?'

Jane took Stern by the arm and guided him out into the garden, the girl who had been reared on *The Iron Heel* and Mike Gold's

Jews Without Money by an autodidact father who taught in a Lower East Side school and delighted in expounding connections. Jane looked back on it all with more affection and amusement than Paul – her father explaining how the Nazi-Soviet Pact had been the 'objective outcome' of cynical collusion between the City of London and Polish feudalism to use the Nazi war machine to dismember 'the first people's republic in the world'. The plot had failed. Reports in the American press of Molotov cavorting with Ribbentrop were 'lies'. Always lies. 'Don't believe what you read. Jane, go down to the A&P, your mother's in pain again.'

'So what was all of that?' Jane asked as they walked under the avocado trees. 'I haven't seen Vishnu that angry.'

'It would be rather hard to explain.'

'You don't trust us, is that it?'

He thought of Cubans's favourite damper: 'need to know'. Jane and Paul didn't need to know.

'You took some money from Desai's uncle?' she persisted.

'Not I.'

'I suppose you realise that bastard Vishnu is bleeding Paul to death? If it isn't him, it's Frieda. Vultures.'

'Money, you mean?'

'And how! Paul has cut a few corners in his time – currency offences, funds in Botswana, unauthorised export of emeralds. Now they've got him for not repatriating the profits of his South African company.'

'He has a company in South Africa!'

'Boy, that nose of yours. Don't you know how the capitalist system works? Paul learned survival when Harry S. Truman was saving the Free World and we were waiting for McCarthy to subpoena Almighty God. It was my Dad who taught me what the phoney message on the cereal packet *really* means – the multinational tie-ups behind the homely brand names.'

'How does Desai figure in all this?'

'The "internals" have got a grip on the Exchange Control guys – everyone's thinking of the future. They can bring charges or not bring charges. Either Paul greases Muzorewa's campaign fund or we take the consequences.'

Stern wondered whether Cubans Urimbo had been aware of the blackmail. To pose the question was to answer it – he now understood the expression Cubans had worn while mau-mauing Shoeshop Desai. But how had he known and why should he care?

'And Frieda?'

'Ugh, that woman. She can smell carrion. The Hershes are hedging their bets, laundering local currency into a South African account. Paul has the Rand, you see.'

'And if he refuses?'

'Dick, fear is fear. If the "boys" ever get predator Hersh and slit open his stomach, they'll find it stuffed with foreign currency.'

Later Paul pulled Stern up to his study for the second time that day, carrying the big transistor in whose company he drifted round the house, like a kid, fiddling with the cassette, backing his thoughts with Bach or Baez or the peachy speakerines of RBC radio sending messages of comfort to troopies in the bush: 'Head down and chin up, Neil, from Sharon, Lynette and Mum.'

Paul locked the study door behind them.

'Couldn't you turn that noise off?' Stern said. Sometimes every diurnal routine motion of Paul's cycle irritated him: slurping food as if each meal might be the last, licking his fingertip every time he turned the page of a magazine, the constant radio.

'What? Oh sure.' Paul turned it down, not off. Now it murmured like a bee under a glass jar.

'Dick, I wanta to know where Esther is. She's with the Catholics, isn't she?'

'I don't know where she is.'

'Frieda says ya do know. Dick, that woman is screwing me white. I've done time as a saint in this world – ten dollars an hour handling United Electrical cases, guys fired straight off the production line for taking the Fifth.'

'Paul, I-do-not-know where she is.'

'Dick, ya gotta get her away from those Catholics . . .'

'I don't understand your obsession about Catholics.'

'Maybe that's because Dick Stern was in diapers when Cardinal Francis Spellman was presenting the Club of Champions medal to J. Edgar Hoover. You don't remember how they hounded Jane out of her job? Ever heard of Monsignor J. Fulton Sheen, Director of the Pontifical Society for the Propagation of the Faith, wooing lousy informers like Louis Budenz into the Catholic faith?'

He slapped his fist into his cupped hand: no sound.

'But Esther's friends aren't of that stripe.'

'How d'ya know?' Paul showed the triumphant gleam in his eye so often seen during games of Scrabble. 'How d'ya know if ya never seen Esther?' But Stern's withering look killed the gleam and Paul began to whine again. 'Dick, the only thing *any* Catholic understands is the Inquisition. OK, tell me Esther's papist friends are progressive, liberation theology and all that crap, but just wait until that leopard shows its spots.'

He broke off and sank into an armchair. Reality had long ago outgunned his imagination; he had spent thirty years quoting himself.

'Help me, Dick. Bring her home.'

'And back to prison, if she's lucky?'

Paul fiddled with his radio, playing with wavelengths, searching for the BBC World Service.

'I've been offered a deal,' he said, avoiding Stern's eyes. 'Jane doesn't know about it . . . yet. A safe conduct out of the country for Esther, gilt-edged, no funny stuff.' He fished in his trouser pocket and blew his nose. 'Actually, it's Zimunya they want. No deal for him, just the gallows. I thought that might suit you.'

Eventually the party ended: another Sunday without Esther. Tomorrow, Tanner. It occurred to Stern that he should have alerted Cubans Urimbo to that particular incoming flight from Johannesburg – though Cubans had been reticent about the two Viscounts brought down by Sam 7 missiles, presumably Zipra's work.

Reaching Baines Avenue, he half-expected to discover District Commissioner Chamberlain standing over his offending typewriter, gun levelled at the door, but all he found was the mess of dirty crockery and smelly clothes that Isaac had neglected for a week. Servants! Then the telephone rang.

'Hi,' said Holz. 'Want to come over and talk about your wife?'

'I ought to work.'

'Forget it. You'll just sit and brood about Tanner. Then you'll brood about Esther. Then Desai. Then the awful man with freckles. Then Tanner again. Better to talk about your wife.'

'I've got to stop talking about her.'

'In my experience, if they run off with your balls in their purse, it takes five years – at the minimum! That's one advantage of a succession of quick marriages: it's like serving the sentences concurrently.'

Stern climbed back into his VW, too weary to check the boot and under the bonnet. He found Holzheimer lounging in drainpipe jeans and bare feet in a spacious Greendale house costing six hundred dollars a month.

'Richard, I've never known a man so surrounded by ugly characters as you. And I know why. You're a misanthropist. You stack the cards against each person in such a way that all potentiality is destroyed. Yours is the glance of the late frost. You grew up anal and English on the wrong toilet training.'

Stern reminded him that his intellect would never recover from his early immersion in the half-baked optimism of flower-power and California junk culture (of which his first wife, daughter to an electronics fortune, had been 'a magnificent specimen').

Holzheimer wasn't pleased. 'I was in Nam.'

'For one month.'

'Won't you give me a whole year? Couldn't you make me the author of Michael Herr's *Dispatches?* Wasn't it Holzheimer who wrote, "He didn't mind his nightmares so much as the waking impulse to file them"? All those hip sentences about "redundant mutilators, heavy rapers, eye-shooters, widow-makers, name-takers" and "classic essential American types". Couldn't I liken life in Saigon to "the folded petals of a poisonous flower"? No?'

'No.'

'OK. Harry Marquis told you everything in American literature has been downhill since Dreiser and Sinclair Lewis.'

According to Holz, the entire cast of the Rhodesian comedy were merely disenfranchised citizens of Stern's imperial imagination. Holz had a way of seizing on casual remarks and gradually inflating them into global fantasies. Stern happened, when drunk on Gerac, to have remarked that fiction might be the way out of the impasse between philosophy and journalism.

'Absolutely,' the American said, thoughtfully adjusting his John Lennons. 'What impasse?'

Holz was bored. Rhodesia was a bigger story in Britain than in America.

'No I do understand, Richard. Your mind was once a precision instrument and also conceptually fertile, yet. You sucked on a hundred creamy teats suspended beneath the lush udder of European culture. What the Common Market calls "a culture mountain". You loved yourself dearly and were about as unselfish as a baby cuckoo. And now you spend your life at sterile press conferences, among philistines, pursuing pseudo-events with the lifespan of a ten-cent firework. You can't go back and what is forward? An interview with Ian Smith? So why not escape from the whole mess into fiction?'

Stern envied Holz the coolness of his house, the high stone ceilings, the expansive verandah overlooking flame trees and poinsettias. His own cramped utility flat on Baines Avenue was hot, noisy and smelly. He reminded Holz that the Greek philosophers had slept all through the summer, rousing themselves only when Spetember brought cooler breezes and rain clouds across the Aegean.

Holz nodded sympathetically. 'But you don't *know* that.'

Stern explained that during our youth life stretches before us like an inexhaustible morning. 'Later we have to adopt the man who came to stay.'

'Really? I'm still very young, of course. I see myself as potential.'

Stern confessed that it was love of Esther that had induced him to abandon philsophy for journalism.

'You're the first person I've told.'

'You mean it's only just occurred to you as an *idée sympathique?* You once warned me to abandon the whole concept of motivation, and *then*, as if that wasn't frightening enough, of *character*.'

Stern indignantly asked him what he believed in.

'I believe in 229 West 43rd Street, New York City, third floor. My alimony also believes in it.'

'Don't you miss your children?'

'Yes, but I don't miss their mothers.'

'What would you do if you found Esther before I did?'

'Found her? Is she King Solomon's mines? But I can read your awful thoughts: you're telling me that two countries divided by a common language is as nothing to two friends divided by a common scoop. I want to ask you something.'

'Ask.'

Holz waggled his toes thoughtfully.

'Do you really *want* to find Esther? Or would you rather pursue her? Don't look at me like that. Maybe you're afraid of what you'll find – no, I don't mean sagging tits, I'm sure she's more utterly beautiful than ever. What I mean is . . . the *existential* Esther.'

'Who she's sleeping with?'

'Yeah. But is existentialism as crude as that?'

Stern told him that the majority of his dreams at night, for years, involved theatres, actors, parts. 'I'm about to go on stage and I haven't learnt my part. I beg to be allowed to carry the text but they won't let me.'

Holz whistled. 'That's serious. *Now* I understand.'

'There's a second version. I'm playing the tragic role of a man who has lost his daughter in a road accident. Night after night I reduce the audience to tears. One evening, shortly before the curtain, a telegram is brought to my dressing room: my own son Jimmy—'

'Jimmy?'

'Don't interrupt – has been killed in a road accident in King Street, Hammersmith. Do you know the zebra crossing outside the entrance to Ravenscourt Park? No? I collapse, but they revive me. Tonight, they say, will be your greatest performance. The dream invariably ends as the curtain rises.'

'Did you report all this to Dr Clausewitz?'

'One shouldn't tell you anything. Give me a drink.'

'You warned me never to give you a drink if you asked for one.'

'I assumed I wouldn't have to ask for one.'

'How's Harry?'

221

'When Ramsay steps down, Harry will be the next Dean. They've become great chums, I'm told.'

'Your words as sweet as watercress. Perhaps he's come back into your wife's life despite that minor disagreement in the offices of *Thought and Action?*'

'McAllisty thinks so. But then he's jealous too.'

'Beth believes you're wasting your time in Africa?'

'Not *my* time – it's quoted at zero on her stock exchange.'

'You still love her? – sorry, that was naive.'

'I've never quite abandoned the hope that she will be reincarnated as Elizabeth in that elegant wardrobe of silks and suedes I once got lost in when searching for oblivion.'

Holz nodded appreciatively. 'Yeah, rip off all that drab Movement gear, all those "natural" colours, those floppy sweaters, and spring forth with pointed breasts and creamy thighs like Barbarella?'

'Silly, I know.'

'Very.'

'In fact she's moving in the opposite direction. She's a political animal. I see her at this moment campaigning for the Labour candidate in Hammersmith North, walking briskly down Du Cane Road, passing Wormwood Scrubs, bravely knocking at the doors of prison warders. She gets short shrift: England for the English is their motto. "*You* should spend a day in *there*," the wives tell her. On she goes, arms loaded with leaflets, window posters and car stickers: "Putting Hammersmith First". When the door is not opened a card is inserted claiming that the candidate himself has called: "Sorry You Weren't In", plus ten reasons for voting Labour.'

'Why Hammersmith? I thought you lived in Notting Hill.'

'That's a safe Tory seat. Hammersmith's a Labour marginal.'

'Don't blind me with psephology. You're sending your wife canvassing in Hammersmith so that she can witness your son Jimmy getting wiped out on a zebra crossing.'

Stern leapt up, ashen. 'Are you calling me a liar?'

Holz shrugged. 'Go on with your report.'

'No!'

'Have another drink. Go on – I want to hear what Beth is up against, it's more aphrodisiac than a rhino's horn.'

Grimly Stern resumed his report from west London:

'Peeling paint, sashes in disrepair, tiles flaking, gutters drooping, cats crouching in front gardens consisting of couch grass, dandelions and overflowing dustbins. Doors of hollow hardwood. She discovers that few women living alone on the working-class housing estates dare to come to the door, even at seven o'clock on a light summer evening, unless the canvasser on the step is a woman. Therefore you position yourself in full view of the front window. "I'm here on behalf of your Labour candidate. Can we count on your vote? Good. And your husband" – she is scanning her street list – "is he at home? He passed away last year? I'm sorry, but I'm sure he'll still be voting for us in spirit, Mrs Phillips." One old woman keeps hovering like a spectre behind blotchy glass panels, screeching, "Who's there, who is it?" Finally the door opens and the old hag snarls, "Don't you keep coming here! I'm sick of the lot of you!" She then dumps into little Beth's arms every campaign leaflet handed out by Tories, Liberals, Ecologists, Flat Earthers, the National Front and Looney Freak-Out Galaxy. Beth doesn't pause to explain that her own husband expired several years ago – unburied and unregretted.'

'So she writes to you? Or is this fiction?'

'Long letters, very cordial. Now that I have passed away, we can be friends. Sometimes she is reflective about our marriage. She accuses me of having employed nursery language during love-making. Apparently I used to call her "my little Piglet" – is that likely?'

'It's likely.'

'She also complains that I never once planted a kiss between her legs. And she knows why: "Because you're haunted by the patriarchy's fear of woman as earth, truth and rebellion." '

'Wait a minute – this is uncanny. Are you sure you're talking about *your* wife and not my second?'

'That was the daughter of an East Coast newspaper fortune?'

'She has two PhDs. Two. Our marriage broke up over a discussion of Elias Canetti's *Auto da Fé*. She told me that the central metaphor was "rebarbative" – the hero being a dear old male bibliophile who loves his 25,000 books but gets no peace from his nagging wife, a domineering creature determined to destroy what she can't understand.'

'You'd recommend the novel?'

'I'd never even heard of it. I majored in Comparative Literature at UC, Irvine, I don't read novels – unless I'm in them.'

'Here we go.'

'I just wondered why Bernard Holzheimer is not only a freaky reporter but also, a few chapters earlier, the disloyal editor of a New York publishing house.'

'Good God, do you deny it? Isn't that how you met your second wife? Surely you admit you turned down Giles Carpenter's book?'

Holz looked sulky.

'You need more wine,' Stern said, filling his glass from Holz's bottle of Gerac.

'It was a lousy book that Giles wrote and you know it. You read it! If I hadn't turned it down you would never have seduced Esther. OK, OK, put that snarl away, I agree she broke off relations for a year but in the end, in the end . . .'

The two friends had developed a nose for the dangerous frontiers. When the cold wind blew the skiers ceased to jump from Berny's. The conversation turned to safer topics. Stern reported a recent telephone conversation during which Tanner instructed him from London that 'Hersh is the man to watch'.

Holz snorted. 'Hersh is a clown. I flew with him to Lusaka.'

'To Lusaka? When? You never told me.'

'You didn't mention the little massacre in Buhera until it struck you that the *New York Times* might pay you five hundred dollars for Leonard Tanner's wastepaper bin.'

'You know I'm grateful, Berny.'

'I saved you from peddling your ass on Union Avenue.'

'By the way, your editor hasn't asked for more of my pieces?'

'More! How about *my* job?'

'Of course. Tell me about your trip with Hersh.'

'I got a message from little Frieda. The whole venture would be off the record if it aborted, on the record if it succeeded. The Hershes wanted confirmation of the deal from West 43rd Street.'

'New York was content?'

'New York could live with it. On the way to Charles Prince airport Frieda entertained me with warnings about "that snake", Vishnu Desai. "Never trust an Anavil," she said. It turns out that the Desais are mainly Anavils, a superior bunch of Brahmins who pray to sticks and stones for limitless power and wealth.'

'Frieda uses knowledge like other women use their bodies.'

'She's dangerous. "We'll curry that little Hindu when the time comes." She also spoke of you. She and the General are after Esther but what they really want is Esther's husband, the enigmatic Dr Zimunya. Oops!' Holz slapped himself. 'Tact is what we don't have in Orange County. OK, have another drink. Hersh's crowd apparently believe that Dr Zimunya is now the biggest wheel in Zanu's underground. They blame him for the destruction of the Salisbury oil storage tanks in December.'

'Fantasy.'

'Oh sure. You and I know that Zimunya doesn't exist.'

'I've never said that,' Stern remarked coldly. As always, Holz hastened to mollify him.

'What else are we dealing with here but fantasy? When history gets to be written Mugabe will be depicted marching up Inevitability Avenue from Chikurbi prison to Government House. All these diversionary cul-de-sacs and meandering dirt tracks will be forgotten. But you and I live by the hour – we're trapped in sub-history. The historians will flip through two years' despatches between breakfast and lunch, shredding us. What we are writing is "News from Nowhere".'

Stern smiled appreciatively. 'You were about to fly with Hersh to Lusaka.'

'Yeah.' Holz sounded doubtful now, as if Stern might steal the story. Sensing this, Stern hung out a little knowledge of his own.

'I suppose you know Hersh flies to London regularly, despite the British blacklist, straight through Immigration with the MI6 man at his shoulder—'

'And Nothing to Declare.'

'A fast car to the Permanent Under Secretary's flat in Albany, a visit to the Ministry of Defence, an off-the-record meeting with the Chairman of the Foreign Affairs Select Committee of the Commons. Maybe a visit to the Soviet embassy – they've been backing Nkomo for years and the Father of Zimbabwe has expensive tastes. For a start, Nkomo fills three seats on any aeroplane – Hersh only two. But in Lusaka, I presume, things are different?'

'Correct.'

'Continue, Berny.'

'Frieda introduced me to the General at Charles Prince. I had something resembling his hand in mine but he just looked through me. They'd hired a Cessna – two Special Branch bodyguards, a couple of aides, and Bernard Holzheimer. He didn't say a word on the plane, just glowered out of the window as if the bush was his private estate infested with squatters. When we landed at Lusaka we were hustled through immigration by a nervous aide from the British High Commission who kept glancing at me in despair. A junior official from the Zambian Foreign Ministry also turned up but no one from Zapu. We blundered about from one bombed-out Zapu office to another in search of a stomach even bigger than Hersh's, but the General betrayed not the slightest interest in the effects of his air raids – maybe it was all familiar to him from aerial photographs. He didn't say a word. We tore out of town along a road where ribbon building seemed to be going up and down at the same time until we came to a high wire fence guarded by Zipra men with AK 47s and painful biographies. You have to heave the imagination to strip away the military macho and set those same faces in the kraals of Tsholotsho and Nyamandhlovu. The guy from the British High Commission was becoming increasingly jumpy – things can go wrong.

'We were led into a building reeking of raw concrete and surrounded by a ghastly mess, the detritus of bomb-shocked refugees with no commitment to their place of exile. A guy with an overflowing bureaucrat's gut conducted us into a room fuggy with sweat and overflowing ashtrays. There were frantic phone calls on lines which didn't function. Hersh's self-control was ebbing: "I 'ave an appointment with Mr Nkomo," he periodically announced in thick Afrikaans gutturals. They treated him as if he'd come to sell toilet rolls. The Zapu officials kept talking among themselves in Ndebele which none of us understood, except as a bad sign. The British High Commission man whispered in my ear that the long delay was an oriental bargaining procedure but then a member of the Zapu central committee arrived and announced that "President Nkomo" was in Prague. We flew back to Salisbury.'

'Never mind, you don't get paid by the word.'

'I should have asked Hersh what he does for sex. I might interview myself on that fairly soon. Is there such a thing as an erogenous drought?'

'What about the third and possibly current Mrs Holzheimer, daughter of a Texas oil magnate?'

'Did you ever try the peep shows in Hamburg? They're putting genuine prostitutes out of business and the city's Social Democratic bosses are now quoting Freud on the evils of self-gratification. The Christian Democrats strike back by citing sociobiology as evidence that devotion to one's own genes is the only biological basis for altruism.'

'What went wrong with Texas oil?'

'She got to Peru and encountered *religiosidad popular*. Soon there were relics and shrines in the bathroom. Eventually I removed them and then removed myself.'

Holz smiled at the splendid Castor Oil plant, *Aurelia Siboldii*, that he nurtured in the shade, diligently spraying the enervating insect webs woven between the elegant tongues of the forked leaves.

Stern yawned. It was late. Tomorrow was Tanner.

'We're living a hundred years too late,' he said. 'Class struggle is now as fashionable as shipbuilding and coal. Feminism is the new electronics.'

'So what? A broken heart is dull luggage. You walk around like Rubik's cube without the formula – doesn't a visit to the tribal trust land remind you that you belong to the lucky ten per cent? Or am I being heavy?'

'That's the odd thing – it doesn't help. I can read of screaming children tossed overboard boats at Da Nang, I can imagine the horror of it, and yet all I can think of is the one *she* decided to abort.'

'And I have four children whom I take for granted and occasionally take to Disneyland. OK. You didn't want a wife, you wanted a . . .' Holz hesitated.

'Say it.'

'I love you too much. You're awful but you're the only real thing I've encountered in this teapot drama. I give you cold beer in the middle of the night, I beg the mosquitoes to bite me, not you, and I'll carry your leg when we both hit a landmine. I even enjoy a clown's role in your novel – you give me a few good lines. When you smile I send a telex to New York. I want you to be happy. Tell me, did you really sleep with Esther three times?'

At four in the morning Stern left him, dragging himself towards Tanner.

TWENTY-ONE

They nodded as Tanner emerged from Customs, pushing a trolley laden with suitcases of genuine leather monogrammed in gold, but didn't shake hands. The suitcases looked in better shape than Tanner.

'Good trip?'

'Spiralled down from twenty thou like a corkscrew.'

Stern heard Beth's mocking laughter: real men always knew at precisely what height they were flying. Tanner's eyes, wary after too many half-digested yesterdays, seemed to be searching the arrivals hall for someone of greater consequence than Stern. But what they discovered were platoons of muscular young warriors wearing Jesus curls, Injun headbands, and pendants over their wide-open chests: welcome to our war. Tanner had never seen shorts cut so obscenely short and tight into the crotch, male organs swelling as proudly as those of medieval archers clad in hose and codpiece. All very different from the awkward serge jackets and Warsaw Pact haircuts he had recently observed in Prague; different, too (and perhaps more to the point, if only Tanner could clear his aching head) – that is to say different *from*, not *to*, or was it 'too'?, the baggy, knee-length shorts and skinny, sheet-white legs he associated with the decencies of the British empire. He didn't like to have his associations scrambled, particularly under Stern's sardonic gaze.

Stern was reading him. 'It's a white sperm war here.'

'Mm.' Tanner could also read, and without moving his lips. Behind the bravado of these hearty, swaggering Rhodesians lay the pain of comrades left behind, the moment when the innocent faces of mother and girlfriend, still ignorant of disaster, shimmer through the elephant grass. Stern couldn't know what he'd never experienced; couldn't – the cliché bounced up brightly – see beyond the end of his nose.

'Did you put your clock back?' Stern asked.

'Back? Forward, you mean.'

'Back by twenty years. You should feel at home here.'

That he should receive the first cut, rather than inflict it, came as a relief to Tanner (though, we must admit, not instantly). Firing the prick would be that much easier.

Stern had begun to lift the largest of the leather suitcases from the trolley.

'Let the boy,' Tanner snapped.

'The what?'

'The porter, for Christ's sake. You're depriving him of a living – or doesn't that trouble you?'

Stern let the monogrammed suitcase drop and heard the shriek of glass bottles. Tanner turned purple.

'You fucking idiot!'

All his working life – he had no other – Tanner had carried half a case of the hard stuff to the remotest corners of the earth. Had he visited the Dalai Lama in Lhasa – he almost did, but that is another story – he would have hired an extra bearer to lug the Black Label up the ludicrous inclines of the Buddhist universe.

'Where am I staying?'

'In Meikles. I've got an imitation of a car.'

'I'll take a taxi.' It seemed ungracious, but it might be harder to fire Stern if he accepted a lift into town. It was at this awkward juncture that a solution surfaced in the shape of a flushed, sweating barrel of a man whose tie cut into his neck like string into braising steak.

'Mr Tanner?'

Tanner's nod was faintly regal – he had recently been with Botha, van den Bergh and Oppenheimer. The Rhodesian extended his hand.

'Mike Gilson, sir, Ministry of Information. Welcome to Rhodesia.'

Tanner and Stern parted without further exchange, Gilson summoning a porter to convey Mr Tanner's baggage to the waiting Ministry car.

'Tail end of the hot season,' Gilson explained.

'Used to it. India, Palestine, Malaya, Kenya . . .'

'You've seen it all, Mr Tanner.' Gilson heaved himself behind the wheel of the oppressively hot car.

'Actually, this is one of the few countries I haven't visited.'

'It's a super country, Mr Tanner. All we ask of the world is fair play.'

As they drove into Salisbury Tanner observed the regularly planted flame trees and poinsettias with mounting fury while Gilson tried to explain why Tanner's requested interviews with Smith, Walls and Muzorewa had not, as yet, been granted.

'In short, I'm required to fire Richard Stern before I walk down any marble corridors?'

Gilson's short laugh got stuck somewhere in his sirloin throat. 'Marble is one thing we don't have, Mr Tanner. I daresay you'll find plenty of that in the presidential palaces of black Africa. As Minister Prinsloo put it only the other day, wouldn't Mr Stern be a whole lot happier somewhere further north?'

They were entering Salisbury now, the rectangular silhouettes of the city centre like candy boxes against the cloudless sky (from which L. Tanner had so recently corkscrewed down). Hanging from every tree and lamp post was an election poster – the marble eyes, executive mouth and swelling cheeks of Ndabaningi Sithole; the crossed hoe-and-spear of Muzorewa's UANC, already the self-styled 'Winners'; and, somewhat rarer, the bellowing elephant of Chief Chirau's Zupo. As Gilson slowed behind a bus belching an oily black cloud both men hastily wound up their windows and Tanner was hit by travel nausea, a sense of his own beaten track – just as the scent of dry, new-mown grass evoked in him memories of English cricket pitches and summer fairs . . . all futile . . . because always, everywhere, Tanner.

Then he heard himself fighting back.

'I suppose your Minister realises that my paper is top of the British quality market with a daily circulation of almost 600,000? I'm not counting the *Telegraph*, of course. Our leaders are quoted in Parliament, on the BBC World Service, and in the foreign press.'

'Mr Tanner, didn't I come to the airport to meet you? We don't lay on that sort of service for just anybody or nobody.'

Tanner was torn between anger and fleeting shame: not only had he added 75,000 to the certified circulation figure, he had also supressed the fact that Labour MPs quoted Stern's reports from Rhodesia as frequently as the Opposition cited Selwyn Foyle's leaders. Or Tanner's. More frequently, in fact – as Gilson probably knew, if the word 'Information' meant anything. He must also know that Tanner, under pressure from his editor, had spiked a story from Stern which was later published in the *New York Times*, to Foyle's fury and Tanner's deep humiliation. Two reporters on the foreign desk had temporarily threatened to resign – there had even been a mandatory NUJ chapel meeting to denounce 'arbitrary censorship and betrayal of news values'. Tanner had lost a large slice of his face.

Perhaps Gilson sensed that the old, travel-worn journalist at his side had been silently battering himself.

'I'll be frank with you, Mr Tanner, when the white man first came out here the Afs were running around half-naked, bare boobs and bums, with no written language, no law and order, nothing you could call a religion, just savagery. I mean, I'll be perfectly honest with you, I'm not one hundred per cent for this internal settlement myself, I mean if you go out to the kraals and ask your average Af who he wants to run this country he won't say Bishop Muzorewa he'll say Ian Smith but times are changing and I suppose we all have to make this thing work. I mean, we feel betrayed by the British. I remember hearing Mr Smith say, I was standing as close to him as I'm sitting next to you, Mr Smith said that if Churchill was alive today he'd emigrate to Rhodesia.'

'*Were* alive. The subjunctive is dying.'

'Ah . . . yees.'

'Turning in his grave all the way.'

'Pardon, Mr Tanner?'

Tanner gazed gloomily at the pretty white women mincing along the hot pavements of the city centre. Boobs and bums not bare but still unbearable. Arriving in a new city, he invariably experienced an acute sexual hunger. 'Ask for number one ass,' the American sergeant had advised him as he stepped off the plane in Saigon.

'It's certainly regrettable that Mr Stern sees fit to describe our protected villages as concentration camps,' Gilson jabbed at him again as they came to a halt outside Meikles.

The honeyblonde girl at reception flashed Tanner a routine-job smile and politely instructed (Tanner noted the politeness for his first report from Salisbury) the black porter to carry Mr Tanner's baggage up to room 217. Invited to sign the register, Tanner's hand brushed hers as he handed back the pen. He would have given anything, anything!, for one hour in bed (nowadays he needed at least an hour) with this gorgeous, peach-skinned honeyblonde, fresh and firm with a bouquet as fragrant as a bottle of Yquem. A sexy Coloured girl walked past; Tanner studied her legs. Anything for her, too.

The old man followed the porter to the lift. And don't forget those hotel girls in Palestine – the ones who'd survived the holocaust behaved as if every day was their last. (Yes, he had heard himself say that many times, the dessicated thought shrivelling on his tongue.) Ascending to the second floor, he noticed that the lift was also occupied by Richard Stern.

'Did Gilson invite you to "let me go"?'

Every time Stern opened his mouth Tanner remembered something else; each sardonic smile, each twitch of the long nose, was like a card-index of carefully catalogued accusations. Pursuing a counter-insurgency operation in the Umtali township of Sakubva, Stern had encountered an outspoken young policeman who had only recently moved up from South Africa ('I'm the restless type, man'), having served in the Port Elizabeth township of New Brighton:

—Man, you should just see the dirt and rubbish those munts leave around. I mean, we actually took our own litter in there to dump on the first bunch of kids who showed us the black power salute. You hear this crunch as a big one hits the armour, so you let them have a 37mm canister of gas and then you're out and after them, anything black, anything that moves, anything that doesn't, birdshot, buckshot, gas, rubber bullets and the good old sjambok, best of all if you ask me. I don't dislike kaffirs, man, I just hate them.

—A base and perverted shepherd, Stern had suggested – it was this comment that Selwyn Foyle had seized on as proof of Stern's unprofessional bias, but Tanner was not unaware of the running battle between the NUJ chapel and the management over the series of full-page advertisements recently inserted in the paper by the South African Government.

Reaching for the duty-free whisky in his genuine leather suitcase, he found the bottles mercifully intact, despite Stern's attempt at sabotage. And 'sabotage' has to be deliberate, doesn't it? You can't accuse a chap of inadvertent sabotage. Tanner stared gloomily from his bedroom window at the flower-sellers on Cecil Square, then glanced at Stern: he had to accuse him of something within the next five minutes.

Tanner poured whisky into two glasses. 'Cheers,' he said, and drank. Aaah: better.

'Well, you've arrived,' Stern said, the precious brown fluid apparently unnoticed in his hand. (Stern's addiction to alcohol is of course the one vice Tanner would never suspect him of.)

'What the fuck does that mean?'

'I hoped they'd shoot down your plane.'

Tanner's whole body eased, as it had eased twenty-seven months earlier when Stern, taunted contemptuously by Tanner after his return from Geneva, had finally hit back: 'Go fuck yourself.' Now Tanner laughed, pouring the golden solace down his throat, and told Stern, 'I've been a rebel all my life.' Unbuttoning his sweat-soaked shirt, Tanner retreated into the bathroom. 'You can tell the wicked white man still runs this hotel,' he called, 'there's even a bath plug,' scattering bottles, pills, tubes and electrical gadgets along the gleaming, mock-marble surface luxuriantly embracing the basin.

Stern was standing in the open doorway, examining the rolls of pasty flesh, the drooping breasts, the too-obvious library of metaphors for Tanner's physical and moral condition.

'What are you staring at? Want to measure my prick? Did you hear the one about the man who was asked whether he was a complete cretin? He said, "No, most people take me for a Jew." ' Instantly regretting the joke, Tanner trundled himself under the hot shower, his voice comfortably clearing the efficient, white-engineered hum of the sprinkler.

'What do you do for sex in this town?'

'Was I expected to fix something up?'

'An early screw works wonders. Everything falls into place, you can do some reporting.' Tanner shot a quick glance at Stern: 'How would you fancy Lagos?'

'You mean the city – or is it old soldier's slang for fellatio?'

'I was in Nigeria in December. A lousy, cockroach-infested room costs eighty quid a night unless you put yourself on the wrong island and then it's a two-hour traffic jam to get to see the upstart whose job is to prevent you meeting anyone of consequence. Oil flows over everything in a great slime of corruption. Just the place for you to study the benefits of black majority rule.'

Dripping on to the carpet, Tanner emerged with a towel round his several waists, his thin, balding hair plastered forward to give the impression of a Roman senator too coarse for the highest office.

'As a matter of fact we need a man in Nigeria. It might even be a staff appointment.'

He grabbed the whisky bottle, astonished and alarmed by words utterly unpremeditated and quite unauthorised. Foyle would never buy it.

'I'll stay here,' Stern said, 'to the end.'

Tanner cackled with relief. 'What have you been reading – Biggles? "Stern Sees it Through." Why the fuck did you want to be a reporter anyway? Weren't you once the brightest fart on the academic Left, occupations, TV rent-a-mob, Bertie Russell's War Crimes tribunal, dinner with Sartre. . . ? Didn't you win the Terrorist-of-the-Year award for tossing fireworks at police horses in Grosvenor Square? Didn't I warn you that journalism is a serious business?'

'You mean creeping up the arse of the Foreign Office or making sure Harry Oppenheimer supports your forthcoming Special Supplement on South Africa?'

'That's bloody insulting.' Tanner padded among his open leather suitcases, searching for appropriate clothes, leaving wet prints on the carpet. What really incensed him was Stern's untouched whisky glass. He found a short-sleeved shirt, drip-dry.

'You know your problem? Guilt. It's the disease of the twentieth century. *I* have nothing to be ashamed of. But you, you're *plus noir que les noirs*. You think it's smart to disparage your own kind.' Tanner carefully hoisted a leg into a pair of freshly pressed cotton trousers – even when turning to monitor a saucy pair of buttocks in the street he was nowadays careful to rotate his shoulders before risking his neck. 'The Rhodesian problem is no longer a racial one. It's simply a contest between moderation and violence.'

'That's what Ian Smith will tell you. It should be a happy interview.'

'If I get one.'

Stern nodded. 'Did Gilson give you an ultimatum?'

Tanner sat down on the double bed and reached for his shoes.

'Listen, I've been in this business for forty years. I was working as an office boy on the *Ramsgate Echo* before you were born. I was wading ashore on a beach in Normandy while you were still clawing at your mother's tits. I was flying three times a week from Seoul to Kimpo while you were swotting for your Common Entrance and learning that sex means six.'

'So Gilson did give you an ultimatum?'

Tanner bent to fasten his shoe and his kidneys screamed.

'He blackmailed you?' Stern persisted.

'Damn it, why abuse the language? We used to be taught precision – even those of us who went to elementary school. When we meant "oral" we didn't say "verbal"; when we meant "afraid" we didn't say "paranoid"; when we meant "a threat" we didn't say "blackmail".'

Tanner lit a cigarette. Stern noticed that the index finger of his right hand was stained to the knuckle. Tanner noticed that Stern badly wanted to swallow the whisky in his glass but was choked by pride.

'I earned my degree in the field,' Tanner said (or concluded). 'What about Hersh?'

Stern's long features betrayed no sign of relief, coded though these three words clearly were to signal a reprieve.

'I'll introduce you to Frieda.'

'Hersh's mistress?'

'His wife.'

'Jesus, you do play it straight.'

Descending to the front lobby of the hotel, Stern was waylaid by a suspicious character wearing an 'I love Rhobabwe' tee-shirt and a pair of John Lennon spectacles.

'Well?'

'I'm reprieved.'

Holzheimer nodded thoughtfully. 'I'm not surprised. The way you bribed him, wow! How come you're prepared to share the central narrative with Tanner but no one else? "Stern noticed, Tanner noticed, Stern noticed . . . " How come we never get "Holzheimer noticed"?'

Five yards on, Holzheimer wheeled like something in the New York City Ballet and came back.

'Just tell me one thing: did he drain your undrunk glass of whisky after you left his room?'

'How would I know, Bernie?'

Holzheimer took Stern by the lapel of his one good safari jacket.

'Don't mess with me, Barthes. Or is it Borges today?'

'OK – he drank the whisky, eighteen seconds after I left the room. He wears my finger prints on his stomach.'

When Gilson pushed the censorship form across the desk, Tanner snorted like a carthorse offered a bag of mouldy oats. But he signed it in his neat, sensible hand – not the ambitious flourishes and extravagant spirals of Selwyn Foyle's signature, or the mean, illegible scrawl by which Richard Stern periodically claimed that he had spent two dollars seventy-four cents on reaching the insurgent peasantry of Buhera.

'Any luck with the interviews?' Tanner inquired.

Gilson offered him a Rhodesian cigarette. 'Did you speak to Mr Stern?'

A thick vein surfaced in Tanner's forehead above his left eye and began to pulsate.

'In South Africa I saw Botha, van den Bergh and Harry Oppenheimer. I'd hardly rate Smith, Walls and Muzorewa in a bigger league.'

Gilson took a sodden handkerchief to his sirloin neck.

'Professor Vishnu Desai would be glad to meet you this afternoon, Mr Tanner.'

'Who?'

'He's very close to the Bishop.' But Gilson's voice lacked conviction. Nothing made much sense any more, even though Mr Smith's frozen portrait continued to squint and squirt integrity at him from the wall above his desk. Gilson's wife was walking further round the bend every day; she had fired two *more* servants in the past week, with the same explanation on each occasion – 'Mike, I could just smell the man'. And now his secretary Sharon was playing hard to get, leaving the office half an hour early on heels higher than ever. No sense in any of it – when he had reported to Prinsloo after driving Tanner into town from the airport, the Minister had almost bust a gut:

—Either he fires that Marxist scum Stern or he spends the next week fucking Coloured tarts in Union Avenue!

—I guess we could always arrange a visit to Victoria Falls, Gilson murmured.

Prinsloo shrugged. —Donna, you mean? You think she might convert the old sod?

Now Gilson sheepishly pushed a travel brochure across the desk to his guest.

'We could arrange a visit to Victoria Falls, Mr Tanner.'

Tanner marched along the corridor of Linquenda House (the corridor where Stern had been kept waiting for his work permit every twenty-nine days), descended five flights of stairs in mounting fury (against Gilson? the Minister? against Stern?), and came across an idle clutch of Africans staring at a large notice, *Hapana basa.*

'What does it mean?' he asked the helmeted security guard.

'Sir, it means "No Work", sir.'

Tanner nodded. 'What's the Shona for "No Interview"?'

'Sir?'

'Never mind.' He took a stroll. It was too hot and he soon succumbed to a pulverising despondency. Better a stringer than a stranger. No one had yet invited Tanner for a drink, not a single message had awaited his arrival; his diary remained empty and all the women parading the shopping precincts belonged to someone else – saucy little bitches in short dresses, their browned breasts bouncing out of low-cut bodices, some of them pushing prams to remind you where it all led.

Salisbury wasn't much. Tanner hadn't seen a single building worth two minutes' concentration south of the Sahara – no mosques or minarets, no wailing muezzins, no teeming bazaars, no desperate young hustlers anxious to sell the potted wisdom of the guidebooks, no history, no tragedy – just a colourless transplant of European suburbia dropped carelessly round a regimented, rectangular grid of intersecting streets designed to promote commerce while regulating anarchic native habits. Tanner bought a newspaper and found a bench under the shade of a palm tree in Cecil Square. Two fat black matrons occupied the other half of the bench.

'So who are you going to vote for?' he asked them, adding: 'I'm a reporter from London.'

'The Beeshop,' said the nearest woman. 'Ever the Beeshop.'

'Does everyone feel the same?'

'Every-*one*,' both women affirmed together.

He asked a few more searching questions, to each of which the two matrons offered an identical reply – 'the Beeshop' – then opened his newspaper with a small nod of contentment. Only a couple of hours after the most fearful corkscrew descent from 20,000 feet, he had already taken the pulse of the population. A real pro on the job again. So much for Stern's analysis of the 'urban grass roots'.

He turned to the entertainments page. A dirty movie might be in order, especially if air conditioned, but the display ads looked unpromising, merely the family films you could see in the London Odeons and ABCs, the space epics, the medieval galactic kingdoms, the unfunny comedies dredged out of the television, the wow-hit musicals featuring the newest of the new. Tanner experienced an acute longing for the X certificate cinemas round the Charing Cross (X) Road. He remembered the film he had sat through the day after Helen's death, the title had haunted him for fifteen years: *Sinful Swedish Nurses*. Three rows from the back, at 5.20 in the afternoon, twenty-five hours and eighteen minutes after he turned his head, he jerked off into a handkerchief as the Swedish 'nurse' Brigitta won her sexy bedroom wrestling match with the rich adolescent boy in her 'care,' straddling his chest with her stockinged legs and unzipping his trousers with mocking panache. As he came Tanner began to weep.

A hospital psychiatrist had promised him that these things do, gradually, 'go away'. Grief, said the doctor, is either 'transitory' or 'terminal' – usually 'the system' rejects it after it has served its 'function'. Vera had accompanied Leonard on his first visit to the hospital – she had wanted to talk about 'guilt' but the doctor would have none of it. 'Fighting your husband won't bring Helen back,' he rebuked her and after that Leonard came alone, though not for long. The psychiatrist had terminated the 'treatment' by bringing his finger tips together as if they were the positive and negative terminals of an electric circuit. Gloomily Tanner studied the Salisbury display ads. Harry H. Corbett of *Steptoe* fame was performing nightly at the Seven Arts Theatre. 'I am very happy to have seen this super country now,' Corbett was quoted, 'because it will never be the same again.' Tanner shifted his weight on the bench and noticed that the two black matrons had slipped away – perhaps his insistent questioning had frightened them. Another old entertainer, Eddie Calvert, 'the Man with the Golden Trumpet', was playing his staple 'hits' at La Bohème – including 'O Mein Papa' and 'Zambezi'. Calvert, too, was quoted: 'Two reasons why I left Britain: Harold Wilson and the wife.'

Tanner groaned.

He feared that if he now – in mid-afternoon – went back to his room in Meikles he might fall asleep and not wake up until after

237

the elections were over – certainly Stern wouldn't wake him. Nobody would wake him. For the first time he noticed how coarse was the newsprint between his fingers – sanctions, probably. Wearily his eye returned to the entertainments page. How about a dinner-dance with Jack Dent, now sixty-seven, at the piano? Jack Dent! – how could Stern know that Jack's career had taken off one night in the early thirties when the Prince of Wales dropped in to hear him at a club called the . . . the . . . Tanner had been a working-class boy much absorbed by the famous and fashionable entertainers, not least the danceband leaders who got invited to perform at the big country houses. The Blue Train, that was it. His eye fell lazily on a small ad.: 'Annabel, 135 Rotten Row. Sympathetic massage for real men. Ten per cent discount for SF.' For some reason – Joburg hadn't been as hot as this – he was reminded of the Profumo scandal; Tanner had not been the first to interview Christine Keeler, but he hadn't been the last, either. 'I hate being called a "scrubber",' Christine had told him, luminously beautiful. Tanner's eyes had closed. The Blue Train, Jack Train, Colonel Chinstrap, *Itma* – short for 'It's that man again'. Jack and Tommy both dead now. Going going gone, for one shilling and fourpence, to Mr James Joyce, Dublin 1904.

A girl with a limp beside the Liffey. A girl without a limp at a zebra crossing in King Street, Hammersmith – the one opposite the entrance to Ravenscourt Park. Tanner heard himself cry out in Cecil Square, Salisbury, and stood up abruptly, bathed in sweat and drugged sleep – absolutely convinced that Stern had just walked through his head. So Stern did know:

'Nothing in your life you've ever kept silent about – or lied about out of shame and misery?'

Stern, who majored in virtue. Stern, with his permanent expression of moral advantage.

Very well, he would confront Stern: 'Sorry it had to end this way but a newspaper is a collaborative enterprise. Good luck. I mean that.' Thank God the supercilious prick hadn't accepted Nigeria – insane offer! Nigeria was real money, two fat advertising supplements a year. Tanner's legs were heading back across Cecil Square towards the hotel, but his head kept repeating, 'ten per cent discount for SF'. *SF?* Science fiction? Stern walked past with a sneer etched into his pale face. 'Security forces,' he explained, and was gone. 'Five Mark for a fuck,' the oriental girl had said in English on the Reeperbahn, not at all the Curzon Street style of his youth: 'Want a nice time, darling? Feeling lonely, dear?' What would Annabel of 135 Rotten Row say?

Stern was waiting for him in the lobby of Meikles, squinting down his long nose as if sighting a rifle.

'Frieda Hersh will meet us here at 4.30.'

Tanner sank into a leather arm chair and ordered a cold beer. He could feel Stern's sly hand reaching for the tiller – when he should have been walking the plank. Then Patrick Warner was standing over Tanner's chair, his smile like freshly applied wallpaper glue.

'Why, I do believe it's Leonard! Where did we last meet – Lagos? Prague? Hong Kong?'

'How's things, Patrick? Still picking the food from the plates of others, then shitting it out on their heads?'

'Leonard, I suppose you realise I know this country like the back of my hand, though I don't brashly boast of the omniscience claimed by certain *arrivistes* . . .'

'I don't care for your "Black Man" column in the *Eye*.'

'Oh.'

'May I quote? "Old Tannhäuser is no longer the fearless, forthright war horse we once knew and loved. Now he cringes before his master's insane political ambitions and sycophantic courtship of the Lady-in-Waiting." '

'My dear Leonard, you can't believe I wrote that! I was *horrified* when I read it – so grossly unfair.'

'You wrote it. You also wrote that I had spiked six of Richard Stern's reports in as many days. A bloody lie!'

'But you did have this one problem about Richard's "Smith Concedes Internal Settlement a Smokescreen" story. It got on to the front page of the first edition while Foyle was with the American ambassador and when he saw it he was livid and ordered it lifted out of the paper.'

'So what? These things happen.'

'I'm genuinely sorry to have offended you, Leonard.'

'You mean you want to sell me something.'

'Is that despicable?'

Tanner sighed. 'Patrick, you may be right that majority rule has led to chaos, bloodshed and nepotism, and you may be right that Africans need firm authoritarian rule, not democracy. But one doesn't say so. Nor does one blather about Cecil Rhodes tossing in his hilltop grave in the Matopos – not in my columns, one doesn't.'

Berny Holzheimer happened to be passing through the lobby with his usual air of distracted intensity. The motto on his teeshirt seemed to have undergone a subtle alteration since lunchtime: it now read 'I don't love Rhobabwe'. Stern introduced him to Tanner.

'Your reputation preceded you, Leonard,' Holzheimer said.

Tanner grinned uneasily. 'What the fuck does that mean?'

'It means that Richard is the best reporter in Rhodesia.'

'Glad you think so.'

'West 43rd Street agrees.'

'What is this – a fucking commercial, or just a forged testimonial?'

'It was Berny who picked up that story of Richard's you spiked,' Warner told Tanner with an eye like a shallot soaked in vinegar. 'Remember that *ghastly* massacre perpetrated by a strangely anonymous District Commissioner?' Tanner flushed. Stern slowly stretched his legs and waited.

Holzheimer gazed at Warner reproachfully through innocent lenses: 'Patrick, you remind me of a tick-bird. You perch on the back of the nearest ox, just beyond the reach of its possibly dangerous tail, and you scavenge.'

Stern laughed. 'For the price of a dinner Patrick will sell you one hundred second-hand words about Ian Smith's love of his farm.'

Warner was furiously jingling the few coins in his pocket. 'How inventive you both are. Last time, I recall, one of you likened me to a "leech looping across the slime of colonialism with blind purpose". Which of you hardly matters, since you are notoriously the same person apart from Bernard's greater wealth and talent.'

'Stop bitching,' Tanner said. 'If any of you had been out on patrol with the Gurkhas in Malaya, hacking through snake-infested jungle in search of lynx-eyed gooks, you wouldn't be wallowing in fancy metaphors.'

'The fancy metaphor is Greene's,' Stern said. 'I believe he, too, was in Malaya.'

Warner smiled at Tanner's scowl. 'Leonard, aren't you going to invite me to sit down?'

'I'm not even inviting you to stand there.'

For Tanner it had become one of those days of arrival which, lost in a time-warp, seem to continue indefinitely, as if the sun had gone to sleep mid-orbit. Whether standing or sitting, his kidneys, gut and clotted veins all registered their protest in one screaming segment of his skull. And who was this little toad of a woman bearing down on him with a grin suggesting a lifetime's familiarity? He heaved himself out of his chair as Stern made the introduction.

'What will you drink, Mrs Hersh?'

'A teeny dry martini, Leonard, though Frieda knows she's being naughty.'

He glanced at Stern but got no response: if the End of the World had charged through the lobby neither would have offered the other a flicker of sympathy.

TWENTY-TWO

'So who's going to win the election?' he asked the taxi driver, from whose mirror dangled a pair of miniature boxing gloves and an equally minute Lonsdale belt.

'Aaah . . . The Beeshop, sir. Ever the Beeshop.'

Precisely! he would fire Stern tomorrow.

Presently a small worm of suspicion uncurled itself: 'What about Mugabe?'

There was no reply. He repeated the question. He had never trusted taxi drivers – even in London the old spirit of service was gone, the cabs were now hugging the square mile round Piccadilly and Park Lane, stuffing themselves with Arabs, two fares at a time, brazenly refusing to travel to any of the suburbs in which native Englishmen were now forced to live. 'What do you think of Mugabe?' he asked for the third time.

Tanner looked out of the window at a darkened city he neither knew nor wanted to know. An immense sadness possessed him. Grief is either transitory or terminal, the psycho had said. As Maugham's China-hand Waddington put it, 'Some of us look for the way in opium and some in God, some of us in whisky and some in love. It's all the same way and it leads nowhere.' Above all others, Maugham was the author to whom Tanner was devoted. He found Helen in virtually every page of Maugham. Had she lived she would have accompanied him on all his travels (but freely, freely), his constant companion and confidante. Tanner's eyes closed momentarily. She would have kept him out of trouble . . . in Moscow (the Metropole) they try to compromise you, in Warsaw they succeed . . . for some reason political oppression worked on him like an aphrodisiac, rendering the yielding flesh more tender . . . only in bugged hotel bedrooms could he be sure of an instant hard-on . . . although the subsequent oozing of what the quack usually called a 'non-specific' yellow fluid was unromantic anywhere . . .

'Moogahbay,' the taxi driver chuckled. 'Aaaaah . . . that one.'

Tanner wondered how to interpret this. It was in such situations that your cocky cub reporter (Stern) invariably got it wrong. Taxi drivers! Leaving the Governor of Hong Kong's dinner after an evening discussing business, sport and Red China, Tanner had been driven to a dark alley behind the docks where two young men were waiting to relieve him of his watch, his wallet and – if necessary – his life. He had asked them for one thing only, the snapshot of Helen in his wallet, and when they gave it to him he heard himself say, 'That's very decent,' – his last remark before he came round in hospital.

It was several days before Tanner discovered that his driver had not dropped him at 135 Rotten Row, or anywhere in Rotten Row, but at a similar establishment in Union Avenue owned – this is hypothesis, according to Holzheimer – by the driver's extremely extended family. 'Cleopatra's Den. Greater Rhodesia Land of Sunshine and Honey' was the message beckoning Tanner on a tatty signboard almost lost among the climbing weeds of a desolate front garden. Hands extended in blindness, Tanner groped towards a bungalow with a corrugated iron roof supported by unpainted brick pillars, only to be waylaid by a huge cactus which clawed at his face with almost Hong Kong-like menace.

A naked light bulb illuminated the front porch without much conviction.

He knocked.

Then again.

'Yes?' The young man confronting Tanner was neither white nor black.

'I saw your advertisement in the paper.'

'Yes? You have an appointment?'

Tanner's heart sank. For years he had sought but never found the ideal whorehouse, a spacious palace of sweetly ventilated rooms, clean bedlinen, hot baths and Indian women with dark, lustful eyes rendered even more provocative by kohl, women with soft, yielding breasts straining out of low-cut bodices, the bare midriff revealed by the cunning snake twist of the sari. A house in heaven: no pimps, no madames, no cash registers, no walls with ears. Cleopatra's Den, of Union Avenue, Salisbury, was not this ideal whorehouse. The small room into which the young man of mixed race ushered Tanner reminded him of all the examination cubicles in which doctors of medicine had charged him twenty dollars, or fifty, for a course of post-indiscretionary jabs – a raised bunk bed covered with a plastic sheet, a cracked washbasin, no soap, a dirty towel.

The young man of mixed race closed the door on Tanner without further comment. Perching himself on the plastic sheet, Tanner lit a cigarette and watched a cockroach move out from under something, on its way to something else, a life hardly more aimless than that of a journalist. As it turned out, the cockroach was heading for a small table piled with old copies of *Playboy*, *Penthouse* and *Stud*, their stained covers curling in the damp heat. The cockroach climbed the table, disappeared into a *Playboy* centre-page spread, then proceeded up the wall to examine the nude posters fixed with irregular lengths of Sellotape – Pirelli girls, Miss Universes, the famous Dietrich garters from 'The Blue Angel', Brando and Schneider in *Last Tango*, Fonda in *Barbarella*, Bardot in *God Created Woman*.

Tanner found these famous stretches of flesh reassuring; less and less did the room remind him of a devious doctor's clinic. He was wondering what to do with his cigarette end (the cracked basin?) when the door opened and a young woman walked in with a bright smile:

'You didn't get undressed then?'

He recognised the accent: Coloured Afrikaans. Her skin was milk chocolate, a gorgeous sheen lavishly layered over broad shoulders, powerful arms and the very breasts he had imagined spilling out of a Bombay bodice – though now supported by a meshed, see-through top belonging to a dress which began in vermilion and rainbowed down to apricot and peach. Her mouth, too, was vermilion – her mother's negroid mouth set beneath a nose which recorded some unknown Boer's loneliness and shame.

'They call me Miss April,' she said. 'I nivver ask a gintelman 'is name.'

He thought: Annabel . . . April . . . ? 'Leonard,' he said. (Indiscreet, perhaps, but he had learned that his pecker didn't respond to pseudonyms.)

'Well, Linard, I'll be beck in two ticks and I want to find you in your birthday suit. You can cover yourself with that towel.'

He knew the tone if not the voice: 'The train now standing at platform three . . .' Wearily be began to disassemble himself – getting undressed was nowadays an exhausting performance. He expected the plastic sheet covering the bunk bed to be cold on his back and buttocks; it was disturbingly warm. What stuck in his memory from the ambulance ride was her terrifying stillness. Unable to see her face beneath the oxygen mask (the ambulance men refused to commit themselves), he remembered his desperately impersonal choice of question:

'How bad is it?'

Quick, practical steps in the corridor and back came Miss April and her generous barbican, wrapped in a wild perfume.

'Now just you relex, Linard, you're as stiff as a tree.'

Feeling her strong fingers probing his neck he closed his eyes momentarily but opened them again because he wanted to watch Miss April's breasts swaying above him like ripe coconuts. How powerful these African females were compared to the fragile porcelain dolls who had soaped him, almost thirty years ago, before plunging him into the purging scalding water of a Tokyo bath-house. But that was a real civilisation, of course, pure-bred, honed to perfection by centuries of devotion and cruelty. After the bath he used to lie in limbo on the futan, suspended in the almost weightless contentment of a man coming round after an operation. Trying to fend off Korea.

'That's a nice dress, Miss April.'

'Thenk you, Linard. I bought it in Durban ectually – you can't git anything reelly naes up heer.'

'Did you buy your lovely body in Durban, too?'

'You men are all the same. Just big babies, reelly.' Her fingers had worked their way down, through the hag's breasts which layered his chest like half-empty Hoover bags, to the pasty flab of his belly. 'You could lose some of this Rhodesian Front,' she said mechanically but he laughed appreciatively. He carried a library of political jokes in his head and was always on the lookout for an audience.

'How long do I get?'

'Half an hour's eight dollars and a shower's fifty cents extra.'

'Do you join me in the shower?'

'I don't want that kind of talk,' she said mildly as her fingers began to probe the suburbs of his erogenous citadel – his penis responded with a quite visible redeployment under the towel, but Miss April's mascaraed eyelids did not bat.

'My earthquake zone.' Tanner affected a grin.

'Pardon?'

'Never mind. Where did you go to school, Miss April?'

'A convent near Plumtree.'

'A convent! They hardly trained you for this!'

'I was always brought up religious, Linard. A girl has to know what's right and what's not right.'

'I'm sorry to hear it.'

'I can see you've been around, Linard.'

Emboldened, he reached up with both hands and cupped them round her breasts. Her response was as rapid and mechanical as that of a nurse to a sudden incontinence: 'Turn over on your tummy, then.'

Meekly he obeyed.

'You git white trash types who walk in heer with the wrong idea, I mean if you do it once for them, you'll do it agin, then one day there's a knock at the door and thet's it.' Rolled on to his stomach like meat on a butcher's slab, Leonard Tanner felt put down, ashamed. *How bad is it?* He heard Miss April say that his jaw line could do with 'a bit of attention' but the words were lost in his rising anger: if she really wanted to be a straight masseuse then why didn't she wear a white tunic, why did she flaunt her body like a tart?

'You've probably got nodules,' she was saying, 'thet's lumps important men in executive positions git from all the tension.'

Wrestling to separate himself from the bloody plastic sheet, on which his sweat now mingled with that of rugby players with 'hamstrings' and 'trash types with the wrong idea', Tanner attempted to roll on to his back and failed – like a misshapen pork sausage resisting rotation in a frying pan. The two hands firmly gripping his waist may have had something to do with it.

'Pelvic,' he spluttered into the plastic sheet.

'You want a pelvic, Linard? That'll be five dollars extra.'

The door opened; it was the young man of mixed race.

'Mr Viljoen is waiting.'

'Tell 'im I won't be long. This one wants a pelvic.'

She rolled him on to his back so that he could see Bardot and Fonda as well as Miss April. As she pulled the towel away from his loins he once again read in her eyes the trained indifference of a nurse servicing a bedpan. At last her fingers found the one part of his body that had been clamouring for attention ever since he corkscrewed down from twenty thousand feet, no, ever since the SAA hostess brought him his whisky in a plastic glass on two long legs that hadn't quite measured up to his standards. Jawline, pedicure and 'facial' could wait.

His hairy hand gripped her wrist: 'Thirty dollars,' he said.

She raised her dark brows like a broker studying the Dow Jones index. 'You want to go the 'ole way, Linard?'

'Yes. The whole way. I'm not a wanker, Miss April.'

'Fifty.'

Leaving Cleopatra's Den (still under the impression that it was 135 Rotten Row), Tanner encountered three lusty, long-haired young warriors in camouflage fatigues, evidently soaked in beer and yelling loudly, the master race at play in this dubious zone of town still reserved for 'Coloureds'. Seeing Tanner stumbling into the night, they fell silent – he might be a General, or merely the fate that awaits us all.

Becalmed, Tanner attended the candidates' press conferences and yawned. His diary remained empty of significant inscriptions. Gilson was unyielding. His generosity extended only to the Ministry's official brochures and the flamboyant exhortations of the Election Directorate:

—Your Vote Means Peace. We are All Going to Vote!

—This is What the People Want!

—A high percentage poll is the way to show the Western world that we have African support for the internal settlement. All white Rhodesians should make sure their employees and domestic servants go to the polls.

('The word "sure" is redundant,' Stern had advised Tanner, another gratuitous prod.)

Thwarted by Gilson, Tanner tried the direct lines to the Prime Minister's Office (Smith) and Combined Operations (Walls) but was inexorably referred back, very politely, with soft, clipped vowels, to the Ministry of Information. To 'correct channels'. Meanwhile, Stern (whose posture reminded Tanner of a martyr confronting the gallows with theatrical dignity) presented him with a long list of police raids and detentions of Patriotic Front cadres in the townships – 'the fifth column', as Stern described them in tribute to the days when Harry and he had been allied.

'If you want to check my sources, I can take you to Highfield and Chitungwiza.'

'I'm not in nappies, you know, and I don't need to be spoon-fed. I've seen what you'll never see – four thousand Moslem refugees butchered on a single train during the communal riots in India.'

Stern shrugged. 'I assume I'm not to file any reports of my own while you're in town?'

'You assume correctly.'

Tanner's first telexed report stressed the heartening mood of racial cooperation 'throughout Rhodesia'. Blacks and whites now frequently dined together in the city's hotels, black and white runners competed in the same marathons, the internal politicians conveyed an impressive confidence, and the Patriotic Front looked 'a great deal less formidable from Salisbury than it does from London'. Tanner particularly liked that touch.

Despite promises, la Hersh did not produce le Hersh. Second-rank businessmen appeared in Meikles to explain to Tanner that what the country needed was 'confidence, stability, something our kids will be proud to inherit'. Tanner drummed his fingers on the arm of his chair, certain that his rivals were getting to Smith, Walls and Muzorewa – and maybe even to General Hersh. He chain-smoked and drank too much: time and again he composed curt messages of dismissal for Stern, but his stringer kept laying scrupulously researched reports of electoral malpractice in his lap with an almost dogged loyalty which Tanner distrusted but couldn't bring himself to guillotine. He told himself, twenty times a day, that if Stern was a shit then he, Tanner, was an even greater shit – though Stern was clearly the greatest shit of all. With decreasing conviction Tanner dialled telephone numbers off a yellowing sheet of paper; often he'd forgotten whom he'd called by the time an unknown voice answered.

'And does little Richard tell Leonard about Esther?' Frieda inquired, purring into the telphone. 'He doesn't? Naughty boy.' Unable to unravel her game, Tanner stifled his impatience, flattered her, even implying that he carried a confidential message for the General from the Foreign Office. He remembered telling Stern that good liars don't make good reporters.

With nothing better to do he accepted an invitation to interview someone called Professor Vishnu Desai at the Bishop's headquarters. Arriving at the Monomotapa hotel, as directed, he was re-routed (after half an hour's confusion) to the chaos of Charter Road where he found a mob of blacks milling about on the pavement, shuffling towards power and patronage like cattle towards water after an eighty-nine-year drought. Two helmeted security guards, who wanted to know his business, didn't even glance at his papers of accreditation when he produced them. Christ! And this was the foreign editor who'd been shown straight up and into the offices of Botha, van den Bergh and Oppenheimer!

'I've come to see Professor Desai.'

'Yeah?'

'I have an appointment for three-thirty.'

'Then you're late.'

'Listen, I was directed to the Monomotapa and—'

'What name?'

'Leonard Tanner, Foreign Editor of—'

'Mr Lenner?'

'Tanner.'

One of the security guards lethargically drifted to the intercom telephone. 'Mr Lenner for 'Fessor Desai.'

Fifteen minutes later, Tanner, jostled, searched, searched again, his name mis-pronounced on every landing by some goon with a walkie-talkie, was pushed into a crowded office with all the dignity of a packet being forced through a letterbox too narrow for it. A delicate, stick-thin Indian gentleman in a beautifully laundered, sky-blue safari suit was in the process of handing out money and what appeared to be petrol coupons to a mob of importunate party activists, watched by more security guards and a colour portrait of a pouting Bishop Muzorewa. (It was Stern who had remarked to Tanner that the Bishop's refusal to display his teeth when attempting to smile to the world was perhaps due to early exposure to the many versions of grinning Black Sambo whom food manufacturers in Africa felt obliged to plaster on marmalade jars, cornflake packets, tins of meat and everything else – until market research indicated that too many potential customers believed that Black Sambo was actually inside the meat tin.

—Yes, I heard that one twenty years ago in Kenya, Tanner had snapped.)

Finally Professor Desai's dark, oleaginous eyes settled on him.

'I hear that you are hopeful of an interview with the Bishop?'

'Yes.'

'The Bishop is the busiest man in Zimbabwe. In truth, Mr Tanner, he *is* Zimbabawe. But honesty also forces me to be frank with you – reports have appeared in your paper which have greatly upset the Bishop. Believe me, the Bishop is no stranger to criticism but he does expect fair play. None of us can understand why a newspaper such as yours continues to employ an apologist for terrorism as its local correspondent. A thief, too. A liar. A Communist.'

Tanner reached for his cigarettes. His hand shook. 'Our leaders—'

'You mean your editorials? But they are constantly contradicted by Comrade Stern's reports.'

Tanner had taken the precaution of clamping his first two despatches from Salisbury under the sweat-stained armpit of his best tropical suit. Producing them with a flourish, he quoted himself: 'Some say the new multi-racial constitution is too little too late, but the vast majority of Africans here hail it as a decisive step in the right direction.'

Desai nodded, bored. 'Yes, we have access to all reports sent by telex or telephone. That is perhaps one reason why Comrade Stern prefers the postal service. And when you have gone back to London, Mr Tanner, to resume your important position, we will continue to suffer the lies and slanders and calumnies of this . . . this . . .'

Desai's confected eloquence brought laughter from the Africans scattered about the office like lethargic plants. Once launched, this high, throaty hee-heeing continued under its own velocity, its own sense of celebration, leaving Desai rigid in his isolation, the long shadow of Uganda upon him. But he still held the Bishop's privy purse and the petrol coupons.

'Take my advice, Mr Tanner – get rid of Stern.'

Half-way down the jam-packed staircase, Tanner ran into the American who'd printed Stern's 'massacre' report after Tanner (at Foyle's insistence, don't forget) had spiked it.

'Hi!' Holzheimer smiled cheerfully. 'Any luck with Vishnu? No? Too bad. They still want you to fire Richard? I guess you've got too much professional pride to let your arm be twisted by a bunch of third-world hoods. Frankly, Desai is too thin to be dangerous. Africa isn't Shakespeare's Rome: here fat is power.'

Tanner nodded, uncertain of this disarming young man who carried the great name, and power, of the *New York Times* so lightly.

'Time for a drink, Mr Tanner?'

'I thought you were on your way up?'

Holzheimer smiled gently. 'Only to find you.'

Tanner let himself be driven out into the residential suburbs and then seated on the cool verandah of the American's rather luxurious house with an iced beer and a generous slug of scotch on the terracotta tiles at his feet. Tanner sensed that Stern had often sat in this same chair, opposite a large potted plant – more uncannily, he felt almost as if Stern now constituted a third, invisible presence on the verandah.

'Understanding this country isn't easy,' Holzheimer said.

'Hm.'

'When I first visited your own country, Leonard – I may call you Leonard? – I soon concluded that the English worship animals, having seen eagles, lions and oxen carved in relief on old churches. Of course I was then unaware that such animals are symbols of the Evangelists, derived from the vision of Ezekiel – well, you know all this, I'm boring you – but also analogous to the Egyptian sun god Horus and his four sons. Only when I began to study Carl G. Jung – that was after my first marriage busted but we won't go into that – did I begin to grasp the *fantastically* potent, though unconscious, role that primitive symbols play in the lives of the English. How's your beer?'

It was a point of honour with Tanner never to be beguiled by hospitality. A reporter on the move was always someone's guest.

'Are you saying something?' he asked with asperity.

Holzheimer's shoulders looked disarmingly frail under his flowered shirt of Indian cotton.

'I don't imagine so. It's just that Richard . . . well, you know, he's read his Jung too. He knows the symbols here, and the visions, and the voices of ancestors through the spirit mediums. Oh my oh my, he'd be angry if he knew I was telling you this . . .'

'He knows Africa according to Karl Marx.'

Holzheimer shrugged. 'He's no Kantian. Tell me, Leonard, do you believe the world's poor are responsible for their own plight? Should we send them powdered milk or lessons in self-help? I'm puzzled.'

Tanner lifted himself out of his chair, damp and crumpled, his white shirt spilling awkwardly from the sag of his stomach.

'I saw them carrying the bodies out of the King David Hotel in Jerusalem before you were born.'

Holzheimer nodded affably: 'While I was still in diapers – let's be accurate, Leonard. Shall I call you a cab?'

TWENTY-THREE

Even at six in the morning the sun was unfriendly. Arriving early at the airport, he bought a cup of coffee and a Dashiell Hammett paperback, then gazed with melancholic lust at the Air Rhodesia posters showing lovely white hostesses flashing smiles beside the Falls, the Zimbabwe Ruins, Rhodes's grave in the Matopos, the Kariba dam. The Rhodesian tourist industry was in desperate trouble – the South Africans had cancelled their package tours because of the high risk factor – and Tanner was in trouble of his own from a late-night drinking session in the home of General Hendrik Hersh. According to Hammett's detective, Nick Charles, hangovers result from going to bed sober; Tanner couldn't remember when he'd last tried it.

He sighed and lit a cigarette; if you start at 6 a.m. thirty will follow. Airborne exactly on time (white mischief – Tanner's joke on Stern), he opened the Hammett then closed his eyes, his face set in a scowl of aggrieved discomfort. Being alive was just death on the instalment plan.

But he had to see the Falls. One more 'wonder of the world' ticked off before the great pencil put a cross beside his name.

Fucking melancholia!

Eyes closed, the engines of the Viscount humming reassuringly, he was invaded by Frieda Hersh dressed in a khaki jump suit with a man-size revolver holster fastened round mid-tub, her legstumps waddling beneath a blancmange bum as she directed her garden-boy's languid efforts to scrape algae off her swimming pool with a long pole. At least Frieda didn't shriek; she was proud of her purr and played Tanner her 45rpm drugstore disc, 'I love Rhodesia', to prove it.

He had followed her into a Swiss-chalet-style drawing room dominated by a large photograph of Ian Smith and his wooden-faced colleagues signing the Unilateral Declaration of Independence. Almost every other photograph in the room was in tribute to the owner of the house – from Hersh the Sandhurst cadet to Hersh the great counter-insurgency commander of the terrorist war.

—Hubby is a great hunter, Frieda leered.

—Indeed.

Here the General holds the gigantic tusks of an extinguished elephant; here he stands, arms akimbo, behind a line of snarling lions whose dead heads are supported by forked sticks; here the victims are human, almost, and have been spared the forked sticks. A barefoot female servant came soundlessly into the room and gracefully sank to her knees before Frieda:

—*Nkosikasi?* she murmured.

—A double scotch for the boss. Frieda's gargoyle grin was fastened on Tanner. The girl rose, inclined her head slightly, and glided out.

—Why does she kneel? Tanner asked.

—Simply good manners, Leonard. It's instinctive. I found that poor girl in a burnt-out village south of Umtali. The gooks had killed both her parents with an axe. Can Leonard guess why? Leonard can't? It was because they persisted in attending the local Christian church, despite warnings. Frieda's pig eyes glinted.

—We don't hear much of that in little Richard's reports.

Twenty (almost unbearable) minutes later Tanner looked at his watch and mentioned the General.

—I had hoped . . .

—Hubby may be delayed. Very big war, yes?

—Hm. I hope he hasn't got cold feet.

—Frieda shares his bed – she knows he's got hot feet.

Gilson had promised that Tanner would be met on arrival at Victoria Falls, indeed the whole excursion was courtesy of the Ministry – but still no interview with Smith, Walls, or Muzorewa. Met he certainly was. Dressed in a two-piece orange uniform and a pert little hat, Donna would probably have been taller than Tanner even without the high heels. White mischief again. Her spoiled, swimming-champ's face apart, she was straight off an ad man's drawing board, with a gleaming VW mini-bus at her disposal. She introduced Tanner to the driver. 'Mr Tanner, this is Phineas.'

All three sat in the front, Donna in the middle, her skirt riding up nicely, too good to be true, any minute now they'd pull into some motel and pick up a bunch of Bavarian Nazis sporting '*ich liebe Strauss*' lapel badges, or a brace of wounded Rhodesian warriors on R & R who would easily eclipse the ugly old journalist with his turkey neck, smoker's cough, pot belly and (Tanner suspected) evil breath. It couldn't last – just as a first-class rail ticket to Greece purchased at Victoria couldn't protect you against a flood of stinking peasants, shitting chickens, drunken soldiers and toilets rendered unusable as you traversed the Balkans.

They passed a herd of zebra which scattered lazily at their approach, then began to buck and gallop. Tanner wanted to tell Donna. 'Fifteen years ago I turned my head at a zebra crossing in Hammersmith.' Returning from Beirut, he had been distempered to discover that the girl, though eight, was still not allowed to cross main roads on her own.—She's pampered, he told Vera, as if it was Helen's own fault she attended the private prep school he insisted on sending her to; her fault that she had not been born into the working class and raised in the same rough school of survival as her father.

—It's how she feels, Vera had said. —She's a nervous child. She shrinks into herself when other children pass in the street, she clings to me like a limpet. Traffic terrifies her.

Approaching a bridge defended by bored, sandbagged police reservists harassed occasionally by Zipra guerrillas and always by mopani flies, tsetse flies and the huge mosquitoes of the Zambezi Valley, Tanner remembered Stern's vivid (he had to concede) report of nights punctuated by muffled explosions as yet another elephant or wild pig strayed into the minefield which now ran in a continuous ribbon along the Rhodesian shore of the great river. Donna waved to the reservists who stared at Tanner with obvious resentment: here today, gone tomorrow. Tanner imagined Stern interviewing them, his sardonic paragraphs feeding off the banalities of dispirited men trapped in a scalding landscape of bleached skeletons.

'A lot of terrs about?' he asked Donna casually, faintly ashamed to have used that term.

'You bet! Zipra gooks. They cross the river in dugouts. The crocs bag some and we cull the rest.'

'I've seen a few wars in my time,' he told her. She hadn't volunteered her second name and he didn't need it.

'I bet you have, Mr Tanner. The Ministry specially said to give you a super day.'

As the mini-bus turned off the airport road and into the small town named after the Falls, Tanner's hangover was beginning to evaporate, yielding to a scenario of exotic proportions: *they*, the Ministry, had resolved to compromise him with the lovely Donna, a peach on a beach, a sunkissed model skipping across the sands of Durban, Florida, California, advertising orange juice or holiday fun in a blaze of English-speaking sunshine . . . Whenever her legs re-crossed, delicately negotiating the narrow gap between Phineas's gear box and Tanner's wide-apart cotton flappers, the swishing of hose carried him back across decades of helpless desire to seamed stockings, Rita Hayworth, a packet of fags for two-and-six, hot afternoons watching lovers miming copulation in Hyde Park within sight of the Park Lane hotels he couldn't afford to enter.

'How old are you, Donna?'

'A gentleman shouldn't ask, Mr Tanner. I'm twenty-three.'

Exactly my daughter's age had she lived: the words flooded into his throat like vomit but he choked them back: exactly my daughter's . . .

They breakfasted together (without Phineas, as he noticed with a qualm – but, hell, would one invite an English driver surely not?) on a hotel terrace enjoying a long view of the railway bridge joining Rhodesia to Zambia and of the postcard-famous plume of spray hanging above the invisible Falls. A waiter brought them coffee, orange juice, fresh rolls, two boiled eggs for the gentleman. Yes, her face wasn't quite up to the rest of her.

'It's bad form, I'm told, to say Livingstone discovered the Falls.'

'Sorry?' She leaned forward politely.

'Most of the rooms here are now empty, I suppose?'

She nodded sadly. 'Even at weekends.'

He saw (private view) her gorgeous brown limbs spread across a freshly laundered bed under a high, turn-of-the-century ceiling . . . drowned in pleasure, thoroughly compromised, he died of cardiac arrest.

'I've just come up from South Africa,' he told her. 'I interviewed Prime Minister Botha, General van den Bergh and Harry Oppenheimer.'

'You've been busy, then.'

Her little finger curled daintily round her orange juice.

Climbing back into the mini-bus (more flashing thigh) he challenged her to name the six other wonders of the world, all of which he had seen. She couldn't so he did. She said she would love to see all those places. Stretching his right arm along the seat behind her shoulder, he challenged her to name the four longest rivers in Africa, three of which he had seen. He wanted to put his hand right up her thigh right up right up right up. Quite suddenly Donna went into a tourist set-piece as if Tanner were a whole party of Japanese businessmen:

'Of all Rhodesia's wonderful resorts, Kariba and Vic Falls have suffered the largest number of 122mm, Soviet-built terrorist rocket attacks from the Zambian shore. However, many visitors continue to enjoy our beautiful climate and scenery, water skiing at the Cutty Sark Hotel or relaxing at the Arabic-style Caribbea Bay with its two pools and lakeside boathouse. On your left you now see the Elephant Hills luxury hotel with the top floor completely burnt out following a terrorist rocket attack. The estimated cost of repair is one million dollars. The famous Elephant Hills golf course now just out of sight was a favourite with such world-famous players as South Africa's Bobby Locke and Gary Player. Among its several unique hazards is a water hole near the eighth green where those of you who are lucky may catch sight of a crocodile which has grown from 1.3 metres in 1975 to over three metres as of now.'

'Lucky or unlucky?' Tanner laughed. Donna stared through him; she seemed to be in a megaphonic trance.

'Do you play golf, Donna?'

'That's a game I might take up later in life, Mr Tanner.'

On the pretext of studying her diamond ring he took her left hand.

'Who's the proud lord of the ring?'

'Sorry?'

Clearly she was hating him almost as much as he hated himself and when they boarded the river boat she promptly deserted him. Taking the public address system in her diamond hand, she waved with the other to a police patrol boat cutting up the river on the frontier of civilisation, her golden hair flowing across her imperfect features as the tourist boat picked up speed towards Kandahar Island. A man with his hair brushed like a Central European joined Tanner at the rail and pointed towards the distant Zambian shore:

'Much good it do you to step over there. Snakes, savages and gooks, you never come out.'

'Now I must tell you all,' Donna was saying, 'that our local people here, the Makaolo tribe, call the Falls "The Smoke that Thunders", the "Mosi-oa-Tunya".'

The delicious sadism of her pointed heels torturing the deck.

A handsome 'pilot', reeking of after-shave and with most of his shirt unbuttoned, announced himself as Warren Jones, ex-Rhodesian Air Force, and offered to take anyone on an 'air-flip' over the Falls at six dollars fifty a head. Warren Jones flashed one of many smiles: 'I guarantee to bring you back safely and if I don't you can sue me.' There being no takers for the 'air-flip', the pilot, looking slightly relieved, began to flirt with Donna. Later, as they drifted downstream, Tanner cornered the pilot (a story here?) and was told:

'We had ten wonderful years and if we must die now, well, I'll certainly give my life for this super country even if we are betrayed by the cowardice and double standards of our kith and kin.'

'You really believe that?'

'Yees I do. I've been working down in the Lowveld, on contract for Comopos, flying over terrorist-infested areas, doing sky-shouts and that kind of thing.'

Tanner recalled Stern's claim that the amnesty campaign had been a washout.

'Did you have any luck with your sky-shouts?'

Warren Jones was now chewing gum steadily. 'I'd rather cull the lot. The gooks read the British newspapers, "heroic freedom fighters within sight of victory" and all that shit. And they believe it. If I had my way I'd take every fucking British reporter in this country and throw him to the crocs in this river.'

These words, overheard, brought Donna to their side with a worried frown.

'Now, Warren, Mr Tanner's our distinguished guest.'

Momentarily her hands folded round his bronzed arm, forcing Tanner to conclude that this unreal, waxworks 'pilot' must be her fiancé, the source of the diamond ring. Adrift in the Zambezi, his loins aching, Tanner was possessed by a heated vision of their wonderful young bodies laced and locked together, sky-shouting and air-flipping in protracted feats of tropical athleticism. Yet the lovely Donna's expression was solemn with piety as she religiously informed him that 'in our country it's not the colour of a man's skin that counts but the colour of his integrity'.

Audible now, downriver, the thunder of the Falls.

Later, back on the hotel terrace, he watched a Rhodesian goods train creeping towards the centre of the railway bridge while a locomotive simultaneously snailed forward from the Zambian side. Halting half-way, they huffed and stomped like mating hippos then coupled with a distant clatter. Tanner felt the jerk in his loins.

'Donna, you're a very beautiful young woman.'

'With a nose like mine? I have to blame my dad for that.'

He didn't want to get diverted into her dad or his nose.

'You're the most charming guide I've ever had – and I've had a few hundred in my time.'

Oh, to have had her!

'Thank you, Mr Tanner.' This time she looked away, rather obviously fingering her diamond ring. But Tanner couldn't be stopped, a terrible need was colonising his common sense.

'I only wish I were twenty years younger . . . Donna.'

She made an effort: 'Well, I always say there's plenty the younger blokes don't know. When my Mummy was a little girl, Mr Tanner, she sat on the knees of the great Pioneers, tough, hardy, straight-backed men with faraway eyes and skins tanned like old leather. My parents brought me up to believe in that spirit of pride.'

The two trains clanked angrily on the distant railway bridge, under the great fountain of spray – a wedding-day quarrel.

Donna looked at her watch. 'I reckon we've just got time for the tropical rain forest if we hot-foot, Mr Tanner.'

'I could stay over-night,' he said.

'Would you prefer to see the crocodile farm?'

'If you were free for dinner.'

Her consternation brushed his absurd hopes like sandpaper.

'There's no flight to Salisbury tomorrow, Mr Tanner, only three a week now.'

'My daughter would have been your age, exactly.'

'I'm sorry,' Donna murmured, looking away from his exploded face of wax and leather.

'I once saw the body of a planter hacked to death in Malaya.'

The fierceness of her reply surprised him. 'Things aren't that easy in Rhodesia either. The man who gave me this ring is as dead as your planter.'

He sat slumped in the Volkswagen mini-bus, heading back to the airport, still damp from the rain forest and the cruelty of a world where baby crocodiles were more loved than old men.

He made an effort: 'Tell me about your fiancé, Donna,'

'You wouldn't be interested, Mr Tanner.'

It was Phineas, the driver, who broke the awkward silence that followed.

'Johnny was a fine man, Mr Tanner, the finest game ranger I ever knew. He loved his work, he loved animals, and when they sent us down to Mushambi Pools on the banks of the Hunyani River Johnny was happy. That's quite some place, elephant and buffalo roaming freely, then the terrs moved in and began to destroy the dip tanks and all the diseases we'd kept in check came back, red-water, heart-water, gallsickness, you name it. That's what your man Mr Stern calls national liberation, Mr Tanner. Johnny loved those tribespeople, he wanted to protect their way of life, he began to take very big risks, following the gooks' spoor for hours. I was proud to work for that man. So one day we came across a group of CTs feeding in a kraal, but when the village kids caught sight of us they stampeded their *mombes* to create a dust storm and the terrs opened up with AK 47s. We took cover under some acacia trees and Johnny got through on the radio to the SF and then we went forward. I tried to grab him, we didn't have the necessary cover, but Johnny just said, and this I won't forget, he just said, "Phineas, I don't hide from any gook." He said that. Then a bullet struck the barrel on his FN, ricocheted through his ammunition belt and tore open one of Johnny's lungs. By the time the choppers arrived Johnny had almost gone but I felt like a

257

brother to that man because he'd always been a brother to me. "Phineas," he said, "take my watch and give it to Donna and tell her that life has been good to me." '

Tanner kept his eye fixed on the narrow strip of tarmac passing under them as they passed the bored police reservists on the sandbagged bridge and headed for the airport.

'You know something,' Phineas continued in the same level voice, 'you people come out from London and tell me I'm suffering from racial discrimination because I'm black. But does it do me any good if I go to my father and tell him that he no longer has anything to teach me? Am I my father's equal?'

'You're his equal before God, Phineas,' Donna said.

Vishnu Desai's Salisbury residence groaned, that last Saturday evening before polling day, with politicians, businessmen, academics and journalists crowding around the lavish display of curries, sweetmeats and black market whisky that the party treasurer had provided in honour of his chief, the Bishop. Resplendent in their saris, the 'Ayshun' ladies who had prepared the feast now withdrew into humble, womanly groups, murmuring in Hindi about births, marriages and (no doubt) the wayward behaviour of Professor Vishnu's young cousin Indira who had returned from London full of 'hot ideas' and was reportedly setting up home in Southerton with an African Post Office clerk. As one lady explained to Bernard Holzheimer, correspondent of the *New York Times*:

'That does happen too often in that Post Office setup. Indira can only blame sheself if she gets she baby.'

Holzheimer circulated with casual affability among the guests, bodyguards and allowable gatecrashers waiting for the roar of police outriders which would signal the coming of the 'presidential' convoy. Desai, who now flitted about the house, cupping his hand under notable elbows, effecting introductions, prodding his guests like prize cattle, had draped a huge banner across his verandah, 'The Winners!', to greet the future Prime Minister of 'Zimbabwe Rhodesia'. Holzheimer was laying bets that the Bish would show up dressed in apple green.

Brimming with affability, Desai took Holzheimer's elbow.

'Berny, I must chide you.'

'Chide me, Vishnu, but don't flay me.'

'Your friend Stern continues to allege that we are financed from South Africa.'

'You were very wise not to invite him tonight, Vishnu.'

'And I informed you, two weeks ago, that 160 Zanla CTs had

come on-sides in Manyeni. This appeared in your famous paper as an "unsubstantiated claim" by a "middle-rank UANC spokesman".'

'Vishnu, when the Bishop appoints you Foreign Minister, I'll appoint you Foreign Minister, too.'

Desai turned away and Holzheimer edged through the throng to the corner of the room where Leonard Tanner squatted in sullen isolation, a plate of chicken vindaloo balanced on his knee, a glass of wine tucked jealously under his leg – invited at the last minute, yet still ostracised, an armadillo.

'Hi,' Holzheimer said.

His mouth full, Tanner nodded, his eye fastening on the American's long, curling hair with the amiability of a Sweeney Todd. Holzheimer read him.

'You think I'd look better in a hair band like John McEnroe?'

Aggrieved by Tanner's churlishness, Holzheimer grabbed two visiting Bavarian 'observers' who were having the time of their lives and introduced them to Tanner, forcing him to half-rise to his feet while endeavouring to keep the chicken vindaloo on his tilting plate.

'Mr Tanner is one of Britain's most senior newspapermen here in Rhodesia at this moment in time,' Holzheimer explained.

Sensing fun, Patrick Warner, who had already squeezed the Bavarians for absurd quotes, jettisoned the President of the Rhodesian Chamber of Commerce and worked his way towards them, repainting his rubbery lips with his tongue as he came.

'Why, Leonard, so they *did* invite you after all.'

'Fuck off, Patrick.'

The two Bavarians exchanged glances. 'Bishop halt Communism Afrika,' one of them ventured to Tanner. 'Man of Destiny. Wind of change.'

'Wind of change equals fart of expediency,' Warner said.

Tanner registered fury. 'Have you no manners at all?' Warmly shaking the Germans by the hand, he furnished them with a brief history of his 'love-hate relationship' with their country, starting with Frederick the Great and Bismarck, proceeding to Konrad Adenauer and Willy Brandt, then concluding with their own Franz-Josef Strauss, whom Tanner had interviewed in Munich in 1975.

'*Sie haben ausgezeichnet Arbeit since den Krieg gedone, München zu rebuilden.*'

Holzheimer thought he understood German but now realised he was under a delusion.

'*Ich immer das Hofhaus bevisite wann immer ich Kann,*' Tanner added, very flushed with this self-imposed effort and Patrick Warner's unrestrained laughter:

'My dear Leonard, one wins wars in order to impose one's own language, not to desecrate that of the losers.' He smiled at the baffled Bavarians, who began to edge away, nodding politely. Warner invariably knew everything, even before it happened, and what he knew he sold. Thus the *Eye* in London was already in receipt of a new 'Black Man' column reporting that 'old Tannhäuser' had been shown round Victoria Falls by the lovely daughter of the Minister of Information, to whom he had made certain 'Ugandan' proposals without ever guessing her identity. Holzheimer and Stern had concluded that Warner must have harvested this damaging item of gossip from Mike Gilson, with the Minister's connivance.

Warner now turned his back on Tanner in favour of Lord Orchard, a member of the six-man Conservative team despatched by the White Hope to monitor the elections. The two men greeted each other warmly; Holzheimer, unashamedly eavesdropping, gathered that they had both attended a recent society wedding in Sussex at the end of which the bride went off with the best man and the bride's father disappeared with the groom's step-mother – or something like that. Holzheimer noticed that Tanner, despite his wounded pride, was also edging towards the peer.

'Frankly,' said Lord Orchard, 'Muzorewa's straight out of a hat box but who else is there? Personally I'm very fond of Joshua but he's too devious for his own good and the Foreign Office have as usual cocked up that option by playing the ridiculous Hersh. As for Mugabe, well he's pure Peking duck, isn't he?'

'Lord Orchard,' Tanner barged through, 'in your opinion will this be a free and fair election?'

'My dear fellow, depends who wins, don't ya know? Oh God, don't quote me – aren't you Tanner, the one who works for my friend Selly Foyle?'

Helen hadn't quite trusted him; perhaps he still smelt of falling masonry, dynamited concrete; perhaps the fatherly hand which gripped hers still carried the tension of Beirut.

—No, *you* must decide when to cross the road, Helen. Don't run, walk. And keep your eyes open.

—Shall I go now, Daddy?'

—It's no use looking at me, child. Look at the road. Look right, look left, then look right again. No, don't swivel your head like a mechanical doll, you must really *look*.

—What's a manical doll, Daddy?

He almost said, —Your life may depend on it, but checked himself in horror: she was only eight!

He withdrew his hand. She clutched at it but he pulled it away again. He wanted Helen to 'be herself'. Tanner was a passionate believer in 'being oneself.' Men should be men, women women, Jews Jews – be true to your biology, your race, your nation, your generation, your class. Don't pretend. Nothing sickened him more than the spectacle of ageing men and women wearing make-up, dressed in bikinis, holding hands and flirting on the beach or jiving gaily in nightspots – ugh! – flaunting the decaying sexual charms of their obese bodies. Be yourself. In forcing Helen to conform to his own standards of self-help he knew he was teaching her to be 'herself', self-reliant, independent, capable of standing on her own feet . . . So he pulled his hand away.

—You must decide, Helen. When the road is clear you must cross. Yes, on your own. No, I shall stand here.

Her trembling almost made him relent. But it was for her sake.

—Is the road clear now, Daddy?

—You must decide, Helen.

When he heard the sharp report directly behind him he was instantly back in Beirut. He prepared to fling himself, for the hundredth time, to the pavement.

From behind his rimless glasses Holzheimer was studying Tanner.

'They're saying that Carrington, not Pym, will get the F.O. What do you think?'

Tanner realised that Holzheimer must have asked him a question. He shook himself like a drenched dog.

'Frightfully sorry,' he murmured, 'I didn't quite catch that.'

'One also hears that Maggie's let it be known that if the F.O. try to block recognition of Muzorewa, she'll purge the whole bunch.'

Normally Tanner would have felt obliged to try and explain the subtle intricacies of British politics to the American, but there was something about Holzheimer which unnerved him, something so incorporeal as to seem almost ghostly.

Desai came past. 'Enjoying yourself, I hope, Mr Tanner?'

'Mm. Excellent hospitality.'

'The Bishop is expected any moment now.'

Tanner felt his sleeve plucked. Turning, he found himself confronted by retired General John Power, one of the unofficial, self-appointed, American election observers.

'You British?' His voice was like a silted estuary.

'Yes.'

'You Leonard Tanner?'

'Yes.'

'Why don't you fire that Communist? Listen, tell your people in Great Britain this: I have spoken with Mr Ian Smith – alone – for seventeen minutes. In my view that is a sincere man much misunderstood. He cares about the black people of this country.

He's got a large vision, that man. It's up to you fellas to clean up his image.'

'Well . . .'

'Listen, if the Soviets ever get their nukes and tacticals installed down here then it will be curtains for our South African partners and you know what that means, Mr Tanner. Having sold ourselves out in Nam we have no choice but to draw the bottom line right here. Pity is that Jimmy Carter's America now resembles a crippled eagle pecking out its own heart.'

Holzheimer intervened. 'Tel Aviv and Salisbury are the same town, isn't that right, General?'

Either the General didn't notice the provocation or he enjoyed it. 'That's correct. If you don't believe in yourself no one else will.'

'We need a new President and the British need a new Prime Minister, is that your position, sir?'

'Correct,' said General Power. 'The way the opinion polls are going, the British will be lucky first. As for Carter, his impeachment is no longer a maybe, it's now a must.'

'And what will you do to Andy Young, General?' Holzheimer asked, abruptly flourishing a notebook.

The General snorted. 'Young is almost black. I wouldn't want to be almost anything.'

'Some of us have our misgivings about the Lady,' Tanner said.

'She's this country's only hope, Mr Tanner, and your country's too.'

'Mr Tanner is Life President of the Middle Ground,' Holzheimer said, his normally reedy voice now carrying a 'caw' sharp enough to rouse a tree full of crows – again Tanner felt disabled by a surreal force that infiltrated every rotting fibre of his being.

The roar of motorcycles outside.

'I hear alarums, excursions, now bugles,' Holzheimer said. 'Look – Vishnu, master of ceremonies and fund-raiser extraordinary, now pushes through the cordon of courtiers to receive the Bishop of the Limpopo and to conduct him to a throne from which his two-tone shoes will dangle several imperial-episcopal inches above the ground. His future subjects line up: the Chamber of Mines and the Chamber of Commerce grapple for precedence while Industry and Agriculture attempt to throttle one another in the receiving line. Importunate hacks kicked aside – wait, dog! a taste of things to come. Finally Leonard Tanner is led forward on a short leash. Listen, now . . .'

'I'm very glad to meet you, Bishop.'

'Welcome to Zimbabwe.' The Bishop was already staring at Tanner's regimental tie as if he wanted to buy it.

'Are you confident of victory in this election, Bishop?'

'Super-confident.' (Courtiers laughed. One or two squealed 'Heav-ee' and 'Aiya'. Businessmen and bodyguards pressed around the garlic clove of power.)

'How many seats do you expect to win, Bishop?'

'All.'

'And what of your rival Sithole?'

'The Reverend Sithole is of today my colleague in the Transitional Government. How can I speak ill of a colleague? I will not do that. Anyway, that man is finished. Washed up. Where did you get that tie?'

'Er . . . it's my old regiment.'

'Yes, yes, where do they sell it?'

'Er, the Army and Navy Stores.'

'Let Vishnu have the address before you leave.'

Tanner asked about Joshua Nkomo.

'Who?' General sycophantic laughter. The Bishop smiled without showing his Sambos and the shirts of the bodyguards flapped out of their trousers as they doubled up – life in the service of the Beeshop was a scream from dawn to dusk. But Tanner was persistent, risking Muzorewa's displeasure.

'Could you work with Nkomo in certain circumstances, Bishop?'

'I don't know this man.'

'And what of Mugabe? You have described him as a "Communist-backed external terrorist".'

'He thinks he can seize power through the barrel of a gun. Maybe he has been led astray. I can pray for him.'

'What success have you had in persuading Mugabe's guerrillas to lay down their arms?'

'All these men you see around you are freedom fighters. The war is over.'

'Will you continue the military raids on Zambia and Mozambique after you become Prime Minister?'

'That's entirely up to Kaunda and Machel. I am a man of peace. I am a dove. I believe in reconciliation. But if others choose to pick a quarrel with me . . .'

Muzorewa released a charismatic pout which precipitated an outburst of raised fists and more cries of 'Heav-ee . . . Ayia'. Professor Desai led the chanting. Tanner was wheeled away. At last he had a story – an exclusive interview with one of the big three; well, the questions were exclusively his, even if the whole of Salisbury was writing down the replies. To his fury he saw the off-white suit of Patrick Warner scuttling into the darkness ahead of him . . . Reaching his hired car, Tanner was nonplussed to find a leaflet tucked behind his windscreen wiper. 'Pasi Puppets!' it declared. Tanner wasn't sure what 'pasi' meant but he noticed that every parked car carried the same leaflet, each bearing a blurred, but unmistakable, photograph of Comrade R.G. Mugabe. Incredulously Tanner gazed at the black security guards – one of them offered him a slow smile.

Holzheimer passed as Tanner fumbled for his car keys, cheerfully waving one of the 'pasi' leaflets.

'It seems "external terrorism" is alive and well in suburban Salisbury, Leonard. Maybe the Bishop prayed for Mugabe too hard.' Holzheimer prodded his glasses up his curling nose. 'I'm expecting to find your devoted man Stern at my place – any message? No?'

'That's wine, Richard, not blackcurrant cordial.'

'You're rich.'

'I was thinking of your liver. Couldn't you close those predator's eyes for a few moments, they unnerve me.'

'To speak of mischief in your underdone Californian features would be like ascribing bad temper to Charles Manson.'

'You've opted out through sheer arrogance. Only God can play the star part off-stage. You offer Tanner the limelight solely in order to torment him – your revenge on Harry. Yeah. And how you cultivate your own silences – the great Baconian garden of a hero's discretion!'

'One does not hear oneself.'

'As for the rest of us, your foils and follies, how we talk! Well, Americans believe in talking.'

'Then why complain?'

'Shall I tell you why your marriage failed and why you still haven't found Esther even though she probably passes you in the street every day? Because you're too lazy to deal with people! Your ideal life is spent in a semi-darkened room, behind locked doors, telephone off the hook, skimming conceits from learned journals in between bouts of brandy and shallow sleep. OK, if some bird would be obliging enough to come and lay you once a week without taking too long on the job you might let her in – though you wouldn't trust her with a key. Three years ago, in darkest despair, you threw yourself on the mercy of a man you despise, Tanner, in search of a new, abrasive, extrovert vocation which might redress the imbalance between your well-muscled *vita contemplativa* and your enervated *vita activa* – great! – yet now the same old corrupting inertia seduces you into abandoning the world for literature, whereupon – oh boy! – whereupon you take the opportunity to blank yourself out of your own life!'

'Berny.'

'Yes, Richard?'

'I've had another letter from Beth. She wants to marry Harry. She's petitioning for a divorce.'

'That might be as overdue as reform of the Irish contraception laws. Who's she citing – Frieda Hersh?'

'She's citing you, Berny.'

TWENTY-FOUR

The Bishop's campaign column had reached Protected Village 10. Hemmed in by gum-chewing Special Branch officers in crotch-hugging shorts, and by his own bodyguards, some of them dressed in the B-movie uniform of the Pfumo reVanhu, the Bishop emerged from his wheeled fortress on short legs, smiled without opening his lips, waved his baton to the village congregation, and said 'Kwenge'.

'What does "kwenge" mean?' Tanner asked the nearest African. (He had tried to hire a local reporter as guide and interpreter, but without success.)

The villagers had been assembled hours ago, men and women in segregated groups, awaiting freedom's carnival without impatience. Life in a 'PV', a 'behind-the-wire', was no fun anyway; as Holzheimer reminded Stern, 'fighting a Japanese quartz watch is a contest for losers'.

The Bishop went into a jig. But his Shona cadences remained flat and soporific. No Martin Luther King, he.

'Shouldn't you be at your boss's elbow, Richard? Look at him, all alone, with that Hogarthian stomach, having to ask kaffirs what "kwenge" means.'

Holzheimer had been treated to a rather severe lecture by his friend during the sixty-kilometre drive from Salisbury, much of it across the twisting, rutted dirt tracks of the tribal trust lands. Almost a castigation, with the nasty kick of a delayed action fuse. Stern had been brooding about 'certain comments'. He didn't entirely deny the charge of laziness but he did resent the 'gratu-itous' remarks about certain women 'in my life' and he did, most indignantly, refute the allegation that he had withdrawn from active service in the political trenches to cultivate a private garden of literary introspection. He had simply been muzzled, silenced, by

266

the convergence of two factors: Prinsloo's hostility and Tanner's arrival.

'Orange groves to your left,' Holzheimer said. 'Have you noticed how an orange tree in life looks like an orange tree in a children's book? Just as trains observed from a high bridge always resemble toy train sets. I'm sorry . . . I just have to tell you these things.'

Stern strongly advised the owner-driver of the car (whom he had generously agreed to accompany to the protected villages of Chiweshe) to interpret certain narrative silences as 'the symbolic context of political censorship'.

'Lots of contexts this morning, Holzheimer commented, as his shock absorbers took a continuous hammering from ruts and anthills. 'I am a man without contexts. It's like being without life insurance. I travel light under the Southern Cross. My rare visits to New York are drenched in invisible ticker tape. The evening begins in the Dakota Building, black tie and artichokes, and then on to a private viewing at the Met on the arm of Mrs Michael Henderson, Friend and Patron of the Museum. She is beautiful and only forty-two; we do not merely pause before Goya's massacre, we give ourselves to it. Later, in the studio-apartment which Mr Michael Henderson, Vice-President of Pepsi Cola, does not visit, we give ourselves to each other and – in the moment of peace between orgasm and sleep – to the not entirely fanciful notion of Stern as disciple of Goya. Wait! You were seen leaving the Prado with Mrs Stern on 14 October 1972. In the morning my slender torso slips out of Mrs Michael's scented bed, showers itself, coffees itself, writes a few alimony checks, and flies back to Rhodesia, refreshed, ready for anything, even the Beeshop – even you. By the way, we were talking – OK, *you* were – about Brechtian alienation and last night, just after I *finally* persuaded you to stop drinking my wine and go home – though at some risk to your fellow motorists – I came up with a rather nice example. Of alienation. A man has been paying life insurance premiums for years but the cut-off date is approaching and he suddenly grows resentful that he hasn't died and made a profit. Like it?'

'All you Americans ever think about is money.'

'Oh sure. And who buys the chewing gum for these trips?'

The Bishop was mocking his 'internal' rivals. Chief Chirau had chosen an elephant as his election symbol: 'Should we bring the elephant to the city or keep him in the forest?' As for Sithole's flaming torch, what did it resemble if not an ice cream cone and at what age do we chase after ice creams?

Stern heard the tinkle of ice cream vans on the housing estates of Royal Oak, north of Wormwood Scrubs; saw his wife pass the kids, arms laden with pamphlets.

Tanner noted Stern and Holzheimer together, the other side of the seated audience. Whenever he looked at them they seemed to be grinning in his direction. He asked the African at his side why the crowd kept chanting 'Heav-ee' but was so bored by the elaborate reply that he saw himself in the mirror of time and knew he was past it. He'd treated life like a national savings certificate whose dividend and bonus were to be paid out in a perpetually deferred future. Success, acclaim, wealth – tomorrow. Life had been a permanent rehearsal for the 'real thing' but the fogged mirror now told him that the rehearsal was the final performance. Nevertheless, in six months he would at last harvest the endowment policy to which Tanner, L. (his parents had given him only one name though his brother Gerald was given two to Leonard's immense resentment) had doggedly contributed for thirty-five years.

The Bishop was waggling his stick angrily. 'Sithole claims he started the war and only he can stop it.' The crowd squatted expectantly through a long, dramatic pause; as a measure of authority Muzorewa kept them waiting.

('When he becomes Prime Minister,' said Stern, 'he'll keep them waiting even longer.')

'It's like a divorced woman claiming she's still my wife,' the Bishop concluded dramatically. The crowd laughed in delight while the bodyguards continued to scowl and finger the bandoliers coiled round their High Noon torsos, tilting their cowboy hats at ever more rakish angles as the Bishop's coming power began to come.

'Is that any way for a Christian Bishop to talk?' Holzheimer complained loudly.

Twenty yards away similar thoughts had occurred to Patrick Warner, now sidling up to Tanner.

'It's the onward march of Islam, Leonard. I see your colleague is still with us.'

'Fuck off.'

'I was the last man out of Saigon,' Holzheimer murmured to Stern.

'Winched off the embassy roof in a zip bag?'

'Correct – the day Charlie really got his shit together.'

'Choppers falling out of the sky "like poisoned birds"?'

'Damn you, Stern, that's my line, you know I'd abandon this mindless job if I could write like that for *Playboy* or something.'

'I don't care what the Communists say!' cried the Bishop into his microphone. 'I put my faith in the good sense of the American Congress.'

Helen hadn't screamed or made any sound at all. He remembered turning his head, then – then? how long? fifteen years to

268

fabricate an answer out of the buried moment – then a sort of thump, very soft, muffled, almost harmless, followed by the more alarming sound of screeching tyres. When the zebra crossing came back into focus (as he tried to explain to the hospital psychiatrist, crying and crying, dear, sweet, trusting Helen) all he could see was nothing, just an unknown car ten yards down the road, I think it was ten, skewered sideways with its front wheel up on the pavement, with its front wheel up, up, but not on the pavement. Where was she? where where where? Rising panic. Only when the young driver of the car climbed out like a man being led to the gallows, forcing himself to bend and look under the front wheel the up wheel . . .

The Bishop had finished. The campaign convoy would now proceed to PV 12 (PV 11 being too risky, due to a strong Zanla presence in the area, though Gilson and the Bishop's officials weren't admitting that). Casually a slender young American intercepted the Bishop as he made for the steel bowels of his vast, armoured truck.

'Holzheimer, *New York Times*.'

'I know you.'

'Bishop, what's your basic philosophy regarding capitalism and socialism in Africa?'

'I am a pragmatist, like Hastings Banda. The OAU can shout at us and denounce us but Banda and I and all our people will shout back with full stomachs.'

When he heard the sharp report directly behind him Tanner was instantly back in Beirut – two hundred hacks sheltering in the basement of the Commodore Hotel under random mortar bombardment. He had told Helen not to fear motorcycles and container trucks – 'so long as you keep your eyes open' – but now he was seized by his own fear and there was no one bigger or older than himself to tell him not to have it.

The Bishop's armoured vehicle roared out of PV 10 with the slow, complaining pitch of a wounded elephant. 'Bloody hot,' Tanner muttered to himself, climbing back into his hired car. Glancing about for anyone in need of a lift, anyone who might speak some English – his spirits were depressed by this stifling journey through desolate countryside strewn with burnt-out stores, shuttered village schools, blasted dip tanks, closed grinding mills, wasted cattle. The hectic zig-zags of the helicopters above the Bishop's convoy had at first reassured him but now it quickened his sense of alarm. The small dusty boys waving shyly as they passed – were they part of Zanla's intelligence system? Were these the notorious '*mujibas*'?

Tanner had seen the driver straighten up, his youthful features stricken, his eyes glazed, and then he said, 'Can you help me, please?' Later, after the two of them lifted the front wheel off her chest, the stranger said, 'I wonder where she lives,' a nice young Australian, his VW beetle covered in across-the-world stickers and wallabies. The front wheels had traversed Asia and the Middle East before coming to rest on this little English girl who (he was trying to explain) had just stepped straight out – 'It all happened so quickly, oh Jesus what have I done, how do we find her parents?' The traffic didn't stop at first, busy people in a hurry, some even hooted irritably, whenever Tanner heard the modern cant word 'community' he . . . until a group of pedestrians began to kneel round Helen and someone ran to the public telephones the other side of King Street, outside Latymer School . . . Ambulances don't come. When the police arrived and the young Australian realised Tanner was the girl's father he leapt back in horror as if Tanner's reticence now struck him as inhuman . . .

At PV 12 the bodyguards spread out and the Bishop began with a short prayer in the name of Jesus Christ. Vishnu Desai was pacing up and down with a hungry look.

'Any minute now, he'll take a collection,' Stern said.

'As soon as you vote, sanctions will be lifted!' the Bishop declared and the village women ululated.

'I guess these peasants miss their imported scotch and video machines,' Holzheimer mused.

Tanner needed a scotch. Pity Zimbabwe if her destiny was this Bishop. Helen had a touching way, before she spoke, of asking: 'May I say something?' and now as he bent over her, touching her frozen face, he silently begged her to say 'May I say something?' but she didn't. She never again asked permission to say something.

—How bad is it? someone asked.

Vera under sedation. Vera devastated and unforgiving. The hospital psychiatrist had promised them that these things do, gradually, 'go away'. Grief either 'transitory' or 'terminal'. Then one day the psychiatrist had brought his finger tips together and that was that. For fifteen years Vera had barely spoken to her husband.

'Do you want me to drive this stretch?' Stern asked.

'Do I look as if I want you to drive? Or maybe you're familiar with every landmine planted by your gook friends? Did Esther send you a street map?'

Sullenly Stern climbed into the passenger seat. He had wanted to drive.

'How old are you really, Holz? You don't look a day over ten.'

'Richard, the mere shuffle of my sneakers on a Haight Ashbury staircase used to herald a riot of *son et lumière* among my fellow creatures. When I lived on Christopher Street there wasn't a single mugging in the West Village for a whole year and do I ever lie to you, my lord and creator?'

Stern sulking.

'I fear that silence of yours, Stern. Too often the republic of letters lapses into empire under its oppressive heel.'

Helicopter low overhead.

'The ruling culture has only one project,' Stern said. 'To hijack the future by cancelling the past. Muzorewa addresses Smith's prisoners in Smith's concentration camps and he doesn't even promise to liberate them.'

'Maybe he hates to make false promises.'

'Let's go.'

'Do we bother with PV 15, chief?'

'*Bado kidogo*, as they say in Swahili – not just yet. The drifting leaf on the sluggish stream of East African liberation. Take the tarred road south of Mazoe, Holz, I want to file my report before Tanner writes his.'

'Wow! High Noon at last! But what of loyalty to your boss? Didn't you attend an English public school designed to produce rubber planters and subalterns in the Grenadier Guards?'

'Everyone north of the Limpopo is on the transfer list, Holz.'

'Should I be taking notes?'

'Roadblock ahead.'

Two Land Rovers supported by a dozen armed police reservists had been parked across a peaceful, tree-lined road on the northern outskirts of Mount Pleasant. A young reservist in a floppy blue hat slowly scanned the interior of the car then showed Holzheimer a cardboard-backed sheet to which three snapshots had been pasted.

'Did either of you gentlemen ever see this woman?'

Both Holzheimer and Stern shrugged negatively. The reservist produced a second sheet of snapshots for inspection. Holzheimer again shook his head, sincerely this time. Stern examined the photographs, then whistled.

'Isn't this Paul Robeson, Holz? Remember Peekskill, forty miles up the Hudson from New York City? Every summer thirty thousand progressives used to congregate at Camp Beacon and who more progressive than Paul and Jane Meyer? In 1949 Robeson went up to Peekskill to give a concert on behalf of the Harlem Chapter of the Civil Rights Congress, which had been cited as subversive by the Attorney General. Esther's parents found themselves caught up in a coordinated attack by local vigilantes, patriots,

Legionaires, all screaming "Kikes niggers reds!" while the Westchester County Police openly fraternized with the mob.'

The bemused Rhodesian police reservist recovered his snapshots from Stern with palpable impatience as the line of cars built up behind Holzheimer's.

'Neither of you has seen the white woman or the African male in these photographs? Both these persons were reportedly sighted in this area last night. The woman was dressed as a nun. They're wanted for terrorist crimes and treason.'

'What's the man's name?' Stern asked the police reservist.

'Sometimes Cubans Urimbo. Otherwise Comrade Doctor Zimunya.'

From Richard Stern, 17 April 1979, Salisbury (telex, UPI, Robinson House, collect, 1630):

The entire white population has been mobilised to deliver black voters – farm labourers, industrial workers, miners, domestic servants – to the polls. The Election Directorate has launched a massive propaganda campaign, said to have cost R$250,000, in the press, television and radio, to persuade every black adult to vote.

In the tribal trust lands the army, the police and the Pfumo reVanhu have been deployed not only to protect polling stations but also to ensure that villagers do not obey the Patriotic Front guerrillas by boycotting the election. It is predicted that government transport and government-hired buses will be used to 'uplift' rural voters to the polls. In several tribal trust lands visited by this correspondent official pressure is already verging on intimidation.

The régime claims that a 50 per cent turnout will be a triumphant demonstration of African support for the internal settlement. But 50 per cent of what? There are no voters' rolls and the most recent census was taken ten years ago. According to some observers, the régime has statistically decimated the potential electorate in order to flatter the final turnout.

Among those who will not be voting next Friday are the thousands of Zimbabwean refugees who have fled over the borders to Zambia and Mozambique. They have already voted with their feet.

Bishop Muzorewa's campaign has been severely restricted by the civil war. Zanla guerrillas have infiltrated the eastern tribal trust lands to the point where district administration has ceased to function. The Bishop's security advisers have wisely confined his rural rides to the 'protected villages' established by the Smith régime to separate the guerrillas from the people. Muzorewa travels in an armoured vehicle of such proportions that it must establish a claim to be the original African 'Trojan horse'.

The Bishop's campaign is based on the slogan, 'We are the Winners!', apparently conceived by Professor Vishnu Desai, the UANC's controversial Treasurer. Little or no programme is offered: nothing on land reform, very little on education and adult illiteracy. Prayer appears to be the Bishop's solution to malnutrition and kwashiorkor.

The war against the Patriotic Front will continue – business as usual – under the same white military commanders who have served Ian Smith. Muzorewa's claim that Zanla and Zipra guerrillas will lay down their arms, accept the amnesty, and come 'on-sides' as soon as he becomes Prime Minister is not taken seriously by any informed observer. Much more plausible is the unhappy prediction that 'Zimbabwe Rhodesia' (as the hybrid state has re-named itself) will continue to provide a happy hunting ground for foreign mercenaries and psychopaths searching for a season's sport.

Like all colonial capitals in the twilight of imperial rule, Salisbury is a hotbed of rumour. Some local politicians and Western diplomats take seriously reports of clandestine negotiations between the veteran Zapu leader, Dr Joshua Nkomo, and Rhodesia's disaffected commander of the eastern operational zone, General Hendrik Hersh. These meetings, which are said to enjoy British backing, are intended to split the Patriotic Front and produce an 'internal' black government with a broader basis of popular support and greater credibility in the OAU and UN.

However, no such meetings have taken place, despite an abortive clandestine journey to Lusaka by General Hersh, and the rumours can be safely discounted – except perhaps by the British Foreign Office – as mere steam from the General's overheated political ambitions.

Predictions that Bishop Muzorewa will emerge as the first black Prime Minister of 'Zimbabwe Rhodesia' seem well founded. A less widespread view, but one shared by this correspondent, is that within two years the exiled Zanu President, Robert Mugabe, will have become leader of a genuinely independent Zimbabwe.

From Leonard Tanner, 17 April 1979, Salisbury (telex, UPI, Robinson House, 17.45, collect):

That Bishop Abel Muzorewa will emerge as victor of this week's black elections, the first in the country's history, cannot be doubted by an impartial observer. Both the electoral process and the new constitution, signed on 3 March 1978, are widely welcomed by the African population as a decisive step towards majority rule and self-determination.

Rhodesians of all races are determined to make a success of the country's unique experiment in multi-racial democracy and power-sharing. The men of violence, who seek to impose themselves through the barrel of a gun (or Stalin organ), are widely feared and distrusted. Ordinary Zimbabweans, who reject white minority rule but possess their fair share of common sense, ask themselves why the Patriotic Front has rejected the electoral process of one man, one vote.

White rule is now a thing of the past. Bishop Muzorewa's abundant confidence and popularity are evidence of this. Despite the mistakes of the past fourteen years, the Rhodesian Front has finally stepped down with commendable efficiency and good grace. Residential and commercial zones have now been de-segregated. Any family can now buy a house in Mount Pleasant or Avondale, provided they can afford it.

The refusal of the British and American Governments to send observers to monitor this week's elections is resented by black opinion here as well as white. As a leading black businessman put it to me: 'Do the British and Americans have a better solution for us? Do they want the war to continue indefinitely? Isn't appeasement discredited in your country?'

I only wished I could have offered convincing answers to these questions.

Tanner discovered that Stern's despatch had proceeded his own over the wires by a full hour when the UPI telex operator at Robinson House handed him a message from London:

'What the bloody hell is going on? Stern's report is not, repeat not, accepted. Convey him dismissal soonest decision final. Foyle.'

Foyle's fury somewhat assuaged his own, he being reluctant to share any sentiment with such an oleaginous opportunist – though Stern's behaviour constantly prompted him in that undesired direction. Tanner allowed himself a decent anger. He had 'come to terms' with his own temper, which he had taught himself to equate with 'standards' and 'standing up and being counted'.

By six o'clock Patrick Warner had telexed the *Eye* in London that Tanner, 'already exhausted by his Ugandan exertions in certain massage parlours', had been so floored by Stern's 'widely predicted treachery' that he had been carried out of Meikles's bar 'too plastered to recognise his own big toe'.

If this is accurate it remains a mystery how Tanner managed to absorb and immediately respond to the message awaiting him from Mrs Frieda Hersn:

'Hubby will see Leonard now. White man's time.'

'Another?'

'Thanks. Very decent.'

"Elp y'self.'

'Elections doomed, you say?'

'Yees. The Bishop's not worth a fart in the Kariba dam. Ectually, we should nivver have flooded those Tonga ancestral spirits, big mistake. Reporter, are you?'

'Foreign editor, actually.'

"Oo owns you? That Australian bloke?'

'That's the other paper. Actually, we're independent, a trust.'

'Sounds socialist.'

'Hardly . . . I used to work for Beaverbrook . . .'

'Still alive? Good man.'

'No, no, I mean after the war. You'd get the summons to the top floor apartment in Arlington House. His mouth stretched from ear to ear.' Tanner laughed, warmed by the General's whisky. 'The Beaver made you stand there while he grinned like a witch doctor. Sort of a loyalty test. "Sit down." he'd say, "pull your chair closer." Then silence again, his hand on your knee.'

'A poof, eh?'

'Not really, no.'

'Ev another? 'Elp y'self.'

'Very kind.'

(Tanner on his feet again, swaying.)

'I once asked a German waitress in Joburg for a dry martini. She brought me three.' Tanner chuckled as he poured, his hand more unsteady then usual. He slopped some on the fake-mahogany top. Hersh's pig eyes, identical (it now seemed) to his wife's, followed him relentlessly as if he were leaving spoor all over the room. The UDI group photograph stared down threateningly from above the mantelpiece.

'She did? She thought you was thirsty, mebbe?'

'No, no: eins, zwei, drei . . . Dry. Drei. Er, well, to business, I suppose. Damned good of you to see me, General, mind if I take notes?'

'I don't give a shit, my life's not worth a baboon's arse. I'm fighting the real war, you see, in the eastern highlands, against the real enemy, Mugabe. *They're* fighting the phoney war against

Nkomo, all those bloody publicity stunts over Zambia, all that Green Leader palaver with Lusaka control tower . . . But in the end you can fool Rhodesians for only so long and I include the kaffirs in that, Hersh is no racist.'

Tanner waited until his host had subsided somewhat.

'You were in Malaya with the British forces, of course . . . a damned fine job. Templer.'

'Yees. The Brits armed the Reds to the teeth then called us in to save their bacon. We sorted that one out. Played the Malays off against the Chinks, no problem. You've got to do that.'

'Singapore, wonderful city. Prettiest girls in Asia.'

'I didn't 'ave time for that.'

'No, quite. I remember when they shot the first two planters in Sungei Seput. I spent some time up there. Terrible life, beleaguered bungalows behind sandbags and barbed wire, too dangerous to drive to the club. And then the silent hour at dusk, when the bullfrogs switched off . . . you'd just lie there, listening.'

'A soldier never lies awake.'

'Can it be done here, General?'

'Divide the Ndebeles from the Shonas. Then divide the moderates from the Reds. Then divide the moderates and you've got it . . . kaffirs eating out of yer 'and. Then you sjambok the terrs. Remember 'ow we cleaned out Jenderam?'

'In Selangor, yes, I covered that.'

'We uplifted the entire population into detention camps. We could do that 'ere but certain persons 'ave other fish to fry.'

'Who?'

'Walls 'ave ears.'

'And Smith?'

'Did I say anything about Smith? Ask me about Prinsloo.'

'I'm asking.'

'Now take the Tunku, that Rahman bloke. "Malay for the Malays," 'e said, but 'e was no fool even though 'e spent 'alf 'is life gambling on the race course. Ayshuns. 'E struck a deal with the wealthy Chinks, gave them fifteen seats, and 'e was 'ome and dry.'

'You could do that here.'

'I could. If they'd let me.'

'With Nkomo?'

'Yees.'

'You've talked to him? I know from my contacts in the Foreign Office that – '

'You 'ave an expense account, I suppose?'

'Er . . .'

'I'll give you four Rhodesian dollars to the pound.'

276

'Ah.'

'Yees.'

'How many do you want to offload, General?'

'Twenty thou.'

'Jesus.'

'Ten then. C'mon, man, put it down to expenses, big story, exclusive. "'Ersh breaks silence – exclusive." '

'Er . . . it's rather unusual. Could you give me any indication of the story . . . ? Nkomo, I assume?'

'Yees. See that lad on the wall? Thet's my son John. Frieda calls 'im Derek, let's 'ope it gives 'im two lives. 'E was 'ead boy at Peterhouse and captain of everything – cricket, rugby, squash, a chip off the old block. 'E's in the SAS, fighting for 'is birthright, 'is 'eritage – not for the organ grinder's monkey, eh? My boy says to me, "Dad, where are we going?" What can I tell 'im – that this country's now run by drunken womanisers who spend their war in Salisbury nightclubs chasing Coloured cunts?' Tanner experienced a discomfort which was both sudden and acute.

'Mind if I help myself . . . ?'

'I never met a Britisher who wasn't 'appy to break sanctions when 'e got thirsty.'

Tanner's laugh lasted all the way to the sideboard. He gazed, puzzled, at the puddle on the mock-mahogany top.

'I don't betray my principles,' Hersh said. 'That's my crime. I was born 'ere and my father before me. "Loved I not 'onour more . . . " – that's Shakespeare.'

'It sounds familiar . . .' Tanner swaying back towards his chair.

'You know the story of the 'edge'og and the fox? The fox knew many things but the 'edge'og knew one big thing.'

'Ah. Nkomo, you mean?'

'Yees.'

'Nkomo's the fox and you're the 'edge'og?'

'Correct. I could settle for five thousand – in cash, of course.'

'Well . . . this would be about a recent meeting with Mr Nkomo in Zambia?'

'You weren't born yisterday. You dine in all the clubs with the ones in striped pants, the Garrick, the Athenaeum, the Reform, regular. Me, I'm just an ignorant colonial, a Boer, yees? Expendable, too.'

'Nkomo's ready to jump, to break with Mugabe?'

Hersh seemed to nod. 'Two thousand in sterling. Just write a cheque, I'll trust an English gentleman. You can 'ave the entire contents of that safe.' He pointed to a heavy, cast-iron strongbox, as old as the flight from Egypt.

'Er . . . mind if I help myself?'

'To the safe?'

'No, no . . . a drink . . . your glass . . . can I top you up . . . ?'

Hersh chuckled. 'You'd 'ave to pin me down first. I weigh 'undred and ninety and you look like you couldn't lift the lid off a saucepan. No offence, Mr Tanner, but you've 'ad enough.'

His hand shaking horribly, Tanner fumbled for the sacred chequebook which only four editorial executives were allowed to carry out of the building and slowly wrote a cheque for . . . one thousand pounds. He tried to rise but couldn't. He stretched out his arm and the General stretched simultaneously but their chairs were too far apart and there seemed no way out of the impasse. He could hardly screw the cheque into a ball and throw it at Hersh. In the end he folded it and left it on the arm of his own chair, whence it soon slipped to the ground.

Tanner summoned a lifetime in an effort at sobriety.

'General, if Muzorewa wins this election, how are you going to remove him?'

'No problem. Botha invites 'im down to Joburg for a new suit of clothes. The Bish nivver comes back.'

Tanner's jaw sagged slackly. 'Ah.'

'It would be bitter not to 'ave the election,' Hersh mused. 'I liked that piece your man Stern just put on the wire. 'E properly rubbished the organ grinder's monkey.'

Silence.

'OK, so 'e didn't give 'Endrick 'Ersh an Oscar either but that's no problem, pull the wool over their eyes I shouldn't wonder . . . Pity you didn't print that piece 'e wrote about Chamberlain's massacre in Buhera. Frieda set that up very good for your Marxist scum Stern but you got yer knickers in a twist.'

'Who's Chamberlain? Are you talking about Munich?'

'Munich?'

'Appeasement.'

'Chamberlain's Prinsloo's faithful assassin 'oo shortly in'erits Miss Donna Prinsloo 'oo's late fiancé was a Special Branch operative working with the Zipra boys in the Zambezi valley under my instructions so Chamberlain goes up there and rubs Johnny out with a shot in the back. Now you tell your Jewboy Stern that I've got 'is future Jewboy father-in-law Meyer by 'is short circumcised 'airs if 'e doesn't deliver that white whore's terrorist doctor to me in very short order.'

Tanner gaped. He didn't follow a word of it. He had no idea that de-colonisation could be so complicated.

Hersh tilted back his head and bellowed: 'Frieda! Frieda! Come 'ere, woman, move that fat arse of yours, shift!'

Frieda Hersh entered with her serene leer. She winked at Tanner.

'Hubby's off to war again tomorrow, the final search-and-destroy operation against Mugabe. Ann Average has packed hubby's biltong, his Bible and his condoms.'

'Ann Average?' muttered Tanner, bemused.

Another wink, so slow this time as to be almost hydraulic.

'Frieda's weekly column in the *Herald* . . . a *nom de plume*, Leonard.'

Then she spotted Tanner's cheque lying on the carpet and pounced on it with a horrible cry compounded of joy and disappointment in equal measure.

Once, home on leave, he had spent an idyllic week (three days) alone with Helen – despite Vera's misgivings – in a rented cottage in Dorset. He bought her a new bicycle, a size too large (to allow for growth), of which she was rather nervous (because it was too large) until she learned to fear her father's irritation more than the prospect of falling off. She rode ahead of him along country lanes between fields of ripe wheat and barley, her little legs pumping the pedals, her hair streaming, he riding a rented machine behind her, happy. Picnicking between the tall hedgerows, they examined her flower book but never quite managed to marry the colour plates to the real flowers. He told her about pollen and stamens and grew faintly irritated when she reported that Miss Pascoe had taught her something different in Form Four. At night he tucked her into bed with her teddy bears and read from her favourite book, *Just William*. A few years after the accident he rented the same Dorset cottage (he wouldn't accept any other) and rode along the same country lanes – the same Great Dane that had frightened Helen came bounding out – imagining her hair streaming in the wind, expecting her to be waiting for him, flushed with triumph, round every bend. Alone in the cottage he drank a lot, purging from his memory the many occasions during that three-day 'week' when his short temper had brought her close to tears.

TWENTY-FIVE

'Holy cow,' Tanner muttered.

Gilson had turned into the imposing driveway of the Minister's residence in Highlands. Seated in the back of a ministerial Peugeot, Tanner found himself confronting a vast bungalow, part Lutyens, part earthquake colonial, part Dallas, fronted by terraced lawns and a curving split drive of vase-like symmetry adorned by urns, statuettes and grinning gnomes. One of whom, artfully breaking his pose as Tanner shoved himself up the front steps to the verandah, turned out to be the Minister of Information and National Guidance.

'Delighted,' Prinsloo said, but his eyes didn't mean it and his hand was diffident. Unhealthily florid of feature, the Minister wore his short, silvery hair wet-plastered either side of a centred parting, reminding Tanner of a professional cricketer of the 1930s passing a hot afternoon in the Tavern.

'And this is Nanette,' Prinsloo added.

He didn't exaggerate; taller than Prinsloo, the wife bore down on Tanner like a pastry chef's fantasy, her beehived hair threatening to burst its clips and explode across her huge bosoms. Clasping Tanner's hand in both of hers, she simply would not let go; he felt as if he were being swallowed by a wedding cake. So this was the Mummy who had sat on the knees of the Great Pioneers, straight-backed men with faraway eyes.

'And you've met Donna,' the Minister said.

The lovely Donna Prinsloo was standing beside one of the pillars supporting the verandah, her golden head leaning on the shoulder of a tall man with sandy hair, ice-blue eyes and dense, almost angry, patches of freckles stretching from ear to ear.

'We meet again,' Tanner said. Donna smiled back dreamily.

'A Rhodesian girl doesn't parade her family connections.' Prinsloo said, 'she just gets on with it. Don't you. darling?'

'Yes, Daddy.'

'And this is our future son-in-law, District Commissioner Chamberlain.'

The freckled man offered his hand without a word.

'Sundowner time,' Prinsloo said. On cue an old retainer appeared, his ancient, long-suffering half-smile crowned by a red fez.

'This is Thomas,' Nanette said. 'Thomas is one of the family, aren't you, Thomas?'

'Meddem.'

'Thomas is a loyal Karanga. Only last month his kraal in Gutu was attacked by CTs. They behaved like animals.'

'They *are* animals,' Prinsloo said.

According to Richard Stern – information which Tanner had naturally not solicited but could hardly avoid absorbing – Prinsloo had first surfaced in Rhodesia after UDI, a South African manufacturer of cheap township furniture with a flair for public relations who had soon taken command of Smith's propaganda machine and supervised a short, nasty battle with the Rhodesian press, installing a Government censor in every newspaper office, until the proprietors threw in the towel and agreed that all the news was all the news that the Government thought fit to print. The Minister of Information's devotion to the internal settlement (according to Stern) was closely related to the protection of his substantial commercial interests in Rhodesia.

Tanner asked for a scotch.

'This is Roddy,' Nanette said.

A muscular youth in bare feet, naked except for the shortest of shorts, had wandered out on to the verandah from the living room where a television set, turned up aggressively high, was urging all Rhodesians to make election day 'our day'. Tanner thought 'spoilt brat' but extended his hand.

Nanette beamed: 'When our Roddy was small, Leonard – *may* I call you Leonard? – Thomas would hide him in his kia whenever Mummy was angry with Roddy. And now, whenever Roddy goes away to fight our war, which is also Thomas's war, Thomas says to him, "Keep alive, Master Roddy." '

'Donna's fiancé was murdered by gooks,' the Minister said.

'Yes,' Tanner murmured.

'None of us will ever forget Johnny, will we, Mummy?'

'None of us, Daddy,' Nanette said. 'But now Donna's happy again, aren't you, Donna?'

'I'm happy again, Mummy.'

'Chris has made her happy again,' Nanette said.

'Johnny was my friend and the finest tracker in Rhodesia,' the District Commissioner told Tanner.

'Have a *super* weekend and put a *tiger* in your tank,' boomed the television from inside the house.

Thomas reappeared bearing a silver tray loaded with drinks. Prinsloo explained to Tanner that the Rhodesian sundowner was more than a 'libation', it was a precious tradition extending back to the Pioneer times when neighbours lived twenty miles apart and –

'More than twenty, Daddy,' Nanette interjected, 'sometimes fifty.'

–and yet would ride over towards evening for a chat on the stoep to show friendship and solidarity.

'Those were the days, Leonard,' Nanette said.

Tanner didn't know why he had suddenly been invited to the Minister's home. Gilson, now standing respectfully in the background, had not been communicative. 'I'm just the chauffeur, Mr Tanner.' But the scotch was real. The first gulp relaxed Tanner; the second emboldened him.

'Naturally, I'm still hoping to see Mr Smith, but my schedule—'

'Now that's a remarkable man,' Prinsloo said. 'Isn't he, Mummy?'

'A wonderful man, Daddy. Mr Smith comes home dead tired from the office but he never forgets to feed his fish. Only last week he said to me, "Nanette, if the future of our beautiful country depends on the spirit and resolve of young men like your Roddy, then we've nothing to fear. Leonard, when I was a little girl I sat on the knees of the great Pioneers, tough, hardy, straight-backed men with — '

'With faraway eyes?' Tanner suggested.

District Commissioner Chamberlain was quick to respond to the sarcasm.

'If the black people of this country had their choice, they'd vote for Ian Smith. We brought them out of savagery and they respect us, just as we respect them.'

'All we ask of the Free World is fair play,' Prinsloo said.

'And if we don't get it, we'll fight,' young Roddy volunteered.

The Minister put an arm round his son's shoulder.

'This young man, Mr Tanner, is a Selous Scout. The finest tracker unit in the world. This time next week Roddy won't be talking to you and me, he'll be fifty miles behind the terrorist lines, living wild, lighting no fires, eating raw game, draining the good green juices from the stomachs of antelopes and other things I'm not at liberty to disclose. *Pamberi Selousie!* Isn't that right, Roddy?'

Roddy had ambled away to lean against his pillar, brown arms folded, examining the resultant muscles. He seemed fascinated by his own arms and legs.

'This generation of young Rhodesians has drawn the bottom line,' Chamberlain said. 'They'll never take the yellow road. If they have to die, they'll die.'

Tanner decided to make an effort with Prinsloo.

'Minister, regarding an interview with Mr Smith and General Walls . . . Perhaps I should mention that while in South Africa I talked to Prime Minister Botha as well as van den Bergh and Harry Oppenheimer. Frankly, I've never believed in economic sanctions . . . your African is invariably the first to suffer . . .'

Prinsloo didn't seem impressed. He nodded as if familiar with this phase of the begging ritual and stared callously through Tanner's empty glass.

'Once the Cape sea routes go, where are you?' Tanner tried again.

'But can we trust Maggie Thatcher?' Nanette put her hand on his arm, beaming at him with a continual animation clearly exhausting to the recipient.

'Mummy, never trust the British,' Prinsloo said. 'The Tories are the worst. Frankly, Mr Tanner, your once-great country has gone. Handouts and dropouts, litterbins overflowing, churches empty, lorry drivers earning more than doctors and not a white doctor to be found in the run-down NHS hospitals.'

The wasp flew out of the jam.

'Balls!' Tanner exploded, smoke billowing through his nostrils like the snort of a cartoon bull. 'You people are the victims of your own mythology.'

The blood flooded up through the smooth silver city of Prinsloo's head:

'It's time the white man was given a break! Everywhere you look he's on the retreat. In ten years' time you'll have a black majority in Britain, a slave depotism, the lowest common denominator! Britain resembles a turd swarming with flies.'

It came back to Tanner for the first time since his arrival in Salisbury. As Minister of Information, Prinsloo had launched a propaganda campaign lauding race relations in Rhodesia and depicting black slums in British cities – but, as it turned out, using photographs taken in the squatter camps of two Salisbury townships, Tafara and Harare. It was Stern who had exposed the forgery and forced a public admission out of Mike Gilson. Yes, yes – that had been one story even Selwyn Foyle couldn't spike.

283

District Commissioner Chamberlain detached Donna's glued head from his shoulder and walked across the verandah to Tanner.

'Some of us are getting reconciled to a bloodbath in this country. There are six million Afs on this plot and every one of them is expendable. Six million zeroes equals zero.'

Tanner caught himself glancing at Donna's long, bespoken legs and Nanette, as if reading the rancid old suitor, quickly said: 'Daddy, I want Leonard to inspect my garden and see the kids bouncing on their trampoline for the Terrorist Victims' Relief Fund.'

Tanner smiled gallantly: the woman was clearly made of marzipan and had spent the last twenty years inside her own wedding cake. His yellow eye cast an almost oriental glance across Nanette's glorious, spreading garden, the purple lantana, the lobelias and petunias and other exotic plants whose names he did not know just as he hadn't known the name of common flowers in the Dorset hedgerows.

'Why did you invite me here, Minister?'

Prinsloo dug his hands deep into his pockets. 'What did Hersh tell you?'

'I beg your pardon?'

'Hersh is a nobody going nowhere. We have bugs up his arse.'

'Daddy!' Nanette blushed.

'Sorry, Mummy. This is man's talk. I'm asking Mr Tanner what the General told him.'

'Obviously he spoke to me in confidence.' Tanner always enjoyed saying that.

'He asked you to launder money, eh? Starting at twenty thousand and settling for two? And how prospers General Coup d'Etat's famous conspiracy with the terrorist Nkomo? Do Mr Smith, General Walls and I face imminent arrest?' Prinsloo laughed coarsely; Chamberlain and Gilson laughed in chorus, Nanette and Donna joining in. Tanner was deafened by his own silence.

Tanner's glass had lain empty in his hand for more than ten minutes – it was the measure of the affection he felt for the great, clotted Hersh (or so he dementedly informed himself) that he could shamelessly ask the Afrikaner General for drink after drink, whereas he'd rather die than beg one from this manufacturer of cheap furniture.

'Mr Tanner decided not to fire Stern?' Prinsloo turned to Gilson.

'There was a telex from Mr Foyle in London, Minister . . .'

'Your notion of loyalty, I suppose,' Prinsloo put it to Tanner. 'We have accordingly withdrawn Stern's work permit. He has forty-eight hours to leave the country.'

Tanner was now in the advanced stages of alcohol deprivation.

Crazed images floated through his head . . . Noah without the ark, Dr Dolittle without his stethoscope, Wolfe without Quebec. Richard Stern and Selwyn Foyle abruptly became indistinguishable. Left and Right, Whigs and Tories, Marxists and Fascists – all an elaborate charade played out by the gilded, cynical Oxbridge establishment to ensure and insure its domination. They had granted Tanner a commission but marked him down for retirement at the rank of lieutenant-colonel – didn't Stern's long nose convey the permanent sneer of the public schoolboy who knew he would inherit the city whenever he chose to stop besieging it? Let them deport the sod. Castigated for his treacherous conduct in filing a report on the Bishop's campaign designed to contradict Tanner's, Stern had responded with an arrogant smile:

—Don't you realise that Mugabe will be the one with the presidential palace and the motorcycle outriders before the year is out?

The verandah was empty now and Gilson was guiding Tanner's uncertain legs among the urns and grotesque garden gnomes and Tanner knew there would be no interview with Smith or Walls, he'd blown it. Slumped in the back of Gilson's car, he closed his eyes while Stern, the other side of town and drunk, was insisting to Holzheimer that all through that summer of sixty-eight, along the southern beaches opposite the Isle of Wight, dads built like rubber dinghies and mums shaped like thermos flasks had argued behind their canvas wind-breaks whether or not Harry Marquis had really written that review of Stern's book in the *Times Literary Supplement* – and whether the review had actually been typed out by the beautiful Elizabeth Halliday.

'Let's go,' Cubans hustled Stern and one canvas grip out of his flat in Baines Avenue.

'But my papers, my files!'

'Those belong to Special Branch. If you're not out of here in five minutes you'll belong to them too.'

Old Isaac slowly wiped his hand on his filthy apron and accorded Stern the triple handshake of the *chimurenga*.

'*Pamberi neZanu.*'

TWENTY-SIX

From the diary of Richard Stern, captured by the Rhodesian Special Air Service, 20 April 1979:

I had travelled to Umtali, Gweru and Bulawayo with Cubans and his gangster sunglasses in fruitless search of Esther, lured by a drawing of a small sailing boat bobbing on a pond, but now (Cubans explained, scanning the rear mirror) Prinsloo had made an 'honest man' of me by withdrawing my work permit, closing my options, driving me into the lumpen fraternity of fugitives. Cubans guided me through Highfield, past Gwanzura stadium, where Muzorewa held his triumphant rallies, past the beer hall under the sullen gaze of kids who needed only a nod to unleash their stones in revenge for ninety years of which they had experienced ten or fifteen. Wary for police, liable to instant arrest as a fugitive, I remembered how Tanner had spiked my best piece on the Rhodesian townships, returning the text with whole passages savagely scored by sweeps of his red pencil:

' . . . buses gorging their long stomachs on the raw labour power which services the cement works, the brewery, the fertiliser plant and the vehicle assembly plant . . . The industrial estates are sited, with physiocratic rationality, between the white cities and the black townships. Managers, engineers and supervisors approach from the city by car; the black workforce is funnelled in from the townships by bus; the encounter of the two races is strictly restricted to the working day. But there is progress. The new class of black executives, devoted to the "internal settlement", now occupy first-floor offices whose desks are graced by onyx pen-holders, a gift from the company. The Chambers of Commerce, the Lions Clubs and the Rotarians all welcome members of the new black middle class with "a stake in the country", guarantors of future "stability". But attempts to reduce the ten-to-one differential between white and black salaries have foundered on what business leaders describe as "different patterns of expectation and consumption".'

Tanner had written neatly across the top: 'We are not a satirical magazine.'

A distant murmur slowly expanded into the challenge of drums, mbiras, and marimbas as a long procession of the Bishop's people came shuffling and prancing through the township towards the Mushandira Pamwe Hotel, headed by the local UANC candidate, a tubular building contractor affectionately known as Mercedes waBenzi, surrounded by ululating Salvation Army women wiggling their bottoms. A fat figure in a corn-coloured suit, poised for victory under Vishnu Desai's brilliant slogan, 'The Winners', the candidate wore a boater tilted jauntily on the back of his head like one of Saturn's rings. I had once interviewed the man: according to the local wits, his children ate their sadza out of spare Mercedes hub caps. His faith in free enterprise was so vast that it dwarfed Adam Smith's; he was a man in whose hand a cold beer appeared every time he mopped his brow. Now, as his ecstatic followers threatened to engulf us, Cubans became alarmed, urging me to use my horn to force a passage, to assert the motorist's natural supremacy (greatest in the Third World, I didn't like to point out), but I shared every white housewife's fear of an accident, a black child under the wheels, an angry scene.

Tanner had once informed me that in the British colonies officers in uniform were never allowed to drive their own vehicles. He seemed obsessive about it.

A police Land Rover idled into view on the meandering wheels of authority, scanning and sniffing, Cassius lazily leaning his yellow eye into my subversive but persistent project. 'Shit,' Cubans muttered; never before had he encountered Special Branch officers from Bulawayo in Salisbury.

'Stay,' he commanded and abruptly was gone.

Cassius, his ten-stitch scar and his ever-smouldering cigarette leant into my car, though not necessarily in that order. I studied the petals of hair plastered forward over his blotchy forehead and told him that his breath hadn't improved. In my burning excitement at my imminent reunification with the woman I loved, I forgot Cassius's real name and addressed him as 'Mr Cuckold'.

Symonds leered like a movie villain. 'Now I'll have you both. You can watch us screw her to death in Stops Camp.'

287

I tried to leap out of the car but he knew how to lean on a door, ravaged though his skeletal frame appeared.

'You're no longer living on hope,' he said, 'but on the memory of hope. What have you achieved in your life? You perched on the frail branch of "promise"; when it broke you were the last to notice – just as you were the last in town to learn you'd been cuckolded by Harry. Neither philosophy nor history has compensated for your genetic defect; like a faulty Detroit automobile I once owned, you were turned out on a Friday; beneath the flashy surface energy you were too lazy to accommodate the human beings allocated to the plots surrounding your own. That's why you're alone – with or without the kaffir's whore.'

The Bishop's ululating women peered into our car as I kept the engine idling outside St Andrew's Church, but Cassius's presence ensured that not even the electioneering piccaninnies and girl-mothers scratched the metal.

'I'm told the swishing tails of passing cows never brush the gleaming Rolls stranded on an English farm track,' Cassius said. No doubt he was contemplating his wife's departure to that distant land. There was a hint of genuine respect in his demeanour; perhaps he felt nervous in Mashonaland, perhaps he regretted the imminent conclusion of his long, fantastic pursuit of a legend.

The last I saw of Cassius was a halo of white light enveloping his head. He seemed to lean right into my car as if determined to kiss my knees, hanging through the half-open window and gradually disgorging what might have been strawberry yoghurt on to the seat, my clothes, the wheel, the dashboard. Cubans later claimed that he had thrown the two Chinese stick grenades into the crowd of UANC women, aiming to decapitate the strutting Mercedes waBenzi, but one had bounced out of control like a jumping jack, severing both of Cassius's legs below the knees and 'for one awful moment, Richard' (as Esther put it) placing my own life in danger. I won't speak of the noise of the twin explosions and of my own hysterical reactions – let's begin with Cubans pulling me off the floor of my car, out of Cassius's yoghurt, hissing 'Go, man, go, go, go!'

The crowd had stampeded in terror, milling in every direction, falling over themselves, screaming – impossible to move the car forward a yard without knocking down some petrified young mother, some panic-stricken child. Realising my incapacity for this task, Cubans hauled me roughly into the passenger seat, gripped the wheel, and slammed his foot down on the accelerator. I closed my eyes as a succession of sickening bumps carried me back to Harry's encounter with a flock of sheep on the road to Penryndeu-draeth though I couldn't have spelt it. By the time I opened them we were clear of the carnage, along Mangwende Drive, past the sewage works, through the high perimeter fence with its tall floodlight pylons, and out of the township itself. Racing up Beatrice Road past the great tobacco auction warehouses, Cubans Urimbo had begun to hum 'God Bless Africa' while the unknown black priest in the back of the car was still counting the Bishop's dead on his fingers. According to Holz, this game is called Catholics and Methodists.

Sister Angelica of the Masita eChita chePrecious Blood said nothing, she remaining shrouded in a voluminous habit and crisp white hood from which the third and final Chinese stick brigade protruded.

'Just in case, Richard,' said Cubans, reading my line of vision. He turned derisively to Sister Angelica. 'He's speechless with indignation. His revolutionary theory encompasses terror, Sartre, Fanon and what Auden once called the necessary murder – but only in the abstract!'

Cubans avoided the city centre, taking a long and masterly detour to avoid the road blocks until we finally dropped the excited black priest off on the Arcturus Road, between the Portland cement works and Silveira House. The priest's hand and Esther's clasped tightly in the triple handshake then he was clambering awkwardly from my VW in his crumpled black habit and walking away on stiff legs, watched by waiting bus passengers, hitchhikers, road workers, scavengers, police informers.

'Dear Fidelius,' she murmured. 'He does understand detonators.'

Cubans accelerated away in a cloud of dust, ignoring the pleas of stranded hitch-hikers, forcing the car beyond the limit of its tolerance.

'Don't worry about Fidelius,' he chuckled. 'That one will be Archbishop of Harare and the first African Pope.'

Heading east, the city behind us, trembling with shock, anxiety and burning love – what a combination! – I plaintively reminded Cubans of my blood-splattered clothes and my filthy, shocked condition. Esther's consoling hand touched my shoulder and I saw that it, too, was dipped in blood. Love cauterized the wounds of twenty-eight months; I wanted to protest about that capricious slaughter in the township yet I was as helpless as a victim of drought staring at clear water. As the long, smooth strip of tarmac running east to Umtali passed under our wheels, I surrendered to the dimple playing in her cheek and allowed my parched fingers to twist and twine through hers in a greedy display of passion, shamed by Cubans's outlaw smile in the driving mirror yet driven by a love beyond endurance. Oh, how I ached to kiss her, hold her in my arms, carry her away from this black man who was a stranger to us both!

West of Marandellas Cubans pulled off the main road and followed a farm track until we reached the labour compound – a suicidal procedure on a white farm, I would have thought, but neither Cubans nor Esther displayed the slightest apprehension and quite suddenly we were enveloped by the urgent, gentle hands of the workforce offering us shelter, a change of clothes, sadza and relish. The fat and jovial farm women in their woollen hats and cotton headscarves closed round Esther, pulling back the hood of her habit, touching her long, silken hair for luck, their black throats emitting soft sighs of awed delight. Their adoration touched a depth of almost religious fervour.

I had waited ten years to see Esther among the people of Zimbabwe. I watched Cubans changing the registration plates on my car. 'This place is called Bromley, Richard – just like home, eh?'

Five kilometres from Marandellas we ran into the first police roadblock. By this time the stained-glass window of Rhodesian propriety had been restored – the white man was at the wheel, the white nun beside him, the black male in the back of the car (carrying a pass, or situpa, in the name of Mr Josephat Chigwedere, mechanic-carpenter of Mount St Mary's Mission). A policewoman who wore her tan like makeup reported our new registration number on a two-way radio.

A leather face eaten by seven years of war came through the window, filling the empty frame from which Cassius's petals had been torn by Cubans's grenade. I was not unaware of that third grenade nestling within Esther's habit.

'Heading for the Mission, you say?'

I nodded. 'Yes.'

'With medical supplies, you say? I suppose you realise there's been a lot of terrorist activity down there? There's nothing the gooks would like more than to grab a load of medical supplies.'

Sister Angelica leaned forward, as if to bless the police reservist. I was reminded that she, like Jeanne d'Arc before her, possessed more than one voice.

'Officer, thank you for warning us. One of my dear Sisters was ambushed only last week. Oh, it was terrible. Can you possibly give us an escort?'

'Sister, I wish we could.' He addressed her with the exaggerated respect and consideration white strangers reserve for one another in a black country. 'We're stretched to the limit.'

'Then we can only pray to God for protection,' said Sister Angelica. Her sad but plucky smile irradiated not only her gentle, oval face but also the police reservist – as only half an hour previously it had entranced the black farm women.

We turned right, heading for Wedza along a single strip of tarmac flanked by soft shoulders. I had once killed an owl on this road, at night: for an instant it had gazed at me, wide-eyed with indignation, just like Hattie, before I heard the thump – even faster and more decisive than the bodies Cubans had struck as we fled from Highfield. Now I discovered that each collision had notched in my ear.

I was glad not to be alone with Esther. Such was my passion that Cubans served as buffer and chaperone. I had always anticipated that when I finally caught up with Esther I would submit her to the most intense, detailed interrogation, charting her movements across Mozambique and Rhodesia, extracting every event, experience and narrow escape of the past two-and-a-half years. But now the project simply abandoned itself. The longer the story, the shorter the report. Not even the escapade in Bulawayo, in which I had been involved, commanded my curiosity. Here she was, a creature of myth and legend, hunted by every police unit in the land, in my car; the only history that interested me was the history of the immediate future.

Occasionally she and Cubans would murmur to each other in English and Shona. I noticed that she never addressed him by name – no doubt a habit of the underground.

'Your parents seem well,' I said. It sounded rather pompous.

'Yes, Mum told me she'd seen you,' Esther said dreamily.

'You've been able to write to her?'

The dimple alighted in Esther's cheek. 'Richard, let's just say we have means of communicating.'

'They employ a dark-skinned messenger,' Cubans intervened in his deepest trombone. 'Did Esther ever tell you the truth about her Dad?'

I glanced at Esther; her beautiful oval face had clouded.

'When the crunch came,' Cubans went on, 'Paul was cited for contempt of Congress and faced a year in jail.'

'It was a horrible dilemma,' Esther said defensively.

'Oh sure. So Paul ratted. He named thirty-two names. He destroyed thirty-two people.'

'That's not true. The Committee knew most of the names anyway. It was just a ritual of the witch-hunt.'

'He ratted on his comrades.' Cubans was inexorable.

'He was thinking of Mum and me.'

'He was thinking, as always, of Number One. Naturally it was in all the New York newspapers. Jane was so ashamed that she threatened to quit if he didn't leave the country and start a new life. She should have quit.'

Esther could take no more. 'Shut up, Zim! He's my father.'

The car swerved off the narrow ribbon of tarmac on to the soft dirt shoulder. They both reacted instantly, he lunging forward from the back seat to steady the wheel, she grasping my wavering arm.

'What happened to you, man?' Cubans demanded.

The letters in Elizabeth's filing cabinet, all neatly indexed in folders, lover by lover.

Esther was scanning me anxiously. 'Are you all right, Richard?' She turned to the man in the back seat as if I were a stranger. 'It may be the effect of the grenades, he isn't used to it.'

All I could think of, in Zimunya's presence, was to stifle the long scream rising within me.

'So your father went into exile and made a fortune?' I said casually.

'Paul inherited a fortune and blew half of it,' Cubans said contemptuously.

'Inherited a fortune!' I yelled (the car swerved again), finding a random outlet for my rage. 'I thought he was brought up in the Bronx home of a fifteen-dollar-a-week garment worker.'

'Oh, did he say that?' Esther murmured. 'I'd forgotten.'

How beautiful she is! How I want her!

Behind the mirrored sunglasses of Cubans Urimbo, son of an Umtali railway worker, grimaced the 'doctor':

'Paul's Dad is an eight-figure textiles tycoon – but he did send Paul to City College rather than Harvard. That much is authentic.' Cubans began to laugh uproariously – I heard in his bellowing all the contempt he had kept bottled up for the past year as he and Esther strung me along, securing my loyalty to their cause, ensuring that Zanu and Zanla received a favourable 'press' in at least one English daily newspaper. Oh yes! Had Esther not planted me on Tanner three years ago, before the Geneva Conference, sacrificing her virtue in the service of the Cause? Had she not monitored my usefulness with a calculating, long-range eye ever since I had scrambled to lift her from the pavement outside Rhodesia House?

Ten years of treachery!

Esther leaned forward. 'Slow, Richard, we're turning here.'

I obeyed, my rage now so vast that it disappeared from sight. Turning up the farm track she indicated, I passed through the open security gate, heading not for the labour compound this time but for the homestead itself. A tall, angular woman in plaid trousers was waiting on the verandah, with a cigarette and two Dobermann Pinschers.

'I think you once met Fay's husband,' Esther said.

'Fay? Did I?'

'You must remember Geoff Cowans.'

'Ah! he who told you that I worked for MI6. And where is that paranoid devotee of John XXIII?'

'He's dead,' Esther said quietly.

'He killed himself,' Zimunya said. 'Though a Catholic.' Stern noted the hint of triumph and remembered Cowans's crude confession of lust, made in front of Paul Meyer.

'Fay is of course one of us,' Esther said.

Zimunya grunted sceptically. 'She's everyone's Momma – our boys at night, the security forces during the day. The lion and the lamb could lie down together, says Fay, if only they had "a bit of sense" knocked into them. Frankly, I don't trust such people.'

The woman in plaid trousers stepped down from the verandah to greet us, calming her salivating dogs as they bounded round the car.

'Three years and you haven't changed, darling.' She embraced Esther. Then, reaching into the back of the car to offer Zimunya her hand, she said, 'Good God, how bloody marvellous, Zim,' in a broad Rhodesian accent. But then she said, 'Watch out for the dogs, Zim, they don't like gooks,' and let loose a long, racking, smoker's hack.

'And who's this?' the woman was eyeing me intently.

'My good friend Richard Stern,' Esther said.

'One of us, eh?'

'Oh no, Richard is entirely his own man.'

The guerrilla camp lies beyond the rim of the world, off the map, in a moonscape. Zimunya and his wife drove the last three hours of the journey under cover of night, ostensibly to avoid the security forces, in reality to ensure that I would never know, precisely, where I had been. If Esther trusts me, Cubans does not.

I had not imagined a camp like those I have seen set down on verdant English hillsides, neat rows of smug tents full of whispering Guides who skip down to the sea at reveille before collecting churns of frothing milk from the local farmhouse. Here in southern Buhera there are no green hillsides, no tents and no farmhouses. Nor had I imagined an African version of the cramped armed camp of the medieval drawings, with battlements, moats, siege machines and catapults – men in armour sardine-packed into uniform profile because the artist couldn't face faces. I hadn't imagined anything.

But there are bugles, alarums and excursions in every war.

The liberated zone is an invisible scar on an uncharted map. It is a state of mind, a claim, a fabric of rebellion stitched out of a thousand personal revolts, rather than a zone. There are no frontier posts. Only the clink of weapons, the black bodies coiled in bandoliers, the cases of East European ordnance, signal that here is what Esther's letters to her parents had ironically referred to as Caliban's kingdom. There are very few trees and scarcely any cover: the guerrillas burrow for safety.

'In defiance of our proverbial laziness,' Dr Zimunya remarks. 'As a matter of fact the African is far from lazy, though I have no wish to convince you.'

They have erected a small tent of East German manufacture for me (as also for General Chimurenga, members of the High Command, Esther and Zimunya – there is no shortage of hierarchy here among the comrades).

Inevitably I am an object of intense curiosity – not because I am white but because I am *white and here*. I feel like a camel captured by bushmen. But their scrutiny is discreet and shy – they do not line up to stare at me in the Chinese fashion.

Zimunya, 'the doctor', never touches Esther in my presence. Neither by deed, gesture nor inflection of voice does he hint at any intimacy beyond that of comradeship in 'the Struggle'. Cubans's sardonic drawl has yielded to a more educated sarcasm masked by the most refined good manners – did Esther ever tell him the truth about our relationship?

Mockery is Zim's stock-in-trade. He takes delight in teasing out my fears. 'Relax, Richard, ha ha, the enemy cannot reach us without tattooing his approach in thunder – snarling helicopters, groaning Dakotas, the whole imperialist orchestra. Don't over-estimate your own race, ha ha.'

Esther has emerged from the Order of the Precious Blood into green camouflage fatigues; the adoration with which she was greeted by the farm women at Bromley is reproduced here among the women comrades. She hands me over to Comrade Liberty with an almost malicious smile:

'You'll be safe in her hands, Richard, provided you consider yourself her prisoner.'

I am first introduced to the tall, powerfully built Liberty (born Olivia Mhondadaro) and her ever-present AK 47 rifle at night – and struggle by oil lamp to extract the contours of her face from the surrounding blackness. What emerges is strikingly beautiful in the bold style of a Nigerian ebony carving.

'Look,' she announces, 'a camp bed and a mosquito net for our guest. De luxe first class, eh?' She is a wit and very keen on laughter, is Liberty, but she moans in consternation when she realises that I will have to lie all night bent into an S to accommodate my height to the camp bed. She brings me hot water and offers to wash my dirty clothes:

'You will be dining with the Comrade General tonight, it's strictly black tie but not black collar.'

She then volunteers that she will not wash my underpants. She would only do that for a husband. Whereupon she asks me rather brazenly whether I'm married. I say no and she raises her eyebrows sceptically:

'Esther says you are married, Richard Stern.'

'Is Esther the last word on every question?'

' "The last word"?'

Try squatting with your heels on the ground: you will immediately fall backwards. We can maintain the squat only by balancing on the ball of the foot but an African woman can squat for hours on the flat of her feet, her bum only an inch above the ground. In this posture Liberty is both talkative and inquisitive. Every freedom fighter, she explains, deserves a wife because a man can 'resist' every hardship except loneliness. (This dependence on women is indeed the Achilles heel of the Zimbabwean guerrilla movement, but it would be ungracious to tell her so; just as it would baffle her if I explained that what renders both 'the doctor' and his wife ineffective revolutionaries is their inability to live apart.)

Bitch!

'I can hardly marry you to get my underpants washed,' I reply as Liberty's sponge floods warm water down my bare back. Her troubled eyes rest on me like saucers, this peasant girl whose splendid limbs, given a different dispensation, might have spread themselves across the pages of the magazines men furtively pluck down from the top shelves of corner shops. Despairing of an education, Olivia had left home to work on the Jersey Tea Estates, a dawn-to-dusk régime of exploitation and constant bullying by the 'bossboys' at seven dollars-fifty a month. Then, fired by the armed struggle around her, outraged by the forcible removal of her mother into one of the concentration camps that Tanner calls 'protected villages' – worked very well in Malaya – Liberty had crossed the border into Mozambique, terrified of the wild, empty country and the prowling leopards, until she reached the great Zanla camp at Chimolo and adopted the 'Chimurenga' name of Comrade Tichaona Liberty.

I listen to the discreet sounds of an armed camp at rest, at food, at firelight – the high, gurgling laughter of young men and women most of whom are assumed to be dead by their parents and many of whom will be dead within a week. Hersh will make sure of that. Groomed to her satisfaction – she is fascinated by my battery-powered razor (I wonder how secure it will be in my tent) – Liberty leads me, or marches me in her long, confident stride to the General's fire, where I become aware of a hierarchy of commanders, commissars and central committee men all eyeing me with varying degrees of suspicion. I hear myself referred to in Shona as 'Esther's journalist' and indeed it is Esther who introduces me to General Chimurenga, the firelight playing on her smooth, pale skin and occasionally, when the logs flare under a burst of wind from the veld, illuminating her from within like a halloween mask of luminous beauty.

The General treats me warily, placing Esther between us as a kind of filter – as if to make her responsible for what I might ask and what I might later write. Clearly pride and honour dictate that the General should hide his intense curiosity about my motives, my impressions of his 'camp', and my opinions about the war; this being so, he inclines to direct remarks obviously intended for my ears to anyone but me.

'And what are the fascists claiming this week?' he asks in his deep trombone.

'They win every battle,' Zimunya says.

'Yet lose the war. Soon every white farm will be abandoned. Are the whites so stupid, then?'

'Desperation makes men stupid,' Esther says. It's the first time I have seen her eat without utensils and I notice how easily she consumes the dry lump of sadza on her tin plate. I find myself examining each of her motions out of the corner of my eye. I love her passionately.

General Chimurenga asks Zimunya whether we had been followed during our journey from Salisbury. The doctor nods casually; clearly he is not in awe of the famous commander.

'During daylight.'

'Until we reached Fay's,' Esther adds.

I don't understand – as far as I was aware there had been no 'tail', just a couple of police road blocks en route. Clearly there was tension between Esther and Zimunya over Fay Cowans, the doctor refusing to share her trust in the good faith of the white woman whose farm survived because (as she vividly described to us over dinner, with a fund of fascinating anecdotes which filled several pages of my notebook) she kept on good terms with both the local guerrillas and the security forces. I liked Fay a good deal more than her late husband.

I was alone with her only once. She said:—Geoff lost his head over Esther and she didn't mind.

The guerrilla officers eat their tough, tasteless chicken in constrained silence. What I've been invited to witness probably represents Zanla's boldest and most conventional military performance inside Rhodesia since the war began and precisely the display of strength that Hersh has been waiting for. I have a premonition that we will all die soon; I keep scanning the vast, empty sky if the 'doctor' isn't watching me with that derisive smile.

Fay Cowans added: —I don't believe Geoff killed himself. He would never do that. She was trembling; she had a desperate need to get it off her chest to anyone other than Dr and Mrs Zimunya.

'And how does our distinguished guest find us?' General Chimurenga inquires. 'Animal Farm or the Heart of Darkness?' He tosses another chicken bone over his shoulder.

'The Comrade General missed his vocation,' Zimunya chuckles. 'He should have styled himself General Knowledge.'

A lump of sadza is glued, bland and tasteless, to my gullet.

'I cannot interview the night,' I reply.

'He's a poet, this reporter of yours,' the General tells Esther. 'Tender is the Night.'

The firelight plays across the intricate web of plaits stitched to the roof of Liberty's head. She has been frowning intently while watching me toy with my food, as if I were a child in her care.

'You must eat,' she murmurs, exasperated by the abandoned meal on my plate. 'You will lose strength.'

'Don't bully him,' Zimunya intervenes. 'His stomach will do better empty. Remember that he has developed none of our immunities.' I suspect that Liberty would have accepted this rebuke had not Cubans, on casual impulse, provoked her further:

'She wants to fatten you up for sacrifice, Comrade Stern. When this war is won Liberty and her sisters plan to seize power. We men will have to suffer a second exile in the bush, cooking for ourselves.'

'Chauvinist pig!' Liberty cries, unabashed by the General's presence. 'We will come in our helicopters to massacre you!'

'Crime and Punishment,' the General announces, tossing aside (I shall be accused of exaggeration) yet another chicken bone. I glance at Esther; her delicate profile registers only a faint amusement; I have spent ten years pursuing her across an adventure playground.

Belching and rubbing his stomach, the General rises and shakes himself like a large dog emerging from water. Immediately his aides and lieutenants are on their feet and we all stand up. Taking Esther by the elbow, he leads her to where I am standing. He addresses me with another display of disdain. We used to call it showing off.

'When I stand they all stand. When your brash young Foreign Secretary, Dr Owen, arrives at Dar es Salaam and sportingly removes his jacket, all six of his Foreign Office aides immediately remove theirs. When Andy Young goes for an early morning jog round the harbour at Malta . . . er . . .'

The General flicks his fingers impatiently.

'Valetta,' says Zimunya.

'Ah, Valetta, then all the State Department aides must also jog. Now, Mr Stern, for which master do *you* remove your coat? For which master do you jog?'

'For the truth.'

The General squeezes Esther's shoulder. 'This journalist of yours takes himself seriously, a common failing among the English. Well, to bed: up at five, stay alive, Mr Stern. I was once caught napping before dawn by Rhodesian commandos of the RLI. There was already a big price on my head, dead or alive, maybe ten thousand dollars, I don't know. First thing I knew I was being hauled to my feet, slapped and beaten with rifle butts by white men with blackened faces. "Lead us to your famous gook General," they hissed, "we know he's here." I wear no badge of rank, you see, no gold braid, I was never at Sandhurst, and these white commandos being simple fellows, apprentices from the Trojan nickel mine and homesick electricians, couldn't imagine the first chap they grabbed would be their prize. Of course I played the cowardly gook baboon, stammering for mercy and promising to lead them to my commander. I told them he was asleep the other side of the Hunyani River, a very big river full of crocodiles. They hit me some more and told me they weren't born yesterday and threatened to kill me on the spot. I told them I would cross that dangerous river by night only if they promised me one quarter of the reward money – as soon as I demanded money they had complete faith in me: colonialism has always depended on the cowardice and venality of the kaffirs, has it not, Mr Stern?'

The General squeezes Esther's shoulders again as if my answer, and my soul, reside between them. Would Caliban like to carry her away for the night? Dr Zimunya's spectacles are glinting in the flickering firelight. Come the Liberation and General Chimurenga will be found guilty of treason by a Minister of the Interior with a medical degree.

The General chooses not to finish his story; his escape from the Rhodesian commandos is either a matter for another night or for the imagination.

'For us, Mr Stern, the sky remains the enemy, the great bowl of fire, but one day it will be our sky.'

He moves majestically away with his retinue, as if this were the Palais de Versailles rather than an arid desert. Esther turns to Liberty like a hospital sister to a nurse.

'Did I give you enough insect repellent for Richard?'

'I have two tubes, Esther.'

'Make sure you cover him from head to foot.'

She and I have been together for two days and two nights now, but not once has she made any attempt to talk to me alone – not even in Fay Cowans's farmhouse.

Liberty's eyes shine like those of the owl I ran down at night on the road to Wedza. Taking my hand she leads me through the darkness among guerrillas preparing for sleep without a single blanket to cover them, weapons at their side. An anti-mosquito taper is burning in my tent but the huge, vicious, blood-sucking brutes are all around us, whining like high-speed saws. Pulling my shirt off, her strong, calloused hands begin to cover me in the repellent whose antiseptic smell mingles with Liberty's own – woodsmoke, sweat, some onion root, womanhood. I can imagine Zimunya and his wife together in their tent, laughing at my dilemma: would it be more insulting to embrace Liberty or not to embrace her?

'It's like deciding whether to tip an Intourist guide in the Soviet Union.' The voice is Holzheimer's. In a placatory gesture he shifts his glasses up from the curling ramp of his nose.

I am tormented by dreams all through the night, thrashing under the mosquito net in the stifling, airless tent, and several times crying out so loudly that my faithful protector Liberty crawls in under the canvas to interrogate and comfort me. I can hardly explain that Esther has ceremonially dipped her hands in the blood of Cassius, and of other victims of Cubans's stick grenades, then ripped off her nun's habit and traced scarlet patterns over her naked breasts as my thirsting tongue begins to lick.

—This is only a dream, Esther laughs,—and when you wake up you'll be alone in London and I'll be far away in Africa . . .

I am awoken some time before dawn by cries of command outside, the rhythmic thumping of platoons moving at the double, deep guttural grunts, sudden chants uttered with fearsome, warlike cohesion (like Zulu extras in a film), Shona slogans interspersed with phrases in Swahili and English. I crawl out of the tent into a darkness which is fading into the sky like ink into blotting paper.

Gradually the strange motions of semi-darkness began to define themselves like negatives developing into a print.

Liberty brings me hot tea and – oh God! – more sadza. I shake my aching head.

'You must eat!' she protests. 'If you die, they will blame me.'

I show her my battery-powered razor. 'Look, Liberty, I smile at it and it shaves me. White magic, eh?'

'Aaaaah . . . you want a fight? I warn you, I beat you up in no time. I've killed those Rhodesian fascist commandos with my bare hands.'

I laugh.

'Why do you laugh? When men laugh at women it is always to put them down.'

'My wife is very keen on male "putdowns".'

'But you told me you have no wife!'

Later Liberty asks whether it's true that during 'World War II' – had she been reading an American magazine? – white girls in Europe gave their 'everything' for a tin of corned beef. As she speaks a line of straggling *mombes* come into view herded by two skinny boys who stare at me with saucer eyes, the beasts flapping their tails against their emaciated shanks out of weary respect for routine, yet scarcely bothering to lower their heads to the dust, their hopes invested in the occasional thorn bush. The kites hover overhead. There is almost no sign of a military encampment; General Chimurenga's unarmed army is forced to abandon its own profile at first light.

I do not see Esther all morning. It is Zimunya who conducts me among the freedom fighters (as if it is he, not she, whom I have known and loved for ten years). The guerrillas are happy enough to talk, funnelling their testimony down the limited channels of their English jargon: 'a certain commander', 'a certain directive', 'a certain ambush'. They speak constantly of the 'masses' and the 'struggle'. One young man, describing his narrow escape during a Rhodesian surprise attack in the Mtoko area, explains how he finally found refuge in the home of 'a friendly mass'.

At the midday meal the General again holds court. This time his approach is less regally indirect:

'You have some questions?'

Clearly he enjoys an audience of acolytes for this confrontation with a white journalist – in the late sixties I conducted similar 'dialogues' with the great mandarins of the European Left, notably Louis Althusser, who invariably presented themselves in the company of a devoted audience of graduate students.

I ask the General whether Zanla's official war statistics, as published in Maputo, are really credible.

'You can believe what you like.'

I press the point. '*Zanu News* informs us that, during the past six months, your forces destroyed 73 enemy vehicles, 18 enemy planes, and 1,115 enemy troops. Your victories, like Falstaff's, magnify in the telling.'

Everyone round the two great vats of sadza has fallen silent.

'Unlike Smith, we don't need to invent facts,' Chimurenga replies easily. 'This isn't Penguin Island.'

'You never report your own losses.'

'We don't fight our war to please foreign journalists. This is war, Mr Reporter, and my people are dying.'

'But we mustn't ignore propaganda psychology,' Zimunya intervenes. 'If we are to make claims they should be convincing claims.' Clearly there is little love lost between them; something sub-tribal, perhaps, or factional, or just the frustration of years of imprisonment and exile. Ah yes, I remember now how Cubans casually mentioned in Bulawayo that he'd been in Wha Wha. He was telling me but I couldn't hear.

There is a stirring and murmuring of armed guerrillas, a clinking of weapons and bandoliers around the fires, like bees swarming before a sting, and I experience a familiar flush of adrenalin: once again I am pursuing the unconditional surrender of Esther Meyer. Now that she has confessed that Paul had named names, she has surrendered her title deed to honour. I understand why in London she led a life of rampant promiscuity almost equal to – ha! very probably in excess of – Beth's. The 'doctor' is clearly one of those 'husbands' who assume theatrical airs of menace while contriving to get cuckolded from January to December.

'Another question, General.'

'Yes, Mr Pickwick?'

'Why do your forces systematically destroy clinics, schools and dip tanks?'

Liberty claps her hand to her mouth, aghast, as if her charge has suddenly revealed himself to be a viper; commanders, commissars and aides have all stopped eating. I glance sidelong at Esther, whose long lashes are lowered over her plate in contemplation.

'I'll tell you why,' she says, 'it's because—'

'I will answer!' roars the General. 'Does our guest refer perhaps to *Government* schools, *Government* clinics, and *Government* dip tanks?'

'Certainly,' I say. 'But the children who go without education are not Government children, they are your children. The people whose illnesses receive no treatment are not Government people, they are your people. The cattle who die of tsetse fly are not Government cattle, they are your people's cattle.'

'The fees for these schools and clinics finance the Salisbury régime's war machine!' the General bellows.

'That, of course, is nonsense.'

Esther slowly turns to me with an expression of horror.

'There are more suitable ways of expressing disagreement when talking to our supreme commander, Richard.'

I am angry because I love her. She has never rebuked me like that before.

'Another question, General,' I persist. 'Why do your young men so often abduct the local girls when they occupy a village?'

Uproar. Predictable, I suppose.

'Such lies!' Liberty cries, eyes ablaze. She knows it's true, of course, but national pride stands astride her feminism. 'Tell him it's lies, Esther!'

But Esther bends her head sadly. 'It does happen, Liberty.'

The General himself disdains to answer this vulgar question while Zimunya (I notice) shelters behind an ironic smile. The younger men argue among themselves in Shona until one of them emerges as a spokesman:

'Actually, when we come into a village our main purpose of taking girls with us, er, we do it for security-wise. We know this can help because in actual fact when we come to a village some people go away secretly and report this to the security forces, then we could be attacked and shooted. Taking girls and, you know, sleeping is part of our security because they are the daughters of people who might report us.'

'We also get essential information from the girls,' another comrade adds. 'We do not usually take these girls in respect of bed things.'

'They would not let you!' Liberty cries. The men look abashed.

Zim laughs. 'You see, everyone is frightened of your camp wife, Comrade Stern.'

I ask the General whether he will succeed in halting the internal, Smith-Muzorewa, election.

'You ask a serious question at last. Yes, we can close down that pantomine of puppets. The masses reject this phoney election. The soldiers come to herd the people to the polls at gunpoint and we kill those puppet soldiers. No problem.'

The guerrillas roar support for their chief, AK 47s raised aloft.

'No problem': I have heard that phrase throughout the morning. Halt the election? topple the Bishop? win the war? No problem. At root there is something resigned in their attitude. Stoical, long-suffering children of the tribal trust lands, forced to bury their dead in mass graves, they have numbed themselves into a certain fatalism. The 'masses' will prevail in the end. The worst moment in Liberty's lonely crossing into Mozambique had been when she was caught in the open by a Rhodesian spotter plane; finally she had found refuge in the house of 'a friendly mass'.

'Mr Stern's head is full of Rhodesian propaganda,' the General announces in his reverberating trombone. 'Rhodesia is merely a small, angry baby perched on the lap of the great white mother, South Africa.'

Respectfully I copy this into my notebook. Here, as on a beleaguered white farm anywhere from Mrewa to the Matopos, the essence of independent journalism is subterfuge. The expressions in the circle around me reflect a great elation. The General has spoken. The Negro, like the Arab, mistakes the Word for the Deed.

I ask Zimunya, as loudly as possible, why the comrades do not dispose of their refuse in an efficient soldierly manner. Why these heaps of empty cans, slops, banana skins . . . ? I have already seen rats and maggots; no wonder comrades are suffering from leeches and lice in their hair. Does not he, as a 'doctor of medicine', take responsibility for hygiene? Zimunya's smile seems ineradicable and I hear my voice go up and up, jabbing into the cross-legged uterus where 'the doctor' plants his seed.

I try to read Esther's expression but cannot.

When the Rhodesian spotter plane appears overhead it's almost a relief from the slow, oppressive confrontation I have engineered with a guerrilla army sprawled lazily round the great, bubbling pots of sadza. The distant drone of the Cessna's engine precipitates a stampede (later described to me as a 'dispersal') and I find myself running for the nearest clump of thorn bushes with Liberty at my side and a pleasant hammering in my chest: bombs and blood would make the afternoon worthwhile.

'Don't look up, your face is white,' whispers a young man lying prostrate beside me, his voice hoarse with anxiety – as if the Rhodesian pilot, five thousand feet up in the sky, might hear him. The distant drone of the plane reminds me of drowsy summer days flirting with Elizabeth Halliday among buttercups and daisies in the long sweet grass of England (was it '71 or '72 that we took a picnic to Blenheim after punting up the Cherwell?), but then I observe a column of red ants marching across the dust of Buhera like unpaid mercenaries only inches from my nose and I sit up abruptly to find myself looking into features all too familiar:

'Good God, Oscar! How the hell did you get here? Didn't we last meet on the Meyers' verandah?'

The Cessna is circling us in a leisurely manner, first one wing up, then the other, watching.

'Two Sundays ago,' Oscar says.

'I thought you were working as a journalist for the *Herald*.'

'Nothing in Zimbabwe is what it seems, Richard. I liked the questions you put to the General, by the way – I'm afraid sycophancy is the normal procedure here. The comrades say "Pamberi neMugabe" and "Pamberi neCentral Committee" five times a day like Moslems doing their prayers – perhaps you noticed we turn towards Machel and Mozambique rather than Mohammed and Mecca.'

I study the beads of sweat glistening on Oscar Mucheche's upper lip and chin. There is a hint of a moustache.

'You always were a cynic, Oscar.'

He chuckles. 'Yes, but keep that white face of yours down. Talking of white faces, I see you finally caught up with our St Joan. I remember the day you brought her to address us at the LSE. I'd already made my own pitch but was turned down by that fat bitch Amy Brand. You had status, of course, a noted New Left TV idol in those days, did you screw her before or after that meeting, I often wondered?'

I take Oscar's FN rifle and gently push the muzzle into his mouth. He looks rather surprised.

'For Christ's sake, Richard, this Communist-built junk goes off if you blow your nose.'

I restore his weapon to him. 'And when the Rhodesians come tomorrow, where will Oscar Mucheche be?'

Oscar grins. 'Filing his story in Salisbury.' Gripping my arm, he lowers his voice. 'Watch out for Zimunya, he's already killed three men he suspected of sleeping with Esther, including a white shit called Cowans. No one can touch him, not even the General; after Mugabe, he's the most powerful man in the Party. He might prefer you not to leave Buhera at all. Graves here tend to be shallow.'

Oscar tentatively rises to a squat and scans the vast, scarred plain.

'I'll be perfectly frank with you, Richard: these people here stand no chance, no way. Tomorrow Hersh will come and then—' His hand slices across his throat. 'Visiting this mob is not unlike reading glowing press reports of a new show, the latest production, man, then finally getting a ticket and finding yourself in a run-down rehearsal littered with tatty costumes, unfinished scenery and bemused actors unsure of their lines.'

I nod. 'You sold out, Oscar?'

'I grew up.'

'You really believe in the Bishop?'

He shakes his head. 'I believe in me.'

Later, as the sun slides down the sky, I sit outside my tent in the sulking company of Comrade Liberty, slowly examining her powerful limbs with a brazen scrutiny that causes her to murder ants with her boots. (She is privileged; most wear dilapidated canvas shoes.)

'Would you like to hear a joke, Liberty?'

'No! You are an agent of Ian Smith! A spy!'

'An actor was playing Hamlet, quite a bad actor actually. The director warned him to remain standing throughout the play except when the action required him to kneel. But on the first night the actor forgot his instructions and suddenly sat down on a chair in the middle of the soliloquy "To be, or not to be". The audience burst out laughing and the play was ruined.'

I begin to laugh. Liberty turns her beautiful, sullen ebony features in my direction. Such tranquillity, such dignity, such nothingness.

'Is that funny?'

'Yes. And if you were a good soldier you would be cleaning your rifle now.'

Her eyes blaze, as anticipated. 'I have not fired my rifle.'

'The Rhodesians clean theirs twice a day.'

She lowers her eyes. The white oppressor can be accused of anything except inefficiency. Later she takes my hand and teaches me a song:

> Ruzhinji rive Africa
> Tinokumbira rubatsiro
> Kuti isu Vatema
> VeZimbabwe tizvitonge . . .

her voice trailing away shyly. 'Tomorrow,' she says, 'I may wake you like this—' she thrusts her hip into mine. 'We call that way "*chimutsa nedako*". It will mean you are my husband.'

The night has descended like a curtain – I would like to write up the day's notes in more detail but Liberty, childlike in her rapid alternations of sentiment, is now regarding me with oppressive affection and I fear that she may insist on making herself my 'wife' before the Rhodesians arrive . . . an event I now anticipate with a sense of anticipation bordering on elation. (I mean the Rhodesians, not Liberty, the heat is spoiling my syntax . . . Bloody mosquitoes!)

Yes, Liberty now offers – insists! – on washing my underpants. While she is at the river doing so a note arrives from Esther. It says, simply, 'Tonight.'

Here Stern's diary, captured the following day by the Rhodesian Special Air Service, broke off. It was never recovered.

TWENTY-SEVEN

The Roman legions prepared to retake Gaul. Strapped into their formidable cargo of weapons, ammunition, ratpacks, and parachutes, the fireforce commandos waited quietly on the runway of Grand Reef Air base, west of Umtali, barely exchanging a word. It was too hot for steel helmets; their long, silky hair glinted reassuringly above skins plastered in camouflage cream. The 'scramble' alarm was blaring continuously.

Tanner saw the first of the rotor blades light up as the white braves filled the small Alouettes in 'sticks' of four. He thought: this is it, Leonard Tanner is back at the front line, at the coal face, they never thought I could do it, this will show them all . . . But his stomach was uncertain, like a great-hearted old police horse put on display at Olympia for the last time, and the paragraphs hesitantly forming in his head constantly decomposed into metaphors imposed upon him by that same alien force which had haunted him since his arrival in Rhodesia. Watching the parachute units slowly filing into the 'faithful' old Dakotas whose noses jutted up at an old-fashioned angle, Tanner (or somebody masquerading as Tanner) was reminded of seals begging for fish.

Competent if not entirely considerate hands were packing the old man into the General's command ship, fixing his canvas straps. An Alouette has no door. —You can fall out any time, General Hersh's commando son had joked over dinner in the mess, grinning at the distinguished English reporter with youthful eyes which saw everything and nothing.

—You know something, Mr Tanner? Killing your gook is no problem once you find him. The gook is like the maize-plundering baboon, he comes out of the hills at dusk, ravages everything in sight, then he's off at the first sign of trouble.

For dinner they ate huge steaks and potatoes baked in their

306

jackets which they split open ('like a gook's stomach,' suggested young Hersh) and crammed with melting butter. Rows of white teeth framed in suntan. Tanner imagined that mealtime was less fun at the southern end of Buhera, in the gook commander's camp, and if Stern was really down there, as Hersh's intelligence officers claimed, he was probably squatting under a thorn bush with his trousers down in the company of a battalion of flies. The young commandos took care to convey to 'Mr Tanner' (their mothers had brought them up to be polite) that what they faced on the morrow was not so much an army as 'three field marshals, six generals and twelve commissars fighting over a single banana skin'. Tanned laughter. A boy from a Baptist family in Texas who was draining one 7–Up after another explained that, —After Nam and Angola we can't afford to lose any more countries.

—I was in Korea, Tanner told them. He described the frozen bodies of US Marines, fields manured in human shit, and the young Rhodesians nodded attentively, uncertain where Korea was, or when.

The General sat at the head of the table, brooding, unapproachable. Tanner had observed the great Boer chieftain striding about Grand Reef ('Hubby hates desk-work,' Frieda had confided), a Pompey testing and tasting his Legion's great love, prodding and patting his helicopters as if they were dogs. No one dared speak to him. He had delegated his son to look after the guest – the only journalist he would allow on this operation (Tanner had finally signed a cheque for three thousand pounds sterling in exchange for a sackful of funny money which he had no idea how he would dispose of) – and that was enough.

Tanner drank steadily in anticipation of his long-awaited return to the front-line. The gooks were a rabble but they also had Sam 7 heat-seeking rockets and their bushcraft (attested young Hersh, in a sudden change of emphasis), was 'just incredibly switched on, I mean unreal'. It gnawed at Tanner's gut that Stern should have responded to dismissal and deportation by essaying a front-line scoop which would no doubt appear not only in the *New York Times*, courtesy of that American, but also in . . . Tanner shuddered at the prospect of Warner's 'Black Man' column and the echoing laughter down Fleet Street. Intruding on these sombre reflections was the steady, earnest testimony of a young British mercenary who was informing Tanner how he'd been born in Kenya, studied zoology at Makere in Uganda until things became too hairy under Amin, then renewed his British passport in Nairobi, lost it, travelled to Botswana, the Sudan and the USA on forged passports, then been sent packing by the British consul in Joburg, tried to obtain a Kenyan passport in Jogo House, Nairobi, been rejected as British and advised to try Tanzania because his father had been born in Tanganyika . . .

Slowly Tanner focused on the young man. —That's a lot of bad luck, he said.

The young mercenary bit the metal cap off another Lion lager.

—All right, I'm a soldier of fortune, you can call me a mercenary, Mr Tanner, OK, I've told a lot of lies in my life, I'll be honest with you about that, but I know Africa back to front, Mr Tanner, I mean Uhuru is crap, I mean I hate those gooks right here in the gut, I mean I'm not a religious man but I'm a believer, this life is the only life we have but this world is of no account, believe me.

Tanner knew when a man was drunk. This one wasn't.

Waiting for lift-off, the bulky Hersh sat crammed into his command ship muffled in huge headphones, a radio microphone at his chin, a great wild boar of a man, bloated and baffled in his capsule. Stern smiled at Tanner from a distance of ninety kilometres: ' "The General has been stuffed into the Alouette like a prune into a lark's stomach" – try that in your first paragraph.'

The Alouette lifted sharply in a cloud of dust, then tilted and wheeled. Tanner clutched desperately at a stanchion – for a moment he had feared he would fall out of the open door. Steady, steady. Dakotas airborne on the port side. He remembered lunching with them both at Rowley's in Jermyn Street a few days after that television fiasco, himself cast in the role of rancid old lecher and yet forced to send her cocky lover to Geneva on the payroll. The rest of the afternoon remained hazy in his battered memory; drank another carafe until they politely turfed him out, then a striptease in Old Compton Street or was it the Windmill?

The noise was severe, his head ached already. The Alouette was capricious in the sky and he felt sick. Soon after the accident he'd found Helen's recorder under the back seat of the family car, together with a plastic folder of crayons and her music sheet in brightly coloured dots: green Cs, red Es, yellow Fs, blue As, grey Gs, mauve Bs, brown Ds – but he couldn't recall these details, only the tune: All things bright and beautiful! All creatures great and small/All things wise and . . . The young warriors of Grand Reef reminded him of Olivier's bowmen before Agincourt, Once more into the breach, dear friends, once more; Or close the wall – was that right? – or close the wall up with our English dead. Yes: if you attempted, like Stern, to resist the pull of kith and kin you were no longer 'yourself' and you ended up by dishonouring your mother and renouncing the father that begat you.

The Alouette banked steeply over the empty brown plain of Buhera. Tanner's bowels were churning. His brother Gerald had officiated at the funeral, taking care of everything, former soldier who'd been bitten by God, turned Catholic and began stomping about the East End in his bushy eyebrows. Helen adored him. Gerald used to tell her jokes (which her father didn't) like:

—What are two rows of cabbages? Answer: A dual cabbageway;

—What's a plum that falls off a table? Answer: A damson in distress;

—What's black and white and red all over . . . ? Answer: Daddy's newspaper. (You see, Leonard, I'm not trying to steal her affections.)

Smug bastard, Gerald, very content with his professional poverty, always borrowing sums too small to decently reclaim (Stern thinks split infinitives OK), how he loved to warm his arse in front of Leonard's fire while downing his Harvey's Bristol Cream like a pre-Christmas ad on TV. Gerald had a rich, voice-over pulpit voice, superior to Leonard's sandpaper rasp. Catholics! Mistake to regard those bloody recusants as the underdogs . . .

Tanner could see the gunships fanning out, flies on the window-pane of a sky incapable of rain during nine months of the year. The Alouette had begun to bound like a puppy sniffing rabbit and it was only a matter of time before he spewed up the breakfast he should have gone without.

—As for your *colleague* Stern and the kaffir's whore, we 'ave 'em, Hersh had roared. —Tomorrow. In a zip bag, with that munt Zimunya.

—I have to admire your intelligence service, General.

A wink as heavy as the flap of a vulture's wing: Hersh perambulating, Napoleonically, with hands clasped behind back, occasionally swinging on his heel as if to catch out some knave creeping up on him from behind. Tanner had guessed that not asking the question was the way to elicit an answer, and he was right:

—Game starts in 'Ighfield, St Andrew's Mission, Zimunya tosses coupla stick grenades into a UANC rally, wiping out several including a Special Branch operative from Bulawayo. The bitch does her Sister Angelica of the Precious Blood act, sheds a kaffir priest on the way, wipes off the blood at a farm owned by a white liberal, talks her way through a roadblock twelve ks west of Marandellas, turns south to Wedza and stops off for the night with . . .

Hersh hesitated. Even Hersh. —With our source, he grunted. —What's more this woman tries to call the police on the agric-alert after they've all gone to bed but the kaffir doctor's waiting for her, grabs her, forces her into your *colleague's* room where the two of 'em gang-rape 'er 'egged on by the screaming nun 'erself. This party of 'igh-class terrorists then takes the gap, leaving the

309

poor woman tied up with a personal message from Chimurenga to 'Ersh: 'Come and get me, Boer.'

Absorbed in this account, Tanner had struggled to fit the *dramatis personae* into the proscenium arch of the fabulous journey recounted by Hersh. All he could visualise, as the gunships began their run-in on Zanla's 'liberated zone', was the central image in a despatch filed by Stern more than a year ago, quoting Vittorio Mussolini:

> 'We arrived upon the Abyssinian unobserved and immediately dropped our explosives. One group of horsemen gave me the impression of a budding rose unfolding as the bomb fell in their midst and blew them up. It was exceptionally good fun.'

Now the budding rose unfolded again as the 20-mm cannon opened up and the CTs began to run, scamper, like fucking ants across the brown dust of Buhera.

Dakotas overhead, figures free-falling, no chutes until one thousand feet, the great panache of the SAS. Tanner could imagine the lights flashing relentlessly above the open doors. Go go go go, and the paras went while the General, his lugubrious features scaffolded in command-ship wiring, barked his orders, regretting or not regretting that he had sacrificed the normal preliminary airstrike to the Staff College totem of Surprise. Hersh was happy: he had seen the birds and they were his own.

The Alouette dipped at a steep angle: Tanner gripped the stanchion in an effort not to follow his magnolia vomit out of the open door. The first of the 'chutes opened into little white mushrooms, checking the pull of mother-earth which threatened to splatter them like broken eggs; this was the big one and whatever happened the mission wouldn't be a 'lemon', a zero kill. Tanner saw two paras jerk in mid-air, the ghastly spasm of a body receiving a bullet, then crumple like insects as they hit the ground. A quarter of a mile to the west a helicopter was burning like the struck head of a match and a Dakota was trying to gain height with oil-black smoke gushing from its port engine. For perhaps twenty seconds it sustained altitude, level and loyal, like a prisoner maintaining a gallant silence under torture, then abruptly surrendered and plummeted down into a ball of fire.

As the Alouette dipped and spun to avoid the upcoming tracer fire, Tanner was reminded that war, like love, is never quite what you remember it to be. To plant his two feet safely on the earth had become his only preoccupation – his most constant nightmare had been to find himself slipping off the top of a tall building, as he edged along a window ledge to where *she* was trapped, terrified,

310

begging him for help while her hysterical mother yelled at him to do something . . . an awful giddiness, I can't do it, not even for her . . .

Fumbled at the buckles strapping him to his seat, found himself hauled out, forced to duck under the spinning rotor blades, pulled by young arms, 'Hot foot, Mr Tanner, run!' The earth rose up and up to smack him in the face: take that! A mortar shell, then another, bang! bang! bang! jagged fragments of rock flying in lateral fury. Down! Noise deafening, choking dust, lay panting. No, wouldn't carry a gun, not even in Vietnam, a matter of principle, the Yank reporters used to bait him about it, 'Hey, Leonard, what if a gook suddenly leaps into your foxhole, what d'ya tell him? – "it's OK, I'm from *The Times*"?'

Silence. In Beirut he had learned to distrust that 'final' silence – there was always one more, perhaps two, from the hills above the airport, one more sniper's bullet, one more Palestinian telling the world, one more Shi'ite gunman serving Allah . . . But here the silence held and the smoke slowly drifted like the curtain of a theatre to reveal men gathering in small knots round the dead and the wounded, the 'bad luck' cases, amid the rising stench of distress.

Tanner stood up, wiping the remains of vomit from his chin with his sleeve, screwing his face into the sun, wise and sad, father to them all. He'd seen war before these babes were born yet such is the pace of human growth and decay that they were now better at it than he. He saw more bodies, mostly black, and he remembered how difficult he had always found it, at first glimpse, to connect a dead man to the notion of 'enemy'.

He noticed there were no prisoners. He lit a cigarette and inhaled deeply. No cigarette had ever tasted better.

The battle had been like a game you play until one team leaves the field, then you stop. Delighted to have survived, he drifted with the slow tide of young warriors towards what appeared to be a focus of attention, a dense circle of men gathered round a great, solitary baobab tree. At first he assumed it was a de-briefing, or a first-aid post, but then he realised that the commandos were staring at something with the intense curiosity of spectators, their sweat-soaked, pack-laden backs blocking his line of vision until they recognised Mr Tanner and lazily parted to let him through.

Two white people sat close together under the baobab, not flinching from the hostile stares of the young commandos whose tension-bitten faces were painted in collages of dripping camouflage cream. Tanner recognised her at once. The commandos gazed at her with a mixture of awe and horror, as if at a fabled unicorn, beautiful and deadly. Tanner remembered how she had cashed a blank cheque out of his own, inexcusable lust. Then he examined Stern – their eyes met – and all he saw on that long, saturnine face was contempt. A deep gash ran across his forehead, pouring with blood; some lad had made his statement before authority intervened. But she, she was safe: reared in white suburbs and on white farms, the commandos had been taught that white womanhood is sacred.

'String him up,' someone said softly, but no one moved.

Hersh swaggered through the throng of sweating soldiers to take possession of his prisoners – his only prisoners. General Chimurenga's army had yet again vanished into the vast, unfathomable spaces of Africa, yet again eluded Hersh's super war machine, yet again made mock of the imperial ceremony of war.

Then Tanner heard, incredulous, the twelve words that Esther Meyer spoke to Hersh. (He counted them later, several times.)

'General, I arrest you in the name of the people of Zimbabwe.'

'And where's Dr Zimunya?' Hersh asked her.

'He is fighting for the liberation of his country.'

The mouths of the commandos fell open at the melodious sound of her voice: two more minutes and they would all have been at her feet.

Hersh turned slowly to Tanner with a scowl.

'Is this your man, Mr Tanner?'

There are two versions of Leonard Tanner's reply. It was brutally hot, his stomach was a void, his tongue a purple thong of leather, his nerves still pumping from an hour of fear culminating in ten minutes of pure terror. Vultures wheeled overhead, the air reeked of burning gasoline, gunpowder and exploded rock, huge metal machines collapsed into hideous grimaces as they burnt out, bodies charred beyond recognition lay strewn across the plain, stretcher parties fastened drips to the wounded and carried their comrades low above the ground to the helicopters, cries of anguish frozen on young tongues as black as Tanner's. So it is not entirely surprising that there are two versions of what Tanner replied to Hersh at that crucial moment.

Either he said:

'He's a British newspaper reporter doing his job in strict accordance with international convention. He is not a prisoner of war and he enjoys my full protection.'

Or Tanner said:

'He *was* mine. He's yours now.'

Both versions, however, agree what Esther Meyer said.

PART THREE

PART THREE

TWENTY-EIGHT

'You didn't meet Smith, then?' murmured Sir Frank Fawcett-Ellis.

London: the Reform Club in Pall Mall. Members and guests were gathering under the high Rotunda to drink sherry and bark loudly. Tanner loathed the stuff – the sweet brown piss of a thousand Spanish cats. Selwyn Foyle surveyed the company with large, watery eyes capable of switching off and on like lightbulbs. To greet Sir Frank he emitted a mere forty watts; Tanner warranted ten. They didn't shake hands. Accepting his sherry without interest, Sir Frank remarked that he had celebrated the fine summer day by walking up through St James's Park.

'The truth is I'd completely forgotten I was lunching here until your good secretary called to confirm, so had a spare cheese sandwich to throw to the ducks. The trick is to get the bread into the water; otherwise the pigeons grab it.'

'The pigeons remind one of the Labour Party,' Selwyn Foyle said. 'Filthy parasites.'

'Ah.' Sir Frank's expression went into neutral.

'Their universal shit costs the Ministry of Works millions every year.'

'I've always thought of the pigeons as the true Londoners,' Tanner said. 'The ducks as wealthy aliens.'

'Ah,' said Sir Frank. 'And how would you classify the seagulls?'

'Seagulls? In London?' Foyle sounded incredulous.

'Oh yes,' drawled Sir Frank, one hand jangling his keys, his sherry still untouched. It was then that he turned to Tanner:

'You didn't meet Smith, then?'

'I met Hersh.'

'Ah.' Sir Frank released a thin smile. 'Can't say I found Smith particularly congenial when I was there last year. The man has

315

rather a wet handshake, I recall. He also made some public remarks about me which were distinctly disobliging.'

The crowd of grey-suited men had begun to shuffle out of the Rotunda.

'Lunch?' Foyle inquired, darting a look at the Deputy Under Secretary's glass. 'Why not bring your sherry?'

Moving in procession into the long, tall-windowed dining room, they took their places at a reserved table.

'Local claret acceptable?' Selwyn Foyle asked his guest. He didn't expect an audible reply; 'Fawcy' had never displayed any interest in food, drink (or sex), not even at school.

'How's Tivenham?' Foyle asked him.

Tanner knew this was Fawcett-Ellis's rather draughty place in Somerset – Foyle had once reported to him a 'ghastly' weekend there, longing for central heating, a good meal and a second glass of wine.

'Tivenham? The tractor's on its last legs. The estate manager generously advised me to buy a new one through a friend of his, special discount you know, but then ran off with his deputy's wife. Or didn't run off, worst luck. The two men now communicate with each other about fertiliser, seed and drainage by letter – rather like those early missionaries in Matabeleland who got on such bad terms after years of failing to convert a single kaffir that they had to communicate with each by post – *via London*.'

Foyle laughed loudly. They all laughed. Tanner didn't mind Fawcett-Ellis: unlike the ersatz Foyle, he was 'the real thing', the genuine article, etcetera. Fawcett-Ellis was an honorary member of Tanner's Be Yourself Club – his social origins could be forgiven and it was amusing to watch this skeletal ascetic picking at his smoked salmon as if he couldn't remember why it was clinging damply to his plate. Perhaps it reminded him of Ian Smith's handshake.

'Roofs, sheds, fences, all in disrepair, Selwyn. Haggling with estate agents in Taunton about the selling price of lots and smallholdings. Chasing up delinquent contractors whose robust wives are under instructions to say they are not at home. By the way, some sociologist might do a useful study of how many downright *lies* are told every day in this country of ours in the course of normal business.'

'I suppose the Foreign Office contributes its share,' Tanner said with a twinkle.

'Ah. We have classified our own lies into direct and indirect. The latter are preferred.'

'You know you love Tivenham,' Foyle said.

'Property. Ghastly burden. What did Marx say about property?'

'Is theft,' Tanner said.

'That was Proudhon, actually.'

'Why don't you sell Tivenham?' Foyle asked.

'You always had a nose for a bargain, Selwyn. *I* would. But Mary wouldn't hear of it. She loves draughts. Never had a cold in her life.'

'Have you read the new le Carré?' Foyle asked.

Sir Frank wiped his pencil mouth with a crisp napkin.

'Mm. Mary bought it for my birthday.'

'We were hoping to acquire first serial rights.'

Sir Frank didn't seem interested in this aspect of things.

'I enjoyed it. Couldn't follow the plot, of course – just as one can't really follow the plot inside the Tory Party. Mm?'

Selwyn Foyle reddened and Tanner experienced a small tug of pleasure: Mrs T. had swept to victory on 3 May but little Selwyn hadn't been given anything.

'One hears things,' the Deputy Under Secretary pressed his casual attack home, 'doesn't one? – new think tanks, special Downing Street Pressure Units, instant crisis response, computerised policy decisions, all very baffling to an old Somerset landlord.'

Foyle clearly knew his aspirations were being mocked by subtle indirection.

'And how's little Peter?' he hit back. 'Just the nigger-kissing wet you people must have wanted, eh?'

'You're referring to my new boss?'

'Who else?'

'As far as I know the Secretary of State enjoys excellent health.'

'You can't be sorry to see the back of Doctor Death.'

Fawcett-Ellis straightened his thin back and sighed; everything Selwyn Foyle had said and done during the forty years since they had first been inducted, simultaneously, into the slavery of fagging had reeked of bad taste.

'I am not particularly a socialist, Selwyn, and I may throw bread to ducks rather than pigeons, but I don't lose sleep over serving a Labour Foreign Secretary – even one who is ten years younger than I, knows less about foreign affairs than he imagines, needs no advice and, being a doctor by training, believes in instant diagnoses and quick remedies.'

Tanner wanted to say, 'We won't quote you,' if only because so outrageous a breach of etiquette might have registered his irritation at Fawcett-Ellis's amusement about Tanner's failure to get an interview with that twopenny-halfpenny colonial upstart, I. Smith.

Foyle refilled his own glass then shoved the decanter towards

Tanner; their guest's remained untouched, beside the full glass of sherry.

'Peter is utterly gutless,' the editor said. 'He's planning to sell Muzorewa down the river.'

Sir Frank picked at a piece of veal on his plate, occasionally dabbing shreds of it in a puddle of gravy, then laying it aside, like the more fussy of his ducks. When Ambassador in Egypt the smell of curry from the kitchens had sickened him; in Bangladesh the High Commission had reeked of filthy spices; he had been the only boy at the school who preferred Holy Communion to breakfast. But his silence could not stay the incensed Foyle:

'A Cabinet of eunuchs. Geoffrey's being taught his two times two on the Dame's knee, Francis is being shown how to curtsy in drag, both of Willie's Cumberland balls are on pawn in her handbag, and as for your boss little Peter, he's rushing off to kiss the great Nigerian arse.'

'Well, you know much more about these things than I do.'

'And you know damned well the F.O. has little Peter in its pocket.'

'You're welcome to search my pockets – provided you agree to pay any building repair bills you come across.'

Tanner glanced from one to the other, congratulating himself on his prudent silence. Foyle was still producing leader columns eulogising the Smith-Muzorewa *Wunderkind*, Zimbabwe Rhodesia, while the Lady herself was widely rumoured to be on the verge of a ninety-degree turn. Foyle's fury, however, was at root personal; he'd been led up the garden path.

'So you saw Hersh?' Fawcett-Ellis said to Tanner, changing the subject. 'That normally involves divesting oneself of considerable sums of cold cash.'

'Leonard signed a cheque for three thousand,' Foyle said contemptuously.

'Well, he got a battle as well as an interview – cheap at the price I'd say.'

'I thought so,' Tanner said. 'I also think a viable settlement needs Nkomo.'

'Very speculative,' Sir Frank said – his codeword for 'correct but premature', for the rogue elephant breaking out of the herd of controlled information.

'I wouldn't trust Nkomo an inch,' Foyle fumed. 'Didn't you see that pic of him clowning in the uniform of a Soviet marshal?'

'Joshua is many-sided,' Sir Frank said, playing with a silver dessert spoon as if wondering whether to steal it and pay off his debts. 'Indeed it takes several minutes to walk round him.'

A pale sunlight penetrated the grimed panes of the dining room windows, as if cautiously applying for membership. Tanner was beginning to suspect that Foyle had decided to forget the main point of the lunch; if so, he'd better raise the matter himself without further delay. He glanced laterally at the civil servants, businessmen, bankers, lawyers, publishers and academics who filled the long room with a faintly concerted murmur of reasoned discourse; middle-aged men who had abandoned laughter. A few obviously bought their shirts up the road in Jermyn Street but the majority now settled for Austin Reed's. Sir Frank's collars had always looked a bit desperate; a stud glinted where the tie had slipped; the Deputy Under Secretary glowered at the cheeseboard as if it were a Caribbean archipelago in the throes of insurrection, then abandoned all discretion and took a slice of mousetrap.

Tanner cleared his throat. 'Regarding Stern . . .'

Foyle went scarlet with irritation: 'Oh, for God's sake!' Then he leaned back in his chair and resignedly let his signet ring flop on the tablecloth.

'We want him out,' Tanner told Sir Frank.

Who looked up from his cheese: 'With all your heart?'

'Strictly speaking, he's not even in our employ,' Foyle said. 'We have absolutely no responsibility for him.'

The blood rushed to Tanner's face: 'He's our man.'

'Yours.' He turned to his guest with a faint sneer. 'Leonard is deadly loyal to ye olde union chapel. You know the usual NUJ line: accusations of complacency, negligence, even connivance, all directed against *me*, of course, and all totally predictable.'

'One hears that you sent a telex sacking the man,' Sir Frank mused. 'Was that before or after he set off on his pilgrimage to Buhera?'

'Before.'

'Then you're in the clear, surely.'

'We want Stern out of prison,' Tanner said. 'He was only doing his job.'

Sir Frank smiled thinly. 'As you may imagine, Mr Stern is not idolised in my neck of the woods.'

'He's a British subject.'

Sir Frank sighed. 'There are so many of them.'

'He's even white.'

'Leonard, I think that was unnecessary.'

'In theory they could hang him under the Law and Order Maintenance Act.'

'In theory, yes. I'd be surprised if they did.'

'He's imprisoned by a régime in rebellion against the Crown.'

'Leonard, a parking ticket issued in Salisbury is not invalid simply because the Union Jack no longer flies over Government House.'

'Journalists were told they were free to travel anywhere, without restriction, during the election campaign.'

Sir Frank nodded. 'If I were representing Mr Stern in court, I'd certainly toss that penny into the hat. It's only a penny, of course – fraternising with armed terrorists has always been forbidden, even before Smith's time.'

Foyle threw his crumpled napkin down, rose and led the way into the smoking room for coffee, Sir Frank following with long, countryman's strides, his trouser bottoms flapping.

'Can you get the bastard out of jug, Frank?' Foyle murmured. 'It might help us.'

'The Bishop is due in London next week. We'll certainly raise the matter.'

'What about the Meyer woman?'

The smears which passed for eyebrows on Sir Frank Fawcett-Ellis lifted a fraction:

'Don't tell me *she* works for you, too. A lovely girl, of course, quite the most enchanting lobbyist, I remember dining at her flat in Fulham . . . but not, alas, a British subject. Mm. Mm.' He glanced at his watch, then at Tanner. 'One question, Leonard: Why did Zanla choose to leave that girl behind? You were there, you saw it all – an admirable piece of reporting, by the way, leaving nothing to the imagination.'

'God knows.'

'Here we have a dedicated revolutionary who has survived the massacre at Chimoio then masterminded the underground operation inside Rhodesia for the past year – if our information is accurate, she's even married to a leading member of Zanu's central committee who was most probably at the scene of the battle – though we're not sure of that. So why did they leave her behind? The prize the Rhodies had searched in vain for, served up on a plate?'

'No doubt she and Stern were having it off,' Foyle said.

Fawcett-Ellis looked at him with genuine distaste. Of all the theories of history he had rejected since reading the subject at Balliol, the sexual one seemed to him the least convincing.

'I think I made it clear in my report what the woman said at the time,' Tanner said.

Fawcett-Ellis shrugged. 'Oh you did, yes. What she *said*.'

TWENTY-NINE

Stern waited on the doorstep, wondering whether to use his key. After almost a decade of marriage and three years in Africa, he still had the key to his mother's house. When the door finally opened her head appeared at a lower level than he expected; she had shrunk, or bent; only the heavy makeup and smudged lipstick was immediately familiar.

'I thought you were arriving yesterday.'

'No, Mother, today. It was in my telegram.'

'I'm quite sure it was yesterday, I read it several times. Well come in, then.' She looked at his single, buff canvas bag. 'But where is your luggage, Richard?'

He dropped the bag in the hallway, wandered into the polished drawing room, noticed that one of the Chinese vases had gone, and one of the Persian rugs, spotted the gin glass rimmed in lipstick behind a spray of paper flowers, and sank into a chintz chair.

'I have no luggage. They drove me straight from the prison to the airport.'

'But were you insured?'

He looked at her. The shoulders had rounded and the waist thickened, yet her shot-silk dress (roses, no longer orchids) was wrapped round her middle tighter than ever and she tottered on absurd heels. Eyebrows and mouth, the black and the red, had been applied like a clown's, on a thickly powdered foundation. A copy of *The Times* lay on the floor, messily unfolded, open at the crossword. The new double glazing about which she had (more than once, her letters were repetitive and amnesiac) written to him did indeed leave the house in total silence. The motorcycle hooligans had been routed.

Stern studied the array of bottles on the drinks trolley. He hadn't tasted the stuff in prison and had fought nobly not to drink during

321

the long South African Airways night flight from Salisbury up the west coast of Africa to Las Palmas and London. One drink and he would be finished.

Deborah sat down and slowly crossed her legs.

'You'll be wanting money.'

'No.'

'You always say no. But you take it.'

'When did I last take money from you?'

'How can I be expected to remember such details, I don't want to quarrel, Richard, I'm not at all well, you know, my doctor wants to put me on some new drug, I don't trust the man an inch, he's a charlatan. I see you cut your hair and removed that awful beard.'

'Yes, long ago. The beard only lasted six months.'

'You've taken years off my life.'

He hadn't expected anyone to meet him at Heathrow. Jane and Berny had turned up to see him off but Gilson and the accompanying BSAP inspector had permitted no conversation, no contact at all, leaving Holzheimer gesturing in affectionate despair and Jane staring at him bleakly, her eyes sanded by too much family history.

'I'm sorry about Monty,' Stern murmured.

'If you were sorry you might have written to say so. You haven't been in prison for two years, have you?' Her bejewelled fingers twisted and tears welled. 'That man.'

He saw that the 'genuine Stubbs' had left the wall along with Monty and his two fictitious racehorses. He waited. Gilson had invited him to sign a form declaring himself to be a 'prohibited immigrant', guilty of a capital offence under the Law and Order Maintenance Act. Stern had declined unless his confiscated papers and diaries were restored to him – not only the ones seized from his flat in Baines Avenue but also, and most important, the diary he had kept in Buhera. The loss of that had been the cruellest blow.

'Monty always was a snake. Right from the beginning, a crook.'

He waited.

'I had to sell my share of the business, did you know that?'

'To Monty?'

'For practically nothing.'

'But I thought—'

'You didn't "think" of anything except yourself. You realise I'll have to sell this house?'

He didn't believe her but decided, perversely, to pretend he did. 'I suppose it *is* rather large for one person . . .'

'It happens to be my home. It's where I've lived for thirty-seven

322

years. Are you planning to shunt me into a semi-detached in the suburbs? Somewhere on the District Line?'

In that agonised moment of forbidden contact he had scanned Jane's features for news of Esther, but the deaf-and-dumb signs they had exchanged had meant nothing to either of them.

'Now that Uncle Benjy's dead, perhaps you could share a house with Aunt Orna.'

She slowly shook her head. 'So much *you* understand. Orna always hated me. And now I have to worry about you.'

'I'm fine.'

'You don't look fine! You look ghastly. You look like a scarecrow! Orna told me they were torturing you in that prison, she said they always do – I know what she meant, she meant it could never happen to a son of hers. Never to Micah. My son in prison! But why should I care? You never took my advice about anything. I warned you about that woman but you wouldn't listen, I told you she was a lesbian—'

'Don't start on that!' For the first time since his release from prison he had raised his voice.

'And I would have liked some grandchildren.'

'Rachel obliged.'

'You always were a selfish person. A chip off the old block. And then you had to throw away your academic career—'

'– which you never approved of.' His voice rising again.

'At least it was *something*. And for what? To run around with a lot of half-naked gorillas. I suppose you imagine those Negroes are all wonderful Palestinian refugees. What have those people ever contributed to the art and culture of the world? What music have they created apart from tom-toms? Where is their Bach or Beethoven?' She was weeping freely now. 'After all the advantages you've had. All thrown away.'

Berny had blown him a kiss. Doubtless Berny had applied to visit him in Chikurubi but no visitors had been allowed – except once, when an 'unofficial' representative of the British Government interviewed him through a mesh and kept saying,— Are you quite sure you weren't abducted? I gather Miss Meyer claims you were. It would considerably improve your position.

'I daresay you'll find another woman,' Deborah said. 'How easily your generation rolls out of one bed into another.' She had found a paper handkerchief in her glossy black bag. 'I read in the paper that homosexuals in San Francisco . . . do . . . whatever they do . . . with at least three hundred men a year. One a day!'

His mother asked about the flat in Notting Hill. He shrugged agnostically. She knew that shrug: it meant she had touched the bone.

'Is *she* still living there?'

'Yes.'

'Then you must throw her out. She has no right to it. That flat was bought with *my* money.' A sudden suspicion dawned horribly in Deborah's powdered features. 'You didn't assign the freehold to her?'

He shook his head.

'Richard, you did!'

'I said no.' Voice going up again.

'You're lying to me.'

He had taken the green Customs channel at Heathrow (never had he had less to declare), averting his gaze from the wall of expectant relatives and friends behind the barrier, honing himself down in expectation of a loneliness more threatening than the solitary confinement and ritual beatings of the past two months. Or perhaps it was because of the beatings that he averted his gaze from that wet wall of humanity.

As he headed for the underground train Tanner emerged from the crowd.

—Richard, he said. Tanner had never used his first name before.

—Good journey? Any problems on the way out?

Stern told him about his deadlocked argument with Gilson but little else was said as Tanner drove out of the airport tunnel and headed for the motorway into London.

—Getting you out hasn't been easy, Tanner said at the Heston roundabout. —Foyle's attitude didn't help but the chapel have been magnificent. They're throwing a party for you on Friday.

—Didn't Foyle get his job in the Government?

Tanner might have laughed out of dislike of Foyle but he knew that Stern lumped them together as 'management', as 'them', as the conspiracy that had spiked him and finally sacked him.

—No, he didn't. He now writes leaders fulminating against Carrington's communistic conspiracy to dish the Bish. They say she may offer Selwyn a consolation peerage.

The traffic had slowed to its customary crawl as the three-lane motorway narrowed to two at the long, curving Chiswick flyover. Stern saw the beginnings of London, *his* city, the city where his wife and mother lived, the roofs of Brentford spreading beneath the flyover and the procession of silver airlines creeping low across the sky's undercarriage towards Heathrow.

—I expect you have a story to write? Tanner ventured.

324

—Buhera, you mean? I assume you've already published your own version.

Everything he loathed about Stern came back to Tanner in those three words 'your own version': the condescending sneer, the innate distrust, the assumption that he, Stern, was the only honest man in the world. Straining against his (now compulsory) seat belt, Tanner reached into the back, plucked a photocopy from his briefcase, and tossed it into Stern's lap.

—Yes I did. Take it. What I had in mind (Tanner slowing his words in an effort at self-control) —was your prison experiences. What did they do to you? Anything nasty?

Stern didn't reply.

—Well, it's your story, Tanner said. —We'd be glad to use a couple of thousand words.

Stern laughed like a man out of practice. —Foyle would never publish it.

—I wouldn't show it to Foyle.

At the Hogarth roundabout the traffic thickened ominously down the Cromwell Road extension.

—It might be quicker to go down King Street to the Broadway, Stern said.

—You remember London, then.

Ignoring the advice, Tanner manoeuvred into the fast lane towards the Hammersmith flyover. Immediately he was trapped in the jam, fuming. As they crawled past St Peter's Church Stern again came up with further advice:

—You can turn left at Latymer School into King Street.

—I do know the area. I used to live here.

He noticed that Stern hadn't even glanced at the photocopy of his three-part report, 'With Hersh in Buhera'.

Stern said: —I'm sorry.

—Never heard you use that word before. What about?

—I'd forgotten. About your daughter.

Tanner saw that Stern's face and neck were running in sweat; simultaneously he noticed the constant vibration in his hands.

—Didn't know you knew.

—You've read William Morris's utopia, *News from Nowhere?*

Tanner nodded. —Morris predicted that by our day King Street would have disappeared, leaving a highway running through wide sunny meadows and garden-like tillage. A fourteenth-century future. No zebra crossings – fuck him. In later years I used to sit by the river in Duke's Meadows and read that book. Damned stupid but . . . I liked to imagine I was reading it to Helen . . .

—Oh I can believe it! The books I've read to my son – in his absence!

—You never told me you had kids.

—Jimmy's four now. Don't suppose he'll recognise me.

Tanner's tone was more congenial than Stern had known it.

—There was a fair rumpus in the chapel after I got back. One or two hotheads who had never set foot in Africa explained to me how I could have got you out of prison if I'd tried – no use telling them that it was all I could do in Buhera to save you from a bullet in the neck.

Earl's Court, South Ken, the chauffeured cars outside Harrods.

—Where am I taking you? Tanner asked.

Stern looked at him. —To the office.

—What office?

—My office and yours. I've worked for you for almost three years. Now you're going to put me on the staff payroll.

—Get some sleep.

Anger spurted, like blood from a severed vein.

—Killed fifteen years ago, was she, your daughter? And you had recently returned from war-torn Beirut, thoroughly shell-shocked? That would put us in 1964. Yes? But the only thing that happened in Beirut that year was the defection of Kim Philby to the Russians. No civil war, no bombardments – just lots of fun.

The car swerved and there was urgent hooting from behind them. Tanner's leather face folded further into itself. At Hyde Park Corner he drew into the side and produced an envelope from his jacket.

—Chapel benevolent fund. I've added a bit of my own. It's not much but it may help. The chapel are holding a party for you on Friday, seven p.m. No need to bring a bottle, it's all in your honour.

Stern removed his canvas bag from the boot. Drawing back into the traffic, Tanner lifted a hand in salute but there was no response from the tall, gaunt figure on the pavement.

Stern wandered to the window, negotiating the blank stare of polished furniture and fighting his craving for a drink – for ten drinks. A depleted room. The beautiful weather outside taunted the funeral parlour within; Stern stared at a fat ginger cat basking on a wall.

'Is that damned motorcyclist there?' Deborah asked. 'The one with "Chelsea Rules" all over him.'

'I thought your double glazing had solved that.'

'It doesn't stop him being there. I know he's making a filthy noise even if I can't hear it. I told him, I said, "Young man, you may as well put a silencer on your machine because I can't hear you anymore." '

'What did he say?'

'Say? Those animals scarcely enjoy the gift of language.'

Stern thrust his hand into his trouser pockets as he might have done twenty years ago when public school boys and undergraduates still walked about in that fashion.

'Mother, perhaps you and I should make a suicide pact.'

'You must eat,' Deborah said. He wasn't hungry but he followed her dutifully to the kitchen, appalled by the slowness and pain of her movements, tempted to believe it was a performance for his benefit. But what couldn't be affected was the walled-in look of old age, the blank shuffle along a geriatrics' corridor.

'I'm afraid this will be yesterday's dinner warmed up. I thought you were arriving yesterday.' Bending to open the oven door was clearly an agony for his mother. Stern took the oven glove and lifted out a pie majestically crowned in pastry.

'You didn't hear about your cousin Micah?' Deborah said. 'He's now an established soloist, concerts in Paris, Frankfurt, Tel Aviv, believe me Orna never stops ramming it down my throat. Well, now she's free of poor Benjy, she made his last years a misery, did you know that? Let him try to make his own way to the bathroom and she scolded him. Your uncle Benjy was the best friend I ever had.'

Stern didn't remember hearing this during the life and times of Uncle Benjy.

'She killed him,' Deborah said.

Stern and his mother ate in silence, all energies spent. Outside the window the long July evening showed no sign of relenting; momentarily a tennis ball floated above the line of trees while 'Chelsea Rules' revved his motorbike, unheard.

He also had a key to the flat in Notting Hill but inhibition (again) overcame him and he rang the bell. After a long, suspecting pause a solid young woman, but no longer so young, stood blinking at him from behind owl glasses, her short thatch of mousy hair lank on her head, her arms folded across her chest in a posture of *No pasaran!*

'Hullo, Hattie.'

It became clear that she genuinely didn't recognise him. He smiled gently. 'Out of sight, out of mind?'

'Bloody hell!' she said. 'Shit. Oh, fuck.'

'My wife at home?' Stern pushed past her into the hallway,

once elegantly furnished *après* Habitat, now cluttered with posters, anoraks, boots, rucksacks and piles of unopened second-class mail. Hardly a recognisable item of furniture remained – the flat had been exorcised. So radical was the purge that Stern experienced the sharp, jolting sense of a personal insult inflicted by the debris of burglars. But the scale of the wound surfaced slowly; the prospect of their first encounter in almost three years had clamped his facial muscles into a deep freeze.

Beth was writing at a pine table in the kitchen. She looked up and smiled as if she had expected him.

'Richard! Thank God they let you out! How are you, poor man?'

She rose and filled the electric kettle, her body lithe and slender and small; her body unchanged. The rigid pencil line of his mouth parted with desire – the lust he felt was the kind excited by the person, the body, of whom one already has carnal knowledge. He had somehow expected her dowdier, more puritan, more 'closed shop soiled' (in Holzheimer's phrase) than she actually appeared. Her complexion was as fresh as ever, her blue eyes as crystalline, her small, determined bud of a mouth as worthy of kisses.

Hattie was sourly monitoring his gaze, her direst predictions on the verge of fulfilment.

'Did the Rhodesians give you the works?' Beth asked swivelling with the filled kettle in hand. 'I even went along to the Foreign Office once, disguised and dressed as Mrs Richard Stern. I was finally shown into the office of a mandarin stickman called Somebody-Ellis who told me that you weren't helping HMG, or Somebody-Ellis, or yourself, by stubbornly denying that you had been abducted by . . . what do they call themselves?'

'Zanla.'

'Right. Sugar in your coffee but not in your tea?'

'Yes.'

'See what a good wife I was, Hattie. Where are you staying, Richard? Look, do sit down, you must be knackered.'

'At my mother's.'

'How is she?'

'Older.'

Beth sat down, lit a cigarette with several nervous flicks of a junk lighter, tossed her flaxen hair, and finally forced herself to look him in the eye through the smoke.

'Did the Rhodesians bash you up? I think I've now asked you that question already – don't answer by all means, so long as I'm not later accused of callous indifference.'

'It could have been worse.'

Hattie whistled. 'Good God, Africa has turned him into Biggles.'

She remained planted on her feet, arms folded, a sentry of the senses.

Stern bit his lip; Tanner had once flung the same hero at him.

'Shut up, Hattie,' Beth murmured gently, as if her friend's offence was one of form rather than content. 'And what news of Esther? One gathers you were taken prisoner together.'

He noted the sudden clarification of her populist vowels, the drawl in the 'one'. Her composure was flawed. Momentarily he felt like a man offered a brandy after walking across ice.

'She's brave,' he said.

'Oh, she always was. And how are things between you? – none of my business, just making conversation.'

Was that why she had never, quite, divorced him – to prevent him marrying Esther? The thought no sooner presented itself than he heard the grim click of the coupled chain:

'I've applied for a divorce, by the way.'

He looked around the kitchen; it reminded him of a refugee camp. Linoleum was torn, wallpaper was grease-stained and peeling, anti-bomb posters leap-frogged to the ceiling. The pine table was piled with pamphlets, drafts, carbons, proofs. Idly he picked up a sheet of typed copy paper:

'For many women "thin" is too vulnerable a bodytype to own. Being thin means handling male aggression. It means competition with other women. It means asserting themselves verbally, rather than with their largeness. Many of us are not willing to approach life without fat,'

and felt Hattie's furious stare.

'Couldn't you leave other people's property alone?'

'That's what schoolgirls say.' He let the sheet drop. 'Who lives here?'

'Ah!' said Hattie, owl eyes widening in anticipation of the night. She had opened a tobacco tin and was rolling herself a fag; Stern noticed that Beth plucked her cigarettes from a glossy gold packet on which the words 'Special Filter' were stylishly inscribed.

Beth lifted her small, neat, booted feet up on to the pine table. 'Me, Hattie, some comrades, to each according to her need.' Her vowels had thickened.

He nodded, masking his anger. 'So how are things?'

'Busy. I'm hoping to be nominated for the East Cheam seat.'

'Some hope! ' cried Hattie. 'There are eighteen males and two females on the selection committee.'

He smiled at this good news. 'You never can tell.'

Hattie snorted. 'In the last elections ten per cent of the candidates were women. Ten per cent!'

'As of now,' Beth said, 'our bread comes mainly from the GWU. I was appointed their Equality officer in November and ran straight into a recently negotiated agreement at Tidworth which in effect made women workers more vulnerable to redundancy than the men. We took it to the Equal Opportunities Commission, who declared the agreement illegal. The male shop stewards then threatened to bring their men out on strike. It's an uphill struggle because the male workers persist in regarding the women as usurpers. The average male wage remains one-and-a-half times that of the average female wage. I've been trying to talk the women out of their passivity, their fatalistic acceptance of second-class status, their fear of speaking out, of being branded as unwomanly.'

'Don't forget the constant sexual harassment.' Hattie said.

'Well that's another thing though really it's all part of one pattern of cultural and social subordination. How does one persuade class-conscious male shop stewards that posters of nudes all over the shop floor might seem offensive and threatening to women?'

'Don't forget the bomb,' Hattie said to Beth.

Beth nodded. 'I suppose you've heard, Richard, that following the recent NATO decision the first generation of cruise missiles will reach this country in 1981?'

'Cruise?'

'Jesus,' sighed Hattie.

'Yes, Richard: an American-controlled, first-strike nuclear guided missile. Land-based and mobile. Coming here.'

He shrugged in mock apology: 'I'm afraid "here" still means Zimbabwe to me.'

'Nuclear extinction will be universal,' Hattie said.

'It must keep you busy,' Stern said.

Hattie blinked at him: 'Don't be so bloody patronising.'

In retaliation he picked up another of the carbon copies lying on the pine table. At a glance he could tell that this, too, was Hattie's work – the content had changed since the time when she had been his pupil at the LSE, but not the aggrieved polemical tone.

'Gayle Hoffnung's article "Lesbian-Feminism and the Sexual Revolution" is so full of malice, cowardice and false assumptions that I'm not sure where to begin. She insists that lesbians sever themselves from sado-masochists and the male gay movement in order to prove that "lesbians do not, in fact, molest children". Is she insinuating that there is no such thing as inter-generational relationships between women? Does she mean one needs a cock

330

to molest? Finally I must protest against the tired old argument that we should put off the struggle "to fuck whomever we please" until we have won "the right not to be fucked".

Stern shook his head. 'You always were a theologian at heart, Hattie.'

'Don't you bloody patronise me!'

He wondered why Beth didn't send her out of the room – she reminded him of the indulgent mother of a constantly interrupting, innately disruptive, small child. Politely he asked about the current membership of the GWU.

'We have 756,000 members, a third of them women. Yet there isn't a single woman among the thirty-four members of the national executive. Of 203 full-time officials, only ten are women. Am I boring you?'

'On the contrary.'

'You look a bit bored. If you wanted to talk about yourself I'd be much happier.'

'No, I've got a block about the whole thing, can't write a word.'

Her appraisal was slow and searching.

'Working people in this country never particularly interested you. Do you, I wonder, really care about the peasants of Africa, or do you just pretend – to please Esther?'

'You've been saving that up.'

His heart sank at the resumption of hostilities. The four eyes of sisterhood stared at him. Desperately he desired Beth's esteem; he ached for her.

'Colonialism is right under your nose,' Hattie said. 'You don't go to Africa to find it, you go to Africa to escape.'

'Are you two still passionate lovers?' Stern asked.

Beth took a strand of blonde hair and wound it round her finger. 'Is that your business?'

Hattie had gone scarlet. 'I warned you he'd want you back. Not for yourself' – her voice was rising as Stern's had done with his mother – 'just for the ego-trip, the re-conquest, to make you his private possession.'

'These are just the clichés of the hour,' Stern said. 'How can you possibly know what I want or feel?'

Beth sprang up from the pine table and slotted a cassette into the player: Françoise Hardy, her romantic side, mocking his desire, her hips swaying almost vampishly in jeans which refused not to fit her perfectly.

'So what is it you want, Richard?'

'I wouldn't mind a bed in my own flat.'

'For starters,' Hattie said.

331

'Well, he is a prison graduate and a refugee,' Beth said, standing over him, running a hand through his hair.

Hattie was on the verge of tears. 'No, no, no!'

Beth clearly enjoyed the competition for her love. Stretching seductively, she yawned.

'The problem is, Richard, we have four or five sisters constantly moving in and out of the flat at all hours, none of them great admirers of the male sex, and I can't really believe you'd be happy.'

Despite the note of conciliation in her voice and his desperate desire to recover his wife – a project entertained on the way to Notting Hill and passionately embraced since his arrival – Stern felt incensed by her indifference to his moral and legal rights in the matter. The flat was his. His! He owned the freehold. Furthermore – it was the only thing he did own. To reclaim this modest possession was neither bourgeois avarice nor landlordism nor anything to be ashamed of: socialists are allowed to own four-roomed flats.

He was about (perhaps) to ventilate these thoughts when the front door closed loudly and a tall black girl strode in wearing an Afro hair-do, threw Stern a glance, dumped down a plastic carrier bag of food and toilet rolls (for some reason Stern had the feeling that she had been out shop-lifting rather than shopping), lit a cigarette out of Beth's packet, then sat down with her boots on the pine table.

'Who's this?' she asked, gesturing at Stern.

'This is Richard Stern.'

'Gawd.' Then she relented, grinned, and offered him her hand. 'I'm Jo.'

'He wants a bed here,' Beth said.

Jo shrugged. 'Why not? We might open his eyes to the possibilities of his own nature.'

'No!' cried Hattie. 'You don't know him!'

Françoise Hardy continued serenely in the background.

'Jo, you always under-estimate the hormone factor,' Beth said.

'I don't!' Jo protested cheerfully. 'He looks all right to me. Maybe what he needs is a quick toss in the hay. Must have been lonely in that African jail.' She winked at Stern.

'Jo,' Beth said sternly.

Hattie exploded: 'He only has to step through the door and there's bloody conflict at once!'

Jo's mocking smile broadened as it settled on Stern again.

'What you want is cunt, dear. Preferably Beth's. He'll happily sleep in the street if he can get that. D'ya fancy me, darling?'

Hattie ripped the wire-framed glasses from her doorknob nose and flung them at Jo:

'You're a junkie! a junkie who kicked the habit, a junkie who sees the needle and swears she only wants to look at it, touch it, but no jabs of course, oh no!'

Stern noticed that neither the wire frames nor the plastic lenses suffered in any way; he assumed this gesture was well practised. Beth grabbed a pink cotton jacket; he watched the stretch of her T-shirt across her small, firm breasts as she slotted her arms into the sleeves.

'C'mon, Richard, there's a new café round the corner, they do quite a decent taramasalata.'

THIRTY

On the Friday he took her to an Italian restaurant they both remembered from their life together in Notting Hill Gate, a crowded place with red tablecloths and candles with fake drippings. With a spurt of pleasure he saw that she had dressed for the occasion, her unbound flaxen hair tossing over bare shoulders. Gazing across the table at her like any young lover, he reached for her hand, twining his fingers through hers. The engagement and wedding rings had gone – into trade union funds, no doubt.

'You're looking lovely,' he said.

'You need a pair of legs in your life?'

He leaned forward: 'Beth, I want *you*, not your legs. I want us to start again.'

The extent of his capitulation, abasement almost, startled him; as soon as Beth explained that Friday was the only evening she could manage during the coming week – 'No, days are impossible' – he had decided to skip the party given in his honour by the NUJ chapel. And now he found himself confessing as much to her, as evidence of his love, before the waiter had even brought the avocadoes vinaigrette.

'You didn't!' Beth looked horrified.

He shrugged. 'I loathe warm beer and Spanish "Burgundy" from paper cups.'

'But it was in your honour! The union chapel! They agitated for your release, I know they did, I went to see the FoC, he was very, very helpful.'

'They did nothing when Foyle and Tanner sacked me.'

'Well, of course I don't know anything about all that, never having met these two gentlemen.'

'Tanner's daughter was killed in a road accident. Do you

334

remember the old man who was knocked down on our wedding day?'

Beth took a lock of hair between her fingers.

'You should have gone to that party.' She glanced at her watch. 'You could still make it, you'd only be an hour late.'

He shook his head.

'Well, what excuse did you make?'

'None.'

'You mean you didn't even tell them you weren't coming!'

'Correct.'

'Richard, if I may say so, that sums up just about everything that's wrong with your attitude to the world. I mean, you have absolutely no respect or affection for people, do you?'

In her agitation she lit a cigarette from the gold packet marked 'Special Filter'. He remembered Sartre's hand under his elbow, the oyster eye askew when the little man said, *'les classes ne sont pas, on les fait.'* Stern had lost contact with his friends in Paris, as with his friends everywhere, but the French literary periodicals he had picked up in central London since his return told him that the old philosopher was dying. Appraising the subtle swell of Elizabeth's breasts beneath her blue, off-the-shoulder Laura Ashley (he guessed) dress, the beguiling curve of her bodice, the satin glow of her skin, he told himself that if he had to choose between:

– this woman taking him back, abandoning her *pétroleuses* comrades and her cheapjack militancy, and fully devoting herself to the role of Mrs Richard Stern,

and

– Jean-Paul Sartre recovering sufficiently to complete his great work on Flaubert,

if he could have one but not both, then . . .

'Did you ever read the stuff I wrote in Rhodesia?' he asked.

'Of course I did. I've always read what you've written.'

'Really?' Again his fingers attempted to twine themselves through hers, but she withdrew her hand tactfully.

'If you're asking me what I think of you as a foreign correspondent, Richard, it's what I think of you with regard to everything else.'

Stern caught the waiter's attention. 'I did order some potatoes.'

'Potatoes, sir?'

'Yes, potatoes. Ten minutes ago.' He turned back to Elizabeth. 'So beautiful you are – you might have been air-brushed on to the page of a colour supplement.'

She fought with a smile. 'And Esther? Is she still beautiful?'

'Does it matter?'

'No. Just making conversation. I heard a rumour that she was married.'

He noticed that he was refilling his own wine glass more frequently than hers.

'You might have written to me.'

'In Rhodesia? I didn't know what to say.'

'Are you sure it's the Cheam seat you're after – not Hammersmith?'

'Hammersmith? I don't know the area at all.'

'The difference between a carnivorous plant and a carnivorous animal is what?' he asked.

Her delicate shoulders moved agnostically. 'Your taste for riddles has survived.'

'In the case of the plant, it is the victim which moves; in the case of the animal, the predator.'

'I see – I am the carnivorous plant?'

He nodded, again topping up his own glass and pouring a token in hers. 'Shall I tell you what they did to me in prison?'

The waiter brought his potatoes. Beth shook her head: a slice of veal and aubergines was quite sufficient.

'So what did they do to you, Richard?'

She could have used the brief interruption to change the subject, but she didn't. Beth (he told himself) didn't run away.

'They soon spotted that I harbour a particular fear of asphyxiation.'

'Do you?'

'Oh yes. As does my father – that's why he loves birds and the sky. So it was the hood usually, or a plastic bag, and then into a bucket of water. I used to count, imagine I was setting a world record for endurance, but I wasn't setting the record, they were.'

He smiled faintly.

'How ghastly. What did they want to know?'

'Why God appointed them to the universe of the secret policeman; why they spend much of every day possessed by rage; why the universal communist conspiracy they fight lies always out of reach; why their victims despise them.'

Beth was watching him steadily.

He said: 'At first you feel the electrodes quite clearly like the jab of hot needles, one at the neck, one at the base of the spine. For a moment one experiences a ridiculous sense of triumph: "This is bearable! I can live with this!" The next moment they raise the voltage and your body goes into spasms – it's like a pair of bovver boots inside your back kicking in a dozen different directions. In short, you part company with yourself and come apart at the seams. There is no end in sight: it can go on for ever, at their pleasure, and if it ends it can start again, any time, day or night.'

Beth's hand reached out for his.

He felt the tears welling.

They were not an actor's tears, since the actor weeps for the part; no, they were the tears of a man who weeps for the actor's devotion to the part. Stern had not been tortured in Chikurubi Maximum Security Prison, merely beaten, twice on the soles of his feet, and once at random by an indignant Robertson. It was not pain or grief that made him cry now, but shame and loss of control, and then the act of crying itself made him cry. He had even contemplated covering himself with cigarette burns before he paid his visit to the flat in Notting Hill Gate.

'You're still in love with Esther?'

'When the Rhodesian commandos arrived, she stayed behind with me.'

'To hold your hand?'

'She insisted that I'd been abducted by Zanla. She sacrificed her own liberty, and perhaps her life, on my behalf.'

'Just as you once told the Bow Street magistrate that a policeman had stamped on Esther's hand?'

'How did you know that?'

'She told me.' Beth offered him a satanic smile. 'But of course that lie cost you nothing whereas she, well, she must soon figure on the cover of *Time* magazine.'

Delighted by Beth's jealousy, he said: 'Is that how one Sister should speak of another?'

Her face frosted. 'What is it you want of me, Richard?'

'If I had a room in my own flat, we might re-discover our relationship.'

She tossed her flaxen hair in refusal. 'We can't afford to risk a man in the commune. Generations of women have been taught to behave differently when men are around: taught to whisper, taught to conceal their natures, taught to compete for attention.'

He touched her hand. 'No libidinal problems?'

'What?' She seemed genuinely bemused.

'You do whatever you do . . . with Hattie? or Jo? . . .'

'Oh – I see what you're driving at. My mother also plucked up courage to ask. She simply can't understand why I didn't settle for her version of happiness – even though my father has been a fucking philanderer all his life.'

'You haven't answered my question.'

'It's not your business, Richard.'

Anger surfaced again. 'It happens to be my flat that I want to occupy.'

'Richard, whenever you light a bonfire the smoke blows straight in your own face.'

337

'Ah.'
'It's time you picked yourself off the floor.'

From a diary begun by Richard Stern soon after his return to London:

Apathy. I get up late and read the newspaper from cover to cover, killing time, trying to avoid mother. The news stories lie side by side like road casualties in a hospital emergency unit: together but apart.

I watch a lot of television. Sometimes mother and I sit side by side for a couple of hours, drugged by the screen, not exchanging a word, incapable even of changing the channel, receiving whatever is dished up to us. Then I see that her eyes are closed and that she has been asleep. I suppose the TV writers are the new élite; I don't know any of them.

My head jangles with silly jokes: 'Hire Richard Stern, he's a guilt-edged investment.'

A letter arrives, postmarked New York. It's from Berny:

'Dear Richard,

'I continue to miss you. Seeing you at the airport but not being able to exchange a word was only slightly less awful than being refused access to you in Chikurubi. I have taken two weeks' leave in NY and wherever else my wives have moved their thatched huts, so imagine me coming down in the big elevator from the third floor of 229 West 43rd Street, my wallet groaning with money, my head packed with vileness, lechery, hypocrisy, then stepping out of the pale brown brick building and heading for Times Square with my usual cocky stride, passing under the four flags and the digital clock, All the News that's Fit to Print, throwing a glance at the Orthodox Jewish women protesting against the conscription of girls into the Israeli army. You know those long newsprint trucks which stick out of the ground-floor loading bays? Don't they remind you of the tits of a huge sow? They don't? Anyway, imagine Bernard Holzheimer heading away from the dirty movies of Broadway towards the Society of Ethical Culture, 2 West 64th Street, maybe by taxi maybe by the BMT, an A train or an AA to Columbus Circle. Your correspondent is attending a meeting called to protest the impending deportation of foreign-born radicals, there is much ritual clapping, the Rosenbergs come up as usual, which puts Holzheimer in mind of Paul and Jane Meyer and their daughter

Esther and his good friend Richard Stern who almost died in Buhera out of love for her.

'Ought I to tell you that Esther is pregnant?

'Jane told me. She said I was on no account to "leak" this information to you. Why? I understand nothing. Please write and explain.

'I have tried but failed to persuade my masters to appoint you in my stead as Southern Africa Correspondent. I hate the whole region. They want me to stay. They continue to admire your work and promise to "consider" anything you may send them. I worry that you are now completely without work or income.

'Richard, if you have written anything about your experiences in Buhera or your time in Chikurubi, *please*, I implore you, send me a copy.

'Your friend, Berny.'

'PS. All my wives are fine and send you their love.

'PPS. It occurred to me the other day that, whereas the reporter uses reality as a cripple employs a crutch, the novelist's relationship to reality is that of a blind man to his white stick. I'd be grateful if you wouldn't attempt to claim this insight as your own.'

Holz is rich.

Earning none, I am almost morbidly reluctant to spend money. My mother tells me I need a new outfit: 'How do you hope to get a job if you present yourself looking like a beggar?' Mother has been much impressed by some American television serial about a rich family who disguise their slide towards bankruptcy by maintaining their normal lifestyle of yachts, mansions, penthouse suites and lavish parties.

—Believe in yourself, Richard, because if you don't no one else will.

Where have I heard that before?

Each morning I get out of bed determined to begin legal proceedings for the recovery of my flat.

While in Africa I kept a snapshot of Esther in my wallet, wrapped in a cellophane sachet. It survived everything including the trip to Buhera, Hersh's gunships, and Chikurubi Maximum Security Prison. Yesterday, after receiving Holz's letter, I laid it on my desk, removed the sachet to kiss her face, and promptly spilt coffee on it. The stain is irremovable.

There has been no word from Tanner or anyone else since I failed to turn up at the NUJ chapel party.

Inspired by Hattie, I have been writing a few crazy letters of my own. Sometimes I panic that I've put them in the wrong envelopes.

Imagine Beth receiving a demand to re-employ me, Tanner getting an invitation to bed.

The *New Statesman* published one of my letters, badly mutilated. I gather J. R. Tree has been given the boot by the new editor, a wild antipodean who regularly publishes polemics by Beth Halliday. I offered to review a book about Rhodesia but the literary editor told me that was *his* preserve. He sounded rather pompous on the phone; I gather he's at war with a bunch of dazzling *literati* of my own generation who have declared politics to be the mortal enemy of literature. They will win, of course.

What I need is a 'friend' with a country cottage. (A friend without one would be no friend.) I long to escape from this oppressive London summer and my mother's ghastly house. Occasionally I thumb through old address books but there is no one to call. Sometimes I close my eyes in front of the television set and dream of soft clouds meandering across a green valley, the miniature hills and houses printed on the landscape in self-absorbed perfection, each jealous of its own tiny freehold on the weather, its own big tree, its own cube of water-washed light, its own clutch of neurotic wood pigeons which burst from the highest branches, thumping and flapping, as you step out of the kitchen door on to the lawn. I remember how fond I became of the countryside when Elizabeth and I used to go down to Oxfordshire during the early years – both of us bending in concern over a baby rabbit lying dead among the lettuces, not a mark upon it, as if dead of fright. We used to walk slowly, hands entwined, through Constable country, listening to the evening thud of grunting cattle across the valley. Occasionally a desperate pheasant, flushed from his (??? – what do pheasants call their houses?) by our innocent, meandering approach, would scurry out of the long grass, gaining speed like a frantic plane running out of runway, then take to the air in dread of the rifle's deadly report.

Alone in my 'friend's' unobtainable cottage, I have been re-reading *Steppenwolf*. Beth was quite right about Hesse and I would like to tell her so. How can I have ever been taken in by the preposterous notion that this pretentious old bum is really a singular rebel against bourgeois society (even though he clings to the bourgeois comforts and his private income), simply because his 'soul' is in permanent communion with art, music and philosophy . . . while his muddy shoes continue to chase cunt?

I hear distant thunder in the sky but it isn't thunder, it occurs at those times of a day's night when I reach out to Beth.

Detecting footsteps on the gravel path, I find two women standing at the kitchen door. Beth is wearing a bare-sleeved summer frock in primrose yellow with a loose bodice flowing around her exquisite bosom. Planted beside her, blinking suspiciously, Hattie looks like a Hobbit.

'We happened to be passing,' Beth says rather formally. 'We've come from the base.' I don't know what she means but I invite them in and make lemon tea. Hattie glowers mistrustfully at my pictures but Beth is perfectly at ease making small-talk about the local countryside and its footpaths.

'Toast?' I suggest.

'That would be lovely. Have you been to the base?'

'The base?'

Beth looks at me. I long to carry her upstairs. The bedroom has a low ceiling under the thatched roof.

'Don't you hear?' she says gently, as if to a child.

Again I pick up that distant, unaccountable thunder in the sky.

'Galaxies,' she says. 'They're preparing the silos for the cruise missiles. You're almost under their flight path.'

'But what do you do at the base?' I ask.

'We take ladders. We lay carpets and blankets over the barbed wire.'

'Non-violent direct action,' Hattie says almost addressing me. 'We're preparing. Some of us even play the part of the police, you know, harassment, trespass, breach of the peace, what to do when arrested, legal rights . . .'

'Preparing?'

'We're preparing our minds and our bodies for the struggle. We listen to our feelings. But it's not easy. We're not after transcendental passivity or any of that crap: we want to stop the deployment of cruise missiles. That means, as women, we have to suppress a number of deeply conditioned reflexes.'

'Such as?'

'Such as avoiding physical violence.'

'Hattie just said you were non-violent.'

'We are. *They* aren't. We chain ourselves together. They cut the chains. We climb their fences. They haul us down. We lie in the mud in front of their bulldozers and trucks; they lift and cart us away.'

'Beth had a vision,' Hattie says.

Beth laughs. 'I wouldn't call it quite that, but I did have a dream, one night, of us women marching more than a hundred miles, two years from now, for Life on Earth.'

'With mirrors,' Hattie says to Beth. 'You said we were all carrying mirrors to hold up to the soldiers and police so they could see themselves.'

' "*Mirare*" ,' I say, 'meaning "to wonder". Hence mirror, mirage, miracle.'

'Stop showing off, Richard,' Beth says gently.

'As soon urge a swallow not to fly,' I say.

She looks at me, then lights a cigarette.

'The thing is, Richard – shall I tell him, Hattie? – the thing is, Richard, Hattie and I have decided to have a baby.'

'Sugar or honey in your lemon tea? I always take honey.'

'Neither of us is getting any younger. We'd like to have a child.'

'Butter with your toast? Do smoke if you want to.'

'We hoped you wouldn't mind impregnating us.'

' "Us" you say? Both of you?'

'Me,' Beth said.

'Ah. You will be the mother.'

'We'll both be the mother.'

'Do you remember that Polish documentary they showed on television just about the time you were getting rid of our last foetus? It was like a western but located entirely in the human reproductive organs – High Midnight instead of High Noon. By a miracle of miniaturisation – yes, don't the clouds cast enchanting patterns of shadow across the valley – the film-makers inserted a camera inside the penis to observe the helpless tidal wave of love-crazed semen hurtling suicidally into the great, pitiless female vault of No Return. Bomber pilots return and survive. Salmon return and die. Spermatozoa never return. Tails wagging with passion, they brave the furious acid attacks launched by the womb until the last survivors stagger exhausted up the canyon of the fallopian tube towards the mute, motionless object that has inspired the whole crazy odyssey: the ovum, leaning passively against the wall of the uterus like any slut, any streetwalker.

'More tea? More toast? No?

'And now the twenty super-sperm who remain alive begin to batter and bite at the soft wall of the ovum herself, crazy with love, lust and animality, all the forces that drive gentlemen of intelligence and sensibility to chase after skirt. Alas, the sperm proposes, the ovum disposes. As soon as one favoured fellow is admitted, the walls close up and the remaining suitors, stranded far from home, exhausted and demoralised – perish.

'Now I call *that* sexual harassment. Yes? Do smoke, Beth, if you wish . . . You don't happen to have a fag . . . ?'

Both women are silent. They must either abandon their sacred quest or suffer my taunts in silence. According to Hemingway, Gertrude Stein insisted that the sexual act between women was much less 'ugly and repugnant' than its male counterpart. 'They do nothing,' she said, 'they are disgusted by and nothing that is repulsive and afterwards they are happy . . . ' Pondering this (rather sceptically), I remain unconvinced that my wife could even contemplate so ghastly a perversion, let alone practise it.

I have an old green notebook which sometimes does duty as a breadboard. Clearly the heavy themes of literature are dying like the great staple industries, coal, steel, shipbuilding, heavy engineering. Dickens and Zola launched their novels like passenger liners gliding down the slipway at Southampton or Bremen. But now the future lies with electronics, microchips, computers and the novelist, too, is engaged in a sophisticated light industry, thinking about thinking, words about words, polished miniaturisation, Rubik's cube.

Knowledge is a mistress whose beauty is a joy in union but an agony in times of infidelity.

I miss Berny.

Beth had agreed to meet him in the park, by the statue of Peter Pan. It was a warm day but wet; the rain came in short, aggressive showers. He arrived early, she late. He had begun to fear she wouldn't show up.

'So what do we talk about?' she asked.

'What it's like to be a Parlimentary candidate.'

'OK.' They fell into step, three of hers to every two of his (the metronomic perception was Stern's), both sheltering under his umbrella (but she didn't take his arm).

'You get to know people by their appearance,' she said, her accent riding easily between what Holzheimer had dubbed, 'Halliday camp' and the broader, lazier, demo-English of a general management committee. 'There is a well-groomed look, male or female, which is predictably Thatcherite if it consents to speak to you. Anyone carrying an executive briefcase and a well-pressed suit – forget it.'

'Invariably? No surprises?'

'And if a woman has taken real care with her appearance then she too will tighten her mouth, avert her gaze and march past. For her Labour is common, you see. Labour is shabby. Labour is about not getting out and about, not marrying a young man with prospects.'

'Depressing.'

'Yes, it is depressing. It's the same with houses you know. I can smell a Tory household even before I ring the bell. They paint their fences, they varnish their doors, they tend their gardens, they make sure their bells tinkle nicely. They have letter boxes which bite your fingers off, snap, and sometimes they site them almost at ground level.'

'In short they own their own homes.'

A faint shadow of irritation crossed her face though he didn't see it; she remembered his old habit, reaching back to the seminars and tutorials at the LSE, of summarising what she'd just said, as if one word could have done the work of ten.

They reached the Round Pond.

'When I last came here you were pregnant.'

'Oh?'

'Do you ever think about that?'

'It would be odd if I didn't.'

'I just wondered.'

After a pause she said: 'Sometimes I lie awake at night thinking of that child.'

'Jimmy?'

'I never thought of a name,' she said quickly.

His long arm tightly enfolded her shoulders. He checked his stride and held her.

'Don't you ever hear Jimmy cry out for a reprieve? I remember the foetus calling to me, "Daddy, Daddy, save my life."'

They walked round the pond in silence. He saw the little blue boat bobbing among the ducks, and the haggard Giles Carpenter slowly drifting round the geese-fouled rim in the wake of his kids' expensive bicycles, and he saw Esther, once more a prisoner, once more at the mercy of Snyder, Kepler and Robertson.

Beth said: 'You want to throw us out of the flat, don't you?'

'I merely want a room in my own flat.'

She shook her head. 'I wouldn't mind but the others are adamant.'

'Do the "others" have status in this matter? Do they pay me rent for the use of my flat?'

'We knew you'd say that. It isn't your flat, anyway. It's ours.'

'Really?'

'The law is changing about married property.'

'So that is why you've been so slow to divorce me?'

'I'm sure your mother will pay for a lawyer if that's what you want. It could prove a useful test case.'

'I see. You're threatening me with headlines – you're prepared to turn a personal relationship into a political one.'

They had reached the exit from the park on to the Bayswater Road through which he and Esther had walked on their way to the Italian café where they had encountered Giles Carpenter and his boy.

'All personal relationships are political. They're about power,' she said.

'You were once a woman of honour, Beth.'

He had stopped walking but she didn't, she simply continued briskly on towards Notting Hill Gate. Watching her grow smaller, he remained convinced that he would set off in pursuit of reconciliation, of love even, but he didn't and she was gone from view. Finally, he drifted down the Bayswater Road to the Gate Cinema, opposite the tower block where he had once lived. For all he knew Beth, or Hattie, or Jo or one of the other faceless four was looking down from the sixth floor as he entered the cinema, to spend a couple of hours with Fassbinder, holding the evening *Standard*, whose banner headline had arrested him in his slow melancholic progress:

POLICE SWOOP ON SQUATTERS

THIRTY-ONE

'My dear Dick,

'Jane returned from the prison today with Esther's "permission" to inform me that she is five months pregnant. Jane admits that she has known of this for some time. Frankly, Dick, it has taken me thirty-five years to realize what kind of a woman I'm married to. She won't let me visit my own daughter.

Five months – does that strike you as a coincidence, Dick? Isn't it precisely five months since you went down to Buhera with my daughter and got yourself arrested in her company? Now I understand why she insisted on staying with you when your capture became inevitable, and why she stuck to that unbelievable "abduction" alibi on your behalf.

I thought you were an honourable man and one of the tribe of Abraham. I know you are the father of my daughter's child and by God you will marry her even if I have to shoot you first – no doubt you recognise that old joke. No, seriously, when is that divorce of yours coming through?

Jane insists you're not the father, but then Jane always had this pseudo-romantic thing about black men, I never told you that when we went Underground in 1950 Jane moved up to Detroit and had an affair with a Negro Party Organizer who was a notorious anti-Semite, even though we Jews fought the Southern Senators like Rankin (who said slavery was the best thing that ever happened to the niggers) and Eastland. Did I ever tell you how James Eastland of Mississippi had me thrown out of a hearing when I advised two clients, both civil rights activists, to plead the Fifth Amendment? He even accused the Warren Supreme Court of being a Commie front. It's not lost on me that as of today it's the KKK lobby in the Senate that's urging the US Govt to recognise the

Muzorewa régime here in "Zimbabwe Rhodesia". Jesse Helms is the worst.

I have faith in my daughter. She has always loved the black people of this country but not in *that* way – whatever Jane may say. Strictly between ourselves, Dick, Jane is merely exacting revenge on me for never having strictly married her. Maybe that is a clumsy sentence by your high standards but I think you'll get the point.

Dick, I've got to be frank, I've never trusted you one hundred per cent. I remember coming to London when Esther was arrested in '74, and you turned up late for lunch at the Connaught and I knew you'd been talking to "Someone". I don't miss a thing, by the way. Geoff Cowans smelt British Intelligence as soon as you stepped in the door. Poor old Geoff. Recently I've asked myself how the Brits managed to spring you from Chikurubi after only a couple of months while my daughter stays inside, threatened with a capital charge under the Law and Order Maintenance Act. I'm not quite the fool you may take me for, Dick. You certainly have a long nose.

However, my philosophy is to give a guy the benefit of the doubt and so I shall continue to regard you as a friend and future son-in-law. I am having some financial difficulties here which I cannot explain by letter but if you should receive a call in this connection from someone introducing himself as "Vespasian" please give him all the help you can, for my sake and your Future Wife's.

Cordially,
Paul Meyer.

PS. According to Jane, Esther has received no word from you since you got back to London. She assumes that your letters have been intercepted.

The day after he received this letter Richard Stern moved out of his mother's house and rented a basement room in Earl's Court. Here, working in permanent twilight, cut off from the world, only dimly conscious of the pedestrians plodding along the pavement above his head, he blasted a tunnel through the intractable rock of manhood and boyhood, excavating his own history until he found, at the bottom of this bottomless hole, himself. It was like a long, wasting illness.

Exhausted, famished, yet incandescent with achievement, he surfaced from his basement half-blind, then made his way through streets almost entirely populated by foreigners to a photocopying agency where he watched with intense, brooding, concentration as page by page the manuscript multiplied itself by ten. An hour later he was at the Post Office with a clutch of envelopes stamped first-class, each bearing a copy of *Buhera and Beyond – A Report from the Future*, by Richard Stern.

Having posted them, he went to bed and slept for thirty-six hours. Emerging again into the twilight, he took himself to St John's Wood and played Monopoly with his mother. Fudging the fall of the dice, he put his own silver boat on Park Lane, paid her £1,500 in respect of the hotel she had built on the site, and left the house, an hour later, with a cheque for £200 in his pocket.

On the way home he read an obituary of Giles Carpenter. It didn't say how Giles had died, merely 'on Thursday'.

Leonard Tanner invited him to dinner.

'Make it 7.45 for eight.'

'Did you read my piece?'

'We can talk about that. By the way, it might be a good idea to wear a tie. My wife's a bit fussy.'

The Tanners, no longer denizens of Hammersmith, lived on the third floor of a mansion block in Marylebone, reachable by means of a creaky, reluctant lift with difficult metal gates. The flat was spotless: Maples furniture with a preponderance of heavy brocade, drinks on a trolley.

Stern was the first to arrive.

'Make yourself comfortable,' Tanner said. 'Scotch?'

'Thank you.'

Mrs Tanner came out of the kitchen wiping her hands on the flowered apron she wore over a shapeless dress cut out of a heavy maroon cloth that Stern didn't notice. She looked older than Tanner. Tanner didn't introduce them.

'I've heard so much about you, Mr Stern.' Her hand held his for a moment.

'I'm sorry to hear it, Mrs Tanner.' He tried a small laugh.

'My name is Vera. Leonard doesn't believe in introductions.'

Tanner handed him a generous tumbler of whisky brimming with ice cubes while Mrs Tanner fussed around a gleaming table in the dining alcove, adjusting the silver candlesticks and embroidered mats. Stern had already noted that the table had been laid for five. Then Mrs Tanner walked to the mantelpiece and took down a large, coloured, studio-portrait of a shyly smiling young girl with pigtails. She handed it to Stern, forcing him to hold its gilt frame.

'That was our daughter Helen. I always think it's best for guests to meet her as soon as they arrive since she's very much alive in my head if not in Leonard's.'

'You haven't met Hugh Parker?' Tanner cut in.

Stern said no.

'It clears the air,' Mrs Tanner said. 'Helen doesn't like to spoil a social occasion, do you, dear?' Recovering the portrait from Stern's hand, she seemed to be waiting for her daughter to reply.

'He said he might be late.' Tanner said. 'Hugh is a prodigious workaholic, I doubt he's snatched more than four hours sleep a night since he took the job.'

'What job?' Stern asked.

'Good God, where have you been?' Tanner chuckled, crossing his legs contentedly and settling deeper into his chair. 'Hugh is our new editor.'

Stern didn't believe in Tanner's contentment.

'What happened to Foyle?'

'Jesus, don't you ever read the papers?'

'In my opinion,' said Mrs Tanner, 'one can waste one's life reading the newspapers, just as one can waste one's life writing for them or ruin one's life being married to someone who does.'

Stern glanced between them.

'For God's sake, Vera, put that thing back on the mantelpiece,' Tanner growled, forced at last to acknowledge her presence. He turned back to Stern. 'Selwyn got his marching orders after he mistook the Lusaka Commonwealth Conference for Canossa. Poor Selwyn. "*Nach Canossa gehen wir nicht*," as Bismarck assured the Reichstag, but Selwyn is no Bismarck, not in our proprietor's opinion, at least.'

Tanner rose and poured himself another scotch.

'It all came to a head after Selwyn insisted on publishing an attack on Mrs T.'s "sell-out" of Rhodesia at the Commonwealth Conference. You must have read it, surely? The proprietor called him in, treated him to a short sharp lecture on loyalty to the leader of the Tory Party, blamed him for excessive editorial expenditure – unfair to Selwyn actually, but let that pass – then sacked him. The man was shattered. He wandered the corridors in a trance, looking for support and finding none. The proprietor then took off for America in Concorde, leaving Selwyn to the untender mercies of a cutthroat lawyer who kept thrusting statements of resignation under his nose until the poor sod began to plead for a generous pay-off.'

'Wouldn't you?' Vera Tanner said. Stern noticed that she had not been offered a drink.

'Wouldn't I what?' Tanner looked at her as if her presence was something he was for ever trying to forget.

'Plead for a generous pay-off?'

She had robbed him of his pleasure in the story.

'Did you hope to get his job?' Stern asked.

Tanner stared at him as if he had only just realised who it was he had impetuously invited into his home.

'I knew they'd appoint a younger man.' But the words trod on each other's heels.

'Leonard wanted the job very badly,' Mrs Tanner said. 'He believed he would end his career as the editor of a major national newspaper, and of course this was his last chance.'

Tanner went again to the drinks trolley, ignoring Stern's very empty glass.

'As a matter of fact, the proprietor did approach me with some vague promises and propositions over dinner. I told him that the job of Foreign Editor suited me fine.'

'Leonard is a great liar,' Mrs Tanner said gently, 'as I've no doubt you have discovered, Mr Stern.' She looked at her wrist watch which, to Stern's astonishment, turned out to be a child's. 'I'd better turn the oven down,' she murmured.

'I told you, Hugh may be tied up,' Tanner said.

'Oh yes, you always tell me, Leonard.'

She left the room in her apron. Stern wondered who the fifth, so far unmentioned, guest was to be.

Tanner planted his feet wide in front of the fireplace, his back to the portrait of his daughter.

'Actually, I was pretty certain Hugh Parker would get the job. Hugh's a professional in a sense that Selwyn could never understand. Hugh knows his job is to print a wide variety of viewpoints while holding the editorial helm steady down the middle course.'

'Did you read my piece?' Stern asked. After almost three years he still couldn't address the Foreign Editor either as 'Leonard' or as 'Mr Tanner'.

'Er, yes, yes. I mean, take the EEC, for example: Hugh's for membership but remains critical of the Community's budget. He's sympathetic to the Palestinians but very firm on Israel's right to exist. He has no love for apartheid but realises that economic sanctions would do more harm than good. Regarding defence, Hugh's firm on the need for an effective deterrent but questions the capacity of the coming generation of tactical missiles to provide that deterrence within the available budget. Hugh looks before he leaps.'

Stern stared into his empty glass. 'Will you publish my piece?'

Tanner did, now, take Stern's glass. 'Same again?'

'Please.'

But instead of pouring whisky he took up position in front of the fireplace, like a burgher posing for his portrait.

'You're quite serious about that piece, then?'

'Perfectly.'

'But what is it? I've never read anything like it in my life. William Morris may have given us *News from Nowhere* but a journalist who starts sending in reports from "the future" is either a nut case or a novelist manqué. I mean what's it meant to be: fact or fantasy or what?'

Stern controlled his voice though his hands were shaking.

'I don't acknowledge the distinction.'

Tanner nodded politely; the man, after all, was his guest and had clearly suffered some kind of breakdown following what had presumably been an unpleasant interlude in a Rhodesian prison.

'I'm sure one of the literary mags would be interested, Richard.'

Mrs Tanner did not reappear. The conversation faltered. The two absent guests were beginning, as the clock swung to nine, to haunt the feast. Then the phone rang. Tanner took it, listened, grunted and turned his back on Stern, shielding his crumpled leather features. He replaced the receiver.

'Your friend Holzheimer.'

Stern sprang from his chair like a young stag stricken by an arrow. 'That was Berny?'

'Mm.'

'He's in London?'

'Passing through. I was hoping he'd come to dinner but I gather he's all tied up.'

'But . . . I mean, did he know I was here?'

'Of course. We all want to help, you know. I'm not always sure you quite appreciate that.'

Stern was choking with anger and grief. Tanner could so easily have handed him the telephone, but the bastard was playing power games because he'd been stood up by two guests in a single evening. Clearly Hugh Parker wasn't coming either.

Tanner poured himself another scotch. 'Holzheimer suggests you call him at his London office early tomorrow . . . I gather he's due on the mid-morning Concorde to New York.'

Mrs Tanner came back into the room. 'How much longer do we wait for them?'

'Holzheimer just phoned with his apologies.'

Her mouth tightened. 'And your new boss?'

'Give him ten minutes,' Tanner growled, incensed by the deliberate insult. As for Stern, the prick was clearly sinking back into the pit of his own bruised ego, oblivious to the fact that *Buhera and Beyond* was defamatory, criminally libellous, and certifiably

351

insane. One woman after another, white-on-black, crawling into his tent and under his mosquito net to fuck him!

'Why did you invite me here?' Stern asked.

'Look, Richard . . . I'd like to get you back to work. You're not exactly your own best ally, you know. A man who fails to turn up to a welcome home party held in his honour by the NUJ chapel without even a word of apology might be considered beyond the pale. Let's hope Hugh does show up . . .'

'But why?'

Tanner looked at the long, fair-weather, nose and wondered why, indeed, he had bothered. He hadn't forgotten Stern's tone when he first mentioned *News from Nowhere* in the car – and then the cynical 'exposure' of the 'Beirut' alibi for Helen's death – just wanton carelessness on Tanner's part, was that the line?

Stern surveyed the cracked parchment and saw only a fragment of an old testament lost in a silted sea of the dead.

Vera Tanner returned bearing a casserole whose sodden texture and flat, spiceless flavour Stern could deduce from its hospitalized smell. With a theatrical display of stoicism she put the casserole on its mat and sat down behind it.

Each of them unfolded their napkins with slow deliberation.

'The wine, Leonard,' Vera said primly.

'Oh fuck, yes.'

'Leonard!'

Tanner had forgotten to uncork the wine. That smug bastard Hugh Parker had called him into his office only three hours before he was due to be Tanner's guest at dinner.

—Leonard, I'm moving you sideways. I want you to take over Features.

Tanner told him that Features wasn't sideways from Foreign, it was down. Features was for girls with honours degrees and bearded lefties like Tree who hoped to edit the *New Statesman* or the *Listener;* Foreign was for men who had seen service and survived wars. Hugh Parker sat back in his swivel chair and swivelled – the proprietor's new darling, oh you just wait, you little cunt . . .

—Sorry, Leonard, it's Features or a redundancy settlement.

—I'd like a night to think about it, Tanner said. Damn it, if you don't do that you're left with no fucking dignity at all. Parker just smirked:

—Make it a short night, then.

When Tanner reminded him that his wife was expecting him to dinner, Parker looked faintly surprised and glanced at his desk diary. —Oh yes, he murmured,—I'll make it if I can find time after teaching our Business Manager, James Ellis, how to use a pocket calculator.

A good description of Hugh Parker, Tanner reflected: the pocket calculator. Was poor Jim Ellis, Tanner's friend of many years (Tanner decided) also to be given a 'short night' to consider a 'sideways' demotion?

Tanner uncorked a bottle of the worst wine he could find.

'Do you have any children, Mr Stern?' Mrs Tanner asked.

'Unfortunately, not.'

'But you were married? A child might have kept you together.'

'Actually, my wife did become pregnant once. But then she decided she didn't want it.'

Mrs Tanner stopped eating. She looked horrified.

Tanner slopped some of the plonk into Vera's glass (a waste, she scarcely touched the stuff) and Stern's. He'd heard a rumour that Stern's wife had turned feminist and aborted a child – hardly surprising, married to a prick like Stern. Tomorrow Tanner would make a few phone calls – show Parker that genuine quality still had its price, there were still places on the Street where the name Tanner meant something.

'Oh your poor, foolish wife,' Vera Tanner cried, 'how could she murder life, the precious life of a child?'

She pushed her plate from her with a small, fastidious motion but Stern ate and gulped wine greedily, mechanically, as if these overdone cubes of animal swimming in Thames water were his only means of escape from the enormous burden of being himself. God, he looks threadbare, Tanner thought, hardly able to sustain his clothes, the tie he'd asked him to wear stained with grease, everything hanging off his skeletal frame like a tent without pegs, a man locked into self-destruct and when his time came you wouldn't be able to gather ten guests for the humanist memorial service in Stationers' Hall, the usual trendy wash of Shelley and Mozart to fill the gap left by God. Giles Carpenter's suicide had brought in a couple of hundred, the man had success, wealth, style and genuine tragedy on his side, but Stern, whom Tanner had spotted alone in the back row, ostentatiously clutching a copy of *Loyalty*, would remain as isolated and disregarded at his own death as at Giles Carpenter's.

Stern looked up. '*Loyalty* was never published.'

Tanner flushed. 'What are you talking about?'

Stern turned to Vera Tanner. 'I invented your husband. He's a liar. It was the unkindest thing I ever did.'

She didn't seem to hear. Only Tanner heard – and possibly Holzheimer. A peculiar smile had invaded the area round her mouth, but it didn't extend to her eyes.

'Did Leonard ever tell you about our daughter, Mr Stern?'

'Er, no.'

353

'I don't expect he did. Leonard likes to bury his mistakes. He forgets. He's very good at forgetting.'

'To forget is to forgive,' Stern said.

The telephone rang. Tanner snatched it.

'Tanner,' he said.

'Look, Leonard, my apologies to Mrs T. but I'm really not going to be able to make it tonight.'

'Well . . . better luck next time, Hugh.'

'Can I assume that you'll be saying yes to Features tomorrow morning?'

'As I said, I'd appreciate . . .'

Vera was gazing fixedly at Stern. 'I suppose you know what he did?'

'Did?'

She had straightened her back regally, hands clawing and kneading the napkin crumpled in her lap, like talons stretched out to her squirming prey.

'He turned his back!'

Stern nodded. 'He did the same to me in Buhera.'

'Turned his back. Insisted on forcing her to cross the road on her own, then turned his back on her because because . . . because a pair of tarts walked out of Ravenscourt Park.'

Host and hostess had simultaneously risen to their feet, crouching like two wrestlers.

'A motorcycle backfired!' Tanner yelled. 'I've told you a hundred times! For a split second I was back in Beirut – '

'Hearing gunfire? In 1964?'

Vera Tanner gazed at her guest, stunned, yet Stern seemed not to have spoken. When she turned back to her husband it was with the glass eye judges insert on the day of reckoning.

'Yes, that's what you've told me a hundred times. But when I spoke to the man who . . . that Australian, yes *him*, he admitted that he'd turned his head from the road because two flashy tarts in mini skirts came out of the park and he remembers you doing the same.'

'It's a lie! You never spoke to him!'

Stern didn't bother with the reluctant lift and its difficult metal gates, he flew down the stone stairs two at a time and galloped out into the night holding the copy of *Buhera and Beyond* that Tanner had thankfully relinquished.

They met in Terminal 3 (Concorde) and shook hands. Holzheimer's impudent face had been emboldened by a wispy moustache.

'Wistful,' Holzheimer corrected him. 'If you don't mind.'

Stern's dark eyes were heavy with reproach: Holz had come through London without even contacting him.

'Is that the accusation?' Berny complained. 'I may not have "contacted" you, Richard, but I sure as hell "contacted" your lady wife and your lady mother. Finally it had to be Tanner – so why don't you grovel?'

Stern shrugged. 'I'm not on the phone.'

'That means you're into one of your "genius" trips.'

'Actually, I can't afford a telephone.'

'When an Englishman says "actually" he's invariably telling a lie to someone who loves him.'

A trace of a smile at the corners of Stern's tight mouth.

'Richard, a personal question: are you the father of Esther's baby?'

Stern looked him in the eye.

'Now you're looking me in the eye,' Holzheimer said, tossing a palmful of peanuts in his mouth and ordering two more whiskies. 'I may as well throw up all over this Anglo-French cigar tube I'm travelling in.'

Stern handed him the large brown envelope he had been clasping under his arm.

'Something you've written?'

'Yes.'

'Does it reveal whether you're the father of Esther's baby?'

'Yes.'

'Can I read it now?'

'No.' Stern examined Holzheimer's expensive leather jacket, lazy cowboy shirt and slick executive briefcase with a mixture of envy and disgust.

'Well, which is it, Stern – envy or disgust?'

A stilted voice on the public address system was coaxing passengers aboard the supersonic flight to New York.

'Out of work?' Holzheimer asked casually.

Stern nodded.

'Like to cover the Lancaster House Conference for West 43rd Street?'

Stern nodded again and almost said 'thank you'. At the entrance to the Concorde departure lounge, reserved for ticket-carriers only, Holzheimer turned and blew him a kiss, but as soon as he was out of sight the Englishman began to reflect bitterly on what his 'friend' had held back from him: the view, shared by every case-hardened hack in the business, that a terrorist as dedicated to survival as Esther Meyer did not surrender to enemy troops out of sentiment for a man she had conspicuously avoided for more than two years.

355

Stern strode from Terminal 3. As he passed a staircase he cast an evil eye on a very fat Indian lady who was carrying a small girl and a parcel; she immediately slipped and fell a whole flight of stairs, landed with a sickening thump, and lay still. The child began to scream. Stern hurried on. Oh, he knew what they all believed, Tanner, Warner, Holz . . . They were in no doubt that Esther and Zimunya had led him by the nose down to Buhera to gain maximum publicity from his arrest, to steal the headlines on the first day of the internal elections, and to choke the Rhodesian boa constrictor on the sacred cow it could neither swallow nor vomit up: Esther.

Opening the brown envelope on Concorde, Holzheimer read the note paper-clipped with the longer text.

'By coincidence, on the day of Giles's death I saw a chalked notice beside the ticket barrier at Earl's Court station: "We regret delays on the Circle and District Lines due to a person under a train." What I never did explain to Esther was Giles's unequalled charm in his Oxford heyday – how, meeting one in the Broad or the High, he would simply turn and walk with one wherever one was going, his arm linked through one's own, his eyes fresh as dew, his lips swollen with the kisses of midnight girls – his trousers flapping cheerfully though torn by College railings.'

Twenty-four hours after Holzheimer's arrival in New York Stern received a Western Union cable: 'Confirm your coverage of Lancaster House stop Telex daily report stop Letter follows stop Insist you install telephone soonest stop Love Holz.'

A letter did follow but it said nothing about *Buhera and Beyond – a Report from the Future.*

THIRTY-TWO

It was five years since Stern had last climbed the narrow, littered staircase piled with cardboard boxes of unsold copies, pushing into the cramped office with its permanent atmosphere of skin-of-teeth survival, cracked a few desperate jokes with Tom McAllisty, sipped instant coffee ('the cheapest brand in London') from paper cups, and awaited the terrible vengeance of the *tricoteuses*. Harry had come late that day, a stumbling footfall on the stairs, a clumping cloven hoof in the corridor, the unoiled crank of the toilet chain followed by the slum flush. Harry on a stick; Harry carried out, half-an-hour later, to a waiting ambulance, almost dead.

Now, five years later, Stern found Harry Marquis seated behind the editor's desk, correcting proofs, wreathed in pipe smoke, the founding father of *Thought and Action*. Harry looked ten years younger; he'd shed weight in the most determined manner and the pouches under his eyes had reduced themselves from several slack sacks to a single pocket of menacing energy.

The composition of the editorial board had changed. Of the young Turks of the early Seventies, only McCallisty himself and the erratic psychiatrist Brendan Hogg had survived.

'You could call it a purge,' McAllisty murmured to Stern, with his usual easy smile. 'The empty chairs have been divided between Harry's lot and Beth's lot – one is reminded of the Nazi-Soviet Pact.'

Stern didn't recognise most of the new faces and they for their part showed no disposition to welcome him: grim scowls and averted eyes seemed to characterise the New Order. Only McAllisty, Hogg and a friendly young Irish writer called Neil (whose second name Stern didn't catch) made sympathetic inquiries about Stern's imprisonment and expulsion from Rhodesia.

Beth, Hattie and the black woman, Jo, arrived together and sat together. Only Jo threw him a friendly smile:

'Had any luck bedwise?' she winked. 'If not, remember We Try Harder.' Laughing at his discomforture, she began to exchange banter with McAllisty and Hogg, who responded (Stern was aware) with better grace and style.

'Shall we begin?' Harry glanced at his watch. 'Minutes of the last meeting. Any corrections?'

'Yes,' Beth said. 'Minute eight, section (b). "Consciousness raising among women" should read "among women and men".'

'Agreed?' Harry barely looked up. 'Any other corrections?'

'Yes,' Hattie said. 'Minute seven, section (c). "Women's issues" should be put in quotation marks.'

Harry tamped his pipe with a blackened finger tip.

'Why?'

Beth shot him an icy glance of warning. 'To convey that they are so-called women's issues as well as genuine women's issues.'

Harry shrugged. 'Agreed? Anything else?'

'Yes,' Jo said. 'Minute four, section (a). "The struggle of women workers for equality" should read "The struggle of women workers and in particular of black women workers for equality".'

'I've no doubt it should,' Harry mused. 'The question is, what was actually said at the last meeting. Does our secretary and minute-taker recall any reference at that juncture to black women workers?' He fastened a sardonic eye on Tom McCallisty.

'He does not,' Tom said, 'but he has a notoriously unreliable memory.'

'Do we doctor the minutes in the interests of social hygiene?' Harry asked.

Stern observed these exchanges with fascination; he suspected that they were partly enacted for his benefit.

'Move that Jo's amendment be adopted,' Beth said mechanically, raising her hand immediately, as if in contempt of the chairman. The women's hands went up automatically; the others followed. Doodling on a pad, Beth had not even deigned to glance up during the vote.

'The Tammany Hall machine is well oiled,' Stern observed.

They all looked at him.

'Remark out of order,' Beth said.

'Seconded,' Hattie said.

Harry sighed. 'Richard, you are here as our guest. Any matters arising?'

'Yes,' Beth said. 'Minute two, the IMG meeting at Newham Town Hall to adopt a new Anti-Harassment Charter. Only seven people turned up. That's a disgrace.'

Harry nodded and ran a hand slowly through his great mane of hair: 'Minuted: "a disgrace".'

'Also,' Beth said. And waited. Stern saw her jog Hattie's elbow.

'Also,' Hattie said, blushing in shame, 'the Conference of Women Historians to be called in conjunction with History Workshop at Ruskin College in December has been refused a grant by the Arts Council, the British Academy, the Leverhulme Foundation, the TUC and the Labour Party.'

Stern burst out laughing and was the object of venomous looks. The next twenty minutes was taken up with a discussion of what should and could be done to rescue the project.

Then Harry cleared his throat. 'Today's agenda, item 3, Richard Stern's essay, or "Report" as he calls it, *Buhera and Beyond*, which the author has submitted to this journal for publication.'

'Point of order,' Beth said.

Harry looked at her.

'Why is this item so high on the agenda? I'd have thought we had more important things to discuss. I mean, if we start debating this now we'll be here all night, won't we, and everything else will go to the dogs.'

Her vowels had broadened as she spoke.

McAllisty moaned softly.

No one looked at Stern.

'I shall give the item twenty minutes,' Harry said, 'and no more.' He raised two bushy, nicotine-stained eyebrows in anticipation of consent, and got it.

'Anyone want to begin?'

Stern saw that each of the nine people round the table had a copy of his typescript before them. A lugubrious silence suffocated the office.

'Must I bite the bullet?' Harry asked. 'I would rather not – for reasons of personal history with which most of you will be familiar. Indeed my attitude towards anything submitted to this journal by Richard really ought to be one of profound abstention. We were comrades and colleagues once, but then there was a painful and protracted falling out involving that deadly concoction, philosophy, sex and the Academy, and then – '

'Objection,' Beth said.

Harry halted, trembling: momentarily he had lost his composure, his authority. Stern had glimpsed, briefly, a part of the old Harry, the several old Harrys. Beth cracked the whip.

'Let us stick strictly to Richard's text,' she said. 'Shall I begin with this person called Comrade Liberty, a black woman guerrilla who enters the narrator's tent at night and engages in sexual intercourse with him?'

'Some chance!' Jo chuckled.

'Why "Liberty"?' Beth asked. 'Isn't the name itself a putdown? Isn't the whole episode designed to denigrate blacks and women?'

'May I answer that?' Stern asked Harry.

'Of course.'

' "Tichaona Liberty", which means "We shall see Liberty", is her adopted Chimurenga name. Her real name is Olivia Mhondodoro. These Chimurenga names are frequently more fanciful than hers: among others to whom I was introduced in Buhera were Comrades Kid Colt, James Bond, Paul McCartney, Killer, Bvisai Mabunhu (Cast out the Boers), Spill Blood, Mick Jagger and Dracula.'

Silence: a sullen shuffling of paper.

'You describe the Zanla camp as "Caliban's kingdom",' observed a new member of the editorial board whom Stern didn't recognise. 'Is this a reference to Mannoni's celebrated work, *Prospero and Caliban*, or merely an indication that the narrator of this "Report" regards himself as Prospero?'

'Comrade Liberty is also reportedly described as "your jungle princess",' Beth commented.

'But not by Richard himself,' McAllisty intervened. 'By Esther Meyer.'

Stern saw a red spot light up in Beth's porcelain cheek.

'Ms Meyer, though accompanied by her husband, loses no time in demanding that our hero fathers her child . . . These slanders are clearly directed against women who take an active part in revolutionary movements.'

'Are you about to defend the proprieties of bourgeois marriage?' McAllisty asked.

'Order,' Harry growled.

From the look she accorded McAllisty, Stern gloomily deduced that Tom must be rather good in bed – one might have guessed anyway, just look at the man. Stern leaned across the table towards his wife:

'Anyway, you yourself made precisely the same demand of me only four weeks ago.'

Her brow furrowed: 'Demand?'

'You and Hattie . . . came to my cottage, together . . .'

Hattie emitted a shriek. 'He has a cottage – Wordsworth!'

Stern's glare was manic with sincerity. 'You asked me to impregnate you.'

'Cut!' laughed McAllisty.

'I hope this all appears in the minutes, Comrade Secretary,' sniggered Brendan Hogg.

McCallisty nodded solemnly. 'Call me Proust.' Hogg bellowed

and the Irish writer Neil began to laugh. Jo looked as if she wanted to laugh but the grim Roundhead expressions along the distaff bench forbade it.

'I was fascinated.' Harry addressed Stern, 'by the enigmatic figure of Dr Zimunya, alias Cubans Urimbo. Your narrative constantly refers to him as "the doctor", suggesting that he may be a doctor of medicine or he may be a charlatan. Could you enlighten me?'

'No,' Stern said. 'I've never been able to enlighten you.'

Harry nodded patiently but made a note on the pad in front of him.

'Does General Chimurenga *have* to eat with his fingers and toss chicken bones over his shoulder as he eats?' Beth said.

'All Zimbabweans eat with their fingers,' Stern said.

'Oscar Mucheche didn't.'

'Not in the refectory of the LSE. He does in Zimbabwe.'

Harry said: 'You pass over your two months in Chikurubi prison rather rapidly.'

'I have to agree,' Tom McAllisty said. 'I assumed that what transpired was too painful to recall.'

Stern seemed incapable of any response. He was chewing one particular fingernail.

Harry resumed: 'Your narrative then announces that six months after your release from prison you were back in Salisbury when the telephone rang early one morning. I quote from page 9 of your text: ". . . Liberty reached across the bed to take it, her breasts pressing into my open, snoring mouth like melons. It was Gilson . . ." And so on. A simple man might ask, Richard, how a "Report" written in August can possibly describe the events of the following February.'

'It's subtitled "A Report from the Future",' the Irish writer pointed out diffidently. 'Now that's a definable literary tradition, surely – Wells, Zamyatian, Huxley, Orwell – even a heroic tradition.'

'But not when projected as a description of the actual behaviour of real people,' Harry said. 'I know of no such tradition.'

'A tradition has to begin somewhere, Harry. But you're the prof., of course . . .'

Turning back to Stern, Harry let his half-lens reading glasses ease down his nose.

'Your account of this man Tanner's behaviour at the moment of your capture by the Rhodesians is highly discreditable to him – by your account, he virtually disowned you.'

Stern nodded.

'According to Tanner's own story, published while you were still

361

in prison, he virtually saved your bacon. The Rhodesian commandos wanted to string you up from the nearest tree.'

'There was only one tree. A baobab. I haven't read Tanner's version.'

'And you tell us that in December – that's still three months ahead of us – you returned (if one may use the past tense to describe the future) to Rhodesia as a correspondent of the *New York Times*, by courtesy of your friend Holzheimer?'

'By virtue of my capacity as a journalist.'

'Obviously,' Harry said.

'Holzheimer is certainly an engaging character,' Tom McAllisty said. 'I'd like to meet him – do you think he might give me a job, too?'

Stern turned his long nose on the man seated beside him.

'Et tu, McAllisty?'

'Richard, why does this man Holzheimer keep speaking your lines?' Beth asked. Her tone was almost friendly.

'He doesn't.'

'Oh, but he plainly does,' cried Brendan Hogg. 'He speaks your best lines, too, mm.'

'Brutus McAllisty agrees,' said McAllisty. 'Odd, really,' he mused, tilting back his chair, planting one foot on the edge of the table, and examining the worn knees of his jeans, 'though I don't appear in your narrative I occasionally got the feeling that I was an early sketch for this Holzheimer.' He shrugged. 'Pure megalomania.'

'You're a fucking prototype, Tom,' Jo said. She turned to Stern. 'We're all ganging up on you, aren't we.'

'I expected it.'

'Well, you got your old grappling hooks into me. I mean I really want to know if this baby of Esther's really is going to be Richard's or that black doctor bloke's, I mean it's a real cliffhanger, isn't it? I mean, how long have we got to wait to find out . . . ?' Jo was counting on her fingers. 'Another four months?'

'Unless she aborts it,' Stern said, staring at Beth, 'like you did.'

Jo's mouth fell open.

'Bastard!' Hattie hissed.

Harry was stretching himself. The notional twenty minutes he'd allocated to item 3, Richard Stern's 'Report', had long since passed but no one, not even Beth Halliday, seemed anxious to raise the point of order.

'As a structural analysis of the armed struggle in Zimbabwe,' said one of Harry's new protégés, 'this piece is virtually valueless. One notices occasional concessions to fashionable semiology and deconstruction theory; but one also notices a protracted ego trip by a disturbed spirit. It seems that for Richard Stern, *"l'histoire, c'est moi"*.'

Harry nodded. 'I'd like to display my proverbial naivety and ask Richard what we are reading here. A dream?'

Beth jumped up. 'What we're reading is a load of monomaniac shit dumped on the heads of all women – the psychopathological face of frustrated patriarchy.' She tossed her copy across the table at Stern. 'Try *Playboy:* they pay real money for a quick dip into pseudo-revolutionary black cunt. Sorry, Jo, but this has to be said.'

The Irish writer Neil stood up, slowly, relectantly, shyly. His physique set him apart from the others: the hands, neck and shoulders of a labourer, large rings in his ears, a building site donkey jacket which had clearly seen some building sites.

'I'd like to speak,' he addressed Harry.

'There's no need to stand, Neil.'

'No, don't patronise me, Harry, I spend my life with a travelling theatre working in the streets of Derry and Republican Belfast and you're a fool over there if you don't stay on your feet . . . Er . . . Yes, well, a good deal of this discussion strikes me as . . . er, it's my belief, actually, that a prose narrative like Richard's has to be read, so to speak, between the lines . . . I mean, all writing is about itself, isn't it, it's coded.'

Unchallenged, his diffidence evaporating, Neil's voice picked up.

'Frankly, I don't know the ins and outs of the various, er, well, biographies round this table, but if our work is to be judged by our ex-wives and ex-professors then heaven help us, none of us would ever get a word into print.'

McAllisty and Hogg laughed appreciatively.

Harry banged the table, his avuncular equanimity exploded by the first display of genuine support for Stern.

'Then why did Dr Stern deliberately submit his prose master-piece to *this* journal – if not to revive old feuds and settle old scores?'

'Uncomradely language,' McAllisty complained.

'Maybe Richard thought it was still a journal capable of resisting or transcending the current orthodoxies of the Left,' Neil suggested mildly. 'Ask him.' He gestured vaguely towards Stern. 'I'd just like to say one last thing – '

'On a point of order,' Beth said, lifting the slender wrist which still carried the Longines watch he'd given her as a wedding present.

'Just one last thing,' Neil persisted. 'I've had the feeling this evening that Richard has been put on trial not only for heresy but also for insanity. If I were in his shoes I'd plead guilty to both

363

charges. A true poet is always a symbolist; an authentic symbol is always subversive; a writer blessed with sanity is simply a bank manager in drag – we have too many of them. Richard's piece told me things I didn't know. I liked it. I'd print it.'

Neil sat down, rather flushed, took out his tobacco tin, and resolutely avoided looking at anyone else seated round the table. Stern thought: happy to fight, glad to lose, a true Irishman.

'I move that we reject this article for publication and proceed to next business,' Beth said.

'Seconded,' Hattie said.

'Richard has scarcely spoken,' McAllisty protested.

'Speak, Richard,' Harry said.

'No, a motion has been put!' Beth said.

Stern reached across the table and gave her a hard slap. Her head jerked in surprise; the ensuing backhander, more casually delivered, brought a gasp from Beth and a scream from Hattie. The lazy, lateral blow he gave Hattie was powerful enough to send her glasses spinning; she emitted a long howl, then descended to the floor in a desperate search for her owl eyes, wailing continuously.

A trickle of blood ran from Beth's nose. She looked round the room in astonishment; no one, not even Jo, had moved to her defence.

'As I was saying,' Stern turned back to Harry. 'What is needed is a new kind of historical narrative. The long argument between the Braudel school of narrative historians and the structuralists is redundant; similarly, the stale, tired distinction between fiction and "non-fiction", the Torah of librarians and literary editors, is merely a decadent convention. We live in an age of relativity, the age of the cinema: the true algebra and geometry of relativity is fantasy and fable.'

Stern again reached across the table, but this time to collect the copies of his article from each member of the editorial board. He paused only to consider the blood oozing down the pretty hollow above Beth's upper lip.

'One day someone will break your neck.'

Neil would not relinquish his copy of *Buhera and Beyond*: 'Richard, I'd like to keep this.'

'Then resign from Tammany Hall.'

Neil shrugged his broad shoulders and followed Stern down the narrow, twisting staircase in a painful gesture of solidarity which came to an uncertain conclusion when they found themselves out in the street.

'Have you time for a drink?' Neil suggested.

They walked across the road to the local.

'What will you have?' Stern murmured, his eyes swivelling impatiently along the bar for attention.

'No, Richard, this is on me. A pint? You'll need a few after that. My God, you English!'

Stern smiled a pale smile into space. Holding his spilling pint he led the way from the bar to a corner table. 'Backs to the wall.'

'Well, cheers, Richard.'

'Cheers.'

Stern wondered what the man's second name was. It seemed rather late to ask. Neil began talking about a film project he had in mind, apparently there was some prospect of feed-money or seed-money or up-front money from the British Film Institute, from a Nigerian oil millionaire, from the Irish Rastas . . . Neil proclaimed himself fascinated by Zimbabwe but he talked about Ireland, oblivious to the restless motion of Stern's dark eyes, the impatient jerks of his angular limbs, the way he kept refolding himself. Maybe not oblivious.

Stern saw that his companion's glass was empty. Neil was gazing at it wistfully. It was Stern's round.

'Richard, I admire your guts, you know.'

Stern glanced at his watch; he knew Neil would be drinking with the editorial board within half an hour – the gravediggers descending in single file, holding aloft poor Yorick.

'Must fly,' he said.

Neil looked disappointed, then bereft. 'Are you sure you won't have another, Richard?'

'Wish I could.'

His diary was without a single entry; there was nothing but the basement flat in Earl's Court and the rented TV. He hadn't changed the sheets on his bed for more than five weeks despite frequent discharges occasioned by two phantom females, the grime in his 'kitchenette' was such that he now ate his daily meal 'out', and every attempt to read a book – any book – had aborted after a few pages. Only TV kept him awake. His notebook, largely neglected but still subject to occasional bursts of activity, observed that solitude becomes a habit compounded of self-indulgent egoism and an aching anguish for 'the Other'.

It also observed that Elizabeth had begun her withdrawal seven years ago (at least) and that he had been unable to respond by finding an alternative 'partner' (ugh word) to co-habit (ugh ugh) as a friend or lover.

A man with a soft Irish voice was offering him the back of an old envelope.

He scribbled his Earl's Court address but deliberately scrambled the new phone number. Neil held his hand in a powerful, building-site grip.

'It's been a pleasure and an honour, Richard. And good luck with *Buhera*. Man, it's a masterpiece.'

Stern looked at him. 'Do you really think so?'

'Don't forget what she wrote in *Middlemarch:*

"I would not creep along the coast, but steer
Out in mid-sea, by guidance of the stars." '

'I won't forget, Neil.' He left the pub clutching half a dozen copies of his 'Report'. Soon he would be alone and free to delve, like a deep-sea diver profiting from disaster, between the pages in search of their obscene, vicious, philistine marginal comments.

He found a shadowed doorway, a point of observation.

Ten minutes later they began to emerge into the autumn twilight in talkative pairs and groups, lingered, coalesced, split, some crossing to the pub, others hurrying away. Stern moved back into the shadow of his chosen doorway, a goods entrance bolted for the night and piled with black plastic refuse bags. He saw McAllisty and Hogg enter the pub and knew they would soon be drinking with Neil. The women came out as a group, drifting slowly along the pavement opposite him, their strides faltering at the pub; he turned his face into the shadows. Jo and Hattie entered the pub but Beth, whose porcelain complexion showed no sign of a recent battering, began to walk briskly towards Oxford Street – now as ever a small, neat, elegant woman with a tight bottom and slender thighs of fine design. He could still feel her soft, surprised face in his hand.

He thought: she could be anybody.

Harry emerged from the staircase alone, wrapped in thought, oblivious to his surroundings. Passing the pub without the slightest falter in his stride, he headed north on automatic pilot with flapping mane and hunched shoulders and the old, familiar rolling gait – the ancient mariner all at sea. Stern smiled grimly and set off in pursuit, soon shortening his stride and slowing his pace to avoid overtaking his prey.

Turning into Oxford Street, Harry Marquis and his battered briefcase rolled towards the Academy Cinema, whose lights glowed brighter as the darkness deepened. There were three films showing at the Academy and only one box office to service them, so Stern was compelled to close up behind Harry as the distinguished political philosopher, author of *Reason and Revolution, Socialism with a Human Face*, and a celebrated study of the Utopian Socialists from Robert Owen to William Morris, fumbled for his wallet. As Stern anticipated, Harry chose Cinema 2: Henri Bresson.

Stern bought a ticket. 'Bresson,' he said.

He followed Harry into Cinema 2, saw him hesitate, scanning the darkened auditorium, then respond to the magnetic flash of her beckoning arm. She had (of course) selected an empty row of seats. Harry eagerly stumbled forward in the dark, two hundred pounds of passion; Stern waited until their long embrace had subsided, then took a seat immediately behind them.

The programme began with a Czech cartoon, high-class animation, a witty expressionist comment on the trials of modern urban life. Kafka would have permitted himself a discreet smile. Stern noticed that Harry found it difficult to sit still, as if his age and bulk rendered him permanently uncomfortable, but then he said something and her blonde head tilted back in laughter; Harry produced a corduroy arm and cranked it up, like a girder being crane-lifted into position, until it encompassed her shoulders.

Stern experienced no difficulty in concentrating on Bresson's austere tribute to Saint Joan, even when Harry's paw planted itself high on her thigh and she responded by unzipping him with a deft, practised motion of her left hand. At every juncture of the film Stern discerned a clear parallel between Joan's life and Esther's – a theme he would develop in a long, indeed monumental, essay, a sequel to the masterpiece, six copies of which he now held in his lap over his own, reluctantly rising cock.

It was not during the fiery execution of Joan at Rouen but in the course of a rather dull, pedantic interrogation by her English inquisitors that Harry finally came in row 'M' of the stalls (a bellow accompanied by a great flap of his mane was evidence enough). The following morning a cleaning woman discovered some typed pages under a seat in row 'N'. They duly joined the discarded ice-cream cartons, empty popcorn containers, abandoned *Standard*s, cigarette packets, sweet wrappers, ticket stubs, and paper hankies in the Academy's dustbin.

THIRTY-THREE

Buhera and Beyond – a Report from the Future by Richard Stern

Liberty made herself my wife the night before the Rhodesians came on a narrow camp bed shrouded in coarse netting in a hot, stifling tent reeking of gun grease. Mosquitoes whined like angry dentists' drills from outside the net while the alien breath of a peasant girl whose diet was not mine assaulted me from within it. Liberty's bush-hardened muscles were uncompromising; she grasped my hips with calloused hands as practical and urgent as a midwife's and the transaction, though not soundless, was completed without verbal exchange. It didn't take long.

Yet Liberty was a most sensitive woman who loved, above all, to talk.

After the ceremony she dutifully re-coated my body in mosquito repellent, carefully fastened the net under the bed, coiled the bandoliers round her splendid body, took up her AK 47, and then settled down outside the tent on the hard, cooling earth of Buhera to guard me with her life. Again not a word had passed between us.

I lay tossing in the oppressive heat, increasingly awake, the luminous hands of my watch inexorably quartering what was left of the night – the Rhodesians would come soon after first light. But they were scarcely on my mind; I had spent ten years waiting for Esther. No inoculation – not anger, not even betrayal – could immunise me against that passion and that longing. Whether it was a real woman I loved or my own Hegelian 'idea' of her, I was hooked.

I may have fallen into a shallow sleep because I heard nothing until I became aware of a soft hand on my drenched brow, murmured words of affection, and the most extraordinary sense of transport, as if my body had become weightless with happiness. It was almost three years since I had last folded my arms round Esther's naked body but what sounded bugles of triumph was the knowledge that I was now to possess her on the soil of Africa.

'Your jungle princess is fast asleep at her post,' Esther whispered. 'I stepped over her prostrate body – the sentinel who reminds us, hourly, that we must "ever be vigilant".'

'Poor girl, she's tired,' I murmured.

Perhaps Liberty's uncharacteristic dereliction of duty uncurled in Esther's mind a worm of suspicion; perhaps her gently roaming hands were worldly enough to discover evidence of the truth. Abruptly they recoiled in anger:

'Liberty was with you!'

My silence was my admission. One smells of the woman one has been with.

'It was her wish,' I said, 'I could hardly refuse.'

'You knew I was coming, Richard.'

'No, my darling. I received your cryptic note with its one-word message, but assumed that it represented another of your husband's dangerous jokes.'

'So you took Liberty in revenge?'

'Haven't I suffered enough for my love of you?'

Esther's head sank on to my shoulder, her rich chestnut hair brushing my face.

'I want a child, Richard.'

I understood at once.

'You mean I am the only man whose hair moves in the wind within a hundred kilometres. Why not wait for tomorrow – you'll have five hundred Rhodesian commandos to choose from.'

Her beautiful oval face touched mine.

'Whatever I say, you won't believe me.'

To which I might add: whatever I write about that night in Buhera will not be believed.

I am neither a war reporter nor a gifted cartographer of violence. I lack the necessary physical self-possession, the capacity to seal off my screaming nerves and pick my way clinically between the living and the dead.

In film mythology heroes are mute in the heat of combat, whether with gun or fist; the reality is noisy. The deadly machine gun crew screams louder than its victims, drowning its own heart beat, expecting retribution. Each survival is a miracle later described as an achievement. I saw the Zanla men pouring fire from their hand guns into the sky, their faces gashed by cavernous mouths in which hung tongues coated with brown dust. The dust storm caused by the descending rotor blades of the gunships and the mounting crescendo of explosions wrapped every running, falling body in its impartial embrace, obliterating friend and foe, until all streams of fire coalesced in a single, indiscriminate funnel of murder.

I remember Liberty clutching me, pulling me to the ground, gallantly wrapping her body over mine, but I never saw General Chimurenga, nor his aides with their East German briefcases, nor the 'doctor'. I heard men stampeding as animals do, that's all. Did I imagine two helicopters mushrooming into fireballs as they descended, their occupants falling from the sky like burning matches? Was it Tanner I saw, flopping out of Hersh's command ship and sinking to knees sixty years old as his Rhodesian breakfast poured into a magnolia puddle? (A message to Professor Marquis: years ago I made you my enemy by demonstrating that the problem about Marxism with a human face is the human face. That message is worth repeating and if one day your creaking heart expires inches from my wife's, you'll know why.)

We were standing, Esther and I alone, beneath a tree, her fingers lightly touching mine. The Rhodesians surrounded us in tight, concentric circles, like boys staring at circus freaks, helmets removed, their flaxen hair plastered to their skulls, camouflage cream dripping down their bronzed faces (collages worthy of Christopher's contribution to the Prague Spring of '68), staring bewitched at a legend of infamy: the beautiful woman whom their mothers and sisters called a 'kaffir's whore'. But rape never crossed their minds. You don't lay hands on a white woman. Me, I was something else. The warriors had crouched, weeping, over their dead and dying and each of the living suddenly knew that each of the dead had been his best friend. The gooks had fired the guns but a gook is just a gook. It was the civilized world which was responsible for this betrayal of kith and kin – calculating bastards devoid of loyalty like this tall, morose shit holding Esther Meyer's hand in the shade of the baobab.

A young brave said, very softly: 'String him up.'

They had been weaned on photos of moustachioed Pioneers standing, arms akimbo, beneath trees from which hung the stick-thin, rag-clad limbs of the defeated black rebels of 1896 – the first Chimurenga. The executioners faced the camera poker-faced; decency forbade a smile.

General Hersh, the stubble-chinned lover of biltong to whom Frieda dedicated her regular 'Ann Average' column in the *Herald*, strode past his braves like a Teutonic chieftain to glower at his captive princess and her pale acolyte. Tanner trailed behind, his folded leather features green beneath a coat of brown dust.

'General,' Esther addressed Hersh quietly, but loud enough for a thousand commandos to hear, 'I arrest you in the name of the people of Zimbabwe.'

Hersh's brow furrowed but nothing came out. He examined me: 'Is this your man?' he growled at Tanner.

I observed my foreign editor weighing the situation.

'He was,' Tanner replied. 'He's yours now.'

When they released me from Chikurubi two months later I was taken straight to the airport and put aboard a South African Airways flight to London. Ushering me through immigration, my old sparring partner Mike Gilson invited me to sign a form declaring myself to be a prohibited immigrant, guilty of a capital offence under the Law and Order Maintenance Act – consorting with terrorists – and liable to instant re-arrest should I ever again set foot in Rhodesia. I declined. More accurately, I indicated the price of my signature: the return of my papers, diaries and address book confiscated from my flat in Baines Avenue.

'No way.' He looked genuinely indignant. But when the phone rang in my Salisbury apartment six months later, and Liberty reached across the bed to take it, her breasts, like melons, pressing into my open, snoring mouth, it was Gilson. I was not the only 'prohibited immigrant' back in town. A tall, florid man with generous, wine-washed jowls and the glass eyes of the imperial family had descended from the sky to declare himself, in the name of the Queen, once again Britain's Governor. The terrorists followed, black with suspicion, coiled in bandoliers, and were promptly corralled, with their nervous weapons, into sixteen assembly points around the periphery of the country. To fight the forthcoming election the political cadres arrived in town, men feared, hated, loathed, reviled, cheekily occupying key buildings and buying houses in the white suburbs, and no one was allowed to shoot them, though there were freelance attempts. I came back thanks to Berny Holzheimer and a few days later Liberty walked through the stained plywood of my front door, no doubt courtesy of the Central Committee. I embraced her with fervour.

'You're alive!'

She eyed my filthy, disordered room guardedly.

'And why shouldn't I be alive?'

Did she know that Esther, released from prison by the British and now eight months swollen with my child, received a stream of callers, comrades and sycophantic enemies alike, on the verandah of the Meyer home in Avondale while her father skulked in his study, waiting and hoping? I had not been invited and was too proud to impose myself, though I once spoke to Jane Meyer on the telephone:

'She's angry with me?'

'Esther's never angry. It's not in her nature.'

'She's offended by what I've written – by this narrative?'

'Dick, get this straight – it will be Zim's baby.'

'If, as Sartre tells us, "a man is what he does", then surely "a woman is whom she loves".'

But Jane could not be provoked; nor (I guessed) the daughter standing at her elbow.

How much of this did Liberty know as she walked into my flat and took a bath? She knew. It was a political question. The prestigious 'doctor', Esther's Zim, was back in town, reputedly the young godfather of the Central Committee and no doubt soon to be Minister of the Interior very regretfully administering the old colonial Emergency Powers, detention without trial, the lot, to fend off the machinations of the Imperialist Enemy. When the 'doctor' eventually threw me into Chikurubi there would be no exit. He'd already seen off our old friend General Knowledge, mysteriously killed in a 'plane crash' only hours before he was due to return to Salisbury. For him, burial in Heroes' Acre; for Zim, the Politburo.

The longer the phone rang the angrier it sounded. When Liberty finally lifted the receiver the sudden silence was that of an irate infant suddenly granted its tit.

'Comrade Liberty, Zanu PF!' she announced.

My growl was matched by the one at the end of the line. Sulkily she handed me the receiver, glowering reprovingly at the litter on my bedside table: a glass still carrying a puddle of ersatz whisky, three inhalers, a small alarm clock left in my home by a German publisher pursuing the Wunderkinder of the late Sixties, not least Richard Stern, friend of Rudi Dutschke and Daniel Cohn-Bendit, and the notebook in which I trapped the evidence of my dreams. Liberty made a close study of these when my back was turned, and then when it wasn't turned, even complaining about my tortured script.

'You describe your wife as a "creature of circumstance",' she complained. 'What can that mean?'

I took the receiver. 'Stern.'

'No way you can answer your own phone, Mr Stern?' Gilson said.

'At five-thirty in the morning? What does one have domestic servants for, Gilson?'

I could hear him shoving his thick gear lever into Self-Control.

372

'On behalf of the Ministry of Information and National Guidance—'

'Yes, yes.'

' – I'm instructed to inform you that a special facility trip will be leaving New Sarum at 0630 hours prompt and no delay for latecomers.'

'Why?'

'There has been a major incident. I'm not authorised to say more at this moment in time.'

'Another dirty trick to discredit the "Marxists"?'

'Listen, man, if you want to spend the day in bed with black terrorist cunt it's no skin off my nose.'

Liberty was sitting upright in bed, her powerful arms folded across her breasts, her hair still parted and braided close to her skull with soldierly precision, though I had not only caught her in front of the mirror wearing saucy underwear from the OK Bazaar but also found her with a copy of *Ebony* displaying slinky West Coast models in a variety of blooming Afro hairstyles. (And she continued to ask me, never satisfied with my affirmative reply, whether the women of Europe had commonly sold themselves for a tin of meat during 'World War II'. I suspect this topic fascinated her because she herself had experienced protracted, debilitating hunger in Mozambique.)

Grabbing my leather shoulder bag and a scarce spool of Kodak, I told her to be good.

'Look at your hair,' she protested. 'What would your mother say?' Liberty loved her own mother, miraculously still alive after two years in a 'protected village'.

'Smile,' I said.

I liked to observe her teeth, which were set both together and slightly apart, like strangers in a waiting room.

But the expression she offered me lay somewhere along a jungle frontier between a pout and a snarl.

'Tell them we're planning to abolish Christmas and put all white women in state brothels.'

Pointing my old Renault towards New Sarum, I imagined Tanner roused in Meikles Hotel from the flooded basement of a hangover by Gilson's early call.

('What the fuck?'

'Ah, good morning, Mr Tanner, the Minister apologises for disturbing you at this uncivilized hour but feels it is his duty to inform you that–')

Did I do I shall I feel pity for Tanner? Like so many other senior correspondents, he continued to measure his status by who received him and who didn't, gratefully licking the crumbs offered to a select band of British reporters on the shaded verandah of Government House by the newly installed Governor, a plum-voiced aristocrat who contrived most discreetly to hint, unattributably of course, strictly *entre nous*, that the Rhodesian rednecks at the helm of Combined Operations didn't always heed the referee's whistle when they got embroiled in a loose scrum – though the worst fouls – this is 'attributable' – undoubtedly emanated from the other, blacker, side.

'Governor, do you hold Mugabe personally responsible for the prevailing intimidation?' Tanner would ask.

A bland smile. 'Leonard, I suspect motive is best left to philosophers.'

They all agreed it was a minor miracle of mercy that Tanner was here at all, having been kicked sideways into Features by his new editor, Parker, then let out on a short leash for the duration of Rhodesia's second general election within a year.

At New Sarum I clambered out of the car, my back already sticking to my shirt, to be confronted by the eager greetings of the new boys and girls from Denmark, Sweden, Kenya, Japan and Germany, all flooding in for the election, a world story, latching on to the half-famous reporter the Rhodesians had put in prison because he knew too much. Most dreaded was the Japanese photographer who constantly reminded me that he worked for 'Tokyo main pepper'.

Tanner and the old Fleet Street sweats stood apart, aloof and contemptuous of the ignorant newcomers, preferring to exchange dire predictions with the Rhodesian journalists who had served in the security forces, half-listening to Mike Gilson's monotonous liturgy about the country he loved going, going, gone. 'Frankly, I don't understand the Brits, gentlemen, I wish I did, I really do. They're handing God's country to the gooks on a plate. That's off the record.'

Tanner and I scanned each other, briefly. I smiled at the handsome French woman newly arrived on behalf of *Le Monde*, who had rapidly concluded that Holzheimer and I were the most likely to know what was really going on.

'The name of the cast is the name of the drama,' Holzheimer told her, eagerly monitoring her enigmatic smile for appreciation. Then he turned to me: 'I called your apartment. I believe I was answered by the third Mrs Stern. Am I late or are they still laying out the bodies?'

'Are we both going on this?'

'You want the story?'

It was true. I wanted it. But perhaps I owed something to Berny. He nudged me at the approach of tiny Frieda Hersh, her frog smile

374

fixed in atonement for the recent disgrace and exile of her husband, the General. Seeing the lie of the land, Frieda veered, the wet-lipped Patrick Warner in tow, towards Tanner and his veterans. They ignored her. Beyond her waddling bum the Air Force rugby ground spread its sun-wasted turf towards a wall of flame trees, its four uprights padded at the base to protect the collar bones of reckless pilots. Gilson himself had once flown Dakotas, slow, steady: looking down on the killing fields of the veld he had seen the gooks scurrying 'like ants' and had known where civilization drew its bottom line. At the nearside of New Sarum, on a plinth, stood the mascot of civilization, a 1940 Spitfire.

Out of sight, a Hawker Hunter soared into the sky. There were still pilots itching to 'take out' the terrs in their assembly points, given a wink from above. Might the Governor himself be overheard to murmur, distractedly, 'Who will rid me of these awful guer-rillas?' – only to deplore the carnage the following day? 'These colonials never could distinguish between a sniff and a sneeze' (as Berny Holzheimer put it).

A convoy of three official cars was now racing towards us along the curving slip road, nose to tail, with the self-dramatising urgency of power. Brakes screeched, Special Branch bodyguards leapt out, and the dapper figure of Prinsloo emerged with inflated chest from the second Mercedes.

'Remind me what I think about Prinsloo,' Holz loudly asked the world at large in his high, nasal voice, his new Lexington Avenue bifocals glinting. It was Holz who had greeted the temporary return of the British under the Lancaster House agreement with the remark, 'This must be the only time in the history of de-colonis-ation that a black President was replaced by a white Governor.'

Like cattle converging on the arriving farmer, the reporters closed round the Minister of Information and National Guidance – who seemed not to have noticed that his and every other Rhodesian Cabinet portfolio had been abolished when the Governor assumed all executive functions.

Prinsloo cleared his throat. 'Gentlemen, in Churchill's day Britain was once a great nation. Then came the welfare state. And now she's a nation which has lost the will to govern. Frankly, the Afs are just laughing: they'll wipe their arses on this new constitution.'

The Danish, French, Swedish and Japanese correspondents gaped in amazement.

'Did you bring us here at six-thirty in the morning to tell us that?' Holz asked, not dignifying Prinsloo with his ministerial title. Prinsloo looked at him as if pondering the proper punishment while his Special Branch bodyguards stood impassive and watchful in the background, their huge legs sheathed in mini-shorts, their jaws steadily rotating on banana gum. Holzheimer had not grown more popular with Salisbury's internal establishment; only the previous day he had walked into a press conference given by the desperate Bishop, Prime Minister for 'a day and a night' but now on the skids, cracked a loud remark about the electronic security gate reminding him of an airport, and impertinently asked Muzorewa why he was flying around in South African helicopters. The tiny prelate had glowered:

'That is no business of any-body.'

Now Holz went for Prinsloo again: 'Where are the Governor's men this morning?' No answer. Holz turned to me. 'I want to know whether the Gov's bowels were functioning normally at 0815 Eastern Standard Time.'

'Gentlemen!' Prinsloo now raised his voice, fanning out chest and bum like a turkey cock, 'the Marxist terrorist has only one weapon in this election. Intimidation. He means to come to power through the barrel of a gun.'

'Wasn't that how you guys kept power for ninety years?' Holzheimer inquired innocently.

Prinsloo grappled with himself in a sublime effort at self-control. 'Gentlemen, what your Af wants is to live in peace with his wives, his *mombes*, his patch of mealies. So Mugabe goes to him and says, "Right, man, you want peace and I'll give you peace, but first you vote for me, for Jongwe, for the Cock. And if you don't vote for Jongwe we have a magic black box which will tell us." But some of our good Africans refuse to be intimidated. They want a moderate solution. Today, gentlemen, you'll witness the fate in store for them.'

Ten minutes later the Dakota lifted its seal nose into the eastern sky with thirty reporters and cameramen lined along the walls of the windowless fuselage like invalid paratroopers, each clutching a white cardboard box containing a chicken leg and lettuce leaf. To be heard you had to shout. Gilson was shouting a message of warning at the South Africans: evidently the KGB were already licking the caviar from their lips as they prepared to move south from Lusaka.

'Man, if I'm the last to leave I'll switch out the lights.'

'The third Mrs Stern.' In referring to Liberty as the 'third' of the species, Holz had generously thrown Esther into my polygamous empire of the night. 'There's one thing that bitch will never be,' my mother used to reiterate throughout my childhood, 'and that's the second Mrs Stern.' She referred of course to a lady who, I'm told, is now dead. According to the same source my father is still alive, lost in a botanical garden three degrees north of the

Equator. He sent a cheque for my thirtieth birthday. That was five years ago. The cheque would have been generous had it triumphantly concluded with a signature. There was none. I wrote 'Conrad P. Stern' in the empty space and my account was duly credited with the sum of thirty pounds. A year later the bank wrote debiting my account by the same amount, plus bank charges. I haven't heard from Conrad P. Stern since.

Holz, of course, knew all this. My only friend. He brought his mouth to my ear and roared against the roar:

'Last night a guy tried to sell me a "secret" film about Zimbabwean spirit mediums engaged in various ritual dances. He told me the first was a war dance, the second a hunting dance, the third was thanksgiving for rain and a good harvest, the fourth was some kind of trance by which they contact the ancestral spirits, the fifth was all about what to do with a village orphan, and the last one was a big lament for a dead chief. Frankly, I was puzzled.'

'Why?'

'Every dance was identical.'

The Dakota descended at an angle which brought pain to the ears – doubtless the pilot's way of reminding us, under instructions from Prinsloo, that the war wasn't necessarily over just because the British said it was. Berny was swallowing hard to fend off the pain and Tanner was grimacing pathetically as a ten-whisky hangover sloshed round his skull. Flopping out of the Dakota into an arid, grassless, wasteland graced only by a few, thin, contorted trees, the international press corps were confronted by a murderous sun and an arc of police pickup trucks carrying heavy machine guns.

'This certainly isn't Durban beach,' Holz protested. 'Maybe it's the Congo river. Anyone seen Kurz?'

'Buhera,' I told him.

His eyes widened. 'Oh sure. Wherever Stern finds himself, it's Buhera. *Buhera and Beyond and Back*, by Richard Stern.'

'May all your wives never die.'

The woman from *Le Monde* smiled faintly. Holz and I had begun to banter for her benefit, a recipe for disaster.

Prinsloo, secreted throughout the flight in the cockpit, had fallen into urgent conversation with a younger man whose sandy hair and glassy, china-blue eyes I knew well. I glanced at Tanner: no doubt he remembered the humiliating scene on Prinsloo's verandah, the lovely, long-legged Donna folding her diamond-glinting hand round her fiancé's while the Minister delivered his ultimatum? (Not that I was there.) As for Frieda Hersh, her frog grin now settled on me in plainest entreaty: 'Little Richard mustn't be a silly, impetuous boy.'

Prinsloo, donning a floppy bush hat against the sun, addressed us. 'Gentlemen—'

'We are not all gentlemen,' said the woman from *Le Monde*.

The veteran reporters slowly shifted their weight from one foot to the other. The muscle men on the TV camera crews sighed softly.

'I stand corrected,' said Prinsloo. 'Gentlemen, I shall now introduce you to a man who knows this area like the back of his hand. A man devoted to his people. They trust him like a father. Whatever happens here, he knows the score. Gentlemen, District Commissioner Chris Chamberlain.'

'That rings an unpleasant bell,' Holz murmured.

Chamberlain addressed us in the short, clipped tone of a busy man, a practical man, an administrator impatient with politicians and ideology:

'We in Buhera want to stage a free and fair election. But we have elements here who aren't playing ball. To my certain knowledge, terr – , er, guerrilla elements from assembly point X-Ray are regularly breaking the ceasefire agreement and intimidating our local population on behalf of Zanu-PF. As you know, we have no authority to enter any assembly point. We can only complain to the International Cease Fire Monitoring Force. We might as well complain to the moon about the heat of the sun. What we face here in Buhera, gentlemen, is part of a nation-wide conspiracy to subvert the process of democracy. Today we will show you the tragic victims of that conspiracy. Let me warn you: this isn't a spectacle for those with weak stomachs. OK, any questions? No? Good, let's hotfoot.'

The reporters were loaded into two open trucks, the police vehicles closing fore and aft as we set off along a rutted dirt track through desolate countryside strewn with boulders and kopjies, villages abandoned, deserted fields of wilting maize, the occasional skeletal *mombe* on its last legs observing our passage with reproachful eyes. The convoy threw up a dense cloud of dust which forced the cameramen to pull off their shirts to cradle their lenses.

'I recall you had a previous encounter with this man Chamberlain?' Holz murmured. 'Didn't we publish that story in the world's greatest newspaper?'

'He was head ephor.'

'A magistrate or censor in ancient Sparta? Must I suspend disbelief yet again?'

'It's what they call prefects at the Edinburgh Academy. It's nineteen years since he took off the blue blazer with its silver laurel leaf on the breast pocket, put down his clacken for the last time, bid farewell to the avenging tawse in the Doric-pillared Academy, and decided to lead a man's life in Southern Rhodesia. His father, once a missionary in Nyasaland, became Moderator of the Church of Scotland. His grandfather knew Livingstone and MacKinnon.'

'And he murdered some women and kids, is that it?'

'Yes. He's a psycho.'

'Ah.'

Frieda Hersh grinned as she listened in, her face grease-washed in fear.

I bit back the rest: this was going to be my story. A bad dream was gliding up at me like the fin of a surfacing shark; like the spike on Tanner's desk, the spike in Selwyn Foyle's vicious but now gouged-out eye. This time Tanner could only spike himself. I smiled at the woman from *Le Monde*.

Holz's elbow in my side. 'The fourth Mrs Stern?'

Removing his new bifocals, he slowly wiped off the coating of brown dust with his shirt.

'Hemingway always did this,' he explained. 'Tell me when we see our first vulture.'

The convoy lurched to an abrupt halt. Groping for their stomachs, the reporters waited passively to be offloaded, paralysed by anticipation of calamity. As the dust cloud settled we were beset by a stench of spilt petrol, and of something else. I glanced up: vultures.

With a commendable effort of will Tanner heaved himself to his feet, the doyen of the press corps.

'Well,' he announced, 'whatever it is, I've seen worse in the Punjab.'

The roof of the bus had collapsed; the overturned vehicle seemed to cry out for help in obscene dismay. Picking their way through the pools of oil and broken glass, the reporters gagged at the stench of burnt metal and fried flesh.

District Commissioner Chamberlain stood over his temporary morgue, instructing his black police constables to pull back the tarpaulin covering rows of bodies; men, women, kids; whole bodies and bits and pieces. Fragments of charred stickers, banners and UANC flags told their story. A journalist from Denmark vomited, precipitating a chain reaction.

'Sick is like laughter,' Tanner announced to no one in particular. Perhaps he was remembering thirty-nine Syrian soldiers blown to pieces on the Golan Heights after their tank convoy had been hit by Israeli Phantoms.

No one asked for the names of the dead. When white missionaries were slaughtered in the Vumba mountains we had demanded to know every detail of their biographies, ransacking their belongings for family snapshots, telephoning anguished relatives in

England as if their first duty was to flesh out our stories. But these corpses were just blacks; just so many 'Zimbabweans'.

'What's the story?' Tanner asked Chamberlain.

'The bus whose remains you see was hit by a Communist-manu-factured rocket while returning from a lawful UANC rally at 4.15 yesterday. The rocket penetrated the driver's cab, killing him instantly. The bus overturned and caught fire. Those passengers who managed to crawl from the burning wreckage were then met with murderous small arms fire.'

He gestured to one of his black District Assistants, who prod-uced a sack full of spent cartridges. Chamberlain plunged his hand in:

'These are Communist-manufactured AK 47 bullets, calibre 7.62mm, weight 7.89 grammes.'

'Ballistics?' I said.

The District Commissioner's blue eyes focused on me. Clusters of freckles spread across his face like iodine stains.

'Yes, Mr Stern. Ballistics.'

'District Commissioner, where are your Pfumo reVanhu auxili-aries?' I asked.

'There are no SF auxiliaries now operating in this area.'

'Since when?'

'Since the Governor, in his wisdom, ordered the SF auxiliaries, a fine bunch of men, withdrawn.'

Frieda Hersh had wriggled to my side. 'Silly little Richard,' she whispered.

'You claim these people were massacred by Zanla guerrillas from one of the assembly points?' Holzheimer asked Chamberlain.

'From X-Ray.'

Prinsloo spoke up. 'Gentlemen, we have leant over backwards to be fair to all parties. And this is our reward, this is the factual situation we find ourselves in. Frankly, it makes me weep.'

A police officer led forward the prize exhibit, a handcuffed prisoner dressed in the camouflage fatigues commonly worn by Zanla guerrillas. The reporters stared at him as at a caged beast, immediately identifying the facial tattoos, the broad nose and the heavy lips as evidence of barbarous debasement.

I remembered the distinctive quarter-moon tattoos on the auxiliary sergeant's cheeks; did Frieda remember? I glanced side-ways and down; her fixed and frightened leer yielded its answer.

The police officer now produced a neat array of supplementary exhibits, all reportedly found on the prisoner: a box of Australian matches (Australian troops formed part of the Monitoring Force); a finger ring embossed 'Zanu PF'; an AK 47 rifle with ammunition pouches; and a diary.

Asked whether he admitted he was Comrade Elias Rusike (Chimurenga name 'Rolling Stone'), the owner of the diary, the prisoner nodded in sullen confirmation. And yes, he also admitted he had strayed out of X-Ray assembly point in contravention of the ceasefire terms.

'Did you take part in the massacre of these people?' Tanner asked. 'Did you kill them?'

The prisoner lowered his eyes. 'No, sir, I never. I never seen these dead peoples until they bring me here to this place. I was far away, sleeping under certain trees and watching Security Forces helicopters coming . . .'

Neither Prinsloo nor Chamberlain looked irritated by this denial. They were almost nodding encouragement.

Tanner grunted sceptically: 'How could you be both sleeping and watching?'

Frieda Hersh grinned. 'Leonard, the Shona word "*kurara*" means both to sleep and to lie down. He means he was lying down under a tree . . .'

I saw her look appealingly towards Prinsloo and Chamberlain. The great Hersh had crashed into exile and now Frieda was licking the boots of his conquerors. She had nothing else to offer but her moist tongue.

The police inspector led forward two witnesses, introducing them as the only bus passengers to have survived the massacre. Shown the prisoner, they had no hesitation in identifying him as one of the 'several' guerrillas who had attacked the bus.

I asked the prisoner the name of his Zanla section commander in X-Ray. He hesitated and Chamberlain immediately intervened: 'Those terrorist elements in X-Ray will deny all knowledge of this man.'

'I'm still asking him to name his section and his section commander.'

The prisoner caught the District Commissioner's eye and threw a name at us.

I asked the prisoner when he acquired his embossed ring. He shrugged. 'In seventy-seven,' he said after a pause.

'Which finger do you wear it on?'

He produced his right hand, which didn't surprise me, since the fourth finger of his left hand was missing.

Presently the reporters withdrew from the stench to open their white cardboard lunch boxes, instinctively moving into two sympathy groups: the veterans who gathered round Prinsloo, Chamberlain and the police inspector, seeking further corroboratory evidence of Zanla's guilt; and the 'progressives' who instinctively smelt another 'dirty trick' behind this charnel-house.

Leonard Tanner wandered alone in no-man's-land, grim and suspicious, unable to affiliate to either party.

Holzheimer drew me aside: 'Your question about the guy's embossed ring: what was the thrust of that, Holmes?'

'Elementary, my dear Watson. The term "Zanu PF" was imposed on Mugabe's party only four week's ago by court order—'

Holz whistled in remembrance. 'To distinguish them from Sithole's Zanu, right?'

'Correct.'

'And he didn't seem to know the name of his section commander in X-Ray.'

I nodded.

'So the whole operation's a fake designed to force the Governor to ban Zanu PF on the eve of the election?'

'Of course.'

'In short, Chamberlain killed forty-one people.'

'Aha.'

'Single-handed!'

'He used his faithful Pfumo reVanhu auxiliaries.'

'But he denied they were deployed in this area any longer.'

'I know he did.'

'But can we prove it?'

I shrugged agnostically: was this the most dishonourable moment in my entire life? Had Holz pressed me further I might have capitulated to my love of the man, but the shot that rang out caused us all to jump out of our skins and hurl ourselves down, cowering and sweating. Only Tanner stood his ground, though he did turn involuntarily, as he had turned sixteen years ago at a zebra crossing in King Street, Hammersmith.

Twenty yards from the official party the prisoner lay stone dead, a neat hole through the back of his skull.

'Shot while attempting to escape,' Chamberlain calmly announced. The proverbial smoking gun lay, as might have been anticipated, in the District Commissioner's hand. I experienced the same lurch in the gut I'd felt when the same gun confronted me one Sunday in Paul Meyer's house. But it was the loyal auxiliary sergeant who had been sacrificed, not the white jackal: that's colonialism.

I had never seen Holz so far advanced into rage.

'You really expect us to believe that! You really take us for dupes!'

The photographers were hard at work on the corpse – I took a few more shots myself of the half-moon tattoos and the hand with the missing finger. Unfortunately I had never been given the photographs Frieda had taken that day when the young *mujiba*, only eleven years old, Sorgachas was his name, had been hanged on Chamberlain's orders by the Pfumo reVanhu sergeant who now lay dead. Nor had she given me her pictures of Chamberlain's 'ballistics' massacre. I hadn't delivered Esther to her hubby and when I did it was by accident.

Four hours later Tanner was first on his feet after the Governor's spokesman concluded his statement to the evening press conference in the Stewart Room of Meikles Hotel.

The Governor's spokesman nodded smoothly in his direction. Tanner usually asked the right questions. 'Yes, Mr Tanner?'

'After forty years in this profession—'

'Oh God,' Berny murmured.

'I believe I know cheese from chalk. Chalk doesn't stink. What stank today in Buhera wasn't simply forty-one corpses. My question is this: before reaching any final conclusion, with possibly momentous consequences for the future of this country, will the Governor meet a delegation of correspondents who today witnessed this appalling scene?'

I thought: at the last post on the course, those who write for *The Times*, the *Telegraph* and the *Guardian* invariably wish they had been politicians rather than journalists.

Even so, the Governor's spokesman was disconcerted by
     Tanner's talk
     Of cheese and chalk.

'Well, yes. I think I made it clear that Government House does not by any means regard the investigation into this dreadful incident as concluded.'

Berny sprang to his feet, discarding his round shoulders.

'Holzheimer, *New York Times*.'

The Governor's spokesman regarded him warily. And nodded.

'With respect, sir, you didn't give this correspondent quite that impression. I understood you to say that you were satisfied with the report of the District Commissioner for Buhera.'

'By his *interim* report. Two nations divided by a common language, Mr Holzheimer.' The Governor's spokesman offered the ghost of a smile.

Holz sat down. 'I try not to hate the British.'

'They're all masters of the dead bat.'

'Of the what?'

'Cricket.'

'A dead bat's a cricket? Is this the newest thing in the British school of natural history?'

A Scandinavian correspondent was now on his feet trying to channel his 'ten urgent questions' through the English language. The Governor's spokesman smiled affably, agreeing to everything and nothing. Likewise with the urgent Japanese from Tokyo main pepper.

'Thank you, Mr Yamomoto.'

I stood up. 'Stern, *New York Times*.'

I am very tall and quite noticeable, but the Governor's spokesman had gradually perfected the art of not seeing me. He pointed to someone behind me. 'I believe the lady was first,' he drawled into his microphone. I turned; it was the handsome woman from *Le Monde*.

'I give my question to Mr Stern,' she said. 'Otherwise I think we don't hear from him.'

And I knew, then, that Madeleine would indeed become the second Mrs Stern – though she herself has always insisted that she had no such premonition and thought only of the forty-one pathetic corpses laid out on a dirt track in Buhera. A burst of applause from the newcomers and idealists greeted her gallant challenge to the Governor's spokesman. The temperature was rising in the Stewart Room of Meikles Hotel, where Ian Smith used to tell the press, 'We have been betrayed, but I try to resist bitterness.'

With a shrug the Governor's spokesman accorded me the floor.

'A question please, Mr Stern, not your nightly statement.'

(A trickle of laughter from the back rows, where Gilson and the Rhodesians customarily sat out these conferences in sullen isolation.)

'One gets one's laughter where one can, Mr Fenn,' I said. 'What steps is the Governor taking to bring to trial former-Minister Prinsloo, District Commissioner Chamberlain and the Pfumo reVanhu detachment under his command for the murder of forty-one black civilians in Buhera?'

Uproar. The Rhodies were all on their feet. The Governor's man looked as if he expected an immediate military coup by Combined Operations.

'I suppose,' sighed Holz, 'that's what I would have said had my psychiatrist permitted it.'

The Governor's spokesman assured me, in the urbane tone cultivated in the Foreign Office's language laboratory, that, as usual, I was well able to answer my own questions without his assistance.

'That's not an answer!' cried the woman from *Le Monde*.

Uproar again. I could see Frieda Hersh quivering with mounting excitement, jelly-roll and Michelin tyre, desperately weighing the odds – did she still possess those photographs? Would Prinsloo, Chamberlain, Desai and the Bishop's communion cabinet ever accept surrender terms from hubby? – then she was up on her stumps crying out her Canossa:

'Given the incontrovertible evidence of Zanu-PF's responsibility for this atrocious massacre, and in the light of the Governor's many warnings to that Marxist party about its systematic policy of intimidation, will His Excellency now take the only step consistent with a free and fair election, not to mention Britain's honourable reputation, and ban Zanu-PF forthwith?'

The Rhodesians applauded, much as they detested her. She beamed, radiant: the exiled Hersh had only to say, ' 'Oo's Nkomo?' on South African radio and all would be forgiven.

'The Governor does have that course of action under constant review,' his spokesman assured Mrs Hersh.

The reporters stampeded for the telephones and telex machines. The British and Europeans had only half-an-hour to meet their deadlines, whereas Holzheimer and I enjoyed (a fatal?) five hours' geographical grace. Through the milling lobby of gossip and intrigue I saw the lonely Tanner stomping away; the bottle would open before he faced his typewriter and would stay open until after the vans had carried his front-page story from Holborn to King's Cross. Or would Hugh Parker relegate him to page 6: 'Buhera Incident Raises More Questions than It Answers, by Leonard Tanner'?

I offered my hand to Madeleine. 'Thank you for your support.'

She appraised me with the slow, searching scrutiny she accorded to everything and everyone in this dubious universe – even our baby son Jimmy if he performed his natural functions with less than Gallic precision.

'You're sure the District Commissioner was responsible for the massacre?' she asked.

'Yes.'

'Minister Prinsloo was definitely involved?'

'Yes.'

'They shot the prisoner because you knew something about the man?'

A thick circle of bystanders was eagerly pressing round us, reporters, Special Branch informers, the Governor's retainers, news agency men, diplomats, a couple of officers from the Cease Fire Monitoring Force who had already announced that no such Zanla section commander existed in X-Ray assembly point as the one named by the prisoner shortly before he 'attempted to escape'.

Madeleine did not repeat her question. 'Well, it's your story,' she said and walked away.

Holzheimer dragged me down the stairs and out of the hotel towards his car, which was parked on the Stanley Avenue side of Cecil Square, opposite the long line of flower sellers. The tip of the Pioneer flagpole appeared between the exotic trees imported by the old, colonial municipality – or would have done were not darkness rapidly descending.

'How about my place?' Berny suggested, nervously reading me from behind his bifocals. 'I suppose we never did cover the same story before.' I was silent. 'There's no harm in a joint by-line, Richard. OK, you want to sulk. I think that's unprofessional. The first rule of 229 West 43rd Street is "never sulk".'

'And the second rule is "Give your story to Holzheimer"?'

An African poked his head through the open window of the car, offering a carved chess set wrapped in greasy paper.

'Twenty dollar, bargain price. Beautiful, beautiful, look, sir, look.'

'Berny, I think this is my story.'

'Yeah? Must I remind you that we work for the same newspaper, the greatest in the world? Must I remind you that I had something to do with that?'

'All right, sirs, only eighteen bargain for you special special for you.'

'And the salary, Berny – why not mention the handsome salary? Why do you have to have *this* story?'

I had never seen Holzheimer tremble before. The whole cool West Coast façade peeled away; his crow's voice rasped like a metal saw.

'Because this is the big one! Because I was there! If I'd been in Zambia or Mozambique I'd have called to congratulate you, but I am Southern African correspondent of this goddam paper and I was there and I do not wish to . . .'

'Worth fifty dollar! Look, look, thirty-two pieces, made in Great Zimbabwe.'

'Wish to what?'

'OK. OK. Fifteen dollar, very last offer, sir, sir . . .'

'Oh, fuck off,' I said – but to whom? – climbing out of Holz's car, recognising myself in myself, the apparently predetermined chain of impulses and reactions which is the true, unwritten, biography on every man's headstone. I hailed a Rixi taxi and drove, for the first time since my return to Rhodesia, to the Meyer home in Avondale. Striding through the open french window of the living room, I was waylaid by Jane, a cigarette dangling from her lips.

We embraced rather cautiously. During the months of Esther's clandestine activity Jane had treated me as a friend, but now the heavy, tanned woman faced me with manifest animosity, folding her arms across her breast.

'It isn't your baby, Dick. My daughter is a married woman –

yet you have the audacity to announce to the world that you are the father of her coming child!'

'Where's Esther?'

Jane shook her head in refusal. 'Go upstairs, you'll find Paul rotting in his study, terrified by the prospect of a black grandchild.'

'The Governor is about to ban the party.'

Jane screwed her eyes against the smoke drifting up from her cigarette.

'Try party headquarters.'

I pushed my way up through the excited crush of black bodies on the stairway of Zanu PF headquarters in Manica Road, stopped on every landing by excited ex-guerrillas equipped with walkie-talkies who rummaged through my shoulder bag, squeezed my balls to see if they were really grenades, shouting, shouting, 'Your business? Your business?' The Intercontinental Hotel in Geneva all over again.

Never during the war itself had I experienced such racial tension in the city.

Reaching the top landing, I saw the 'doctor' emerge from the room in which the central committee was meeting in emergency session. Once again Zimunya sported the mirrored sunglasses Cubans Urimbo used to wear in the days when the game was to let me sniff the bitch behind every tree in the park. He greeted me with lazy affability.

'You've come to tell us that the Governor is about to ban the party.'

'The massacre in Buhera was a put-up job.'

He nodded. 'Of course.'

'I can prove it.'

He laughed. 'Oh yes. Just as you "proved" how my wife's child is really yours. You have a gift for hyperbole.'

'I can also prove that you were involved in the murder of General Chimurenga.' This was said loudly, in the hearing of the ex-guer-rillas crowded around us, men devoted to the memory of General Knowledge. In the hearing of Esther, too, for she had emerged from the committee room in a billowing beige maternity frock, her long brown hair tied in a severe bun. But which hospital would she choose: the Andrew Fleming, strictly for white infants out of white mothers, or the sprawling clamour of Harare Hospital where anything comes and anything goes? I always wanted to tie a tin can to a cat's tail but never had a cat. I constantly asked for one as a boy but mother said it would claw and spoil the furniture (which she and Monty sold to foreign dupes as 'antique'). Mother preferred to use her own claws on the fabric of souls – I simply can't comprehend how my sister Rachel grew into the generous, well-adjusted anthropologist and mother-of-three who occasionally writes to me, 'Dear Bean' – having dropped the 'stalk' I remember not when.

'Well, Richard?' These were the first words Esther had spoken to me in eight months; the first since she stood with me under the baobab tree in Buhera and told Hersh that I had been abducted by Zanla. They had not allowed us to speak to each other after that.

I said: 'Are you well, Esther?'

'Yes, thank you. And you?'

'You realise the Governor is about to ban the party?'

Zimunya said: 'Richard claims he can prove how the fascist régime staged the massacre in Buhera. I gather he wishes to offer the treasure to us – or to you: I suspect there may be a price.'

I nodded and held out my hand to her. The bodyguards, militants, place-seekers and petitioners parted on the staircase to let us through: each and every one of them murmured to Esther with deep affection.

We drove through the city in silence. And when we reached my flat we found the place ransacked, with poor Liberty crumpled against my desk, the fine weave of plaits across her skull soaked in blood, one half of her face shattered by an immense blow from an axe.

Esther sank to her knees by her friend, sobbing.

I found a screwdriver and removed the back plate of the refrigerator – Frieda's photographs were intact, securely wrapped in layers of cellophane. She had given them to me after all, of course she had, and never mind the seizure of my papers from the flat in Baines Avenue after my arrest, I had taken certain precautions . . . I pulled Esther to her feet, lifting her off her comrade's body, and threw her across the bed. Only then did I see how pregnancy had stolen her beauty; thick at the throat, dull of eye, her once-luminous skin opaque, the seductive dimple now lost for ever in the swollen yeast of her cheek, she was already a solid matron who had surrendered to biological destiny. I saw the vast line of patient black women sitting outside the hospital on a low brick wall, waiting through the day to display the effortless fertility which Mrs Tanner dreamed of, the mechanical reproduction which would subvert every education programme, every economic plan, every stab at progress. Occasionally the women looked in my direction and laughed shyly – the only white men seen here at Harare Hospital were doctors and secret policemen. Watching the children weaving along the hospital verandah, enjoying the constraints of a man-made space, I tried to imagine a birth, the moment of birth, where neither the mother nor medicine had predicted the child's colour. But all my imagination would yield was the Charles Addams cartoon of a screaming nurse bursting out of a maternity ward and passing the bemused father, from whose innocent brow sprouted two devil's horns.

Then I saw Mrs Jane Meyer emerge from the hospital, walking towards me across the stony ground with the lowered head and cautious step of a woman suddenly invaded by old age.

THIRTY-FOUR

'I've been trying to reachya. Whereya been?'

Paul Meyer's new home in Highlands was even more opulent than the one he had recently vacated in Avondale. Invited to Sunday lunch, Stern parked his hired Renault in front of a car porch graced by a Mercedes and a BMW. Hearty guffaws and girlish shrieks interspersed with splashes greeted him from beyond a fake Moorish wall, but when he turned the corner and saw the verandah the sound effects suddenly died, they too were a fake. This wasn't the over-spilling Meyer gathering he had inspected, week after week, in Avondale, this was Paul and two unknown young women waiting for the only other guest; Paul had sought him out so that the two pariahs might consume each other in a slow feast of mutual loathing.

'Hey, Dick, come on in!' Paul yelled, hauling himself from the chlorinated water with a thick mat of sodden hair clinging to his chest and back like seaweed. The two girls were basking and giggling in the pool. One was pretty, one was plain: both American. Paul mumbled their names but Stern didn't listen.

'It's great,' the plain one called.

'Nice house,' Stern murmured.

'Yeah, it's an investment – though I guess real estate prices will fall through the floor as soon as the Brits wave goodbye.'

'I assume you're delighted by Mugabe's victory – as any Marxist would be?'

'He'll slap a fifty dollar minimum wage on domestic service.'

'At least fifty – surely you approve?'

'Yeah. The number of blacks in service will be halved overnight. Capital will take off.' He thumped his right fist into his left hand, but more silently than ever.

Towelling himself, Paul headed for the verandah, where a servant was laying out cold meats and salads for lunch.

'Drink?'

Turning, Stern saw the pretty one emerging from the pool looking half-way to Hollywood.

'Doreen's hard to get, I warn ya,' Paul growled. 'Try her at tennis after lunch. She doesn't like losing.'

'Sorry about everything,' Stern said.

'You're sorry and I'm sorry, so now we've said it.'

The two girls came and spread their bodies in sundowner chairs on the verandah, the plain one choosing to lie in the sun, the pretty one preferring the shade.

'So what brings you to Zimbabwe, Dick?' the plain one asked.

Paul handed him a scotch on the rocks. 'I'll show ya the house. It cost me in excess of one hundred thousand so ya'd better like it!'

Paul stomped from one show-room to the next, like a museum guide who'd forgotten to wear a shirt, his voice throttling down to a purr every time he contemplated another item of 'unobtainable' furniture: a desk of Finnish beech, a Klober Sitzcomfort desk chair on wheels, a lamp by Ingo Maurer, 'Japanese-influence'. A salmon-pink sofa by Conran. 'Maybe *after* Conran,' Paul murmured doubt-fully, 'you have to live with ersatz in this part of the world.'

The prevailing motif was black leather and chrome, awful.

'What's the use of a hi-fi without cassettes?' Paul asked the world at large. 'Jane kept the lot, did I tellya that? Vindictive, Dick, but thereyare. Can't get a videocorder, no way. Next time ya come out from London bring me a Sanyo, I'll pay a good commission.'

Stern trailed after him into a kitchen fitted with chrome stools shaped like tractor seats and a shy 'cookboy' whom Paul identified out of the side of his mouth. 'Wanna see the bedroom?'

'Must we?'

'Dick, if ya knew more about bedrooms I'd have a white grandson.'

Nearing the air base the traffic had slowed to a crawl. The coach in front of him carried a German registration plate: it was full of peace women from Hamburg. Police motorcyclists with crackling radios sprinted up and down the jam like despairing sheepdogs, and the great motoring public, facing a ruined Saturday, dreamed of firing nuclear warheads at anti-nuclear demonstrators. Stern saw pink faces blistered with rage at the entrance to the local golf club as two women in anoraks, gum boots and woolly caps walked along the line of cars distributing leaflets describing 'The Coming Holocaust'. The appended map showed a small section of southern England dotted with missiles, bombs and warplanes: USAF, RAF Strike Command, NATO Air Command, bunkers, bolt holes for the warmongers. '*Your* future in *their* hands. Take it back.'

Stern smiled at the two busy women in anoraks. 'I agree,' he called.

Finally Stern pulled his car off the road on to the grass verge and began to walk. After half an hour he saw wire and gates; the crackling of police radios grew louder and there was always the sense of something more important, 'the real thing', the weapon itself, just out of sight. A group of young women in drab colours, insulated like Tibetans, were dancing clumsily to recorders; passing them, two elderly women hesitantly picked their way through a quagmire of mud under the banner 'Grannies against the Bomb'. (Catching his stare, one of them turned on him with a fiendish grin as relentless as an electric light.) He noticed that the crowd round the outer perimeter remained an aggregate of individuals, each jealous of its independence, hesitating on the brink of total, collective commitment like sinners peering warily from purgatory into heaven.

The mad lady was still grinning at him.

'You can't sit on the fence round here. Pull it down!'

She had said that perhaps a hundred times since she crawled out of her tent or survival bag at dawn.

He progressed as if at a fair ground, admiring the 'exhibits' affixed to the outer fence – a teddy bear, photographs of children, a cardboard cut-out of a family, a clean nappy, a wedding dress – moving from one 'stall' or 'event' to the next until he reached the 'real thing', a group of women who had fastened themselves to the wire by means of a bafflingly intricate skein of coloured wool. Policemen stood around them, non-plussed, their eyes in neutral, waiting for an order. Other women watched the police watch the tied-up women. Stern watched everyone and occasionally noticed someone watching him. Police excepted, there weren't many men about; he wondered whether it would be Beth or Hattie who emerged from the crowd to order his expulsion from the peace camp.

The voices – encouraging, exhorting, demanding – over the loudspeakers were women's voices. Welcome to the sisters from Holland. Welcome to the sisters from Hamburg ('his' bus in the traffic jam). Greetings to our comrades in Holloway gaol.

From behind the wire baby-faced soldiers watched. The Action Men and pocket computers they had been given for Christmas had not prepared them for this baffling outburst of inchoate uxorial wailing and wire-cutting.

It wasn't Beth he'd come for, but Harry. If he found Harry, he would kill him. Stern pushed on through crowds of women with crow's feet of concern etched under their intelligent eyes, until he reached the bivouac area of flapping fly sheets, polythene shelters, straw bales, blackened kettles suspended over fires, clothes lines sagging under the weather. Here, then, was the bandits' camp: the core of the hard core; the ones in and out of court. You can't kill the spirit, she is like a mountain old and strong, she goes on and on . . . Here pale skins were shyly illuminated by the reluctant light of a northern winter, the light that clears the head and disperses lethargy, the light that had launched the great Scottish engineers and the industrial revolution.

'Nuclear stockpiles and first-strike missiles represent the suicidal aggression of patriarchy!'

The megaphone distorted the urgent voice; it required a moment's audit before he was sure it was Beth's.

'Sisters, we are embracing this air base and we will go on embracing it by non-violent action until our love suffocates the men of war!'

Pressing towards the source of this hugely disseminated woman-voice, Stern realised too late that he was passing the notorious Gate 4, site of the Gulag marquee where rows of captive men sat chained to tables, making marmite sandwiches. Attempting to gallop past, he was instantly grabbed by a woman steward of horribly familiar physiognomy.

Hattie held a small, forlorn boy by the hand.

'Don't just stand there doing nothing, Richard. Take Jimmy for a walk round the play area. He may want to wee.'

'Wee? Pee? Where's his mother?'

Hattie studied him with owl eyes. 'She's liable to be arrested any moment.'

'God.'

The boy looked up at him sceptically, trailing snot, saw a camel among the pyramids, then lowered his head to level with the intelligible universe. Beneath the little red trousers Stern discerned the bulge of nappies.

Beth's voice rose over the horizon again, remote, huge, distorted, almost stranger than the giant Galaxy transport planes remorselessly landing and lifting against a pale, autumnal, water-washed sky a mile away: 'Sisters, we stand shoulder to shoulder, twenty thousand of us here today, against the patriarchy which would plunge our children into the final holocaust.'

He smiled grimly down at the boy then picked him up and smelt stinky pooh.

—You can pretend to want a child, Richard, she had said four years ago, on the telephone from Leeds or Manchester,—because you won't have to shovel the cabbage in one end and the shit out the other.

'Stinky poohs,' he told the boy.

'Mummy,' the boy said.

Stern nodded sympathetically. 'Who's your Mummy?'

'Mummy.'

'What's Mummy's name?'

'Name.'

'Mummy's name?'

'Mummy.' The boy paused, then jabbed Stern in the eye. 'Daddy,' he said.

Stern said: 'Jimmy, the world is made of marzipan and methodical constables. Of nectar and neat, clean policewomen in penguin-starched uniforms. Of anorexia and anoraked health-food women, successors to Orwell's bearded fruit-juice drinkers, with heavy, resistant, sack-bodies destined for the waiting vans. Yes, Jimmy?'

Paul began heaping food on to his own plate. 'Helpyaself, helpyaself.' Stern studied the plainer girl: she knows she's overweight but she can't help herself, she's going to eat.

He had toyed with the idea of bringing Madeleine but decided against it.

Faced with a mound of meat cuts, pâté, cheese, beansprouts, beetroot, potato salad, Paul settled down to wolf his last meal on earth.

'Didya know my father's dying, Dick?'

'Is that the presser who stood for thirty years over a steaming iron in a West Side factory? The one who always bought tickets to the Yiddish theatre in the Bronx because he thought it was a scandal to see fellow Jews "dying of hunger three times a day"? The party militant who sold the *Daily Worker* down at the bus terminal every Sunday?'

'Yeah.'

'He's dying where?'

'Miami.'

'Did the International Ladies Garment Workers' Union buy him a little bungalow down there?'

394

'He's worth seven figures, my Dad,' Paul said, refilling his wine glass and pushing the bottle towards Stern.

'Only seven? Esther told me eight.'

Paul almost dropped his fork. 'She talked t'ya about my Dad? Did Jane also talk, eh?'

Stern shrugged. 'Merely that he's a textile tycoon.'

Cautiously Paul resumed his eating, as if it were now safe to do so. The plain girl was ingesting steadily; the pretty one, Doreen, who had hardly touched the food, was patiently massaging her limbs with suntan cream. Stern wanted her.

'When McCarthy chased my ass out of America, my Dad cut me out of his will,' Paul said.

'Was that before or after you named names to the Committee?'

Paul wasn't thrown. He was waiting for it. Presumably the poor man had spent much of his life expecting people to find out.

'Ya nose was always high in the air, Dick, but a girl can't go to bed with a nose. Ask Esther.' He turned to the pretty one. 'I bet Dick makes love like an intellectual.'

'Is that bad?' the plain one asked.

Paul sighed. 'A khaki grandson, Jesus. Heaven help me if my Dad ever hears of it. *She* would tell him of course but she daren't because she wants to grab half his estate.'

'I thought he cut you out of his will.'

'Yeah but then he had this major operation some years later and I flew home and showed him photos of Esther and he forgave me. Cancer of the throat, it was. The doctors thought it would finish him but only atomic war will finish him.'

Pushing through the crowd, he headed for Gate 6, sometimes slipping in the mud, his breath cloudy in the frosted air, his bare fingers blue and numb round the little boy. Pulled by the loudening crackle of police radios, the urgent signals of counter-insurgency, the cries of women being surprised and hurt, Stern strode on in pursuit of Harry's white mane which kept vanishing in the mists of England, into the double line of women fifty yards along the outer perimeter fence, heaving, straining, striving in concert to uproot the ten-foot-high wire mesh.

'Mummy,' the boy told him.

'Pigs!' he shouted. 'We've evacuated ourselves!'

The boy burst into tears because the man carrying him had unexpectedly raised his voice and because the boy had seen the raven's beak suddenly grow longer and sharper. Jimmy stopped crying equally swiftly when a metallic shriek of triumph from the women signalled that a section of the fence had finally peeled away from its concrete supports and collapsed.

'Fight!' Stern cried. 'Fight!'

Women eyed him with suspicion. Had he not carried a child in his arms, this tall, lunatic male, they would have fallen upon him and savaged him with tooth and claw. Avoiding a police cordon directly ahead of him, Stern veered off the muddy track and plunged into the surrounding woodland, tripping over roots, stumbling in ditches, his face slapped by naked winter branches. The boy began to cry, his little soft cheeks suddenly red and sore.

Stern stopped. 'Sorry, Jimmy.' He kissed the boy's cheek and ruffled his flaxen hair, then found a handkerchief to wipe the snot from a nose whose length Stern was moved to admire. Reconciled, the two of them plunged back out of the wood and into the thick of the fray, at the point where a chain of women was blocking the exit of two buses loaded with American servicemen at Gate 6. Beth's voice rose again on the megaphone, closer, more urgent:

'Don't use your hands, don't fight! Don't give them a pretext to arrest you, Sisters, just stand your ground. Remember this is *your* country they're condemning to death! It's *your* children who *they've* decided are expendable!'

'What does she know about children?' Stern asked the boy. 'Didn't she find you expendable, Jimmy? Didn't she abort you?'

'Mummy,' Jimmy said.

Stern saw that he was the only male demonstrator in sight, apart from Harry. But Harry was hiding. Stern plunged towards the lines of police.

'Lackeys!' he yelled. 'Mercenaries!'

A woman shouted a warning to her comrades; several hands grabbed him, but gently because he held the child. Feeling like Gulliver among the Lilliputians, he thrust laterally through the crowd of women which parted before him almost in revulsion, as if he were a creature monstrous of aspect, and then he saw the bravest ones being dragged through the mud, wet and filthy, hurled into the blue vans. The continuous shrieking chilled him; the boy had begun to scream.

'Mummy!'

Stern saw two policemen converge on Beth. One ripped the megaphone from her hand; the other grabbed her round the neck. They lifted her, little light Beth, kicking and screaming – this was the sort that refused to be bound over, defied injunctions against trespass, or jumped bail and came straight back like a jill-in-the-box to resume the whole cycle of civil disobedience, bringing chaos to a quiet rural community, filth, toilet paper and sanitary pads in

the bushes, police leave cancelled, an urban agitator, a
cunt.

'Mummy!'

The boy was reaching out to her, straining. Stern took a step
towards her through the mud, small restraining hands clutching at
his clothes from behind . . .

'So I said to Jane, "Whatya want those cassette tapes for, since
when didya ever listen to Barbirolli and Horowitz?" Dick, that
woman is screwing me for half my Dad's fortune. Oh, she's smart.
She sends private eyes up here to spy on me. I offered her the
house in Avondale and twenty thousand a year in return for a
written declaration of "no interest" in my Dad's will. No way.
You bet some sharp lawyer is right behind her, pushing her on'.

Doreen recrossed her lovely oiled legs, dutifully shielded from
the sun.

Paul couldn't be stopped. 'Ever hear of a nuisance action, Dick?
Ya challenge a will, ya litigate, ya hold up a settlement for years.
Finally ya force ya victim to compromise, to settle. He shells out.'

'But you and Jane aren't even married,' the plain girl said plaintively, 'I can't see how she can do that!'

Paul Meyer was staring at his swimming pool and the avocado
trees beyond.

'I've always rejected bourgeois conventions,' he muttered. 'I
guess I'm an anarchist at heart . . . Jane knew how I felt . . .'

'And you wept the day Kennedy was assassinated,' Stern said.

'Yeah . . .' Abruptly Paul reached forward to grab the last slice
of beef, dipped it messily in horseradish, smeared it in Dijon
mustard, slapped his tongue against the roof of his mouth, then
gouged angrily between his teeth.

'They're in the game together, mother and daughter,' he said.
'They're goading me into evicting Jane from Avondale so that the
whole town will turn on me and drive me out of the country. As
for the black doctor, he's no fool either: having put the bun in the
oven he means to pull out a loaf with at least three zeros.'

Silence on the verandah.

'Isn't black good?' the plain girl said.

'Black is good for black.'

'You didn't *have* to leave your wife and daughter,' she whined.

'That's my business.'

'Sorry I spoke.' She looked up longingly at Stern. 'Dick, forgive
my asking this but were ya Esther's lover or something? I mean
Doreen and I only flew in from the States last week. . . '

Paul snorted. 'What Dick's got between his legs is a fine prose style.'

Doreen stirred, stretching her arms behind her head to display the curve of her breasts. 'I'd like to see this man's fine prose style,' she purred.

This was too much for Paul. 'And if he has a friend in town apart from me, black or white, I'm the flying Dutchman. Jesus! Ya should hear Berny on this guy. Berny was his *only* friend, his meal ticket. Talk about professional ethics!'

'I've never had an Englishman,' Doreen said.

Half-a-dozen paces across Paul's verandah and he had picked Doreen off her feet, another small, light body, smelled her cologne and suntan cream, stood very still as her tongue slid into his mouth, his fingers impaled in the meat of her thigh.

She pulled her pretty face back from his, glanced at the empty swimming pool, then looked him in the eye.

'Fuck me under water?'

'Hey . . .' Paul protested feebly, ' . . . tennis . . .'

The plain one ran into the house.

The two policemen swung Beth like a child, like you swing a child when you're just pretending and the child knows you're pretending and they carried Esther out of Rhodesia House in the Strand and dropped her from a height of three feet on to her spine and they just hurled Beth against the tree like a rag doll, she crumpled without a sound. Jimmy's face also crumpled. In the deep end Doreen's dream loins absorbed his huge cock and began to digest it. He saw Esther emerge from the house on to the verandah, the khaki baby in her arms, and he heard the women singing in the distance: 'Three minutes to midnight . . . and now it's time to say goodbye. Two minutes to midnight . . . and now it's time to say goodbye.'

'You feel good, Dick. . . ' Doreen's predatory eyes had finally consented to close.

'I'm leaving Zimbabwe tomorrow.'

One minute to midnight . . . and now it's time to time to time.

EPILOGUE

Tanner died within the year. A memorial service was held in the Stationers' Hall. The front benches were filled. Wreaths and telegrams of condolence arrived from several of the correspondents Tanner had posted abroad and also from one or two members of his own generation. These messages, for the most part conventional in form (only one risked an elegiac metre), were read out by Tanner's priestly brother Gerald, who also delivered the eulogy, in the course of which he mentioned the great love Leonard had felt for his only child, and the terrible suffering experienced by Vera and Leonard after 'disaster struck'. Neither of them, added Father Gerald Tanner, SJ, 'ever quite got over it.'

Mrs Tanner sat in the front row with the dry-eyed rigidity of a woman under a hair dryer. Few of those present knew her well. She had rarely been seen in her husband's company.

Hugh Parker sat in the second row – a courageous gesture since no one doubted that his sudden (if necessary) demotion of Tanner had brought on the high blood pressure which resulted in the first heart attack. But Parker could hardly be blamed for the self-inflicted wounds Tanner had suffered after he announced his availability to virtually every newspaper in Fleet Street.

I happened to be in London that week and dropped in on Tanner's memorial service to fill an empty hour and maybe catch up with friends. After the service I joined the line threading towards the exit where Mrs Tanner was shaking hands and when I got to her I said fine man, total integrity, deepest condolences . . . She had no idea who I was.

Outside, in the light rain, I nodded to Patrick Warner. He read my shifting gaze with that wet, rubbery smile of his:

'Don't tell me you were hoping to find Richard here?'

I shrugged. 'A faint hope.'

'My dear Bernard, he's in France, attending the state funeral of Jean-Paul Sartre. Surely you read the ten-part eulogy with which he's been filling the *New Statesman?*'

I flew on to New York for the usual happy reunion and meeting-of-minds with my wives and children – so much water has flowed under the bridge since the chapter when I discussed them with Richard that I can't even recall how many wives or children.

Occasionally our paths cross. We met in Lagos, expecting a military coup, didn't get one, but had a pleasant and humid evening together, sweating in anticipation of malaria.

'I hear Tanner died,' Richard said casually.

I stared at him with rising dismay. 'You *heard!*'

'My dear Berny, I was at Sartre's funeral. Only Tanner could be thick enough to die at the same moment as the twentieth century's greatest writer.' Richard looked at me with a sort of sly intensity. 'I don't suppose you're accusing me of killing off Sartre?'

I sighed as theatrically as possible – and asked him whether he had ever regretted giving up the academic life.

'After all, what's a mere reporter compared to a scholar?'

'I shall never be a "mere" anything.'

I *swear* he said that! It was then that he handed me the manuscript you have read.

'I'd value your opinion. If you like it, I might even dedicate it to you.'

Then he was gone or I was gone, it's all the same, what a life. Well, I lugged that manuscript around, paying excess baggage and half-hoping I'd lose it. I read a chapter in a Hilton, was interrupted by the assassination of a President or a Pope, picked up the threads again in a Holiday Inn, was diverted to an earthquake or tidal wave, made a really big effort in a Sheraton and fell asleep watching the Ayatollah on Iranian television.

I was fascinated, of course, but really the sane, Protestant, practical Holzheimer had to protest: Wait a minute!

I tried to list my logical objections to the narrative. I had of course suspected for many months that in one of my dizzying incarnations I was living inside a novel and inhabiting a skin on hire from the Great Taxidermist – and this suspicion had ripened into the fruitiest paronoia when I sat down on Concorde in September and read how I was destined to quarrel with Richard the following February! I mean to say! OK, so Richard has tea leaves, but surely predicting the future must itself alter the future? I have to admit that when I first read *Buhera and Beyond* I didn't believe a word of Richard's predictions and when they began to happen a few months later I had this dreadful sense of *déjà vu* but could do absolutely nothing to climb out of the nightmare.

The next time we met was in the Beaubourg – an exhibition of Senegalese sculpture. He was with Madeleine but they weren't married and I detected a coolness between them, the raw edges of two lovers interrupted in the middle of a quarrel. However, the gods had thrown us together and we made a gastronomic night of it – with an accent like mine there are some Parisian restaurants I never get into unless riding piggy-back on a frog. I had been longing to discuss Richard's novel with him (I'd made pages of notes), particularly how he'd managed to turn himself into a *mhondoro* spirit medium and describe events at the USAF base at Greenham Common two or three years before the cruise missiles actually arrived – but now, somehow, well, I kept deferring that conversation, maybe there was something in Richard's manner that I found inhibiting, even alarming – certainly he didn't mention the manuscript himself, I wondered whether he'd abandoned it, authors sometimes do.

I asked Madeleine about her work for *Le Monde* and she seemed rather surprised I should take an interest. Apparently she had been re-assigned to education, having once been a teacher herself, the big issue of the moment being the struggle between the Church and the Socialist Government over the *écoles libres* – she gave me the whole history of the conflict extending back to the Third Republic and she was far from boring though Richard was looking increasingly bored and distracted, his dark eyes roaming the restaurant from one pretty woman to the next. Clearly Madeleine was not unaware of this because she suddenly broke out of church-and-state:

'Enough of that. You must hear about Richard's new job.' The last word came dressed in the quotation marks of irony.

Between Richard and myself this was the most sensitive subject of all; it may come as no surprise to the reader to learn that soon after R. Stern published his famous scoop, *The Last Dirty Trick – Massacre in Buhera*, in the *New York Times*, I made it clear to the editor that either Richard quit or I quit. The odds were not long; I had a contract of employment and he didn't.

'A new job!' I cawed desperately. 'Great!'

Richard told me that he now worked for BBC External Services. Quite frankly, I was astounded.

'Great,' I said again.

'And what about all the MI5 vetting?' Madeleine said.

'One must live in the real world,' he told me, ignoring her.

Apparently he occupies an office on the sixth floor of the south-east wing of Bush House (an edifice whose sheer monumentality makes it worthy of Hapsburg Vienna) writing scripts for a department called Central Talks and Features. Yes (he was quite aggressive about it), he *had* been vetted by MI5; and yes, he had also signed a piece of paper presented to him by the Senior Personnel Officer, English Services (Room 413, South-East wing, Richard's passion for precision is nowadays approaching pedantry), by which he acknowledged that he was subject to the provisions of the Official Secrets Act. He'd also been warned that as a 'Restricted' employee of the Beeb he could not undertake any literary or journalistic work without first seeking permission. Anything he wrote had to be vetted.

'Are you quite sure this is the Richard Stern I knew and loved?'

His laugh was rather more worldly than the one I remembered.

'The Foreign Office pays the bills,' he said.

Madeleine emitted a moan of disgust. Richard didn't react well (as usual he'd been in charge of pouring slightly more wine into his own glass than into ours) and told her that 'France without Sartre stinks from top to bottom' – though he obviously didn't mind the food.

'I might as well tell you, Berny, that according to a circular issued by the Controller of Administration (Room 314, Centre Block, if you're interested) I am breaking my conditions of employment by even talking to you about the Corporation.'

'About the *what?*'

'The Corporation.'

'Richard, I don't know what to say. And do they actually censor what you write?'

'Of course. Until you learn to do it for them.' He leaned across the table with that intense expression I knew so well.

'You've got to work *inside* the system, Berny.'

Madeleine let out a little cry of horror and turned on him with an emotion akin to anguish.

'Why not admit the truth? – you're tired of fighting, you need a regular income, and you're almost forty.'

'Great! We'll give a party!' I wailed, hating the evening more and more. Richard looked almost haggard at the prospect and I realised that he had probably never had a birthday party, or even mentioned his birthday to a soul, for more than twenty years.

'Divorced?' I asked casually. (It was folly, of course, but you can't be *any* kind of friend to a man and yet not inquire about his divorce.)

He shrugged shiftily. Madeleine's eyes had filmed over. Yes, it must have been a blessing to them both to have bumped into Berny in the Beaubourg. To try and keep things going and to demonstrate my congenital insanity I asked about Esther.

He snorted. 'The "doctor" is now Minister of the Interior. His main job is detaining political opponents under Ian Smith's

402

Emergency Powers. If anyone he doesn't like should happen to be acquitted in a court, Zimunya's police immediately re-arrest them on the courthouse steps.'

'But Esther?'

He turned rather desperately in search of the wine waiter. The bottle was empty.

Madeleine smiled sadly. 'He will always love her. The last time he was in Zimbabwe she refused to see him.'

'Really?' I feigned astonishment, though I'd heard a rumour.

'Because of his published attacks on her husband.'

It wasn't an entirely happy evening and when we came out of the restaurant together we needed three taxis and for some reason this reminded me of the scene in which Richard describes how he, Harry and Elizabeth took separate taxis at Victoria station after arriving back from revolutionary Paris – this very city, but no longer worth a barricade or a mass. I flew on to Beirut because the *New York Times* had the awfully good idea of sending me to Lebanon. Nice place.

So far Richard's manuscript has survived the combined enthusiasms of the Phalange, the Israeli Air Force, the Druze, the Shi'ites, the Syrians and I almost forgot the PLO, what's left of them, poor bastards. The news is that Richard is due here any day, so all factions will no doubt call a ceasefire in his honour and the US Marines 'guarding' the airport will stop firing thousands of rounds into the surrounding hills which they do every day as evidence of good will. I have placed Richard's manuscript on the window ledge of my apartment; if that doesn't attract accurate fire, I'll try the balcony.

Oh shit, that was in the next street, they're coming closer again. Time to

Fiction in Paladin

The Businessman: A Tale of Terror   £2.95   ☐
Thomas M. Disch
'Each of the sixty short chapters of THE BUSINESSMAN is a *tour de force* of polished, distanced, sly narrative art . . . always the vision of America stays with us: melancholic, subversive and perfectly put . . . In this vision lies the terror of THE BUSINESSMAN'
Times Literary Supplement

'An entertaining nightmare out of Thomas Berger and Stephen King'
Time

Filthy English   £2.95   ☐
Jonathan Meades
'Incest and lily-boys, loose livers and ruched red anal compulsives, rape, murder and literary looting . . . Meades tosses off quips, cracks and crossword clues, stirs up the smut and stuffs in the erudition, pokes you in the ribs and prods you in the kidneys (as in Renal, home of Irene and Albert) . . . a delicious treat (full of fruit and nuts) for the vile and filthy mind to savour'
Time Out

Dancing with Mermaids   £2.95   ☐
Miles Gibson
'An excellent, imaginative comic tale . . . an original and wholly entertaining fiction . . . extremely funny and curiously touching'
Cosmopolitan

'The impact of the early Ian McEwan or Martin Amis, electrifying, a dazzler'
Financial Times

'It is as if Milk Wood had burst forth with those obscene-looking blossoms one finds in sweaty tropical palm houses . . . murder and mayhem decked out in fantastic and erotic prose'
The Times

To order direct from the publisher just tick the titles you want
and fill in the order form.   **PF1**

Arts in Paladin Books

Moving into Aquarius   £2.50 ☐
Sir Michael Tippett
One of our greatest living composers asks: How does music, the most
expressive of all forms of communication, relate to a technology-
obsessed society in which aggression and acquisitiveness have
become an index of personal worth?

The Jazz Book   £4.95 ☐
Joachim Berendt
The revised edition of this authoritative and comprehensive guide
which documents over 100 years of jazz.

Miles Davis   £3.95 ☐
Ian Carr
Penetrating biography of one of the world's most original and
enigmatic jazz performers.

A History of Jazz in Britain 1919–1950   £4.95 ☐
Jim Godbolt
From the arrival of jazz in Britain with the Original Dixieland Jazz
Band in 1919 to the early postwar years, this is the first truly
comprehensive study of the phenomenon of jazz from a British
perspective. 'Friendly, refreshing sceptical, very well documented.'
Max Jones. Illustrated.

Cult Objects   £5.95 ☐
Deyan Sudjic
A witty and stylish guide to contemporary design successes – objects
that have a special kind of attraction and personality that has nothing
to do with cost, utility or even neccessarily fashion. Illustrated
throughout.

To order direct from the publisher just tick the titles you want
and fill in the order form.   PAL3082

Original Fiction in Paladin

Paper Thin   £2.95 ☐
Philip First
From the author of THE GREAT PERVADER: a wonderfully original
collection of stories about madness, love, passion, violence, sex and
humour.

Don Quixote   £2.95 ☐
Kathy Acker
From the author of BLOOD AND GUTS IN HIGH SCHOOL: a
visionary collage–novel in which Don Quixote is a woman on an
intractable quest; a late twentieth-century LEVIATHAN; a stingingly
powerful and definitely unique novel.

To order direct from the publisher just tick the titles you want
and fill in the order form.   **PF2**

Biography in Paladin Books

Mussolini £3.50 ☐
Denis Mack Smith
'Will be remembered . . . for the exceptional clarity and brilliance of
the writing. His portrait of Mussolini the man is the best we have.'
Times Literary Supplement.

Karl Marx: His Life and Thought £3.95 ☐
David McLellan
A major biography by Britain's leading Marxist historian. Marx is
shown in his private and family life as well as in his political
contexts.

Miles Davis £3.95 ☐
Ian Carr
'For more than a quarter-century Miles Davis has personified the
modern jazz artist. Mr Carr's biography is in a class by itself. He
knows his music and his Miles.' *New York Times Book Review*.

Freud: The Man and the Cause £3.95 ☐
Ronald W. Clark
With great objectivity, Ronald Clark provides a new, human and
revealing portrait of the physician who changed man's image of
himself. He also gives a clear and balances account of the medical
world of Freud's early professional years; the conception of psycho-
analysis; Freud's struggle for recognition; and how his achievement
can be viewed in the light of contemporary knowledge. Illustrated.

Chaplin: His Life and Art £8.95 ☐
David Robinson
In this definitive biography, the only one to be written with full
access to the Chaplin archives, David Robinson provides a uniquely
documented record of the working methods and extraordinary life of
the mercurial genius of early cinema. Illustrated.

To order direct from the publisher just tick the titles you want
and fill in the order form. PAL4182

Fiction in Paladin

In the Shadow of the Wind   £2.95 ☐
Anne Hébert
Winner of the Prix Femina
'A bewitching and savage novel . . . there is constant magic in it'
Le Matin

'Beautifully written with great simplicity and originality . . . an
unusual and haunting novel'
London Standard

Love is a Durable Fire   £2.95 ☐
Brian Burland
'Burland has the power to evoke time and place with total authority
. . . compelling . . . the stuff of which real literature is made'
Irish Times

To order direct from the publisher just tick the titles you want
and fill in the order form.

Biography in Paladin Books

Aneurin Bevan (Vols 1 & 2) £3.95 ☐
Michael Foot each
The classic political biography of post-war politics.

The Unknown Orwell £2.95 ☐
Peter Stansky and William Abrahams
Introduces Eric Blair, of Eton and the Indian Imperial Police. In analysing his background, the authors have given us a uniquely valuable key to one of our most important literary figures.

Orwell: The Transformation £2.95 ☐
Peter Stansky and William Abrahams
This covers the period of four crucial years, in which Eric Blair, minor novelist with little or no interest in politics, emerged as George Orwell, an important writer with a view, a mission and a message.

Oscar Wilde £2.95 ☐
Philippe Jullian
Still the best biography of Oscar Wilde, This book presents his astonishing life, work, wit and trials.

Welsh Dylan £1.95 ☐
John Ackerman
This penetrating biography throws new light on Dylan Thomas's identity as a Welshman, showing the close relationship between his work and his Welsh background.

Virginia Woolf (Vols 1 & 2) £1.95 ☐
Quentin Bell each
Acclaimed as one of the outstanding literary biographies of the century, these books trace the troubled development of Virginia Woolf as a writer and as a woman.

Solzhenitsyn £9.95 ☐
Michael Scammell
'A comprehensive picture of the man . . . This superb biography will certainly be the standard account of the most remarkable literary life story of our time.' *Times Literary Supplement*. Illustrated.

To order direct from the publisher just tick the titles you want and fill in the order form.
  PAL4082

Literature in Paladin Books

Fear and Loathing in Las Vegas   **£2.95** ☐
Hunter S. Thompson
As knights of old sought the Holy Grail so Hunter Thomson entered
Las Vegas armed with a veritable magus's arsenal of 'heinous
chemicals' in his search for the American Dream. 'The whole book
boils down to a kind of mad, corrosive poetry that picks up where
Norman Mailer's *An American Dream* left off and explores what Tom
Wolfe left out.' *New York Times.*

The Stranger in Shakespeare   **£2.50** ☐
Leslie A. Fiedler
A complete radical analysis of Shakespeare's work which illuminates
the sub-surface psychological tensions.

Confessions of a Knife   **£1.95** ☐
Richard Selzer
In this riveting book Richard Selzer seeks meaning in the ritual of
surgery, a ritual 'at once murderous, painful, healing, and full of
love'. In the careening, passionate language of a poet he speaks of
mortality and medicine, of flesh and fever, and reveals something of
the surgeon's thoughts and fears as he delves into the secret linings of
our bodies. 'I was awed and strangely exalted,' Bernard Crick, *The
Guardian*.

Notes from Overground   **£2.50** ☐
'Tiresias'
Man is born free, and is everywhere in trains. More than a com-
muter's lament, *Notes from Overground* is a witty, wide-ranging
meditation on a horribly familiar form of travel.

To order direct from the publisher just tick the titles you want
and fill in the order form.   **PAL8082**

All these books are available at your local bookshop or newsagent, or can be ordered direct from the publisher.

To order direct from the publishers just tick the titles you want and fill in the form below.

Name _____

Address _____

_____

Send to:
Paladin Cash Sales
PO Box 11, Falmouth, Cornwall TR10 9EN.

Please enclose remittance to the value of the cover price plus:

UK 60p for the first book, 25p for the second book plus 15p per copy for each additional book ordered to a maximum charge of £1.90.

BFPO 60p for the first book, 25p for the second book plus 15p per copy for the next 7 books, thereafter 9p per book.

Overseas including Eire £1.25 for the first book, 75p for second book and 28p for each additional book.

Paladin Books reserve the right to show new retail prices on covers, which may differ from those previously advertised in the text or elsewhere.